W9-CBQ-832

WELCOME TO
BEACH TOWN

WELCOME TO
BEACH TOWN

A Novel

SUSAN
WIGGS

WILLIAM MORROW
An Imprint of HarperCollins Publishers

Excerpt from the poem "B" in the book *No Matter the Wreckage* by Sarah Kay, © 2014. Reprinted by arrangement with Write Bloody Publishing, www.writebloody.com.

This is a work of fiction. Names, characters, places, and incidents are products of the author's imagination or are used fictitiously and are not to be construed as real. Any resemblance to actual events, locales, organizations, or persons, living or dead, is entirely coincidental.

WELCOME TO BEACH TOWN. Copyright © 2023 by Laugh, Cry, Dream, Read, LLC. All rights reserved. Printed in the United States of America. No part of this book may be used or reproduced in any manner whatsoever without written permission except in the case of brief quotations embodied in critical articles and reviews. For information, address HarperCollins Publishers, 195 Broadway, New York, NY 10007.

Artwork by ShutterProductions and Netfalls Remy Musser/Shutterstock, Inc.

ISBN 978-0-06-291416-3

For Dee Neff.
Love of my brother's life.
Sister of my heart.

WELCOME TO
BEACH TOWN

PART ONE

They deem him their worst enemy who tells them the truth.

—*Plato*, The Republic, c. 380 B.C.

1

Commencement Day, 2008
Alara Cove, California

There was a moment—brief, but as palpable as the sting of a wasp—when Nikki Graziola felt her power. When it was time to step up to the lectern, she would have everyone's attention in a way she'd never had before. In all her eighteen years, she'd never been in this position. Now it was her moment to shine. She knew that if she managed to get through today's ceremony, her life would go forward exactly as planned.

That was the whole point of *commencement*, after all.

It was a beginning. A fresh chapter. A commencement was the moment when new stories started. For Nikki and her classmates at Thornton Academy, life itself was meant to move ahead, not backward. Yet she couldn't stop thinking about senior night, a mere six days ago, after the program committee had approved the written final draft of the speech she'd been chosen to deliver.

The commencement ceremonies had almost been canceled due to the tragedy. But it was at the insistence of Mark McGill's own family that the event was going forward as planned. Mark would have wanted it that way, his parents assured school officials. For the sake of his classmates, and especially for the sake of his twin sister, Marian, the show must go on.

Out of deference and respect for their beloved classmate, every student and faculty member present wore a black armband. Amid the alphabetically arranged graduates, Mark's sister sat next to a vacant chair. Actually, the chair had started out vacant, but as the graduates filed in to take their seats, the chair had filled up with tokens and memorabilia, spontaneous offerings from people whose youth and privilege had thus far shielded them from grief. Now, shocked into adulthood's worst transition, most of them were at a loss. They brought flowers and candles, handwritten cards, photos, a soccer ball, a theater mask, an antique vinyl record. A stuffed toy slumped atop a debate trophy.

Awaiting her part in the ceremony, Nikki took in the crowd gathered at the hilltop stadium. It was late afternoon, the most beautiful time of day in the small seaside town, when the lowering sun drenched everything in deep golden hues. From her vantage point on the raised dais in the middle of the stadium, now filled with an emotional crowd, Nikki could see where the land, sea, and sky met. She had never viewed the landscape from this angle before. The coastline defined a series of curves from south to north, each curve forming a different beach. At the north end was the arch of the bridge that connected the mainland to Radium Island, a decommissioned Navy power facility. The old military station had given the town its name, ALARA being a radiation safety acronym for "as low as reasonably achievable."

The next inward curve was one of the middle coast's best surfing beaches, known all over the world as the ideal place to catch the best waves of summer. To the south lay family-friendly Town Beach, adjacent to the marina with its forest of masts and radar equipment, connected to the yacht club by a network of docks. And then, just before the curve of the earth, there hovered a faint hint of the amber miasma of sky over LA. From Alara Cove, the big city was as distant as a dream.

Chasing dreams was a central theme of Nikki's original speech, the one she had written, deleted, and rewritten over the past few weeks. She had labored over the commencement address. She had lost sleep, waking up in the middle of the night in her room at Miss Carmella's to work by flashlight, pen, and paper, crafting the speech that would be immortalized in the annals of Thornton Academy, one of the most famous schools in the country. But now how would she get the words out without bursting into tears?

She tried not to fidget from nerves as she waited for her moment. The keynote speaker was talking now—a famous Thornton alum who was serving as an ambassador for the State Department—but Nikki couldn't focus on his words.

Prior to the senior night incident, Nikki had been filled with a sense of wonder and gratitude for the school, and yes, of purpose, as she sought the right tone for her speech. Mr. Florian, her English teacher, had been her first reader and advisor. She gave him the first draft, and when he looked up from reading the pages, she had caught a glimmer in his eyes.

"Well done, Nicoletta," he said, taking off his rimless glasses and rubbing the lenses with a polishing cloth. "It's very well written and beautifully expressed."

"You're sure?" She trusted him. He'd been a powerful mentor all through senior year, and she valued his feedback. "It's not too cheesy?"

"What do you think?" Florian was always answering a question with a question. He encouraged her to think for herself. To evaluate her own work. He knew she was harder on herself than anyone else could ever be.

"I suppose I said what I said in the best way I could. But . . ."

"But what?"

"I kind of wish the speech could be funnier."

He pursed his lips briefly. Put his glasses back on. "Do you want to say something funny, or do you want to say something true?"

She'd shrugged her shoulders. "It'd be cool to be truly funny."

"When you play something for laughs," her teacher said, "the message usually goes in one ear and out the other. When you speak from the heart, it sinks in deeper. I think you've accomplished that, Miss Graziola. These words show us your heart. You've spoken your truth."

Had she? In that moment, at her meeting with Mr. Florian, that had probably been the case. She had felt the full weight of her role as the least likely class valedictorian of the class of 2008. In its hundred-and-fifty-year history, the venerable school had educated the sons and daughters of the most important families in the country—governors, legislators, foreign royalty, and even a few presidents. Its graduates became Nobel Prize winners, titans of industry, giants of the enter-tainment world. Given its proximity to Hollywood, Thornton was the school of choice for the rich, the famous, the powerful—and the power-hungry.

And yet this year, after all the grades, faculty and coach recom-mendations, evaluations, and weighted scores had been calculated, the valedictorian announcement had shocked the senior class. Nico-letta Graziola was the chosen one. Local girl. Scholarship student. Practically—though not completely—an orphan.

Nikki was pretty sure she was the first Thornton valedictorian who had been raised in an Airstream trailer at the ocean's edge. She'd grown up with sand in her hair, her face freckled by the sun, her knees and elbows bruised from rough days on a surfboard.

She had not taken the honor lightly. She was not the sort of person to take anything lightly. Deeply aware of her undistinguished status, she had worked her ass off to climb to the top of her class. She'd studied twice as hard as the next student. Trained twice as hard to letter in three varsity sports. Labored like a rented mule at her community service projects, keenly aware that some of the re-cipients of her good works were more well-off than she had ever been. She'd spent twice as many hours as any other student on her art portfolio.

All to prove she was at least half as worthy of a Thornton educa-tion as the other students.

Before the tragedy, this had been the image she wanted to project. *I am worthy.*

The first draft had flowed from her brain to the page in a thin line of peacock blue ink from the fountain pen Miss Carmella had given her for her eighteenth birthday back in April, right after Nikki had received news of her acceptance to USC. The University of Southern California—her dream school. The one people considered a long shot for a girl like her. Nikki had not expected to get in. She'd assumed that she wasn't unique enough, or special enough, or talented enough to make the cut. She knew without a doubt that she didn't have enough money. But she could dream. And by some miracle, she had been accepted. With a generous financial aid package.

Finally, her father's status of being perpetually broke turned out to be useful. Thanks to Guy Graziola's financial disclosure form, she'd qualified for all the grants and loans she needed.

To her knowledge, no Graziola had ever attended college. She would be the first. For that matter, she would be the first Graziola to finish high school, as far as she knew. She didn't actually have that much information about the Graziolas. They were in New Jersey, and her dad had only seen his folks a couple of times after he dropped out of high school and moved to California. But she was pretty sure she'd be the first to go to college.

Back in April, staring at the laptop screen when the decision came in, she had felt like Dorothy before the gates of Oz as they opened to an unseen chorus of voices, welcoming her to her future.

She had written her speech to reflect the pride and empowerment and opportunities she'd found at the school. Once the school administration had approved her speech, she'd had a deep inner urge to rewrite the address for the umpteenth time, and she'd stayed up late, laboring away at the piece.

The glimmer from her flashlight had ghosted the ceiling of her room while the sighs and soft mutterings of Shasta, her foster sister, flowed through the darkness.

And it was this—Nikki's uncertainty about the speech, and her determination to get the words just right—that had sent her off into the night in search of Mark.

Nikki was one of a handful of local students who did not reside on campus at Thornton. Instead, she lived at the home of Miss Carmella Beach, a local artist and third-generation resident of Alara Cove. Miss Carmella took in foster children. Nikki was not in the system, but she might as well have been. By the time she reached grade six in the local public school, she was more trouble than her dad could handle, so he sent her to stay with his old friend Carmella.

Nikki's speech included a special tribute to Carmella Beach. She was one of Thornton's distinguished alumni, having studied fine arts at Occidental College. She'd won many awards for her work. But that wasn't the reason for Nikki's tribute.

Being exiled to Miss Carmella Beach's home at the age of twelve turned out to be the best thing that had ever happened to Nikki. The rambling Beach family estate was a place of stability and routine, a secure haven for kids who were scared or flailing or abandoned, or girls whose fathers had no idea how to raise them once puberty hit.

It was Miss Carmella herself who had arranged for Nikki to attend Thornton, and that was another reason Nikki had worked so hard to excel—to make her mentor proud.

Nikki realized early on that in order to keep her place at the school, she would have to follow the rules as if they'd been chiseled in stone. A single infraction could get her expelled. For four years, she'd resisted the usual pranks and illicit gatherings most of the students indulged in.

But on senior night after lights out, Nikki took a risk. She knew her commencement address wasn't good enough. She convinced herself that perfecting the speech was more important than curfew rules. She needed help, not from a teacher or coach, but from her smartest, closest friend and the best writer she knew: Mark McGill.

From the day they'd met as brand-new freshmen, Nikki and Mark had been a bonded pair. He knew what she was thinking before she thought it. She could take one look at his face and read his mood.

Mark was the one who would help her sort out the jumble of words swirling through her mind. The trouble was, the well-established Thornton rules made it impossible to reach someone late at night without permission. Students at any other school would have exchanged text messages or email notes, arranging an after-hours meeting.

Sending a convenient text message wasn't an option for Thornton students. The school was known for its academic rigor, socially progressive values, outdoor ethos, and its no-exceptions digital lights-out policy. Every night at ten o'clock sharp, the Wi-Fi was turned off and all data connections were blocked. Cell phones were rendered useless, and that included the hot new iPhone, which all the rich kids had. Laptop computers and the big ones in the computer lab became mere data banks. Students were reduced to reading books and talking to one another, maybe settling down for a game of chess or cribbage.

The nightly return to the founders' revered analog world had become a time-honored tradition. Some students tried desperately to find a way around the digital freeze, but most took it in stride, maybe even secretly enjoyed the silence.

All of the day students were expected to follow the same rules as the students who lived in the traditional neo-Gothic dormitories on the verdant, sprawling campus. Nikki herself didn't mind the rule, which Miss Carmella enforced throughout the school year. It wasn't much of a hardship for Nikki. Her flip phone was flimsy, it charged by the minute, and anyway, she liked reading books. She always had.

Nikki's mother, eighteen years gone and unremembered, had left behind a small collection of books and not much else. Nikki had methodically worked her way through the library her mom kept under the banquette in the Airstream—*The Heart Is a Lonely Hunter. The Diary of a Young Girl* by Anne Frank. *Beloved.* The *Lord of the Rings* trilogy. Some Stephen King books. There was a Hollywood novel by Judith Krantz that was completely bonkers, yet Nikki had savored every salacious page of it, wondering if sex was actually like that. *The Joy Luck Club*—a gorgeous novel that had very little to do with joy or luck. One of the pages, where a woman went crazy and drowned her baby, was smudged and crinkled. By her mother's tears, Nikki imagined.

Pretty much everything about Lyra Wilson Graziola was imagined. Had to be, since Nikki was only a few weeks old when her mother had died.

Nikki never even knew what she would have called Lyra—Mom? Mommy? Mama? Never knew what the two of them might have been like together. Would they have played at the beach, surfing the waves that brought people to Alara Cove from far and wide? Made mac and cheese for dinner and snuggled under the covers watching scary movies? Would they have gone shopping for clothes and hair clips and makeup? Would her mom have explained how to use tampons so Nikki didn't have to figure it out on her own? Would they have traveled back to Indiana to see Lyra's mother, the grandmother Nikki had never met? Would her mom have given her advice about boys and school and friends?

Nikki would never know what her mother might have advised her to do about the night Mark McGill died.

Intent on getting help with her speech, she had slipped out of the house around midnight. She jumped on her bike and rode to the school to find Mark. The dorm complex was organized around an oblong courtyard called the quadrangle. His room was on the second floor, three windows from the corner. Mark knew the drill. When she rattled the windowpane with a hail of pebbles—their longtime agreed-upon signal—he would sneak down to meet her. But that particular night, there was no response.

This was her first clue that something was wrong.

On graduation day, the convocation included a moment of silence for Mark, and the moment stretched into endless sadness. A breeze stirred the eucalyptus trees under the stadium scoreboard. In addition to the school song, "Halls of Ivy," there was an excruciating rendition of "Bright Eyes." Then they sang "Hearts Lifted to Heaven," which the McGills claimed was Mark's favorite hymn.

Nikki doubted that he had a favorite hymn. Mark was partial to the Ramones and Cake and seventies rock. He liked Usher and Coldplay and Adele. Ironically, his favorite song was Pink Floyd's "Another Brick in the Wall." She'd never known him to be a fan of hymns.

During the eerie silence, which seemed to go on forever, Nikki shut her eyes and drew a mental picture of Mark, a boy she'd known since they'd arrived for the preterm freshman orientation weekend four years before. They had only known each other for four years, but they had shared a lifetime. Some friendships were like that, she supposed—intense and real.

She tried to relive every moment, because there would be no more moments with him. What would he want her to say now that she had everyone's attention? He was no longer here to speak his truth.

Four years ago, neither of them could have foreseen this unimaginable loss.

2

On freshman orientation day, Nikki's father drove her to school in his battered white delivery van. The old van wasn't used for deliveries anymore, but the ghost lettering of the previous owner's logo was visible: *Alara Cove Catering: We Bring the Good Stuff to You.* Her dad had bought the van for a song and used it to transport surfboards and gear for guests of his Airstream park, Beachside Caravans.

Since Guy Graziola was always dodging bill collectors, the van was supposed to be anonymous, blending in, not drawing attention to itself.

It didn't exactly blend in that day, parked in the bumper-to-bumper line of families delivering their kids to the West Coast's most exclusive boarding school. Instead, the thing stuck out like a black eye amid the gleaming luxury SUVs with tinted windows, the flashy European sedans, the polished limos and bulletproof secure cars like the one that was tightly wedged directly in front of the van.

Nikki's gaze darted around in nervousness. Incoming freshmen, including a handful of day students, would all move into the dormitory for a three-day orientation program. Dressed in their khaki and navy school uniforms, they would take a tour of the gorgeous campus, learn where all their classes took place, set their sights on the clubs they wanted to join, the sports they wanted to go out for, the challenges they wanted to take on.

To Nikki's eyes, all the students swarming the campus were ridiculously attractive and polished and filled with exuberant confidence. The sight of them made her feel self-conscious, with her home-barbered short hair, sun-drenched freckles, and ropey muscles formed by long summers of surfing and cycling around town.

A guy in a dark suit with an earpiece got out of the shiny black vehicle in front of the van. He was followed by two students, a boy and a girl. Nikki recognized Mark and Marian McGill, because their image was plastered, a hundred times larger than life, on a billboard at the side of the coast road on the edge of town. It was one of their mom's campaign ads. The brother and sister looked as wholesome as a glass of milk. In person, they were even more attractive, with shiny blond hair and clear, pale skin, brilliant smiles displaying expert dental and orthodontic work, and the perfect posture of trained dancers.

The McGill twins needed extra protection because their mother, Senator Barbara McGill, had recently introduced a controversial bill, and she had been getting threats. As a little kid, Nikki had first heard the name McGill during a political discussion. A group of guests at her dad's caravan park was having a heated debate around the communal fire pit. Later she'd asked her dad, "What's a same-sex marriage?" She couldn't recall his answer—probably a shrug of genuine bafflement.

Mark was slender and unassuming. Marian's face was lit with wonder and delight as she looked around the campus, her bright-eyed gaze following a group of jocks who were shoving each other toward the main gate to the dormitory quadrangle. Mark seemed more cautious, even vulnerable, as he spoke to his parents at the curb. He hugged his mother, then turned to Mr. McGill and shook hands. He stared down at their joined hands as they shook. Then he took a step closer and hugged his father. To Nikki, it looked like a one-sided hug.

In the van, her dad drummed his fingers on the steering wheel. "Yeah, yeah, let's not be in too much of a hurry, people."

"You can't wait to get rid of me," Nikki said, only half joking.

"Don't give me that," said Guy. "I got work. Unlike these yay-hoos, I don't have all the time in the world."

Nikki doubted a US senator had all the time in the world.

"What even is a yay-hoo?" she asked, fixing the collar of her polo shirt. The school uniform felt strange to wear. She'd never owned a polo shirt before, and she wasn't quite comfortable in it. Collar up or down? Top button undone or fastened? The knee-length khaki skirt was stiff, too big in the waist, and it sagged around her hips. She'd traded her summer flip-flops for closed-toe shoes, which made her feet look weird. "And what makes you think these people are yay-hoos?" She watched Mark reach into the car and emerge with a small, squirming dog in his arms.

"Oh, now we got Timmy and Lassie in the picture," her dad said, shaking his head. "Take your time, fellas. We got all day."

Nikki rolled her eyes, then climbed behind the passenger seat, stepping over a litter of fast-food wrappers and CD cases, wetsuits, board fins and leashes, pots of Sex Wax and wax combs—the flotsam and jetsam of a talented but not-very-neat surfer. She moved a mildewy-smelling wetsuit out of the way and slid the van door open.

"Well," she said. "I guess I'll get going now." She dragged out her battered overnight bag, which hit the ground with a thud. The bag had a preprinted tag that had come in the mail along with her student orientation packet. *Suite 4C.* That room, shared with a group of girls she'd never met, would be her home for the weekend. Even the day students were required to stay on campus for orientation.

She tilted her head to look up at the grand iron and stone arch that marked the gateway to the school. There was some kind of Latin motto spelled out in formal lettering. Everything about this place seemed important; she felt the weight of it. This would be the start of a new chapter in her life. That was the Thornton promise, after all.

Her dad got out of the van and hurried around to the curb. "I'll give you a hand," he said.

"I got this." She hoisted the strap onto her shoulder. The bag bore a Ralph Lauren logo, but it had the name *Amy* embroidered on the side, because she'd found it at the local thrift shop.

"Yeah, so listen," her dad said. "It's a big deal you got into this school. Don't blow it."

Meaning, she knew, don't screw up. Don't go skipping class just because the surf's up. Don't get caught shoplifting tampons because you're too embarrassed to tell your dad that you need them. Don't let the assistant coach find you making out with some boy under the bleachers at the stadium. Don't pick a fight with a kid because he called your best friend fat.

Now that she was going to Thornton, she didn't have a best friend anymore, fat or otherwise. She and Shasta swore, of course, that they would be friends forever, but this—the start of a new school—was a dividing line, and they both knew it. They'd still share their room at Carmella's, yet each sensed that things would never be the same.

Nikki was a grade ahead of Shasta in school, so Shasta wouldn't even start high school until next year, and she would attend the public high school. The gulf between them might prove to be too wide for the kind of friendship that had bound them together for the past two years.

"I'm not going to blow it," she told her father. Their hug was brief, just one beat of the heart, and then they broke apart. Her dad wasn't a hugger. Nikki wasn't either, even though sometimes she wished she could be one.

The McGills' car finally pulled away from the curb, and her dad climbed back into his van. The exhaust pipe coughed as he revved the engine, then left a puff of blue-gray smoke in his wake as he drove away, garnering disapproving glares from some of the other parents. It was not the first time her father had dropped her off somewhere. Far from it. She was used to him leaving her places.

She joined the stream of students heading toward the quadrangle, the vast green space meticulously tended by her friend Cal's dad.

It would be weird not to see Cal Bradshaw anymore. They'd spent their early school years together, but now Cal would be a freshman at Alara Cove High starting next week. Mr. Bradshaw was the groundskeeper at Thornton.

Upbeat music drifted from hidden speakers. At the far end was the Sanger Residence Hall, named after a famous donor family. Its twin wings opened like a wide embrace. A few upperclassmen and proctors were greeting the new students and helping them find their way around. Beyond the quadrangle was the stadium, which overlooked the inward curve of the bay, its grand entrance shaped like two sentinels on guard duty.

A tall, russet-haired boy with a backpack and leather duffel bags in both arms blew past her like a football player rushing the end zone. The backpack bumped into Nikki and she nearly lost her balance.

"Hey," she objected. "Watch it."

The kid swung around, an insolent grin on his face. "Oh, pardon me, your highness."

Nikki recognized him. Like her, he was a local kid—Jason Sanger—same name as the residence hall. Unlike her, he was as rich and privileged as any Thornton student. Everyone in Alara Cove knew who the Sangers were. His house—the Sanger mansion—was so fancy it had a name of its own—*Quid Pro Quo*, a nod to their success at winning lawsuits. The Sangers had made a fortune in private practice. Their public service, as DAs and county solicitors, gave them enough political clout to do favors for their friends, and to go after their enemies.

Generations ago, there had been bad blood between Charles Sanger and Henry Beach, who was Miss Carmella's grandfather. Charles Sanger, the county prosecutor, tried to indict Henry for his interracial marriage back in the fifties, and to prohibit him from building a home inside the city limits. The suit failed laughably, but it left a bad odor behind.

Still, the Sangers rose in power and wealth and influence. They served on city council boards, held positions in the Department of Natural Resources enforcement agency, ran the county solicitor's office, and built a private law firm founded on personal injury lawsuits. They were close pals with the Navy administrators of Radium Island. It was thanks to the Sangers that the power facility was located on the island so close to town.

Several times, the Sangers tried to shut down Guy Graziola's Beachside Caravans park for code violations, but their efforts failed. "Bunch of troublemakers," Nikki's father often declared. "I got no use for 'em."

Jason Sanger had no idea who Nikki was, though. Why would he? Even though they were from the same hometown, they hardly breathed the same air. Alara Cove was sharply divided between the locals who made the town a town, and the rich people who owned everything and ran everything.

With hot, squinty eyes, Jason gave her a once-over that felt intrusive, borderline rude. His gaze lingered on her chest, then slipped lower to her hips and crotch. Boys did that. It had been happening a lot lately, ever since she had grown boobs.

"*What?*" she demanded in an annoyed tone.

Being challenged for staring made his eyes turn mean. "Nothing," he said with a curl of his lip. "Just wondering what a trailer park mongrel's doing here at Thornton."

Ah, so he did know who she was. Maybe he'd seen one of the features about her in the local paper. She'd won her share of amateur surf competitions and her picture had appeared several times in the sports pages. She looked a lot different in those pictures, wearing a swimsuit or wetsuit, her short hair mussed by saltwater and wind. "I guess you're about to find out," she said to him.

"I guess I'll see you around," he said, then focused on her bag. "*Amy.*" Since he probably couldn't think of anything else to say, he gave a snort of sarcasm. Then he pivoted and strode toward the residence hall, barging past other students. A few yards ahead, Jason's backpack smacked into Mark McGill, who lurched sideways, seemed to trip over his own feet, and fell to the ground. His bag hit the sidewalk. It popped open and a few items spilled out across the grass.

Jason didn't seem to notice the impromptu yard sale. He just kept striding forward.

Nikki set down her bag and hurried over.

"You okay?" she asked.

"Yes, sure. Bruised ego, maybe." Mark brushed at the grass stain on his khakis. He groped around, gathering his things and stuffing them into his backpack. Nikki pitched in, retrieving a hacky sack ball and an iPod player that had landed on the preternaturally weedless, groomed lawn. There was an awkward intimacy in seeing a stranger's personal things strewn about. Socks and underwear, and one of those athletic cups boys wore to play sports, a Speedo swimsuit, rolled up shirts, pajamas with a designer logo, some books, a JCPenney sale brochure and a boys' magazine she didn't recognize, an alarm clock— the prosaic contents of kids' baggage.

She handed over the Penney's circular and a copy of *The Hunger Games*. "That's one of my favorites," she said. "I like to think I'd be that brave. Have you finished it yet?"

"I just started reading it," he said, tucking it away.

"Then I won't spoil it for you. I'm Nikki Graziola," she said, grabbing her overnight bag.

"You travel light," he said.

"I won't be living on campus," she said. "Just here for the weekend orientation. I live in town." When school properly started, she would go back to staying at Miss Carmella's. She wondered if she would feel like an outcast because she didn't live in the dorm, sharing late-night whispers and after-hours games with the other kids. Although she liked living at Miss Carmella's, and she liked sharing a room with

Shasta, Nikki hoped the boarding students wouldn't treat her differently. They probably would, though.

"That's cool. I'm Mark McGill," he said.

"I know." She flushed. "I mean, I know your mom is Senator McGill."

"Nice to meet you."

Ahead of them, Jason Sanger was engaged in a game of keep-away with some girl's faux fur pillow. He held it out of reach while the girl nearly cried in frustration.

"That's Jason Sanger," she said. "He's a local kid, too."

"He seems nice." His deadpan expression underscored the irony. She liked this kid already.

In the lobby of the residence hall, there were tearful farewells to the families, promises to call and write and visit. Nikki was glad her dad hadn't insisted on coming in with her. The outpouring of emotion would have made him gag.

Eventually, the group of one hundred awkward fourteen-year-olds was left in the hands of faculty, staff, and proctors. There was a bit of a scramble as people found their rooms and beds. Everyone had a twin bed, a study carrel, and an armoire. Nikki's meager belongings took up only one shelf. She hung up her dress uniform—navy blazer, blouse, skirt, necktie, socks with those ridiculous tabs, and lace-up oxfords. The dress uniforms were for assembly days, field trips, and visits from VIPs. She'd never worn anything remotely like it, but Miss Carmella said the uniform would simplify things—probably a diplomatic way of saying it would keep people from being snobby about her clothes. Nikki usually wore cutoffs and tank tops and flip-flops. When she had to dress up, she could usually find something nice at the local thrift shop.

An announcement came over the PA. They were to proceed to the assembly hall. Miss Carmella had told her that it used to be called the chapel a hundred years ago, but now the school was neutral on the subject of religion.

Mr. Ellis, the headmaster, gave a welcoming speech ("we are all equal here, blah blah blah"). *Yeah, right*, thought Nikki, picturing the limos dropping off the kids. Ms. Chenoweth, the dean of students, promised them an orientation full of fun challenges, supportive group talks, and the chance to make lifelong friendships. They would soon dive into the signature Thornton experience—a diverse panoply of events that reflected the school's distinctive outdoor spirit and its proximity to the beach.

An a cappella group of upperclassmen performed the school song, which they would all soon learn by heart. The voices echoed like a chorus of angels up to the high, arched ceiling, bouncing off the jewel-toned windows. Although the song was old-fashioned and sentimental, the sound of it made Nikki's heart swell. Everything felt so shiny and new—this school, these students, the eager teachers, her *life*.

They proceeded to the open-air atrium to visit the booths and tables that had been set up to welcome them. This event was meant to offer the incoming students a look at all the clubs. They were invited to sign up for the ones that appealed to them. Chess. Glee club. Mathematics. Drama. Robotics. Art club. Archery.

"What are you interested in?" she asked Mark, who was hanging back, looking slightly bewildered.

"Drama, I guess," he said. "Glee club."

"You should try both. I could hear you singing at assembly. You're good."

"Thanks," he said. "Oh, and orchestra, for sure."

"You play an instrument?"

"Cello and piano."

"Wow, that's cool." The only thing she played was the tabletop jukebox in her dad's Airstream.

"Also, I need to join the Buccaneers," said Mark.

"Who—or what—are the Buccaneers?"

"It's a club. It's *the* club. My great-grandfather, my grandfather, and my dad were all Buccaneers. They kind of turned it into a family tradition."

"Okay, but what do they do?"

"Raise funds for the school, boost the sports teams, and probably have unauthorized parties. The Buccaneers earn badges like Boy Scouts for their feats. My dad collected quite a few." He showed her a small, stylized pin depicting crossed swords.

She studied it. Maybe when a kid already had everything, he craved the things he had to earn. "If that's your thing."

"It's my dad's thing." He tucked the token into his pocket.

The Buccaneers table was manned by a group of seniors dressed like Jack Sparrow and talking out of the sides of their mouths. One of them brandished a fake sword and pretended to slash some kid's throat.

"They seem nice," Nikki observed, echoing Mark's ironic tone. "Do they allow girls in their club?"

"Only girls who are willing to be called wenches."

Nikki grimaced. "I'll let you get to it, then."

"Wish me luck."

She circulated among the tables. After some consideration, she signed up for swim team and water polo club. She knew she was a strong swimmer and the coach, a woman with a gentle smile and kind eyes behind cat's-eye glasses, welcomed her. Nikki had never played water polo or even seen a water polo match, but she said she'd like to give it a shot. The coach looked relieved when Nikki expressed her interest, since most students took one look at the singularly unflattering headgear and avoided the sign-up table.

Then Nikki saw what she was looking for—a booth with a buzzing crowd around it and a backdrop of fake palm trees and a vintage Jacobs longboard polished to a high sheen. It was a handmade beauty and had probably never touched the water.

"Ever done any surfing?" The guy asking wore a name tag—
Ramses Barr, Club President. He had long, straight hair parted on the
side, and he wore a team tank and shorts. He had the slim build and
muscular shoulders of a seasoned surfer. She recognized the type.

"A bit." Nikki didn't want to oversell herself.

"We'll have some boards out at the beach party this afternoon. A
few of us'll be around to help you beginners."

"Cool," she said. "Guess I'll see you there." She left the event as
a new member of the swim and surf teams, the art club, the water
polo team, and the Spanish club. Thanks to Miss Carmella, Nikki
was crazy about art. She knew a bit of Spanish from middle school
classes. After school, she hung out with her friend Irma, whose
parents owned a convenience store near the caravan park. When
she was little, she would go there to hang out with Irma on the days
her dad wasn't around, which was most days. More than once, she'd
overheard Irma's mom saying, "Someone should remind him that he
has a daughter."

As she filled her new school logo backpack with more information
cards and pamphlets, she felt a surge of hope and delicious antici-
pation. The other kids all seemed as excited and nervous as Nikki
was. There were the obvious brains, the artsy types, the jocks, the
goths, the skaters, the slackers, the posers—same as you'd find at
any school.

"Get involved in things," Miss Carmella had advised her. "That's
the way to meet people. Look them in the eye and tell them your
name as if they should already know it in the first place."

Nikki noticed a group of girls who were huddled together, scanning the area like a tactical team conducting a recon exercise. Kylie
Scarborough was instantly recognizable, as she looked so much like
her famous mother.

Although they were all the same age as Nikki, something about
the girls made them seem older. The shiny, expertly styled hair, the
light, fresh makeup, the manicured nails, even the way they wore

their polos and skirts gave them an air of polish. They looked as if they'd just stepped out of a Rodeo Drive salon. Kylie and her orbit were clearly the power squadron, the ones who would call all the shots.

Nikki held back, thinking about her short, blunt-cut hair and freckles. Then she remembered Miss Carmella's advice: "Look them in the eye and tell them your name as if they should already know it in the first place." She took a deep breath, squared her shoulders, and strode forward into the squad.

"I'm Nikki Graziola," she said, indicating her name tag.

One of the girls, a tall, pretty blonde who could probably pass as a Paris Hilton look-alike, gave her a quick assessment with expertly shadowed steel blue eyes. "Name tags don't lie," she said.

Nikki felt a sting of embarrassment, but she made sure her smile held steady. "Just trying to be friendly." She glanced at the girl's name tag. "Storm." Storm Jarrett was probably another celebrity's kid. Famous people seemed to like unusual names for their kids.

As Nikki walked away, Kylie Scarborough—equally tall and even blonder—called out to her. "Hey Graziola. Maybe don't try so hard."

Nikki paused and turned to look back at the group of girls. "Why not?" she asked, genuinely mystified. A person didn't get anywhere without making an effort. She'd known that all her life.

When there was no answer, she pivoted in the other direction to hide her burning cheeks. Trying hard was the only way she ever got anything done.

As she headed for the snack buffet, she heard someone say, "Townie. Probably a scholarship student. There's a few mongrels every year."

No one was supposed to know which students received financial aid, but somehow, everyone seemed to.

Another girl fell in step with her. "Rohini Nakshatra," she said, tossing a look over her shoulder to indicate the power squadron. "They're pathetic. They think the villains in *Mean Girls* are the good guys."

Nikki laughed. "I loved that movie. But . . . you call that mean? Believe me, that wasn't mean. I'd agree with lame, maybe." In public school, Nikki had learned that *mean* meant getting rolled in the hallway for your lunch money every Monday. Mean was having your head plunged in the toilet for a swirly. Mean was making sure everyone knew your dad ran a trailer park.

Rohini turned out to be supernice. She didn't boast about her parents, but Nikki found out later that they were famous physicians and her mom was actually a corecipient of a Nobel Prize.

The beach party that took place later that day worked out better for Nikki. The beach was her natural milieu, and surfing was a key component of Thornton's physical education program. While most schools lionized football, Thornton set itself apart with its surfing and water sports programs. The athletic department had a quiver of surfboards, a fleet of Laser 2s, the rowing team's boats, a couple of Jet Skis, and the seventeen-foot Triton console speedboat used by the surf and sailing teams. Although some of the girls complained about the drab team suits and wetsuits, Nikki didn't mind one bit, and she could tell from the way kids stared at her that her wetsuit was flattering. The hipster bottom and skintight long-sleeved rash guard were fine with her. She wasn't tall, but she had curves and tight abs and muscles that had been shaped and elongated by hours in the water.

Ramses and another guy offered to help her carry a board into the surf, but she assured them she could do it on her own. Then she headed out into the water with the board, dipping the nose under each incoming wave as she made her way to the first break. Although she was a total misfit at the new school, Nikki was in her element now, surrounded by the power of water and wind. It was like a certain mechanism kicked in, moving her mind into a state that flowed like the ocean itself.

A few other students made a run at some of the waves. A couple of guys were pretty good. Nikki straddled her board and watched the action for a bit, letting the rhythm find her. She took her time waiting for the right wave to come to her.

"Need some help over there?" called one of the guys. "First time can be scary."

"I'm good," she replied nonchalantly. She waited some more, knowing the other kids probably mistook her patience for fear.

When the moment arrived, she popped up into attack position and started out with a quick turn at the bottom of the wave. Now she could feel the attention of the team members and coaching staff on her. Several of them dropped what they were doing to stare. She pretended not to notice as she threaded a nice hard curve, savoring the momentary rush of water-cooled air.

Nikki had learned long ago that surfing soothed her emotions and focused her mind, and that the best surfer was the one having the most fun. When she rode to a casual standing exit and picked up her board, kids from the team gave her a thumbs-up. They knew a good surfer when they saw one. She grinned and made the shaka sign with her hand. Then she turned and went back into the waves for a few more rides.

Surfing was one of the few things she could thank her dad for. He had never been the dad who coached soccer or taught her to ride a bike or even remembered her birthday with any regularity. But he was a damn good surfer. When Nikki took an interest at a young age, he'd taught her to swim and to surf. He showed her how to balance on the board and to read the rhythm of the waves. The sport was simple in concept, endlessly complicated in practice. She learned to respect the power of the water, not to fear it. She was indefatigable as she figured out how to read the waves. After a few seasons, her father declared that she was a natural, and that one day, she was going to be better than he was. Nikki wasn't so sure about that, but it was true that she could ride. And for a while, surfing was the thread that had bound them together.

By the time the beach party concluded with a bonfire, Nikki was welcomed by the team. She even noticed a couple of cute boys checking her out, including Mark McGill. She was savoring a carefully built s'more when he sat down next to her. "You're really good," he said.

"Thanks. Have you ever tried surfing?"

"Sure, a couple of times. Just enough for my mom's media manager to do a photo shoot, anyway."

"Did you like it?"

"I liked the surfing. The photo shoot, not so much. My sister likes that stuff." He eyed Marian, who sat on the other side of the fire pit, gabbing away with a group of students. "She definitely likes the attention."

"What's it like, having a twin?" she asked. "I'm an only child."

"It's fine," he said. "It's cool to have somebody who lives the exact same life as me, but sees things so differently."

At night, the new students experienced the school's digital blackout for the first time. Internet and data connections were shut off, eliciting groans of protest from most of the kids. Nikki didn't mind, since she didn't have a mobile phone, unless her dad remembered to pay his bill and his old Nokia was working.

The proctors and upperclassmen kept everyone busy with getting-to-know-you games. There were puzzles meant to get students to learn their classmates' names. Some were easy, because they looked like their famous parents, like Kylie Scarborough, whose mom was known as America's sweetheart because she starred in the current number one hit show. Another kid was the face of one of the biggest Christmas movies of all time—Hugo Harris—and had been a household name from the age of five. Now he claimed he wasn't really fond of acting and wanted to be a writer instead. A girl named Monica Mulli was an actual Kenyan princess. Even Jason Sanger was a surprise. In addition to being a douche, he played the trumpet and had a newborn baby brother by his dad's third wife. A boy named Tombo went by one name and had performed at Lincoln Center, and Kendra Watson had a national golf title. Judd Olsten's dad was the head of an evangelical megachurch.

Nikki was mesmerized. She felt as if she had been drawn into a special world populated with beautiful, mythical creatures. She imagined them living in fairy-tale castles surrounded by perpetually blooming gardens. They probably had their own theme songs that played in full symphonic sound whenever they made an entrance. Their lives seemed entirely different from hers. Effortless and filled with wonderful things.

So it was a shock when she went into the girls' bathroom and heard an unmistakable sound from one of the stalls. A few minutes later, there was a flush and Kylie came out. Scarcely acknowledging Nikki, she bent over a sink, rinsing her mouth out with water.

"Um . . . are you all right?" asked Nikki.

Kylie ripped off a wad of paper towels and dabbed at her face. "Mind your own business, Graziola."

"Just checking," Nikki said, impressed that the girl remembered her name.

"I don't need you to check on me." Kylie leaned against the edge of the counter and took a deep, shuddering breath that turned into a sob.

Nikki had learned about bulimia in health class. If someone did it a whole lot, it could cause major damage. She moved closer and lowered her voice. "Hey," she said.

"Back off," Kylie told her, but not forcefully enough for Nikki to take her seriously.

"Look, you don't have to be my friend," Nikki said. "I'm sure I can't fix whatever is wrong. But maybe—"

"You got that right." Kylie pressed a wet towel to her face.

"No one wants to see you get sick, or . . . or hurt yourself."

"You don't know that."

"It's a guess," Nikki admitted.

Kylie shuddered and braced her hands on the edge of the sink as she glared at her image in the mirror. "You know what hurts? Rhinoplasty, that's what."

"A nose job?" Nikki studied the other girl's nose. It was just . . . a nose. A pretty one, the kind you saw in the "after" pictures in the magazines. "Have you had one?"

"Of course I've had one," Kylie said. "It hurt like hell."

"Well, it turned out really good," Nikki said. "I mean, I'm sure it was fine before . . ."

"I didn't want to do it. My mom made me." Although her mom was America's sweetheart, to Kylie she was probably just a mom.

"You mean she forced you?"

"No, but . . . almost everyone gets it done and I felt like I had to."

"I'm sorry. That must suck."

"You think?" She looked immeasurably sad as she gazed at her image in the mirror. "I miss my normal nose."

Nikki wondered if she would miss her face if something about it changed. She didn't consider herself a beauty queen, but it was her face and she was used to it. "Don't you have, like, somebody you can talk to about stuff like this? A therapist or counselor, maybe?"

"Why would you assume I have a therapist?"

Nikki shrugged. "Don't most of you rich kids?"

Kylie gave a snort that was almost a laugh. "I started play therapy when I was two years old. So yeah, I've had a therapist all my life."

"Then you have someone you can talk to."

"Sometimes it'd be nice to talk to somebody who isn't getting paid to listen to me."

"I could listen. I wouldn't charge you."

That elicited a burst of genuine laughter. "You're all right, Graziola." For the first time, she studied Nikki, her eyes unexpectedly soft. "You've got that rockin' bod. Everybody noticed you at the beach today. And I like your hair. Have you always worn it short?"

Nikki touched her dark hair and decided to be brutally honest. "Ever since my dad got a Flowbee."

"You mean one of those dog-grooming things? Seriously?" Kylie leaned in for a closer look.

"Yeah. It was cheaper than the barbershop. Eventually, I guess I just got used to keeping it short," said Nikki.

"With a Flowbee."

"Well, not now. Now my foster mom cuts it for me."

"You're a foster child?" Kylie looked incredulous.

"It's complicated. Come on, let's go watch *Ferris Bueller.*"

They were playing an eighties double feature in the campus theater. There was popcorn and root beer and way too much candy. Nikki found herself sitting between Mark and Kylie, which caused her status to rise considerably. She was even able to relax and laugh at the movie. There was nothing not to like about *Ferris Bueller,* and everyone was in a good mood by the end.

Kids lounged around in a pit filled with throw pillows, talking about anything and everything.

"What's this place really like?" Mark asked Nikki.

"Alara Cove?" She frowned. "It's just a town. A beach town." She wasn't sure what he needed to know. There was the backdrop of the Santa Ynez Mountains, which she and Carmella painted sometimes on their plein air expeditions. The town was not too far from Santa Barbara, where the rich kids lived in Montecito and Hope Ranch, the middle class in between or in Goleta. A hike up into the foothills offered views of the red tiled rooftops of the adobe buildings, with palm trees and ocean breezes through the archways.

"What do you even do around here?"

"Well, you saw the beach. There are at least three good beaches. At my old school, we usually ate lunch outdoors. In town, there's a long dock with touristy businesses, and an art walk along Front Street on weekends. The country club has a golf course and a pool, but that's just for the rich people." She flushed, remembering who she was talking to. "The Driftwood Drive-In theater shows a different movie every weekend. And the marina has kayaks and paddleboards to rent. I never have to pay the rental fee, because my friend Manny works there . . ." She caught Mark eyeing her. "What?"

"Just thinking. Must be nice to be a regular kid," he said.

Nikki laughed. "Right."

"What's funny?"

"I was just thinking it must be nice to be a rich kid like you."

Mark paused, seriously considering this. "Sometimes it is, I guess. Some of that stuff weighs you down, though. Makes you want to hide."

Everything has its price, Nikki thought.

Not long after orientation weekend, Nikki told Miss Carmella and Shasta that she had cracked the code at Thornton. They were in Carmella's art studio, and Nikki was organizing the paint box attached to her Jullian easel, which she brought on her plein air expeditions.

"There's a code?" Shasta asked, peeking over the pages of her book. She always said she had no desire to go to Thornton. Sports and outdoor activities—and cutthroat competitiveness—had never been her thing.

"Of course there's a code."

"And you figured it out already?"

Nikki nodded. "All I have to do is be the best at everything, and I'll end up with a ton of friends."

Miss Carmella looked up from organizing some brushes. "What if all you had to do was be yourself?"

Nikki rolled her eyes. "Right. A local from the Airstream park? The kids would all flock to me."

"Maybe they would. Maybe not. You don't have to prove anything to anyone but yourself."

"That is not compatible with life in high school."

"Yeah, every school needs its share of mediocre kids and losers," Shasta said with a snort of laughter. "If everyone was the best, there would be no diversity."

"Very funny," said Nikki.

"There are a lot of ways to have value besides simply outdoing everyone else," said Miss Carmella. "You're there to find a path to your life. It's up to you to make the most of it. To find your way."

"People like me better when I win a race or nail a surf competition or get the highest grade. I bet you did the same thing when you were my age."

"I . . ." Miss Carmella paused. "Times were different then. As a student of color, I faced issues you have no notion about."

Nikki's cheeks heated. "You're right. I'm sorry."

"Tell us about Thornton when you were young," Shasta urged Carmella.

"Oh my goodness, it was considered an enormously progressive institution. Even scandalous by some measures. The school was fully integrated, coed, with an outdoor program that was second to none. My grandparents thought it was a safe, positive place for me. But at the end of the day, I knew I was different. I was either shunned because of my race or tokenized because of my race. I'm certain I did have a few friends who genuinely liked me for exactly who I was. Sometimes it was hard to tell, though."

Nikki had never been treated a certain way because of the color of her skin. She'd been teased about being poor, about living in an Airstream, about having a dad who ran a trailer park and drove a van from the last century. But never because she was white.

"That's too bad," Shasta said. "Because you're awesome."

"Why, thank you, baby girl. That means a lot to me."

"So far, I have one friend I'm pretty sure of, and one genuine enemy," Nikki said.

"An enemy? Already?" Shasta tucked her finger in the pages of her book. "Who? How? Why?"

Nikki gave a short laugh. "Jason Sanger, no surprise. How?" She shrugged. "Maybe because I know about the Sangers so he can't even pretend he's not a dick." She glanced at Miss Carmella. She didn't usually approve of crude language, but this was about the Sangers, after all. "From a long line of dicks. And why doesn't he like me? I haven't figured that out yet. Could be, *he's* still figuring it out."

"What about the friend?"

After the incident in the bathroom on orientation weekend, Kylie Scarborough had granted Nikki conditional approval to hang out with the popular girls. But Nikki knew better than to call that an actual friendship. She considered it an alliance, but not one to be trusted just yet.

"Mark McGill," she said. "He and I . . . we just get each other, you know?"

"Ooh, do you like *like* each other, then?" asked Shasta.

"Not even close." Nikki surprised even herself with the swift reply. "I mean, no. We're just . . . he's just . . . he's great, you know, but there's no liking other than friend liking." Attraction was a funny thing, she reflected. A boy could be perfect like Mark—cute, funny, kind, smart, thoughtful—yet she had no urge to make out with him. On the other hand, a boy could be tough, sarcastic, and sometimes even rude, yet something about him excited her. A perfect example, though she would never admit it in a million years, was Jason Sanger.

She and Mark had even talked about the issue. It happened one day after an excruciatingly awkward moment that could have ended their friendship once and for all, if they'd let it. The two of them were down at the beach after surf practice, finishing up their chores. Mark wasn't much of a surfer, but he was working as a volunteer judge, learning to properly score the rides he observed. It was Nikki's turn to sweep the surf shack that day. She hurried through her shower, peeling off her rash guard and bottoms and scrubbing the sand from all the places sand tended to collect after a day in the rough surf.

Wrapped in a towel, she swept the concrete floor, singing "Toxic" along with Britney Spears on the radio. She got into it a bit too much and spun around the broom, which caused the towel to drop.

At the same moment, Mark McGill came through the door.

"Shit!" she said, snatching up the towel.

"Shit!" he said, bolting for the exit.

She scrambled for her locker and yanked on her team sweats, trying not to be too mortified. As a surfer, she'd had her share of wardrobe malfunctions, but it always happened when she was out in the waves, not up close and personal like this.

Mark was waiting for her outside, pacing in the sand, his face on fire. "Hey, I'm really sorry about that," he said.

"Don't worry. Um, I mean . . . it's cool. We didn't mean . . . it was an accident, right?"

"Right. Totally."

They walked back to campus together, moving on to other topics—English class, Mark's gloating joy that he'd managed to secure tickets to an Usher concert, and his uncle's wedding in Massachusetts, which was a bigger deal than it seemed because it would be one of the first gay marriages in the country.

When they reached campus, she headed toward the library. Then she paused, feeling as though she should say something. "Hey," she said, turning back to him, "I'm glad you didn't make a federal case out of seeing me naked."

He shrugged, and a blush stained his neck and face like a harsh sunburn. He was so blond, and so damn cute. Most of the popular girls had a crush on him. "No big deal," he said.

"Huh. In that case, maybe I'm insulted."

"What, that I didn't look at you like you're dessert?"

"You don't like dessert?" she asked.

"I'm kind of picky about dessert," he said with a crooked grin.

3

Four years after that moment, Nikki could still hear Mark's funny, ironic voice. As she waited to step up to the lectern to give her speech, she shut her eyes and pictured her lost friend as he had been that day—impossibly young, vulnerable, and maybe a bit intrigued by her.

From that moment, she and Mark had formed an unbreakable bond of trust, right up until the night he died.

All through high school, Mark had embodied the very best of Thornton. He was exactly the sort of student who had given the school its sterling reputation. In fact, people assumed he would be class valedictorian. Yet when the honor fell to Nikki, Mark had been genuinely thrilled for her. "You're gonna knock 'em dead," he said when she told him the news.

Her speech today was meant to extol the excellence of Thornton. Even a local kid with nothing, a kid like her, could make something of herself here. She was a perfect example of the school's power to elevate a person's potential, even someone like Nikki.

Thanks to Thornton, she had a shot. The school had prepared her to live the life she dreamed of—a chance to study and travel and make art. A pathway to a future filled with love and adventure. One day, she might even create an actual family for herself, perhaps.

But only if she kept her mouth shut. Only if she didn't make waves.

Yet how could she praise the school now, knowing what she knew? Mr. Florian's words haunted her: "Do you want to say something funny, or do you want to say something true?"

Breathless and nervous, she looked out at the crowd, only half listening as the dean of students introduced her, the words ringing across the field with a slight echo.

"It is my great pride and honor today to present Miss Nicoletta Graziola, a young lady from right here in Alara Cove. She grew up surrounded by the ocean and the salt air, in the shadow of Thornton Academy. Some might say Nikki was lucky to be chosen by Thornton, but I believe Thornton was lucky to be chosen by Nikki. She exemplifies the qualities this institution values most—Sincere scholarship. Compassion. Athleticism. Striving. Personal integrity. As a student here, Nikki has achieved the number one rank in her class. She has lettered in three competitive sports—swimming, surfing, and beach volleyball. She's earned a commendation for her service at Helpline House, a local charity. I'm delighted to share that Nikki has been accepted to the University of Southern California to follow her passion for art and to develop her talents to the fullest. At this moment, I'm proud to present to you our 2008 valedictorian—Nicoletta Fabiola Graziola."

There was a brief eruption of applause, and a few yells from the student body. When she stood up, Nikki's legs felt stiff, her feet leaden, though it wouldn't be apparent thanks to the shin-length graduation gown. The applause crescendoed and then quickly tapered off. She hadn't expected much of an ovation. These people had no idea who she was. She didn't have a well-known name. She didn't have famous parents. She was a nobody.

As she stepped up to the lectern, her teammates offered their signature cheer—"*Go Nikki go!*" Some of the guys howled like wolves—the school mascot. Mark would have howled right along with them.

The support of her classmates used to mean the world to Nikki. The need for approval had driven everything she'd done at Thornton. She had not earned top grades and top honors in pursuit of some lofty personal goal. Far from it. She had done so in order to be accepted. She was not from one of the richest families in the country like Audra Biltmore or Jason Sanger. She wasn't freakishly talented like Victor Gomez, who had already performed at Carnegie Hall. Her parents didn't have a gleaming collection of Oscar statues or a Nobel Prize. No, she was as ordinary as a box of cereal, so the only currency she possessed was to be outstanding whenever possible. So people would approve of her. So they would treat her like one of them. So she would be accepted. Maybe even liked.

Mark had liked her. Mark had loved her.

Mark deserved so much better than to be dismissed as a drug addict.

As a breeze swept in from the west, where the sky was taking on the deep golden color of late afternoon, Nikki scanned the crowd again. Some students had whole entourages to cheer them on—not just parents and siblings, but grandparents. Aunts and uncles. Former nannies and siblings and au pairs. Tutors and therapists. A couple of the kids had bodyguards, and one notable family was discreetly shadowed by Secret Service agents.

Nikki had requested only three tickets to commencement. One for her father, who had tried to wriggle out of the commitment as usual; another for Miss Carmella; and the third for Shasta. The three of them sat together about halfway back. Carmella's scarf, displaying school colors, fluttered like a flag in the breeze. Even now, decades after she had been the first woman of color to graduate from Thornton, she was considered a VIP.

Guy Graziola had never been comfortable around the sort of crowd gathered at today's commencement. He told Nikki that he'd never attended a graduation ceremony, not even his own back in Cape May, New Jersey, because he'd dropped out of high school in order to drive across the country on a teenage whim. That was his explanation, anyway.

Nikki's dad had arrived late as usual. He'd cleaned himself up in his own way—khakis instead of board shorts, an aloha shirt with a vintage blazer, cowboy boots instead of flip-flops, his ponytail neatened up. People often said he had Hollywood looks, and he'd been mistaken plenty of times for a TV star, maybe like a dude on a sitcom or cop show, thanks to his working-class handsomeness. People often wondered why he was still single after being widowed so young—"a good-looking guy like you"—and he would just laugh it off, saying, "You'll have to ask all the dames who rejected me."

Even though he never remarried, he still dated plenty. Women seemed drawn to his good looks and easy charm, but they never stayed. The Beachside Caravans life didn't seem to hold much appeal to women hoping for a future. And when they met Nikki— gap-toothed, unkempt, almost feral—they headed for the hills. Guy didn't know how to do hair, so he kept Nikki's short. When she was very small, people sometimes mistook her for a boy. She had been as cute as any little kid, but according to the parade of babysitters who kept quitting, she was hell on wheels.

During Nikki's time at Thornton Academy, her dad had kept his distance from the earnest, intensely ambitious Thornton parents. For four years, he'd managed to dodge parents' weekend, grandparents' weekend, and all the other family-oriented events. He'd already warned her that he wouldn't be attending the various receptions and parties that would take place after the ceremony.

This was fine with Nikki. People seemed to like her dad, and it was embarrassingly obvious that women loved him—for a while, at least. He was a popular figure around town. But he just didn't seem like the other kids' parents.

Now her legs trembled as she stood at the lectern, clutching her printed speech in both hands. From this perspective, the gathering looked huge and intimidating, a sea of blue and gold graduates, and behind them, the well-dressed, scrubbed, and shiny families and friends. She laid the pages on the slanted deck and leaned forward slightly, her heart pounding. There was a flicker of feedback from the microphone. The panoply of expectant faces blurred before her eyes.

Nikki drew a deep, steadying breath. She felt as if she were teetering on some unseen precipice, about to take a plunge.

She looked down at her painstakingly typed document—the speech the committee had approved and expected to hear. Then she looked out at the gathering. All the faces seemed to meld together.

The afternoon sun rimmed the distant coastline with flame. A breeze lifted the pages, and Nikki laid her hand on them to keep them from blowing away. She took another deep breath, then cleared her throat.

"Ladies and gentlemen, fellow students, faculty members, and distinguished alumni, let us commence. It is my honor to stand here before you today." Her voice sounded flat and lifeless, devoid of the passion that was supposed to animate her delivery. Her heart wasn't in it. Her heart was broken. Her words were hollow lies. She felt as if she might burst into tears at any moment.

She swallowed hard and started to read. "Four years ago, I came to Thornton not knowing what to expect. My first impression . . ." She stumbled, remembering her first encounter with Mark—hugging his dog, dealing with his spilled suitcase, offering her a warm smile.

Impulse drove her to look up from the words she was reading. She had a decision to make. She considered not speaking up. There was a strong case to be made for keeping her mouth shut. Sticking to the script. She knew perfectly well that if she simply left things alone and didn't rock the boat, then her silence, her complicity, would lead to the life she had imagined for herself. If, on the other hand, she said exactly what was on her mind, she would be putting all of that at risk. They might withhold her diploma. Her four years of hard work might lead to nothing. No scholarship. No USC. No way out of Alara Cove.

Nikki shut her eyes. Then she lifted her hand from the printed pages and the breeze took them, blowing them away on a fresh breath of air. Someone on the dais tried to collect them, but the papers were swept to the ground.

She didn't flinch, didn't blink. Didn't think. Instead, she leaned toward the mic and spoke in a clear voice. "I had a lot to say to you today about what the past four years have meant to me, and what they meant to us all. Thornton was a place of safety, that's what we all thought."

Her delivery wasn't flat now, but sharp and strong, ringing with conviction. Only a few people had seen her speech. Only a few would realize she had already veered off script. "We were taught to think for ourselves and to speak our truth. So that's what I have to do today. Our hearts are heavy in this moment, and now I have an obligation to voice the truth for someone who is no longer with us to speak for himself."

She felt a slow trickle of sweat between her shoulder blades. She sensed someone shifting behind her in the faculty section. Going down this path would lead to trouble. Nikki was aware of the risk. She'd been warned.

"By now we've all been told that Mark McGill had a drug problem, and that he died of an overdose. But the reports in the media are wrong. Mark wasn't an addict. That's not what caused his death."

A chorus of murmurs rolled through the crowd. A mad shuffle erupted on the dais behind Nikki. She knew she probably had only a few moments before someone shut off her mic and hastened her offstage. "Mark McGill did not use drugs. He was not an addict like people are saying. It was a hazing incident at this school, and they're trying to cover it up."

"Miss Graziola! Step down immediately," hissed an urgent voice behind her.

Nikki forged ahead in a strong, clear voice. Her legs weren't shaking anymore. "The Buccaneers Club had one of their secret revels no one is supposed to know about. The thing is, everybody knows, and the school turns a blind eye to them."

The Buccaneers Club had probably started innocently enough many years ago, with a group of seniors who organized fund-raisers and boosters, hosting what they called revels with their fellow members. Over the decades, it had somehow morphed into an exclusive clique dominated by the worst and most influential kids in the school. At the revels, members had to pass through a gauntlet of dares and challenges.

When Jason Sanger became head Buccaneer this year, the challenges became increasingly risky. He and his buddies created a drink with whiskey and crushed pills, and they dared the other students to try it. Students like Mark, who just wanted to belong.

Her heart in her throat, Nikki scanned the sea of blue-gowned graduates, and her gaze fixed on Marian McGill, who was seated next to Mark's empty chair, piled high with flowers and mementos. Marian was the person she needed to reach. Because Nikki knew something. She knew Marian had been at the party.

Now Nikki was talking to an audience of one. Mark's twin sister. She drilled Marian with a stare and let the words rush from her. "The Buccaneers do oxy-bombs at those parties—that's a crushed oxy dropped in a shot of Fireball. They fed those to Mark. You can deny it all you want, but the people who were there—you know who you are." Even from a distance, Nikki could see the color drop from Marian's face. Marian slowly shook her head back and forth, back and forth, her mouth forming an oval of horror. Nikki didn't relent. "You know what happened. And now a student is dead because of—"

There was a screech of feedback, and then the mic went dead.

Nikki wasn't surprised. Obviously someone had guessed where she was going, and didn't want this crowd to hear the truth from her.

"Step down, Miss Graziola," the dean of students commanded. "Don't embarrass yourself further."

She swung around and glared at the faculty, the men and women who had shaped the past four years of her life. They had been her mentors. Her encouragers. Now they formed a frieze of fear and outrage, their faces aghast. Nikki had tried to tell the school authorities at the time, but they'd refused to listen. Worse, they'd implied that she was just hysterical, her teenage mind addled by grief and shock. They'd tried to tell her all the clever ways an addict might hide his habit; they'd suggested she didn't know Mark as well as she thought. They tried to make her doubt herself. To doubt the truth.

Now she turned back to the crowd, cupped her hands around her mouth, and shouted, "Justice for Mark!" Obviously, there would never be justice for him, but she wanted to make sure people realized he didn't overdose; it was a cover-up of hazing to save the school's reputation.

She knew there would be pictures and maybe even video. Everyone brought a camera to commencement. A lot of the rich kids had camera phones.

Then, spotting Coach Lambert making a beeline in her direction, she knew her time was up. She turned and left the dais, chin held high. Face aflame.

As she stepped down onto the close-cropped grass of the playing field, Nikki began to absorb the full impact of what she had just done. She had set the commencement ceremony on fire. In one impulsive moment she'd put her entire future at risk. Now she felt trapped like a sacrifice in an arena. The sea of gowned graduates rippled before her, emitting waves of outrage as people realized she had just blown up their graduation.

Nikki caught a glimpse of Mark's sister, but Marian sat with her eyes cast down, her shoulders hunched. Nikki lowered her head and hurried toward the exit.

"Keep walking, you stupid twat," Jason Sanger said to her as she passed him on her way down the aisle formed by the rows of chairs. "You might as well walk straight into the ocean and disappear. Stupid fucking c—"

Inundated by jeers and boos from other students and by ear-splitting feedback from the sound system, Nikki lengthened her strides. She didn't try to find her dad or Shasta or Miss Carmella. Everything was a blur, and all she knew was that she had to get the hell out of there.

4

Nikki didn't break stride as she peeled off her cap and gown, dropping them on the ground by the registration table outside the stadium. She continued walking across the quadrangle, passing through the massive wrought-iron gates that arched over the main entrance of the campus.

At the top of the arch was the school motto, *Audentes Fortuna Iuvat*, a line by the Roman poet Virgil everyone eventually learned in Latin class but no one really thought about. *Fortune favors the bold.*

Had she just done something bold? Or totally foolish? She was sure everyone thought she was a complete blithering idiot. The crazy girl no one believed.

She headed for the ocean. For Nikki, it had always been a place of refuge. Over the past four years, she had made this hike countless times—on foot, on her bike, on the team bus. She gravitated toward the sea like those newly hatched turtles, irresistibly drawn to her natural milieu. Other people were happy enough hanging out on the beach, basking in the sunshine, and playing in the shallow rushing waves, but Nikki had always wanted to be out in it, part of it. When Nikki started school, the teacher said she couldn't sit still for anything except art, lunch, and PE. Some parents wouldn't let her play with their kids because she liked the shock value of using her dad's best swear words, and she tended to have adventures, like climbing the water tower, riding her bike off the end of the marina dock, or swimming out too far. The beach patrol made her wear a neon orange suit just so they could keep track of her.

When other grade-schoolers were practicing their cursive writing, Nikki was studying hydrodynamics, though she couldn't have known what it was called. She was mesmerized by the ocean's power and movement. It beckoned to her, invited her to explore its mysteries.

The only danger, her father used to say, was failing to learn the ways of the ocean. The most rideable waves on the coast happened to be right here at her doorstep. Her excellence at the sport had opened doors. But it was her love for surfing that had saved Nikki.

College team scouts had come here to watch her surf, and her talent on the water had been the key to her acceptance at USC. Mark, her best cheerleader, always thought she could compete in the Global Surf League, the elite professional organization. With Mark gone, who would cheer her on?

She made her way to the surf shack, where the school stored its gear. *Shack*, of course, hardly described the modern-designed facility set seamlessly into the brow of the cliffs that faced the beach. The donor family's name was featured on a plaque over the door. The key-pad code still worked for her, since she had been team captain this year. She knew her status was about to change. Everything was about to change. After what she had just pulled, she would be surprised if they gave her bus fare out of town.

At the moment, out of town sounded like a good plan. She was pretty sure she had just blown up her future. She already knew she'd turned herself into a pariah. She had sabotaged herself, but she felt no regret. She was the only one willing to speak up for Mark. Because he deserved better than to be dismissed as some psycho addict.

She unlocked the quiver—the team's selection of boards—and got out her favorite longboard, propping it against the building outside. Then she opened the shack, went to her locker, and changed, leaving her dress draped across a bench.

She and Shasta had shopped for days to find the perfect graduation dress. They'd discovered the fitted silk jersey sheath at the
Village Thrift Shop. Nikki wasn't too proud to wear secondhand
clothes, and Shasta swore she'd seen Rihanna wearing the same dress
on the red carpet at the Teen Choice Awards.

Before Mark died, Nikki had planned to wear the dress to the
reception after the ceremony, and then to the after-parties. But the
reception had been canceled. Everything was canceled. *She* was
canceled.

She put on a practice suit, a sleek, long-sleeved one-piece that fit
like a second skin, the deep blue of a storm-driven wave. This early
in the summer, some people still wore wetsuits, but she didn't feel the
need. It was a hot day, and she was on fire with what she had just done.

Then she picked up her board and headed for the water. The
heat of the day lingered into late afternoon, with high, puffy clouds
crowning a golden sky. The beach was scattered with the usual
assortment of tourists and locals. She could see a few surfers sta-
tioned out at the first break, bobbing leisurely as they waited for the
wave they wanted. Manny and Chassie and others in the local surf
squad weren't around, though. They had jobs now at the country
club, and their Saturdays were toast.

Nikki paused at the wrack line to fasten the leash around her
ankle. She shaded her eyes and faced the horizon, and then waded
in, welcoming the mild shock of the water. The ocean was a cleansing
anointment as it swept across her bare skin, and the salt water buoyed
her up as she went deeper. This was her home, her natural habitat,
the place where she felt most like herself.

A group of guys—likely frat boys from one of the colleges in the
area—made some noises to get her attention, but Nikki ignored
them. She had learned several ways to handle the unwanted attention. It was a pain in the ass that she had to handle it at all. Did they
really think she might say, *Hey, thanks for the catcalls, let me have sex with
you immediately?*

The sounds became more aggressive and they moved in closer, four of them. Yes, college guys—one wore a baseball cap with the Cal Poly logo. They were lean and tanned, and they acted totally full of themselves, which was usually a cover for a crushing insecurity. She had learned this from Mark, who had insights into male behavior. The world didn't make sense without Mark.

"Want to hang out?" asked one of the frat boys.

Great. The perfect ending to a perfect day. "Uh, no," she said, and stayed focused on the break.

"Come on, babe, we'll show you a good time."

Babe? *Babe?* She stopped and turned to them. "Has that ever worked to get a girl to hang out with you? Ever?"

"There's always a first time." One of the guys had the grace to blush.

"I said no. Anyone care to translate for your friend?" Without waiting for a reply, she surged away from them with the next wave, ducking under the rush of water and emerging on the other side, her short hair slicked back.

She paddled out, taking her time, observing the glassy undulations of the water and the shape of the incoming waves. Alara Cove offered rolling waves breaking in a stable pattern. Nikki actually enjoyed dumping and surging waves, just for the challenge, but most surfers preferred predictability.

The ocean was not just her refuge; it was her teacher. So many important lessons she'd learned in life had been taught to her by the sea—power, respect, humility, awe, vigilance, patience, timing, rhythm. She had learned her place in the world on the back of a surfboard. She learned balance. When she was surfing, her mind emptied of everything else. She had perfect clarity.

She worked her way toward the surf line, welcoming the wash of the incoming waves. She reached the spot of open water and the break where she could sit and watch the waves roll in toward the shore. She assessed each incoming wave. The swells forming today were big but stable. She plunged under the next wave, then slipped down the backside and scanned the break again.

Timing was everything when it came to surfing. It wasn't enough to spot the right wave. You also had to know when to make your move, when to go for it. Let the wave come to you. Don't bother chasing it. You'll never catch it. The ocean taught her that you had to know when to rise, and, most important of all, it taught her not to be afraid to fall.

Maybe that was the reason she'd risked blurting out the truth today. She wasn't afraid to fall.

The shifting water under her board carried away the thought. After a while, she sensed that the moment had arrived. The wave came toward her like an approaching friend, offering a ride home. This was hers, all hers.

There were unwritten rules of the sport—don't steal a wave if another surfer is positioned for it. No one else was nearby at the moment.

She paddled fast to match the speed and rhythm of the surge, positioning herself relative to the wave in order to drop in at the right time, and whether to drop in left or right. Then she extended from her belly to her feet in a single fluid motion that felt like a breath of fresh air. There was a glorious feeling that occurred when the wave took over her forward momentum. That split-second decision to yield taught her about trusting her gut and committing to an action. The visceral, overwhelming power of the ocean beneath her board put everything into perspective as she rode the fast-moving, curved wall of water. The speed, the wind in her face, her bare feet on the board connected her to the brutal strength of the sea. In sync with the ocean's glorious power, she rode the wave toward the shore. She exited before it weakened, then lowered herself and paddled back through the surge for another ride.

The ocean and the air cleansed her mind as she rode again and again. She didn't think, didn't worry. She let the day take her. She lost track of the time, but the sea told her when enough was enough. After the last ride, she eased ashore and crossed the beach, heading for the shack.

"Hey!" called a voice from the lifeguard station.

She turned to see Cal Bradshaw climbing down the timber ladder. The station was a painted wooden structure set on a raised deck, surrounded by surf rescue sleds and lifesaving gear. Cal hit the sand and jogged toward her, undersized and slightly awkward, but always earnest.

"Hey, yourself," Nikki said.

Calvin Michael Bradshaw was one of her oldest friends. She had known him since grade school, when she'd hit him in the face with a dodgeball, breaking his glasses. She'd felt so terrible that she had cried—so long and hard that he'd ended up consoling her. At the age of nine, she learned that he was the very definition of a good person. She already knew from any number of frustrated teachers that she was not, so she made friends with him in the hope of learning how to be good.

Nikki and Cal were both raised by single dads, but their situations were very different. Cal's father was always around, making stuff with him, teaching him to play chess and cribbage, and how to carve wooden signs for local businesses. Nikki's dad was usually out surfing, managing caravan park guests, hanging out with fellow surfers, or having a woman over.

Cal and Guy got along great, though, because Cal loved to talk and Guy was a good listener. Cal went on constantly about traveling the world, a notion Guy barely understood. He never wanted to go anywhere. When Cal asked him why, he'd encompass the area with a sweep of his arm and say, "Why do I need to see the world when my whole world is right here?"

Cal had always liked a good debate—Don't you want to see the big waves in Portugal and New Zealand? What about the world's ancient monuments and cities and art treasures? Her dad cheerfully indulged Cal's high-flown ideas about places he hoped to go one day. Unlike other adults, Guy never challenged Cal about how he was going to fund his travel. So mostly, it was just talk.

When their paths to high school diverged, Nikki's friendship with Cal distanced. And he was so different from the boys at Thornton. When it came to appearances, Cal didn't sweat the details. Short of stature, slight of build, he looked like a person put together from mismatched parts. He wore an oversized stenciled LIFEGUARD T-shirt and had a prominent Adam's apple. Bony legs protruded from his red logo trunks, which sagged around his skinny waist despite being cinched in with a drawstring. He had a shock of nut brown hair that his father cut at home. Judging by the uneven spikes peeking out from beneath his lifeguard's bucket hat, Cal's dad was still at it. The lenses of his glasses were so thick they magnified the bright blue of his eyes.

"Aren't you supposed to be, what, graduating at the top of somebody's class?" he asked her.

"Yep," she said, "but I totally blew my speech. Right in the middle of it, I switched gears. I had to say something about Mark."

Calvin and Mark were not exactly friends, but they knew each other. In the past four years, she'd introduced them and tried to get them to hang out. It was awkward for her to straddle the line between her townie friends and her Thornton friends, but the two boys were important to her for different reasons. They got along fine, but sometimes it seemed like the only thing they had in common was Nikki.

"What do you mean, you said something?" Calvin asked.

She told him about her blurted-out accusation and its aftermath. "I was so scared. But I kept thinking about Mark and I couldn't hold it in."

"Not surprised," he said. "I figured you'd have a hard time keeping quiet."

"*Everybody* should have a hard time keeping quiet when a kid is dead and there's no investigation," she said. She felt depleted by the day. "You on a break?"

"Uh-huh. Want to hang out?"

She rinsed off in the beach shower, then ducked into the surf shack to towel-dry her hair, shaking out as much sand as she could. Then she swapped the rash guard for a denim shirt from her locker and joined Cal outside. She left the fancy silk dress on the bench like a skin she'd just shed. She and Cal fell in step together and walked away from the main part of the beach. There were three cypress trees at the far end of the strand jutting out like triple exclamation points. When they were little, she and Cal used to play at Three Tree Point, building forts out of driftwood and hiding out among the wind-harried trees.

They found a patch of shade and sat on a big fallen log. The throaty boom and watery hiss of the surf continued its endless rhythm. Nikki glared out at the horizon.

"So what do you think? Is that Buckhorn Society going to get what's coming to it?" Cal asked her.

She shrugged. "Buccaneers. You know, like pirates. It's out of my hands now. I kicked the hornet's nest."

"Well, you know the problem with that. The person who kicks the hornet's nest is the one who ends up getting stung."

"I know. But I had to say something. Nobody else would, not even his damn sister. Not even his . . . his closest friends. They were all too scared of getting in trouble. Mark was . . . he deserved better. He was really something, Cal. Such a good guy. All he ever wanted was to make people happy."

"Isn't that all anyone wants?"

"I suppose." She mulled over the notion. Was that what she wanted? To make people happy? What people? Was making them proud the same as making them happy? In the past week, her life had become very confusing. The world suddenly seemed so complicated.

Grief was a horrible feeling. It made her head and her heart throb with agony.

"What's going to happen to you?"

She shuddered as she told him about the leaden feeling in her gut when she fled from the commencement ceremony. "I didn't really think about that. They might withhold my diploma. Could be I trashed my entire future."

"For telling the truth?"

"I don't know. Maybe. They sent out a memo beforehand about not disrupting the ceremony. No yelling, throwing Frisbees, or making unapproved statements . . . Guess I'd better come up with a Plan B." She felt the wind ripple through her shirt.

"What did your dad say?"

"I suppose I'll find out when I see him tonight." She sighed. "This was not how the day was supposed to go."

"No? And how was it supposed to go?"

"I was supposed to deliver the speech I slaved over for days and days. The crowd would go wild, giving me a standing ovation. They would all be like, 'Who is that brilliant girl? She has such a bright future ahead of her.' Instead, they cut off the mic in the middle of my speech and I left the stadium in a walk of shame. Came straight to the beach and grabbed my board."

"That's kind of badass," he said.

"Kind of stupid," she said.

"You're still that brilliant girl. And you still have a bright future."

Something in his tone brought her up short. She looked at him, finding comfort in his familiar, goofy face, his kind eyes and crooked smile. "Hey. Here I am wallowing in my woes, and I haven't even asked how *your* graduation went." Alara Cove High School's commencement had taken place the day before Thornton's.

He shrugged his shoulders. "It went. We all got our diplomas. My dad and Sandy and I went to Doc's for fish and chips. My mom sent me a text message."

She glanced at him sideways. "Sorry about your mom."

"I've learned not to expect much from her."

Nikki nodded, swirling her bare foot in the sand. She didn't know what it was like to have any sort of mother, even one who took off and left her family behind and hardly ever contacted them. When Nikki and Cal were in fourth grade, she got a black eye for starting a fight with a kid who called Cal's mom a loony.

"She doesn't know what she's missing," Nikki said. "She ought to be proud of her awesome son who got into college and is going to take the world by storm."

He grinned. "Right. Hey, I just found out Brown has a program where you can spend junior year abroad."

"Yeah? You gonna do it?"

"*Dub.*"

"Abroad is pretty . . . broad. Where would you go?"

"Freakin' everywhere. Serious. Thailand and Iceland and Senegal and . . . Hell, *everywhere*. Maybe I'll get on one of those boats that visits every port in the world."

"That sounds heavenly. Maybe I'll join you."

He was quiet. There was a weight to his silence; she could feel it pressing against her. "What? You don't want me to join you?"

"It's not that. It's . . . I worry about my dad."

"What's up with your dad?"

"I think his cancer might be back."

Her stomach clenched. "You think? You *think*?"

"He just had a bunch of doctor appointments. Lab tests. Scans. He says they're just being cautious, but he's lost some weight, and they're worried about his vision. Like, there might be damage to his optic nerve."

"Oh, Cal. I'm sorry. And here I am, yammering to you about my graduation shit show."

This was so much worse. Cal and his father had always been superclose. Alfred Bradshaw was a familiar figure around the meticulously maintained Thornton campus. Thanks to him, the school's formal gardens were famous. The sales brochures called it a school in a garden, and the photos usually featured the main quadrangle with its precisely cut hedges, massive eucalyptus trees, and abundant flowerbeds.

Mr. Bradshaw always had a smile and a kind word for anyone. Even when some of the lofty, entitled students ignored him as if he were a piece of lawn furniture, he cheerfully went about his business. He continued to work at his job even while going through cancer treatment, his face gray and gaunt, his bald head covered with a Dodgers baseball cap.

Cal had reacted to his father's diagnosis by growing up seemingly overnight. He went from being a dorky fourteen-year-old riding his bike and building tree houses and forts in the woods to hauling wheelbarrows full of compost on campus in order to help out his dad. A few of the Thornton kids had tried to tease him, but Cal ignored them in a way that just made them look like dicks. Cal's brother, Sandy, who was four years older, had a different reaction. He went out drinking and partying and got in trouble at school. Eventually, he dropped out and went on the road as the bass player for a band. It was a bad time for Cal's family, and Nikki knew it had been a huge relief when Mr. Bradshaw's cancer went into remission and he seemed like his old self once again.

Now she saw new lines of tension in Cal's face and felt guilty that she had not noticed it before.

"I wish I could help."

"Yeah. We're hoping for the best."

She shaded her eyes and scanned the beach. The coast road was crowded with vans and cars, bringing flocks of people from the bigger cities to the north and the south. The crowds seemed to get thicker every year. "I can't wait to get away from this place," she said. "Sometimes it seems like the whole world wants to come here."

"Tell me about it. I had to go in four times before lunch today."

"You're a hero. Did you save a damsel in distress and did she confess her undying devotion to you?"

"Right." A horn sounded from the lifeguard station. "Break's over," Cal said. "Time for me to put in forty-five more minutes of hawklike vigilance. One final shift and then I'm off."

"I'd better go, too. Check on my hornet's nest."

"Don't get stung."

5

Nikki stuffed her graduation clothes into a duffel bag and wore her team shorts, denim shirt, and flip-flops to the bus stop. While waiting for the shuttle to town, she took out the book she was reading—*Madame Bovary*. She'd had to read it for French class last year, but she found the story so fascinating that she wanted to read it again in English. There was something weirdly mesmerizing about Emma Bovary—her persistent discontent, her high-flown dreams, her desperation to escape the drab, provincial life she led. Imagine, a yearning so powerful you would die for it.

"I can relate, Emma," Nikki said under her breath, opening to the dog-eared page where she'd left off. The author got in trouble for writing about a cheating wife, but he wrote the book anyway. He believed the world needed a story about a woman whose passions burned away all reason.

Perversely, Nikki could relate more to Charles Bovary, who as a teenager had attended a rigorous, cliquish school that was not so different from Thornton. Did he feel that he had something to prove because he was poor? Did he strive to inspire kids to like him by making sure he was the best student, the best athlete, the best friend to all the high-and-mighty kids? Did he fail to figure out what his true purpose was?

And Emma. What a hot mess, always reaching for status, never satisfied with anything. She came to a bad end, poisoning herself. But the real poison was disappointment—for chances not taken, yearnings unfulfilled, stupid choices she couldn't take back.

Nikki derived a strange comfort in reading about people who were more screwed up than she was. As the light changed to early evening, she was distracted by the glint of sunshine off the row of windows of the Thornton buildings on the hilltop that loomed over the highway. The stadium would be empty now. The dorms had been vacated, too, being prepared for the annual cleaning and for next year's crop of freshmen. The graduates would all be off to celebrate with friends and family. The florists and caterers would be the only ones left, breaking down the floral arches and the tables laden with hors d'oeuvres.

In a normal year, graduation from Thornton was a huge deal. After four years of paying a fortune each year to send a kid to the school, people were entitled to celebrate. But this year's traditional lavish reception had been minimized, since it seemed disrespectful to have a big party so soon after Mark's death. Families would have to find alternative ways to mark the occasion. Nikki had heard that the biggest private parties were still on.

Up until Mark died, life at Thornton was good. Some of the teachers were flat-out amazing, the way they challenged and encouraged her. Today should have been the culmination of all her hard work. Instead, she felt empty and lost.

Putting away the book, she tilted her head back and shut her eyes. *Why'd you do it?* she asked Mark. *Why'd you have to go to that stupid Buccaneers party?*

The bus lumbered to the curb and the door clanked open. The vehicle was outfitted with a bike rack in front and a surfboard rack behind. A few rowdy surfers clambered aboard and sprawled into the seats, their hair stiff with salt, their skin sun-darkened and filmed with brine from the ocean. Nikki climbed aboard and flashed her student pass.

She nodded a greeting—the locals all had a nodding acquaintance. Then she took a seat and gazed out the window at the passing scenery. The bus route followed the coast road into town. She had made the journey many times—on the bus, on her bike, even on foot. Sometimes it seemed she knew every inch of this coastline.

Like many beach towns, there was a fringe of run-down dwellings in the uplands, where the forest sloped eastward into the hills. Working-class people—those who ran the services and businesses of Alara Cove—lived in the area, euphemistically called "affordable housing." Closer to town, the homes and establishments took on a polished, seacoast vibe, and the welcome sign at the city limits named it AMERICA'S #1 BEACH TOWN. No one really knew what that meant, but it sounded good.

Around the last curve in the road was the marina, with boats lined up like sardines in a tin. There was a forest of tall masts with cables that sang in the breeze. A small fishing fleet moored there, offering fishing charters to tourists. There were powerboats of every size, all the way up to a few monster yachts complete with water slides and helipads. An arched bridge connected Radium Island to the mainland.

The marina district catered to boaters, with a chandlery, a bait and tackle shop, well-appointed restrooms with showers and a laundromat, and a small convenience store called the Marina Mart. Nikki had not entered that store since she was in sixth grade. Even now, years later, the memory of her disgrace there still made her shudder. She would forever think of it as the day of the last straw, when her father had finally given up on her and handed her off to Miss Carmella.

Nikki had been at Town Beach all day, and she'd had to make a pit stop in the marina restroom. The facility was meant to be used exclusively by boaters who paid a fee for showers and the laundry room. Nikki always managed to find a way in. That day, she'd learned the door code by spying on a family that had just pulled into the marina in a Nordhaven yacht. She waited until they entered, then casually typed in the code and strolled to the restrooms.

To her horror, she discovered that her period had started for the first time. A distinct telltale stain had seeped past her undies and all the way through her faded denims. Disaster. Waves of panic left her breathless. She was utterly certain that everyone who saw her would notice.

She tried not to hyperventilate. She was having her period. No need to panic. Of course she had been waiting for this. Of course she had read *Are You There God? It's Me, Margaret.* Of course she'd studied the "Girl Into Woman" chapter of her health textbook. She knew what was going on. But that didn't ease the mortification she felt about the soiled clothes.

Deep down in her most hidden heart, Nikki yearned to be like girls who had real live actual moms. It was a feeling she kept all to herself. She could even picture how this would go if only she had a mother to confide in. She would shyly tell her mom, "I started." And her mother would need no further explanation. She'd go all dewy-eyed and give Nikki a hug, and ask her if she needed a Tylenol and a hot water bottle. She'd coach her about how to actually use a tampon.

Nikki's reality was far different, of course. She would have to figure out tampons on her own, by the pictures in the instructions. She and her dad studiously avoided talking about "that stuff." She would rather eat worms than discuss it with him.

Keeping her back to the wall, she edged her way out of the stall and looked around. There was a vending machine by the sink; she dug into her pocket for some change. Two dimes and two pennies. Not enough. Even if she could get something from the machine, she'd still be walking around the crowded marina area with a big red stain. She couldn't take off her shirt and tie it around her waist, because the shirt was cropped at her midriff. That was the way everyone wore their shirts that summer, showing off their abs.

In the adjacent laundromat, an older lady sat paging through an old magazine. No one else was around. Acting nonchalant, Nikki sidled over to an unattended dryer and opened it. The clothes were still warm. And—jackpot—there was a pair of gym shorts. Surely they wouldn't be missed. She grabbed the shorts, slipped them on over her denims, and went outside.

Then she ducked into the Marina Mart and made a quick glance around. Narrow aisles, shelves crammed with goods. The clerk was busy ringing up a sale, and there were a few customers picking out sodas and ice cream drumsticks. She found a small box of tampons, stuck them in her shorts pocket, and scurried out the door, her heart pounding. It was a desperate move but she was desperate. She would've gotten away with it, except a guy with a laundry basket blocked her way.

"I'll take my shorts now," he said.

And behind her, the clerk gestured at the bulge in her pocket. "Are you going to pay for that?"

The memory still made Nikki wince. She was told to give back the shorts and the clerk ordered her to wait on a bench outside while the shop owner called her dad.

Only she didn't wait, of course. She took off running as fast as she could, jumped on her bike, and rode all the way home without stopping. Driven by panic-induced adrenaline, she barely felt the distance. But when she got to the caravan park, breathless and sweating, her dad was waiting on the stoop.

Guy Graziola was all jaw and brow, with a shiny tumble of dark hair and a swagger to his posture even when he was sitting still. Irritation seemed to roll off him in waves.

"Shoplifting?" he asked her as she tried to push past him. "What the hell is up with that?"

"I needed something." Her tone was defiant.

"Then you should have asked me for it."

"It's personal."

"Then you shouldn't have gotten caught."

"Excuse me." She jerked her head toward the door. "I need to go to the bathroom."

"You're grounded."

"From going to the bathroom?"

"Goddamnit, Nikki, why do you have to be this way?" He raked his hand through his thick hair. "I didn't raise you to be a liar, or a thief."

"You didn't raise me at all," she shot back.

"What the hell do you need so bad that you had to steal it?" he demanded.

Her cheeks were on fire. "Stuff. Like . . . Girl stuff."

"What the—" He seemed genuinely confused. And of course, that was the problem.

"Tampons, Dad," she finally spat out. "I needed some fucking tampons."

That shut him up, long enough for her to brush past him. She stormed inside and grabbed her things, then went to the outdoor shower. Behind the weathered boards, she stayed under the stream for so long that the hot water ran out. Then she stuffed a thick layer of tissues in her undies, closed herself into her cramped bunkroom, and cried so hard that her chest hurt.

When she finally ventured out, the sun was setting and her dad was nowhere to be seen. But outside her door was a paper bag from the local drugstore. It contained a collection of a half dozen different sanitary products.

The day of the shoplifting fiasco was a dividing line in more ways than one. Though she hadn't known it at the time, that day had marked the start of a new chapter for Nikki.

The next morning, her dad took her to Miss Carmella Beach's place.

Carmella and Dad knew each other from way back; Nikki wasn't sure how. But that day, they both looked superserious.

"You're going to stay with Miss Carmella for a while," Dad said.

"Stay. You mean like overnight?"

"For a while," he said.

"What, did CPS finally say you're an unfit parent?" she snapped.

"Hey," he snapped back. "Watch your damn—"

"Let's not do this." Carmella turned and spoke directly to Nikki. "You're welcome here. I'd love to have you."

"So I don't get a choice."

"Look, you're growing up and you could benefit from a woman's influence," her dad said.

And just like that, Nikki became an orphan. She wasn't officially in the foster system, but the result was the same. She was a parentless kid who had to live in a foster home. Her dad was almost never around. He worked all the time at the caravan park, running surf workshops and hosting exhibitions. In the winter, he went down to a surf camp in Costa Rica—for the work, he told her. He said she could come back to live with him anytime she wanted, but the only time she returned to the caravan park was during the summer, when she helped out around the place and gave surf lessons to the tourists. The Beach estate felt more like a home than her dad's beat-up Airstream at the caravan park.

The fact was, Nikki had always liked Miss Carmella for a lot of reasons. They had first met long ago, when Carmella set up her easel and pochade box on the lip of the overlook adjacent to the caravan park. She loved to return to the same scene, over and over again. Her main focus was Cypress Point—a jut of land topped by a brake of coastal cypress trees that grew slanted by the wind, as though they were perpetually in motion, running away from the water. She said it was her favorite vantage point on the California coast. She seemed happy to spend hours painting the scene in all its many moods.

"It's my own personal Mont Sainte-Victoire," Carmella was fond of saying. "That's the name of Cézanne's mountain in the South of France. He painted that mountain over and over again, at every time of day, in every season."

And Nikki would hug her knees up to her chest, rest her chin on them, and contemplate the scene. "It's pretty. It always looks the same, though."

"Yes," Carmella said. "And no. Just like a person, it shows different moods depending on what is going on around it and what is going on in the artist's mind. Some days, it's bright and clear, and other days, it's shrouded in mist or fog. The view is different at sunrise and midday and sunset. When there's a bright moon, you can see its silhouette. Every time I paint Cypress Point, I see something new. Not only in the scenery but in myself."

Nikki had been mesmerized by the entire process—the leggy easel, the paint colors in all their variety, and the swift strokes and contemplative pauses that transformed a blank paper or canvas into a layered scene.

Back then, Carmella had seemed happy to have a bit of company, even though Nikki was very small. She would sit in the dune grass beside the older lady, watching her paint. Carmella explained that *plein air* was simply French for "open air." "It's glorious to leave the four walls behind," she liked to say. "Out here, we're free to paint what we see, but it's just as important to paint what we feel."

One day when Nikki was about six years old, Carmella gave her a few basic supplies—a child-sized wooden easel, a paint box, and some brushes. She showed her how to secure the paper to a board with frog tape, and how to go about capturing a scene by painting from observation. She praised Nikki's early efforts, and the sound of her praise made Nikki feel ten feet tall.

She wasn't exactly sure when her curiosity about painting turned into an almost visceral passion, but she suspected it came to life on a day when she was with Carmella, and the painting on the board in front of her seemed to dance as if with a special energy, as if it were alive.

Carmella seemed to notice that Nikki's interest was more than casual. She spent days on the bluff near the caravan park with her easel and canvas. Eventually, Carmella got more technical. She demonstrated the way to compose a scene by framing it and finding a focal point. Together, the two of them observed the foreground, middle ground, and background, studying the many shapes, colors, and textures in the panorama defined by the canvas. Nikki learned how to use brushes, mix colors, compose a scene, and play up the value of darks and lights. Working side by side with Carmella, Nikki learned to bring a scene to life quickly and with deep absorption, because a shift in the weather could change everything. She eagerly created pictures with the unique, bold confidence of a young child.

Her dad said painting was the only thing that got Nikki to sit still for more than an hour.

As the proprietor of the Carmella Beach Gallery in town, Nikki's mentor shared her work and showcased other local artists. Carmella had amazing taste and the window displays always got people to slow down and wander in for a closer look.

Now Nikki exited the bus at her stop in front of the gallery, four blocks from Miss Carmella's place. It was hard to believe that she'd been living with Carmella for six whole years. It was even harder to believe that she would be moving out. She was eighteen and done with school, and it was time to find her own life.

Flooded with a jumble of memories and emotions, she walked the short distance up to Miss Carmella's house. A third of her life had taken place here, and she tried to sort through her feelings—grief and regret and impatience and breathless trepidation. But above all, she felt gratitude. This was where she'd discovered all the possibilities life had to offer. Maybe her dad had done the right thing after all, sending her to live here. She still felt that sting of rejection, but he'd probably made a good call.

The rambling Beach estate itself was something special— surrounded by gardens that looked as though there were fairies hiding in the shadows. The stone and timber house was called a cottage, but it was huge. Like that old-fashioned game of Clue, the house had a strange variety of rooms: the library, the parlor, the keeping room, the game room, the solarium. The place had been built almost a hundred years ago by the famous Black actor Henry

Beach. He was a pioneer in the film industry and had a scandalous love affair with a white woman, who he married even though it was illegal in California right up until 1967.

Carmella always said she never wanted to live anywhere but here, in the place her grandfather had built, even though it was too much house for a woman alone. She had no particular interest in marriage, she'd told Nikki, but she did love family, and the children she took in were her chosen family.

Now Nikki braced herself, knowing Miss Carmella was going to want to have a conversation about what had happened at the commencement ceremony.

Taking a deep breath, she climbed the stairs to the front porch, which was hung with aspidistra plants and begonia baskets, wind chimes and sun catchers.

"Miss Carmella?" she called out, stepping through the front door.

"We're in the solarium, having a tête-à-tête." Miss Carmella had a fondness for fancy words and foreign phrases.

Nikki carried her duffel bag up to her room and deposited it on the bed. Her mobile phone was on the nightstand, the red light blinking ominously. She pressed the arrow and saw a long list of text messages. The top one was from her dad. She read it and winced. Then she set the phone aside and went to the solarium, a light-filled sanctuary overlooking the back garden.

Miss Carmella waved to a tray of iced green tea, her customary afternoon beverage. Nikki was more partial to Orange Crush, but she took a small glass. The harsh, bitter flavor was like a punishment.

Shasta was lounging on a chaise longue with the cats and a fat novel. Shasta read books the way a gifted athlete played sports, with total absorption and laser focus. She was also obsessed with experimenting with hair and makeup. Today's look featured purple-streaked hair, violet eyeshadow, and a dark burgundy manicure. Miss Carmella urged Shasta to love herself, her mind, and her body.

But of course, kids at school were quick to attack anyone who was the least bit different.

Shasta had learned to ignore them. "Maybe I just need to grow into my face," she used to say, staring at her larger-than-life image in the mirror.

Now Shasta looked up at Nikki, blew a bubble, and popped it. "So," she said. "Your speech."

"My speech." Nikki darted a glance at Miss Carmella. She was always put together like a piece of art that had come to life, as intriguing and as complicated as her mixed heritage. She had a knack for combining colors and textures with a big piece of jewelry, like a cool medallion or bangle bracelet.

"Always dress well, because you never know who you're going to meet. But don't make your outfit the most interesting thing about you," she liked to tell the girls.

Now Miss Carmella studied Nikki with a calm expression. "How do you feel about it?"

Nikki's stomach clenched. "My dad and I are supposed to go to a meeting tomorrow morning with the headmaster. I just saw the message on my phone. So I guess I'm in trouble."

"Like, how much trouble?" Shasta asked.

Nikki picked at her nails. "Not as much trouble as the school is going to be in, I hope." She noticed Miss Carmella's expression change. "I know you love Thornton," she added. "But something bad happened to Mark and they're covering it up, and that's not right."

"Nor is it a good idea to speculate," Carmella said. "Just knowing the boy's character won't convince anyone."

"Not even you?"

"Without evidence, it will only prolong the agony of what happened."

"How can they find the evidence if they don't investigate?"

"Maybe they're doing just that, and you haven't been told. And maybe they will find something. This is not yours to manage. Not your circus—"

"Not your monkeys," Nikki and Shasta said in unison. It was one of Miss Carmella's expressions she used when she wanted them to mind their own business.

Nikki was in agony, knowing there was more she could say about that night. This was Carmella. Nikki could tell her anything. But it was Nikki's word against a conspiracy of silence.

Carmella finished her tea and placed her glass on the tray, and the moment passed.

"Go get changed," Carmella said. "Let's walk down to Playa Bonita for tacos."

Tacos were always a good idea. Nikki and Shasta went up to their room. Nikki put on a clean denim skirt and a T-shirt. She was combing the sand out of her hair when Shasta handed her a gift bag from the White Rabbit Bookstore in town. "I got you a graduation present."

"Aw. Thank you." She looked at the cover of the book, which featured a bright abstract painting. *"Colors of Dreamtime."*

"I read it in one sitting," Shasta said. "It's by an Indigenous artist in Australia. She hated her life, so she painted a new future for herself, and it all started coming true. Sounds bonkers, but I couldn't put it down."

Nikki wished she could paint a new future for herself. She was a pretty good painter—good enough to submit her portfolio to USC—but she wasn't *that* good. Not good enough to paint away regrets and sketch herself a different outcome. "You didn't have to get me a gift, Shasta."

"Well, graduation is a big deal. And the bookstore gives me a frequent reader discount."

"We don't even know if I actually graduated," Nikki said glumly. "I walked out, remember?" She looked around her side of the room. She had already started moving out. She'd taken down her posters and removed the photos from the corkboard over her desk.

"I can't believe you're leaving," Shasta said, collapsing backward on her bed.

"I'm going to miss you. Let's promise to be sisters for life."

"We made that promise on Christmas six years ago. Remember?" Nikki felt an unexpected lump in her throat. "Oh my gosh. How could I forget that?" She collapsed next to Shasta. "I'm awful. I suck."

"You do, but you're still my sister," Shasta said.

The girls exchanged a lingering look. They had shared a lot of looks, here in their bedroom at Carmella's house.

"Maybe I forgot that one thing," said Nikki, "but I remember almost every minute. Not exactly word for word, but every minute, like a movie reel." She had been twelve and Shasta eleven when they'd first met. Shasta had come to Miss Carmella's through the foster system. She had been surrendered by her mother on Christmas Eve. In desperation, her troubled mother had dumped Shasta like a delivery of lost luggage on the doorstep.

Shasta had been in shock, her gaze downcast as Carmella whisked her into the house. The girl said almost nothing as she ate a bowl of chicken noodle soup and a stack of Ritz crackers. While Miss Carmella tried unsuccessfully to reach someone at CPS, Shasta had consumed the meal with dull, mechanical efficiency. She peered at Nikki through stringy black bangs that were too long, forming prison bars in front of her eyes, and her face was filled with a kind of pain and suspicion that made Nikki wonder what she'd been through.

They'd shared this very room that night, the room Miss Carmella called the Royal Dormitory because it was on the top floor and had two queen-sized beds under the gabled roof. That Christmas Eve, Shasta came out of the shower looking damp and chastened, wearing a soft, faded Dodgers jersey and thick socks. She was not small, yet she looked lost in the bed. After lights out, both girls lay in the dark staring up at the vague glow of Christmas lights that had been strung under the eaves. Nikki was beginning to nod off when she heard a faint but unmistakable sniff.

Without a word, she tiptoed over to Shasta's bed and slipped under the covers, scooting close. Shasta smelled of shampoo and toothpaste, and tragedy.

"It's okay," Nikki whispered. "I cried a lot when I first got here, too. It turned out that I was crying from relief."

"Really?" Shasta asked.

"I swear. There was all this trouble I was holding in, like I was scared that if I let it out, then everything would drain out of me and I'd end up on the floor like a wetsuit with nobody in it."

That had been the first of many nights together. Now they faced a lifetime apart.

Shasta sprang up and extended a hand. "Let's get tacos."

They went downstairs and joined Miss Carmella. The three of them stepped out into the evening, walking slowly down to the city center just as it geared up for the early evening crowds. At this hour, the whole town seemed to glow with a special light that emanated from the burning seam of the horizon and spread like golden ink over the landscape. Lights came on in the windows of the shops. Restaurants rolled out their awnings and set up tent chalkboards with the day's specials.

The streetlamps along Front Street were festooned with hanging baskets filled with flowers and herbs and cherry tomatoes. Some of the establishments displayed banners and signs that read CONGRATULATIONS GRADUATES, saluting students from both the local high school and Thornton Academy. Tables at the fancy wine country restaurants had probably been booked for months.

Nikki knew that a number of Thornton families were hosting lavish private graduation celebrations tonight. She had been invited to three of them. Max Romberg, whose dad had directed a string of hit action movies, had rented the Driftwood Drive-In, an outdoor movie theater that showed classic films in the middle of a vineyard in the hills above town. Romberg's biggest movie, *Hello Darkness*, would play on a giant screen while everyone gorged themselves on gourmet snacks.

Jamila, who went by one name only, was celebrating tonight at the Alara Cove Country Club. She came from Middle Eastern royalty and had an extended family that could populate a small village.

And then there were the Sangers. They didn't have to rent a venue at all, because their home was easily as fancy as any commercial place. The Sanger mansion crowned an elevated point of land overlooking the ocean. There was a tennis court, a pool, and a six-bay garage that housed a fleet of fancy cars. At school, Jason didn't boast about his family's wealth and status, but he somehow managed to convey that the Sangers were the richest family in town.

"Glorified ambulance chasers," Nikki's dad often called them.

"Seems to be working well for them," Nikki would point out.

And of course, after today's fiasco, she would be attending none of the graduation galas. Miss Carmella seemed to recognize that and steered them clear of the fancy restaurants. The small, unassuming taco spot catered to locals, and it wasn't set up to host parties. They found a table on the outside deck overlooking the water. Nikki ordered her favorite fried avocado taco, but her stomach kept knotting up and she could only pick at it.

Upbeat mariachi music played through speakers, and a breeze toyed with the flags strung across the deck. "Such a pretty night," Shasta said.

"Glorious weather," Miss Carmella agreed.

"I miss Mark." Nikki started to cry.

"Of course you do," said Miss Carmella. "You two were so close. I know it hurts, but that's because you loved him."

"I did," Nikki agreed, pressing her napkin to her eyes. "Everybody did." Mark used to come around to Carmella's, hanging out in the studio, keeping them entertained by doing dramatic readings of plays, which were his passion.

"Love doesn't stop when you lose someone," Carmella said. "And you don't want it to. Wrap your heart around the memories, honey, and keep him alive within you."

"It's not the same."

"I know. But it's all you have, and it'll have to do."

Nikki stood up, fighting to conquer her tears. "Can I be excused? I think I'd better go see my dad about the meeting at the school tomorrow."

"I can drive you," Carmella said.

"I'll take my bike," Nikki said, "and stay over at Dad's place."

"Wear your helmet," Carmella said. "Keep your flashers on."

"Of course." Nikki leaned down and hugged them both. "Thanks for dinner. I'll let you know how it goes tomorrow."

6

It was nearly dark when Nikki approached Beachside Caravans. The property was magnificently situated on a bluff overlooking the best surfing beach in the area, and that was pretty much its only claim to fame. She'd ridden the sinuous route from town countless times on her bike, pushing hard up the last hill toward the flickering neon sign that marked the entrance at the main road. The old sign had long been missing the E and the A from the word BEACH, so of course people referred to the resort as Bitchside Caravans.

The sign had been a beacon to Nikki when she was little because when she was on the beach, she could see it from the first and second breaks. Sometimes in the fog, or on dark mornings when she went out on dawn patrol with the first surfers of the day, the winking light of the sign was the only thing to guide her home.

The collection of Airstream trailers had been the brainchild of a man named Boone Garrity. Back in the sixties, he had acquired a lease from the city for the ten-acre parcel. Known for his eccentric ways, Boone had rounded up the Airstreams from failed counter-culture communes and set them up for surfers. And people had found the spot in that uncanny way surfers had of somehow tapping into a secret network that spread the word about the best beaches, the best breaks, and the best place for a cheap sleep.

For a long while, according to Nikki's dad, the surf spot was a closely guarded secret. Folks like the Sangers complained that the park was an eyesore. They said it attracted riffraff. They harassed

Boone about the upkeep, hoping he'd move on, but Boone held firm. Serious surfers didn't mind the funky old trailers. They were picky about the waves, not the accommodations.

Guy Graziola had grown up surfing in Ship Bottom, New Jersey. When he was a kid, he'd learned the sport from the legendary Ron Dimenna himself—the founder of Ron Jon's famous surf shop. After dropping out of high school and falling out with his parents, Guy showed up in Alara Cove with his board, his Ron Jon T-shirt, his Jersey accent, and not much else. Boone offered him a job giving surf lessons and waxing boards for tips.

When Boone Garrity got sick, he had no family to help him out. It was Guy who took care of him through the worst of it, all the way until the end. Right before he checked out, Boone told Guy to look after the place, and to make it his home by the sea.

Guy Graziola was as surprised as anyone when he discovered that Boone had willed all the caravans in the park to him, free and clear.

Since the property itself was city owned, it wasn't such a grand legacy. But the city council renewed the lease and Guy took over the operation. Although he readily admitted he had no head for business, he counted on his passion for surfing to sustain him. He hadn't counted on having a family, though.

He met a girl named Lyra Wilson. Fresh out of high school, Lyra had driven with friends from Indiana to California, eager to escape the tedium of midwestern life. She didn't have much money but she got a job waiting tables at the Surfside Café in town, and she flirted with Guy until she convinced him to teach her to surf. He convinced her to fall in love with him. She got pregnant, so Guy married her—the logical thing to do, he explained to Nikki. He and Lyra moved into the host trailer at the far end of the lot.

Less than a year later, Lyra was dead and Guy was stuck with a newborn baby girl.

Running the park and surf school kept him busy. He left Nikki in the care of whoever he could convince to watch her. As Nikki got older, she figured out—seemingly through osmosis—that her parents' young love affair had probably not gone so well. They were nineteen and twenty when she was born, which was hardly a blueprint for long-term success. Her father tended to wave off her questions about the marriage—"*Of course I loved your mother. I married her, didn't I? We had a kid together. If that's not love, I don't know what is.*"

He definitely didn't know. Nikki didn't, either, but she was open to the possibilities. When she was feeling romantic, she imagined that her parents were truly in love, but their love never had a chance to grow and deepen its roots.

As far as she could tell, the one thing her dad loved was surfing. She had no memory of making a conscious bid for his attention, but at some point when she was very small, she somehow sensed that the door to his heart was shaped like a surfboard.

Sometimes he talked about Nikki's mom. "She was a natural on the board," he would tell Nikki. "Like you. She just took to it."

He used to tell her that a lot, and it always frustrated Nikki. "Talk about her, not just surfing," Nikki would say, desperate to construct a living, breathing mother out of air and memories. "What was she *like?*"

When her dad spoke of her mother, a distant look clouded his eyes. "You have to understand, I only knew her for a short time. A little more than a year."

Nikki always found that heartbreaking. They met and fell in love. Within a few months, there was an unplanned pregnancy and a hasty marriage. He told Nikki that Lyra was beautiful and delicate like a butterfly. Trying to visualize her was like trying to tape together a ripped-up photo.

"I never met Lyra's mother," Guy had told Nikki. "She lives back in Indiana. Lyra never knew her father. She moved out here and it was just the two of us, and that was all we thought we'd ever need. When she died it was the saddest thing in the world. The only thing that kept me going was you."

Nikki had never made her dad tell her the grim details of how Lyra had died. He always just said it was an accidental drug inter-action and left it at that. She tried to believe her dad had taught her to swim and surf because he wanted to do stuff with her. As she got older, the bond had frayed and weakened. At some point, she real-ized he just needed a way to keep her busy.

She turned her bike off the road and rattled down the gravel driveway that bisected the rows of Airstreams. Summer had only just begun, but it looked as though every unit was occupied. There had been a green-light report on the radio, which meant the fair-weather riders would be flocking to the beach. The caravan park was the favorite spot for people looking for a cheap place to sleep.

She coasted down the center strip past the Airstream units. At this hour, when the sunset bathed everything in gold, the place didn't look half bad—a collection of cozy units filled with happy campers. The low light of evening transformed shabbiness into nostalgia. There had been a coolness factor here at one time—that sought-after midcentury vibe—but the charm had worn off, eroded by overuse and haphazard maintenance. Still, the guests hanging out on the patios drinking beers or eating cones of fries and clam strips looked happy enough as the sun set on another day at the beach.

Nikki braked in front of Patsy's place. Patsy Hayward occupied a unit with her two little kids. She was a single mom going through hard times, and Nikki's dad let her live there in exchange for house-keeping and maintenance work around the place.

Patsy was on her front stoop, smoking a cigarette and staring at the sunset. The faint sound of a kids' TV show drifted through the screen door of her place. Worry lines creased her face, but she offered Nikki a brief smile. "Hey, surfer girl."

"Hey, yourself. How's it going?"

Patsy exhaled a plume of smoke. "Sorry," she said. "Nasty habit, I know." She stubbed out her cigarette in a coffee can filled with sand.

"I don't judge," Nikki said. "What's up?"

"Ex-husband bullshit. He's delinquent on his child support payments again, and all I ever hear is excuses."

Patsy had shown up one night when Nikki was about ten years old. With two little kids in diapers in a rusty hatchback, Patsy had a black eye and trouble breathing due to broken ribs. Guy let her move into the small vacant unit next to his. Not long afterward, a burly thug with a neck tattoo and a bushy mustache had come wheeling into the park too fast, his El Camino spitting out driveway gravel.

Nikki's dad had ordered her to stay inside while he went out to deal with the situation. Nikki heard some swearing followed by a terrible crunching sound, a gust of air, then more swearing. A few moments later, there was a squeal of tires and a spray of gravel as the tattooed man took off.

Guy came back inside, placed a sack of frozen peas on the knuckles of his right hand, and drank a shot of whiskey.

Patsy's ex never came back. And Patsy never left.

"That sounds tough," Nikki said to her.

"I suppose it's better than dealing with that loser guy or letting him get near my kids. I'll muddle through. Do what I have to do. Sure could use some good news, though."

Bad timing, thought Nikki. "I got nothin'," she said, but offered a smile.

Patsy smiled back. "Join the club, girlfriend. Join the club. You know, when you're young, every bump feels like the end of the road. Turns out, it's actually not. It's really just a speed bump taking you to a new place. And maybe you don't get to see what it is until you get over the bump."

Folks like Patsy put things into perspective, Nikki supposed. Her situation was a reminder that most people didn't get to coast through life. Everyone had stuff to deal with.

The caravan park was always in some kind of financial trouble. The place had never been a big moneymaker, but as long as the city kept leasing the parcel to Guy, they had a roof over their heads. Nikki couldn't imagine how the park could run without Patsy. She did most of the housekeeping and maintenance herself, and she supervised the few day workers who dealt with laundry and gardening.

Some dude sat on the stoop of Unit 7, strumming a guitar while his buddies scraped and waxed their boards. A little boy with long hair and no pants was playing with a toy dump truck while his parents made hot dogs on a camp stove. A few gray-hairs—surfers who had been coming here for decades—were having drinks in the folding lawn chairs and eating snacks like Bugles and chili cheese Fritos. It was a well-known fact that when you went out surfing all day, you came back with a raging appetite.

Her dad's place was the host unit, an old thirty-three-foot Airstream set at the far end of the park near the utility buildings and commercial dumpster. There was a carport next to it and an outdoor shower around the back. Behind that was a mechanical building and a storage barn for the rental boards, wetsuits, and other gear. A couple of lights were glowing in the windows. From a distance, the scene looked neat and cozy.

Nikki had spent the nights of her childhood lying under the curved roof of the trailer, gazing up through a small, rounded window at the night sky, often filled with stars. In the summer, there was one group of stars she learned to pick out every clear night. Her dad told her that this constellation was called Lyra. She decided that her mother resided there now, unreachable but ever present, watching over her.

Heaving an explosive sigh, she dismounted and leaned her bike in the carport.

"Hey, Daddy-O," she said, letting herself in.

"Hey, yourself. You hungry?" He was sitting at the small booth table, reading the paper and having a bite to eat.

"Always." She'd barely touched her tacos from Playa Bonita, and the uphill ride had finally made her appetite kick in.

He was having Frito pie, one of their standards. It was a layer of Fritos smothered in hot chili and cheese. When they were being fancy, they added sour cream and green onions on top. Nikki grabbed a bowl, helped herself, and took a seat across from him. The booth featured an old-fashioned tabletop jukebox that still worked, although the most recent selection was from fifty years ago. When she was little, Nikki would listen to A-7 at least once a week—"Lola" by a group called The Kinks. For some reason, it made her think of her mother.

"You went rogue at your graduation," her dad said.

"I couldn't keep it in. I had to say something. I had to."

"You didn't have to do anything."

"Somebody did. Mark doesn't do drugs," she said. *"Didn't.* But they said he was a druggie who overdosed, and that's just wrong. He was hazed, and nobody else would speak up."

"Sometimes a drug overdose is just that. A drug overdose." He shot her a squint-eyed look. "Almost always."

"Not this time."

He finished his bowl of chili. "Doesn't matter. That school's going to do everything in its power to bury this. Thornton needs to protect its brand. People won't send their kids there if they think it's a dangerous place."

"It *is* dangerous if you get sucked into the Buccaneers like Mark did."

"Then you can take it up at the meeting tomorrow with the headmaster," he said.

"Trust me, I will."

"Just don't expect him to believe you."

"Mark's own sister was there."

"Seriously? Then she's your ace in the hole. And if she's not talking, then maybe there's a reason."

Neither of them spoke for a bit. Nikki felt a heaviness in her chest, yet at the same time, it was hollow. Mark had been plucked from the world, leaving a void of pain and confusion.

"What's on your mind?" her dad asked.

She didn't want to talk about Mark anymore. Thinking about that night only made her feel worse. It created a sadness that bit with the sharp teeth of regret. "I was wondering something. Do you ever dream of a different life?"

"How's that?" He glanced around the room, as if it was a trick question.

"I mean, do you wish you'd done something else?"

"I did dream of a different life," he said. "That's how I ended up here."

Nikki couldn't sleep, so she went to her dad's clunky old computer and logged on to Facebook. The dial-up connection screeched as if in protest, but her dad snored louder. In the past couple of years, everybody had started using Facebook to instantly tell the world what they were up to. Nikki had joined the site, but she didn't believe she was interesting enough to put up pictures or to answer the front-page question, the one her dad had asked her just a short while earlier, "What's on your mind?"

Nobody wanted to know what was on her mind. Besides, she didn't have a digital camera or a phone that took decent pictures. So mostly, she just looked. A lurker, she was called.

That was Nikki, always on the outside looking in, the way she had the night she'd lost Mark. Now, no matter how hard she tried, she couldn't stop thinking about the way the events had unspooled. She ruminated about it endlessly, wondering if she should have done something different, and if so, if it would have made a difference.

It was after ten—after lights out—when she went looking for Mark that night. She had pretty good aim with the pebbles—their usual signal—but he didn't show up at the window. After a while, she gave up trying to get his attention.

As she made her way back across the quadrangle and went behind the theater building where she'd left her bike, she kept to the shadows and avoided the motion-detector lights. Thanks to Cal Bradshaw—who of course knew all about the campus lighting since his dad was in charge of it—she knew where most of them were aimed.

Hearing a thumping beat and strains of "Suffocate," Nikki had stopped to listen. It was coming from the theater building, which had fire doors on the ground level leading to storerooms for costumes and props. A known after-hours hangout, though she'd never hung out there. A seam of light leaked from a ground-floor window, glinting off something shiny in the pathway. It was one of those dumb Buccaneer tokens they gave out for completing challenges.

The sound of laughter mingled with the hip-hop beat. The Buccaneers were having a party. One of their ragers, as they liked to call the gatherings. She'd never understood why the club was so important to certain students—Mark included—especially this year, when Jason Sanger was in charge, calling himself the captain and coming up with reckless challenges.

As she drew closer to the building, Nikki heard a groan of pain emanating from somewhere nearby. She stopped and held still, her skin prickling with apprehension. She tracked the sounds down to a shadowy space in one of the window wells of the building. Someone was there.

Two someones, and the groans she heard were not groans of pain. Two shadows shifted and melded in and out of the darkness.

It seemed, at last, that she had located Mark. She recognized his voice. She could hear disjointed phrases and gasps, sounds of a passion meant to stay private. She didn't linger long, not wanting to embarrass Mark at such a vulnerable moment. Shaken by surprise, she tried to step quietly away. The gravel of the path crunched under her sneaker.

"Shit," said a voice, "someone's there."

Not Mark's voice. Someone else.

The shadows broke apart. Nikki was appalled, but there was no-where to hide, so she stepped toward them. "Hey, um, Mark. It's just me," she said quietly. "I didn't mean to startle you . . ." Two figures scrambled out of the window well, and she found herself face-to-face with Judd Olsten. He smelled faintly of cinnamon-flavored whiskey. Even in the low light, she could see glints of panic in his eyes as he adjusted his clothes, backing away from her.

Judd Olsten was a junior. His father was the head of some mega-church back East. Nikki barely knew him, and she hadn't realized Mark knew him at all.

"Hey, it's okay," Mark said. "She's cool—"

"Fuck off," Judd said, his voice low and harsh. "Just . . . fuck off." He turned and stalked away, then broke into a run.

Nikki scuffed her foot in the gravel. "Aw, Mark. I'm really sorry. I didn't mean to . . ."

He combed his fingers through his mussed hair. "I know you didn't."

"I won't say anything," she assured him.

"I'm not worried about you."

"You shouldn't worry about anybody," she said. "You're entitled to like anybody you want. It's really not a big deal." She felt zero surprise at the discovery. In a weird way, she'd known it without either of them saying anything at all.

Mark scoffed. "Right. Are you kidding me, Nikki? Not a big deal?"

She glared at him. He, too, smelled like cinnamon whiskey. "Why should it be? Nobody cares about that stuff anymore."

"God, what planet have you been living on? Oh, that's right. The planet Alara, where everybody goes surfing and lives in trailers and pretends the world is perfect."

She winced. "You don't have to be mean about it."

"Listen, my mom's up for reelection next November. You think she wouldn't get dragged for having a gay son?"

"Only by stupid people who—"

"Who what? Who vote? And what the hell do you think would happen to Judd?"

"I don't really know Judd, but—"

"His goddamn parents would send him to one of those camps where they force people to pray the gay away."

"To . . . what? That's ridic—"

"It is. And it's also real." He staggered a little and swayed away from her. "Go on home, Nikki. You just don't get it. I'm going back to the party. You need to go home. This isn't your scene."

She winced again. She must have really pissed him off, just by showing up. "Not my scene? Geez, Mark."

She had never been allowed to pierce the Buccaneers' inner sanctum, and it had never mattered to her. But to hear Mark say it cut deep. "Why do you do it, Mark? Why hang out with those guys?"

He scoffed again. "Why do you think?"

"Come on, I'll walk back to the dorm with you."

"I'm not going back."

"You're going to their stupid party? Doing oxy-bombs? Getting wasted? Mark—"

"Go on home, Nikki. This isn't for you." He pivoted away, stumbling a little, and went down the stairs and through the door to the storage room.

Nikki stood alone, close to tears. She started to walk away, then turned toward the window. The party looked like fun, with kids sitting around, talking and laughing. She wondered what it would be like to be part of that. Screw Mark for telling her she couldn't join in. She pictured herself barging in, becoming one of the gang. And that, too, made her cringe. If she crashed the party and got caught, she'd be toast.

Some people were doing shots. Others shared bags of chips and cans of soda. A few couples were making out while sprawled on the furniture that had been used in the spring production of *Radium Girls*. Marian McGill sat in Jason Sanger's lap, whispering in his ear and giggling. Nikki didn't understand why Marian was so into him. She seemed ridiculously proud to be Jason's girl—his *wench*.

Everyone looked silly and happy in their own little world. It was a world Nikki would never be a part of. She would always be on the outside, looking in. It had taken a while, and a lot of discussions with Miss Carmella, but Nikki finally came to understand this clearly. People who were born and raised in wealth and privilege were different. What seemed normal to them—a private jet flight to Sun Valley; a red-carpet movie premiere; an invitation to the White House; a private, illicit party—would never be *her* normal. She could be their classmate. Their teammate. Their lab partner. Some, like Mark, might even call her their friend. But she would never truly belong.

After four years, Nikki deeply understood this.

She saw Jason passing out shots, heard people laughing and chanting, "Drink drink drink!" Then she slipped away and headed home.

Now Nikki was haunted by that incident. She couldn't have known it was the last time she would see Mark alive, but she wished she could turn back time. She wished she'd barged in or reported the party to a proctor—anything that would have stopped the hazing.

She swiped at her cheeks and glared at the computer screen. A lot of the kids from school weren't shy at all about putting up their real-time photos on Facebook. Her current news feed was filled with shots of the graduation parties that were going on right now, in real time. She saw fellow students aboard someone's yacht. Chicken fights in the Sangers' swimming pool. A banquet at the Rombergs' party at the Driftwood Drive-In theater. And—

Nikki did a double take. She clicked on a photo to enlarge it. There was a picture of Jamila's gala at the country club. That was the one Nikki and Mark had planned to attend. They had RSVPed together, and she still had the little mortarboard-shaped entry tickets, right here by the computer. She and Mark thought it would be the best party. Jamila's event planner had hired an almost-famous eighties cover band, and Mark loved eighties music. It was the only music that could get the whole place on their feet, he used to say. He loved to dance the way Nikki loved to surf.

It wasn't the band that caught her eye, though.

It was Marian McGill. She was at the party. In the picture, posted just minutes before, she was dancing and laughing along with everyone else.

"Really, Marian?" Nikki whispered. "Really?" She pushed back from the computer screen as if it were toxic. Then she grabbed the tickets, threw on a pair of cutoffs, and mounted her bike, switching on the battery headlamp. The country club was less than a mile up the road, and she pedaled swiftly, propelled by fury. The night was beautiful, sprayed by stars, the ocean rimmed with bioluminescence.

The party was in full swing when she arrived. A woman at the registration table looked up in surprise and started to say something. Nikki slapped the two tickets on the table and barged into the ballroom. There was a red-carpet setup with a backdrop bearing the school logo and sponsors' names. She didn't slow down for it, but cameras flashed as she strode by.

The band was playing "Love Shack," and people were dancing and laughing under the flashing lights of a rotating disco ball. There was a photo booth set up on one side of the dance floor and a series of banquet tables on the opposite side. Nikki paused, squinting at the strobe-lit dancers as she scanned the room.

This should have been the biggest night of her life. She had planned to wear the silk Rihanna dress and heeled sandals, and Shasta would have done a stellar job on her makeup. Instead, Nikki was conspicuous in her cutoffs and T-shirt, but no one seemed to notice her.

She spotted Marian—her ace in the hole. Marian was with Jason Sanger, who apparently had abandoned his own graduation party to hang out with her. They were the golden couple, the ones everyone aspired to be—attractive, popular, destined for a bright future. According to Mark, his sister had been under Jason's spell throughout their senior year, measuring her own worth by Jason's approval.

As the song ended and a slower tune started up, Marian and Jason retreated to one side of the dance floor, their posture tense. Marian was up on tiptoe, saying something into Jason's ear.

Nikki watched them for a moment. She had never been close friends with Mark's twin sister, but they weren't enemies, either. Marian was not a bad person, but she was spineless. How could she let the world think Mark was a druggie? And why? Somehow, someone had convinced her to keep her mouth shut about the hazing.

Jason was vicious and popular and ridiculously good-looking. Nikki steered clear of him. Not now, though. She thought of Mark and felt the same surge of clarity she'd experienced earlier, standing at the lectern. She dismissed him with a cutting glare and turned to Marian as the band shifted to "I'm So Excited."

Touching Marian's arm, she leaned in and raised her voice over the music. "We need to talk."

"Back off, Graziola, you freak," said Jason, taking a step toward her. "She's got nothing to say to you."

She glared at him briefly, then turned her back on him, inserting herself between them. "Come to the bathroom with me," she said, taking Marian's arm and hustling her along before Jason could intervene. "If not, we can do this right here, and it won't be pretty."

The ladies' room looked like a fancy boudoir with dressing tables and louvered doors on the stalls and a chandelier overhead. At the moment, it was blessedly vacant.

"What the hell are you doing?" Marian demanded, her voice thin with tension. "Like Jason said, we don't have anything to talk about."

"Then how about you listen?" Nikki suggested. "Again. I saw you at the ceremony today. The look on your face. You were there, Marian. You know what happened. Mark deserves for people to know what happened. Was he in obvious distress and you ignored him?"

"No, oh my God, it wasn't like that. It was . . ."

"Then what, Marian? What was it like?"

"Nobody ignored him. Everybody was wasted and he left. If I thought he was in trouble, I would have done something. I'm not a monster. None of us are. But if we bring up the party, we'll all be in trouble."

"Then be in trouble," Nikki shot back. "Deal with the consequences. Trust me, it won't kill you. You need to speak up now."

"Why should I do that?" Marian's eyes darted toward the door.

"Because you don't want to be that person," Nikki said. "You can't be that person who lets everyone believe a lie. Why would you let them think your brother was an addict when he wasn't?"

"Jesus, Nikki, why can't you just leave it alone?"

"Because Mark deserves better."

Tears sprang to Marian's eyes. "How can it even matter now? He's gone, and nothing will bring him back."

"Why don't you want to clear your brother's name?"

"Because it's impossible. Don't you get it, Nikki? We're all hurting so much already. I don't see the point in ruining everyone else's life over a life that can no longer be saved."

Nikki felt a fresh wave of grief. "Oh, Marian. When has the truth ever ruined anyone?"

"Try growing up with a politician. Then you'd know."

Or an evangelical church leader, Nikki thought. She had a point, but it still didn't justify the cover-up. "So when he left, did you . . . didn't you even try to stop him?"

"I . . . He . . . It's not my job to babysit my brother at a party. It's nobody's fault. We were all doing shots."

"Shots with oxy."

"It was a *party*. I didn't know—didn't realize he'd done too much. Nobody knew. He left the party and that's the last time I saw him." Marian wobbled on her feet, then sank into a chair. Her posture was slumped over, defeated. "Listen, you were the best friend he ever had, Nikki. I get that. But this has to stop. You're trying to throw us all under the bus, and for what?"

"Because it's the truth," said Nikki. "And the truth matters. It's also the only way you're going to crawl out of that black hole you're in."

A distinctive noise intruded into the silence. It was a gagging sound, followed by a flush. Marian's face blanched. Nikki froze.

Kylie Scarborough came out of one of the stalls and went over to the row of sinks. She grabbed a small bottle of mouthwash from the tray of amenities and rinsed, then dabbed her lips with a towel.

Then she turned to face Nikki and Marian, who stood gaping at her.

"I was there, too," Kylie said at last. "And I know what I saw."

7

The headmaster's office was in the oldest building on campus, an ornate brick building with figured concrete flourishes adorning the doors and windows. Built long before the advent of air-conditioning, it had soaring ceilings with fans overhead to stir the breeze. The reception area was furnished with antiques and tall plants in pots, and the walls were hung with portraits of distinguished alumni, from Gold Rush millionaires of the 1800s to dot-com billionaires of Silicon Valley. One of the pictures featured Carmella Beach, looking impossibly young and glamorous, posing in the kind of outfit Jackie Kennedy might have worn.

Nikki's dad looked like someone about to undergo a root canal. Her father had never been fond of drama. And she was about to cause some drama.

Joni Rath, the headmaster's secretary, looked across her desk at Nikki and Guy when they arrived, then propelled her wheelchair slightly as she reached for a button to buzz them in. She kept her face arranged in an expression that was as neutral as Switzerland. "Coffee?" she offered. "Some water?"

"We're fine." Nikki's dad answered for them both, which was good, because she was too nervous to talk.

Joni indicated with a sweep of her arm that Mr. Ellis was ready to see them.

The headmaster stood behind his desk as they stepped inside. Mr. Glenn Ellis was Thornton through and through. He himself had attended the school, and he revered the institution, along with the salary and perks that came along with his position. He shook hands with Guy and solemnly invited them to sit. They faced him across a heavy, ornate desk. Behind him was an array of diplomas and certificates on the wall. True to Thornton values, there were no visible computers or cables, just a typical office phone.

Nikki glanced over at her father. Everything about this place seemed designed to make him uncomfortable—the antiques, the framed documents, the shelves lined with leather-bound books, the expensive paintings. Yet Guy appeared to be at ease as he settled into his chair.

"I'm sorry to meet with you under these circumstances." Mr. Ellis folded his hands on the ink blotter. He drilled Nikki with a penetrating stare. "What an unfortunate moment we've come to. And so very unnecessary. You were a Thornton success story until yesterday. I can't imagine what possessed you to make such wild accusations."

"The truth, I suppose," she said. Her voice sounded breathless. Uncertain.

One of the buttons on the desk phone started blinking. Mr. Ellis glanced over but ignored it.

"Did you know about this?" Ellis asked her father.

"Know about what? That my daughter tells the truth?"

Nikki felt a jolt of surprise. Did her dad really think that? Or was it just a show of solidarity?

"Did you know she was going to disrupt our commencement exercises with false accusations, and ruin the day for the entire graduating class?" Ellis persisted.

"He did not," Nikki said, keeping her tone firm. "I didn't plan to say anything. I shouldn't have had to. Finding out the truth about Mark's death was your job, and you didn't do it."

Mr. Ellis's neck turned red against the collar of his white dress shirt. "Your concern for your friend is admirable, and we all deeply grieve our loss. But . . ." *Womp, womp.* That was all she heard of a long, rambling lecture.

"Is there a point you're trying to make?" asked Nikki's dad, interrupting the tirade. "Because I'm not hearing one."

The headmaster addressed Nikki. "Using the school's commencement exercises to broadcast a terrible rumor was very damaging. You're young and I realize you miss your friend, but you've called the school's reputation into question, and you've caused more hurt to a grieving family than you can possibly imagine. We cannot undo the damage you've already caused. Nor can we deny that your performance at commencement will have consequences."

Her stomach knotted and her chest felt tight. She had put in four years of work to get to this moment in her life—college and a future people like her could only dream about. Had she thrown that all away? Then she pictured Mark, who had no future at all. "Do what you have to do. It doesn't change the facts."

"Young lady, if you fail to retract your public statements, the Board of Directors has urged me to withhold your diploma, and that means your acceptance to USC will be under review."

"What the hell is that supposed to mean?" Guy demanded, his Jersey accent suddenly flaring. "*Under review?*"

"Exactly that. A college acceptance is always conditioned on the student completing graduation requirements. As of this moment, Nicoletta has not done so."

"She did everything required of her," Guy snapped. "Performed on all your sports teams—took the surf team to the state championship. Got the best grades in the class. She completed every damn requirement, and then some. You withholding a piece of paper from her won't change that."

"The college will also rescind the acceptance of a student who exhibits controversial or unacceptable behavior."

"Since when is free speech controversial?" Guy shot back.

"Your daughter defamed this institution," said Ellis. "It would pain me to have to report her outburst to the USC admissions committee."

"Dude. That sounds like a threat," said Guy. He leaned slightly forward in his chair.

"It's an opportunity," Ellis repeated smoothly, "to salvage her future."

"By backing off."

"By accepting the truth. Nikki, I'm offering you a chance to make a public apology and admit that you fabricated a story for the sake of your friend."

Fabricated. *Fabricated.*

Guy turned to her. "What do you say? You want to back off and walk out of here with the future you planned?"

Nikki teetered on the precipice. How easy it would be to buy into the lie, to let the Buccaneers get away with murder. *Oh, Mark.* She tilted her chin up. "I told you what happened. I tried to get you—someone, anyone, to listen—"

"And we did," the dean interrupted. "Of course we did. The incident is a tragedy, but no one is at fault. Miss Graziola, I won't offer you a chance to put things right again."

Nikki stared at him. She understood clearly that if she walked out of the office now, she would not go to college. She would not have the future she'd dreamed of. Then she thought, *If that's the case, I don't want their stupid diploma. If this is the world I've been grooming myself to live in, then I don't want to live there.*

Ellis's phone had been blinking throughout the meeting. Now it buzzed insistently, and the button changed from yellow to red.

Nikki felt weirdly composed as she regarded the headmaster, with his clean, manicured hands and effete designer glasses and ice-cold stare. She turned to her father. "We're done here."

Guy Graziola gave a curt nod, and together they stepped into the outer office. When she saw who was waiting outside, Nikki stopped in her tracks.

Senator McGill and her husband, followed by Marian, strode toward Mr. Ellis's office. Nikki locked gazes with Marian. The other girl's eyes were tender and puffy, and her cheeks were blotchy from crying. Kylie Scarborough was there, too, somber-faced as she stood off to one side. Mr. McGill looked haggard, immeasurably sad, but Mark's mother looked as if she was about to explode with rage.

"The sister caved," Nikki told Shasta and Cal. The three of them had met up in town, taking advantage of a rare occasion when they all had the afternoon off work. They sat together on the seawall at the end of Ocean Avenue, dangling their legs over the edge and listening to the boom of the full-throated waves. Nikki stared at the breakers hurling themselves again and again at the craggy rocks, exploding into particles that were as fine as new snow.

"About time," Cal said. "What took her so long?"

"Mark always said she was spineless when it came to the popular kids. You know, always trying to be the person she thought they wanted her to be." Although Nikki would probably never see Kylie Scarborough again, she would always be grateful to her. Kylie, of all people, had cracked the code of silence, pressuring Marian to tell her parents about the hazing. Many people dismissed Kylie as the spoiled kid of a TV star, but Nikki had seen Kylie use her social status, her power and influence.

"Well, better late than never," Shasta said.

"When Marian started going out with Jason Sanger, she kind of became his shadow." Nikki banged her heels against the seawall.

"Miss Carmella says never be anyone's shadow, or you'll miss the sunlight," Shasta said.

"It's not always that easy or clear-cut," said Nikki. She made a practice of avoiding Jason. He either ignored her or acted like a jerk, but for the most part he kept his distance. "I saw him at that party," she said.

"Him. Mark, you mean?" asked Shasta.

"They were outside, and I . . . I tried to get him to go back to the dorm."

"But he didn't want to go," Cal said.

"I couldn't get him to listen. I just . . . couldn't."

"You said *they* were outside. He was with someone?" Cal could read her like a book.

Nikki looked away. "It was private. Something I wasn't meant to see, and it upset him, so he went back to the party. Shit. I wish I'd stopped him. Maybe I could have—"

"You couldn't have known," Cal said. "Kids drink. They sleep it off. Then they get up the next day and feel like crap and swear they'll never do it again."

"Cal's right," Shasta said. "At least now the school and the people involved will have to take responsibility for what happened."

"I don't get why you're still in trouble," Cal said.

Nikki thought about the meeting with Headmaster Ellis. "Because if I hadn't said something, there wouldn't have been repercussions at all. Now that the story is coming out, families are pulling their kids out of Thornton left and right. That's what I heard, anyway. So I guess he's just being a dick."

The unspooling drama was a PR nightmare for the school. People did not want to entrust their children to a place where a kid might be in danger of being hazed to death. An online news blog suggested that there would be some sort of private settlement between the school and the McGills. If that was the case, then probably no one would ever know the details.

"My dad heard the same thing," Cal said. "But he also heard that nobody's going to be charged with anything."

"Because God forbid that the Sangers should take responsibility," Nikki grumbled. "Rich people have a way of not getting in trouble in this county."

"Especially since Jason's dad is the prosecutor for the county. Well, at least you've been vindicated," said Shasta.

"That wasn't the goal," Nikki said, "and it turned into a lousy break for me." She nudged Shasta. "Maybe for you, too, because I won't be going to USC in the fall. My acceptance was rescinded." No one had tried to make things right with Nikki. She was expendable. They didn't care about her or her future. She'd never see her portrait in the hall of distinguished alumni, would never be invited to give a keynote address.

"That sucks," said Shasta. "Just because you told the truth?"

Nikki shrugged. She was still trying to get used to the idea. *Now what now what now what?* "Supposedly I could go through an appeals process, but that's guaranteed to fail. And even if it didn't, I can't afford college without a scholarship."

"It's not the only college in the world," Cal pointed out. "Any school'd be lucky to have you."

"You are way too nice," Nikki said. "Can't I just be bitter and resentful for a while?"

"You can be anything you want. But I guarantee, your buddy Mark would not want that for you."

She nodded, gave a sigh. "You're right, I know. Maybe I'll just be a surfer. Mark used to say I should compete on the GSL circuit—the Global Surf League. He even made me fill out this dumb registration online and send in my high school standings."

"What's dumb about that?" Shasta asked.

"To think I could compete at that level of surfing? Way above my skill set," Nikki replied.

"So . . . What are you going to do now?"

"Go surfing. Seems like the only thing I feel like doing lately." She gestured toward the beach beyond the rocks. "Maybe I'll get swept away by a mysterious stranger and ride off into the sunset."

"Oh, I like that idea," said Shasta.

"What about you?" Nikki asked.

Shasta shrugged, palms up. "I'm still in high school, remember? I'll be working at the library and saving up for college."

If anyone deserved to go to college, it was Shasta. She was totally serious about her studies and she loved books more than anything.

"Your turn, Calvin," Shasta said. "What's your plan?"

"I'm going to earn a million dollars and see the world," he said.

"You always say that," Nikki pointed out.

"I've always wanted that," he said.

He and his dad and brother had never had much. They lived in a place that had been someone's weekend cabin back in the day, in an area where regular folks could still afford to live. They had a woodworking shop and a garden patch. In addition to working at Thornton, Cal's dad carved handmade signs for local businesses and grew vegetables for the food pantry. Unlike Nikki's dad, Mr. Bradshaw was always around for his kids. They made things together and grew things on the scrubby piece of upland outside of town. They had a collection of old *National Geographic* magazines from a library sale, and Cal had papered the walls of his room with the maps. He used a Magic Marker to circle the places he wanted to go.

"So how are you going to earn a million dollars?" Nikki asked.

He grinned and used one finger to push his glasses up the bridge of his nose. "I still haven't worked out the details." The grin faded. "If it turns out my dad's sick again, I'll help him get better and take him with me." He paused and looked out at the horizon. "As long as we're fantasizing here. But I'm definitely going to see the world someday."

"Where will you go first?" asked Shasta. "The world is a big place. You're going to have to narrow it down."

"Angkor Wat," Cal said immediately.

"Anchor what?" asked Nikki.

"It's a place in Cambodia," Shasta said. "Bunch of ancient temples in the jungle. Remember that movie—*Lara Croft, Tomb Raider*? It was filmed there."

"Cool," said Nikki.

"It does look cool. I'll bring you a book about it from the library." Shasta believed everything in the world could be found in the library.

"Don't you want to see it in person?" Cal asked. "The Great Pyramids? Easter Island? The northern lights? Victoria Falls?"

She shrugged. "I like it here." She encompassed the scene with a sweep of her arm. The beach was teeming with people enjoying the sunshine, the sand, and the waves. Gulls and curlews wheeled and dipped like kites overhead. Delicious smells wafted through the air—sugar cones and funnel cakes, hot dogs and French fries. "This place doesn't suck."

Nikki knew that her foster sister had experienced life in some terrible places. Alara Cove seemed like paradise to Shasta. But not to Nikki. Not anymore.

Shasta probably liked the stability of small-town life because her life with her mother was terrifically unstable. Mental illness and drug abuse. Months would pass between letters and phone calls, and afterward, Shasta was emotional for days. She walked around gingerly as if she'd survived a car wreck and ached in every bone. Shasta was proof that there were worse things in this world than having an irresponsible dad like Guy Graziola.

"Let's hit the beach," Nikki said. She jumped up and stuck her feet into flip-flops. The three of them started making their way down the concrete stairs to Town Beach, the most popular of Alara Cove's three beaches. The waves were tame caresses against the hard, flat expanse of sand, and the scene was more varied. The hard-core surfers favored the bigger water up by the caravan park. Here, there was more variety—a volleyball game going on, kids tossing footballs and Frisbees or just hanging out.

Nikki shaded her eyes and scanned the scene. Then they set down their things in the usual spot, a level area in the sand with a horseshoe-shaped border of rocks. Shasta stabbed the shaft of her sun umbrella into the ground, spread out an old blanket, and set down her book bag. She always brought along three books—the one she was reading, a backup book in case she finished the first one, and a third book in case the second one didn't work out for her.

Nikki slipped off her shorts and tipped her face to the sky. The breeze was as warm and light as a caress, and she took in all the familiar sounds of a summer day—the rushing surf, laughing children, music from someone's speaker, birds crying out. In that moment, she felt Mark's absence like a wave crashing over her and then receding, leaving her breathless. He should be here. He'd never be here again. Everything had gone to shit.

"Hey man," Cal said, nudging her, "turn that frown upside down."

She stuck her tongue out at him and tugged her rash guard over her bikini top. "Thanks, coach."

"I've never known a day at the beach to make a bad thing worse," Cal pointed out.

"Really?" asked Shasta. "What about a sunburn?"

"You gotta take precautions." Nikki dug a tube of heavy-duty sunscreen out of her bag and knelt behind Shasta, covering her friend's back with a layer of protection.

Cal dropped his towel and glasses by the umbrella and sprinted across the sand to join a volleyball game. He jumped into the rotation and high-fived a couple of his friends, immediately a part of the action.

Sometimes Nikki wondered what it would have been like if she'd stayed at the local high school rather than gone to Thornton. She'd be surrounded by kids who were from around here. The student body was way more diverse than the one at Thornton. Her swim and surf team uniforms would bear the Alara Cove High School logo—a bolt of lightning slashing through a radiation symbol, which was not very politically correct, but it was a nod to the island's former role in producing power. Her prom would have been held at the funky old Seaside Ballroom instead of the Beverly Hilton. She'd hang out with more regular kids like Cal.

But she never would have met Mark McGill.

She sighed, wondering whether or not she should join the volleyball game. She watched Cal dive sideways to return a shot. He missed the ball and ended up with a face full of sand.

Shasta chuckled. "The comic relief has arrived."

Cal stood up, brushed at his shoulders in an exaggerated gesture, and adjusted his baggy shorts. He was a good sport even though he wasn't good at sports. He didn't exactly fit in with the lean, ripped guys in his group, but everyone liked Cal. They always had.

"I hope he gets his wish," said Nikki, thinking of Cal's worries about his dad. "I hope he gets to see the world."

"I'll tell you what he really wants," said Shasta.

"Yeah? What's that?"

"You."

Nikki snorted. "You're high."

"I'm right. He looks at you like you're his dream date."

"No way." She felt a slight lurch in her gut because, yes, maybe she'd felt that vibe from him a time or two. "We've known each other since grade school."

"And your point is?"

"That you're wrong. Cal and I have always been just friends. If he really had a thing for me, he would've said something."

"Nuh-uh. He thinks you're, like, light-years out of his league. You're this surf goddess who belongs on the cover of *Sports Illustrated*. And he's, well . . ." She gestured toward the volleyball game. Now Cal was maneuvering in a sideways crab walk, trying to get in on the volley, laughing at himself when he missed. It was kind of admirable, the way he embraced his dorkiness. He was on the short side, and he was so skinny that his ribs showed, despite his fondness for funnel cakes and foot-long hot dogs from the beachside kiosks.

"Nonsense. I don't even know why we're talking about this," said Nikki. She jumped up and grabbed her board. "Want to come?"

Shasta shook her head. "I'll stick to reading in the shade, thank you."

"Suit yourself." Nikki toted her board down to the surf. Passing the volleyball area, she heard a sexy growl from one of the guys, and she flipped him off and kept walking. At the exact same moment, Cal kicked sand at the guy and told him to knock it off.

She tried to dismiss the notion that Cal Bradshaw had a thing for her. She and Shasta and Cal were friends, and only friends. The Three Musketeers. One for all and all for one. Getting romantic would ruin everything. It was a universal truth about friends that if they got romantic, they would eventually break each other's hearts, and after that, nothing would ever be the same again. The question was, now that Shasta had brought up the topic, could Nikki ignore it?

The answer was the same as always. Surfing.

One thing was always true about surfing. It could wash your mind the way the waves washed your body. But the ride always ended back at the shore. Right where she started. Sometimes, though, things changed while she was away. The sky changed color. The wind shifted. Something bitter turned sweet. A wound stopped bleeding. One could always hope.

In those moments, she wished the surf would bear her away to a different shore. To a different life. Then, as always, the ocean worked its magic and kept her from thinking for a good, long time. Finally, in a state of pleasant exhaustion, she took her last ride to the shallows and stepped off with a little flip of her foot.

She scooped her hair back and shook the water from her ears. When she picked up her board and started making her way up the beach, a tall, muscular guy walked directly in front of her, blocking her way. She stopped, squinting at Jason Sanger.

Great.

"You're in my way," she said, stating the obvious.

Jason jerked his head toward the surf. "Better watch yourself," he warned. "You might end up drowning out there."

"Your concern is touching."

He eyed her up and down in that insolent, insulting way some boys had, making her feel violated without touching her. "Hey, there's a party at the marina tonight. On my dad's Ocean Alexander."

He said it as though expecting her to be familiar with the fancy brand of yacht. She moved her board so it created a barrier between them. "Oh, cool. So you can poison someone else with your oxybombs?"

"Hey, sweetheart," he said, licking his lips. "You've got to let that shit go. Aren't you in enough trouble already?"

"You're the one who should be in trouble," Nikki snapped, glaring at him. Mark was dead because of Jason and the Buccaneers. She would never be okay with that. "We all know why you're not, but you should be."

"You know what, Graziola?" Jason shoved her board with his foot, trying to push her back into the surf. "Fuck you." He took another step toward her.

"Everything all right here?" Cal appeared, plastered in sweat and sand, his hair spiking every which way.

"No, loser," Jason said. "Don't you have some yardwork to do with your dad?"

"Don't you have some ambulance chasing to do with *your* dad?" asked Cal.

Jason's neck turned red. "Back off, dipshit," he said through his teeth. His big hands closed into fists as he took a step forward. Nikki could tell he was spoiling for a fight.

Cal stood his ground. "Yeah, I will, but I think your little brother's been looking for you." Turning slightly, he indicated the kid behind him.

"Hey, Jason!" The small boy, who was maybe three years old, came running up to them. "Hey, Jason! You're s'posed to be watching me. Mom *said*. Can we get some ice cream now? Can we? Huh? Huh?"

Jason held out a hand but didn't look down at the boy. "Yeah, whatever," he said with a sneer. He kept his stare on Nikki. "We're done here. Come on, Milo."

The little kid followed him like a stray puppy as they headed toward the ice cream stand behind the lifeguard station.

Shasta came over, brushing sand off her legs. "What was that about?"

"Just having a friendly chat." Cal wiped the sweat from his brow, but it only added to the crust of sand.

Nikki felt a wave of gratitude for him. Cal was so mild-mannered, a de-escalator in a world of hotheads. He was thoughtful, too, everything a friend was supposed to be. Then she remembered what Shasta had said and felt a flush come over her. "You're covered in sand," she said. "Let's take a dip in the ocean."

"Good plan." He ran into the surf, diving as a wave rose and the sea-foam surrounded him. She took off her ankle strap, and she and Shasta followed him in, ducking under the surf and playing the way they had when they were younger.

"Much better," Shasta said, bobbing in the waves.

Cal came up for air next to Nikki. "You're right. This is exactly what I needed. What do *you* need?"

"To get out of this town." The instant response startled her. It seemed to be on the tip of her tongue, just waiting to be uttered. She lifted her feet and let the water buoy her up. "There's a whole world out there. I just need to figure out where I want to be."

8

On her final night with Miss Carmella and Shasta, Nikki made a last check of her room. She had already stripped the bed, cleared away the dust bunnies, and boxed up the last of her books and keepsakes. One day soon, someone else would take her place in this room, someone who needed Carmella the way Nikki once had.

She went to the studio to collect her art supplies. It was quiet there, filled with familiar smells and memories. Carmella had brought Nikki into this world without hesitation. She was more than happy to nurture Nikki's passion for art, bringing her along on plein air days, then working beside her in the art studio for hours on end. Nikki loved being in this bright space. It always seemed so alive to her, with the scent of paint and linseed oil, the paintings stacked against the walls, and light flooding in through the skylight. This was where she had learned to turn her dreams into art, where she put her heart on paper and canvas, where she escaped into another world.

Through the years, she and Miss Carmella got a lot of talking done as they worked side by side, either in the studio or in the field. They also got a lot of silence done. The two of them would find their favorite spots overlooking the ocean and set up their easels next to each other. Nikki was always intrigued by the differences and similarities in their paintings. Even though they were both looking at the exact same thing, their pictures always turned out so different.

Miss Carmella seemed to love that aspect of it as well. "A person can only see something through her own filter," she told Nikki. "We paint what we feel and perceive. So the result will be different for each of us. The landscape might not change, but you change. Your perceptions. Your emotions. Your place in life."

A part of Nikki, a very big part, yearned for the days when she used to go with Carmella on plein air expeditions. She hoped she'd have many more opportunities to paint in the future, but now her future was uncertain.

She took out her flat portfolio and glanced through some of the work she had done in the past six years. Carmella offered to store the portfolio here, since space in the Airstream was at a premium. Nikki's pictures were often broad and expansive. Mr. Wendell, the visual arts instructor at Thornton, had commented on her wide-ranging vision. She was always focused on something in the distance, making her paintings bold and grandiose with color and scale yet scant on detail.

Miss Carmella's vision was more intimate and controlled, focusing on microdetails—the shadowy vein of a rock, a glint of light striking a single leaf. "There's a whole world in the middle of a flower," she would say.

"My world is out there someplace far away," Nikki often said. Capturing a scene in plein air was so different from studio art, where the outcome was predetermined. There was something she found so compelling about capturing a scene directly onto the canvas or paper while inhabiting the very space she was painting.

She had spent so many dreamy hours bringing a world to life with color and light and shadow. When she worked, Nikki felt as if she were in an alternate state of mind. She wished she could go back to that place. But there was no going back, she realized. Not now. Maybe not ever. Before Mark had died, her future had seemed so bright with promise. They both planned to attend USC, where she would study art and he'd pursue theater. Now she felt unmoored, and the act of painting a picture seemed ludicrous, but she didn't want Carmella to worry about her. Somehow, Nikki would have to find a way to live with the grief that followed her everywhere.

She planned to spend the summer at the caravan park, helping out around the place and giving surf lessons, as she'd done in summers past. Leaving Miss Carmella's would be bittersweet. Tonight's farewell dinner would feature Nikki's favorite—margherita pizza delivered from Oliva's, and a big Caesar salad. Spumoni for dessert—a nod to Nikki's heritage, which, as far as she knew, extended only to her name.

She and Shasta took turns in the shower, and they dressed up just a bit for dinner, in skirts instead of cutoffs. Miss Carmella didn't have many rules, but one of them was that they should sit down together for dinner as often as possible, and they should show up wearing clothes, not swimsuits or pajamas.

The girls helped set the table with the good china and cutlery. Even when it was just pizza, Miss Carmella liked to use her nice things.

Once they were seated, Carmella made a toast with their lemon sodas. "To your amazing life, Nicoletta. I've done what I could with you. Now it's your turn. The world is waiting for you."

Just not the one I thought I'd find. Nikki smiled at Miss Carmella. "I can't thank you enough," Nikki said. "Seriously. I know I haven't always been easy, right up to and including commencement day. But if I've done anything good or worthwhile—if I *ever* do anything good or worthwhile—it's thanks to you."

Shasta fanned herself. "Seriously, it's getting so emotional in here."

"You are part of the best idea I ever had," Miss Carmella said. "When your father brought you to stay with me, we made a family together. It's been an honor."

"Same goes for me."

They were digging into their spumoni when there was a knock at the door.

"I'll go," said Nikki. "Are you expecting someone?"

Miss Carmella shook her head. Nikki wiped her mouth on her napkin and hurried to the front door. The leaded-glass panes framed a tall, dark-haired visitor standing between the potted ferns.

Interesting. Tall, dark strangers were not a common sight around here. She ruffled a hand through her hair, arranged her face, and opened the door.

It was at that moment that the evening light decided to flood the sky directly behind the person on the front porch, limning him with a thread of fire. It was the sort of light that inspired her to paint. The large male silhouette inspired something else entirely.

"Oh, hi," she said, a little breathlessly, squinting her eyes. "Can I help you?"

"I'm Johnny Mercury," he said, his deep voice seeming to resonate in her belly. "I'm looking for a Miss Nicoletta Graziola."

He had an accent. Not British, but something like that, refined and delightfully different. He didn't say her name quite correctly—Graziol*er*.

Nikki stepped back, feeling a jolt of . . . something unfamiliar. Something she'd never felt before. Fascination. Excitement. Yearning, maybe.

She knew she was staring, but he was staring right back, his head tilted at an inquisitive angle. He had rich brown eyes with the kind of long, thick lashes women spent gobs of money on in salons. His hair was dark and a bit shaggy, and he had the kind of face you saw on movie posters, sculpted and distinct and commanding. He cleared his throat and smiled slightly. "Um . . . is she available?" He held out a business card.

Their hands brushed as she took it from him, and a warm sensation seemed to travel up her arm straight to her heart. Then she glanced down at the card. It had a blue wave logo and the words *Executive Director, Global Surf League.*

"You're the director of the GSL?" she asked, studying his face and then his board shorts and Nehi T-shirt. He didn't look old enough to be an executive anything. He didn't look much older than Nikki.

He offered a brief laugh. "No." The word came out longer and sounded more interesting: *Noi.* "I'm just the messenger, here on behalf of the league. I don't have a business card of my own."

A cahd of my own. For some reason it made her smile. "Then . . . ?" she prompted.

"So you're Nicoletta, yeah?" he asked.

"I am," she said. "I . . . what's going on?"

"I'm here on a surf exhibition tour."

"Pismo Beach, right? They host it every summer." When she was little, she would tag along with her dad and watch from the beach, mesmerized by the confident, nimble surfers. Later, she tried to emulate their techniques.

"Your application came up," he said. "The exhibition committee wants to meet with you. There's always room on the tour—"

"My application?" *Ah, Mark.* Last spring, they had filled it out together, because after she'd been recruited by three schools, Mark was convinced she was good enough to compete. Nikki never once thought anything would come of it.

"Are you serious?"

"I am." He held out a manila envelope. "I have your official letter right here."

In about three seconds, the world seem to change color. It was as exhilarating as her first ride on a surfboard.

"So in addition to being on the GSL tour, you . . . what? Hand-deliver important stuff to people?"

He laughed again, and it sounded like a sweet, fresh waterfall. "My mates and I came up to surf the cove tomorrow, so I volunteered to deliver it in person."

Nikki opened the envelope and scanned the letter. *It is with immense pleasure . . .* They wanted to see her perform in the women's shortboard and coed longboard events. This was no hoax. Her first impulse was to call Mark and yell with excitement. Mark had made this happen.

She caught her breath and looked up at the stranger, knowing her heart was in her eyes—the thrill of opportunity. Sadness for Mark.

What would Miss Carmella make of this guy? Nikki gazed at him for another moment. He didn't seem sketchy or anything. Just open and friendly, undeniably good-looking, and so very foreign. "Is Johnny Mercury your real name?" she asked.

That grin again. "No," he said. *Noi.* "It's my professional name."

"Miss Carmella," she called over her shoulder. "Someone's here. A guy named Johnny Mercury."

Carmella came to the foyer, Shasta close behind. "Yes? What is it?" Nikki introduced them.

"Ma'am," he said, "I've brought an invitation from the Global Surf League. For Miss Graziola. Mind if I come in?"

Carmella hesitated, then gestured toward the front room. It was an airy parlor with nice furniture, a piano, and shelves displaying books and family pictures and Henry Beach's Oscar statue, all bathed in light that filtered through the sheer curtains. This was where Carmella met with social workers and welcomed new children to the house. The walls were hung with paintings, some by Carmella, others by artists she admired. Above the piano was the best landscape Nikki had ever painted. She'd given it to Carmella as a Mother's Day present last year.

"Well then, Johnny Mercury," Carmella said, "let's hear what you have to say."

He sat in one of the wing chairs and indicated the packet. "I came to deliver this to Nicoletta."

Nikki handed the letter to Carmella. Shasta scooted in close and read it over her shoulder. "So cool," she said. "Are you going to do it?"

Oh, hell yes. "I always thought I was a long shot." Nikki spoke quietly, but her mind was racing. Patsy and her dad were depending on her to work all summer, but this was an opportunity she couldn't ignore.

"We're all long shots," Johnny said. "That's what makes the sport interesting, eh?" He looked around the room. "You have a beautiful place here," he said to Carmella.

"It was built by my grandfather." She indicated the portrait of her grandparents on the wall. "My grandmother Edie always wanted to live by the sea. She was a master garden designer. She wrote a book about the design of Central Park." She sent him a polite smile. "And you are from . . . ?"

"Born in Western Australia. Now I live in Surfers Paradise in Queensland," he said. "This is my first trip to the States. I've only seen the California coast so far, but I love it here. We heard about the epic reef rolls at Alara Cove, so my mates and I came up to check out the scene." He took another look around the room, and then stood up. "Miss Beach, it's been a pleasure." He turned to Shasta and then to Nikki. "Nice to meet you."

Nikki was sure his gaze lingered on her. She was sure his mouth curved in a subtle suggestion of a smile.

"We have cake," she blurted out. "And spumoni ice cream. Would you like a piece of cake?"

The suggestion blossomed into a genuine smile. "Thanks, but I need to get going. We've booked a spot down by the beach and I should check in before it gets too late."

Her heart fluttered a little. "Beachside Caravans?"

"That's right. You know it?"

"It's my dad's place," she said. "I'm heading down there myself tonight."

"Awesome. Maybe I'll see you around, then."

She walked him to the door. The moment he was gone, she fake-fainted on the sofa. "Oh my gosh," she said. "What just happened?"

"Was he created in a lab somewhere?" Shasta asked. "Or is that a new level of handsome?"

The thrill of meeting Johnny Mercury took away some of the sadness Nikki felt about leaving Carmella's house for good. Later, when her father drove up in his van, she practically floated out the door, and her duffel bag felt light as air.

The words tumbled from her as they drove to the caravan park.

"That's something," her dad said, grinning from ear to ear. "Really something."

"It might be nothing," she admitted. "But I'll give it my best shot."

"You're good," Guy said. "I always thought your talent would be wasted on a college surf team."

"If being on a surf team gets me into college, I'll be on a surf team," she told him. Her dad was a skeptic when it came to college. "Just because I'm not going to USC doesn't mean I'm not going."

But college was the last thing on her mind when they got home. Johnny Mercury and his mates, as he called them, had checked into Unit 7, and they were sitting around outside, their boards leaning against the trailer. He introduced her to Diego from Costa Rica and Duncan from Hawaii. They were on the exhibition tour as well, and the talk was all surf, all the time.

"Your dad's cool," Duncan said. "He's living the dream right here, eh?"

Nikki shook her head. "Well, what about you guys? Professional surfers. Now there's a dream. Who gets to do that?"

"Maybe you," said Johnny.

"I didn't even think I was a maybe." She shuddered. "I have to try not to get my hopes up."

"Sometimes hope is all you've got," Johnny said.

"What's it like, being in the league?" she asked.

"Well, you probably shouldn't plan on getting rich and famous," Diego said. "Being in the league isn't all partying and traveling."

She eyed their ice chest of beer and bags of chips. "No?"

"There's not a lot of free time once you're on the qualifying tour," Duncan said. "Flights, passports, taxis, baggage claims, customs, and then you have to get into the local wave a few days before the competition starts. Then there are the photo ops and meet-and-greets—"

"Come on, man, you love that stuff," Johnny said. He looked over at Nikki. "Don't let them talk you out of it. Just remember why you started surfing in the first place." He stood up and held out his hand. "Let's go have a look at that beach."

It seemed like the most natural thing in the world to take his hand and walk up over the bluff to the wide, flat beach. There was a partial moon and the waves made a pale, lacy ruffle along the sand. They headed barefoot into the water, walking slowly and aimlessly as the surf swirled around their ankles. Nikki felt breathless, not quite sure this moment was actually happening to her. He seemed like something she had conjured up in all her lovelorn, hormone-powered teenage dreams.

"Do you think I have a chance?" she asked. "You haven't seen me surf."

"Your point total in your school division was in the top two percent."

"But to compete at this level . . . I can't even imagine what that would be like."

"Sometimes it *is* like being in a dream," he said, pausing to look at her for a moment. "Like right now."

She almost couldn't believe her ears. "Is that what you always wanted to do? To compete? To be on the tour?"

"Sure. But it is true what the guys said about the process," Johnny said. "It's a tough way to make a living. I've done my share of side gigs, couch surfing, and hoping the next injury isn't too bad."

She eyed the lettering on his Nehi shirt, which glowed faintly in the moonlight. "Don't you get, like, sponsors?"

"Sure, but you have to hustle them. Then you have to get used to them pressuring you to rack up points. If you're under at the end of the season, you're terminated."

"Now *you're* trying to talk me out of it."

"I'm not," he said. "If you're really into it, then no one can talk you out of it."

"I just can't believe they're actually giving me a shot," she said.

He took her hand again. "Listen, in this business, nobody *gives* you a shot. You take your shot. And you earn your place—or not."

"Understood." She let out a long sigh, thinking of Mark. When they had sent her records off to the league, she'd never dreamed anything would come of it. Mark, though, had believed in her. "Can I tell you something?" she asked.

"You can tell me everything."

"It might keep you up half the night."

"I'd stay up all night, every night for you," he said.

She and Johnny Mercury did stay up half the night. After walking the beach, they sat at a picnic table overlooking the ocean, sharing a bag of pretzels and bottles of cold root beer.

She told him about Mark's death, crying a little, because her grief was still so raw. She told Johnny that Mark was the one who had made this opportunity happen for her.

"He was your boyfriend, then."

"Oh! No. We weren't . . . he wasn't like . . . No." Then she told Johnny about the commencement fiasco and the way she had destroyed her own future by speaking out.

"Maybe you didn't destroy anything," he said. "Maybe you're meant for something else."

Maybe you're my something else, she thought.

"I hope you're right," she told him. "I just want to get away from this place. I've been here forever. I want to live a different life, you know?"

"I do know what that's like, yes. I grew up in a suburb of Perth. I was supposed to stay home and take over my dad's auto detailing business when he retires."

She wrinkled her nose. "My dad doesn't talk about retiring, but when he does, I'm definitely not taking over this place. I hope he doesn't expect me to." She finished her root beer and looked around at the familiar array of vans and family wagons in the parking lot, and the Airstreams with their lights glowing in the small, rounded windows.

Visitors thought the park was funky and charming, and maybe it was—to them. Not to Nikki. "I'm keeping you up too late."

"You're not."

"Best waves tomorrow will be at sunrise."

"Are you going out?"

"Of course," she said, relishing the prospect of surfing with him tomorrow. "We call it dawn patrol."

"Question," said Johnny. "Do you have a boyfriend?"

"No. Why do you ask?"

"Because I might want to kiss you."

She was startled by the words, but at the same time, they seemed inevitable, like something she'd been yearning to hear all evening. They reflected exactly what she'd been thinking. "I might want you to kiss me."

Moving with slow deliberation, he came around to her side of the picnic table and took her hand as though asking her to dance. She turned and stood up, tilting her head back. He touched her cheek lightly with his fingertips, brushing his thumb across her lower lip. Then he cupped her face gently between his hands and gazed down at her.

Again there was that exquisitely subtle smile. Then a cloud obscured the moon, and his face disappeared into darkness. "I want to take my time with you," he said.

"Yeah?"

"This is important. It's our first kiss. But the way I feel now, it might be our *last* first kiss."

She nearly melted. It was the most romantic thing she had ever heard. She stared at his mouth and lifted up on tiptoe as his lips came down to meet hers. The kiss was both exactly what she hoped for but also like nothing she'd ever experienced. He tasted of root beer and something fresh that had no name. His lips were soft as marshmallows, and the scent of his skin and hair enveloped her. Behind her closed eyes, the whole night became a whirlwind of color.

When they came up for air, he held her even closer, pressing her cheek to his shoulder. "Is it just me?" he asked. "Or is something happening here?"

She sighed and felt a fullness that brought her to the edge of tears. Not the tears of grief for Mark, but happy tears. *At last*, she thought. *At last*.

"It's not just you," she whispered.

PART TWO

The cure for anything is salt water—
sweat, tears, or the salt sea.

—Isak Dinesen

9

15 years later
Brisbane, Australia

Nikki Mercury felt dazed and numb as she stepped into the office of the Angel's Rest Funeral Home. She still wore her hospital bracelet, twisting it around and around her wrist. Just hours after the accident, she seemed to float in some gauzy zone of disbelief, an empty vehicle on autopilot.

She was still haunted by the flashing glare and beeping alarms of the emergency room. She'd been only dully aware of people moving her around, pointing her in the direction she was supposed to go because she almost couldn't think about taking the next breath.

Her world had been smashed into oblivion. Everything was gone, and nothing made sense. She felt assaulted, and though her physical injuries were minimal, her ability to cope had been destroyed.

The foyer of the funeral home was weirdly silent after the cacophony of the hospital. She'd walked here, because it was close to the hospital complex. She had no car—the car was wrecked. She had no phone—that, too, had been lost—so she couldn't use a rideshare or transit pass.

Her head was still filled with questions that echoed as if they were being shouted through a long, dark tube: *"Is there someone we can call? Do you have someplace to go? As his next of kin, can you sign this release?"*

At the hospital, a social worker had given her a brochure with an overwhelming list of suggested steps to take.

Notify loved ones. But *she* was Johnny's loved one. He didn't really have others. His family was scattered and out of touch.

When the hospital staff informed her that she was being discharged, she'd nearly lost her mind. How could she be discharged with minor injuries when Johnny would never—

In an attempt to stave off a full-blown panic attack, she had clung to other matters on the social worker's list. *Make funeral arrangements.* There was a card: *Angel's Rest. Open 24 hours.* Less than a kilometer from the hospital. It seemed like something concrete she could do.

The reception area was decorated in muted colors, and soothing, tuneless music played through a hidden speaker. The office door opened and an elegant woman held it wide. "Mrs. Mercury?"

"That's, uh, me." Was it? Now that there was no Mr. Mercury?

"I'm Fiona Costello. Please come in." She had kind eyes, and the sort of style Nikki associated with big-city fashion—silky straight hair, lips shaped by filler, smooth Botoxed brow. Nikki took a seat across from her. The desk plate identified her as the director.

"Ah, you poor thing," said Fiona, her speech flavored by a hint of Irish. "Are you here by yourself, then?"

Nikki nodded and tried without success to organize her thoughts. Sorting out the end of someone's life was a complicated process, and she had barely begun. A "disruptive loss," the social worker had termed this. She explained that when faced with a disruptive loss, recovery would take enormous effort—mental, emotional, and even physical. Nikki didn't know the first thing about dealing with a situation like this. She was so deep in shock and disbelief that she couldn't even think for herself.

"Can I get you a cup of tea, then?" the woman offered.

"I'm okay," Nikki said. "I mean, not okay . . ." *I'll never be okay.* She twisted the bracelet again. It bore a bar code along with her name, a lengthy number labeled "MR," her date of birth, and the date of admission. Yesterday. And yesterday was a lifetime ago—literally.

God, if she could turn the clock back to yesterday. *If, if, if.*

She felt something unexpected—a knife-sharp memory of the traumatic stress that had nearly crushed her when Mark McGill had died. Then, too, she'd been flooded with grief and guilt, ruminating over what she could have done differently. *If, if, if.* Mark's sudden death and the loss of their friendship had reshaped her youth and realigned her future. She had so many lingering thoughts of Mark. She'd run away from her grief over losing him. That didn't mean she'd made her peace with it.

This fresh, even deeper tragedy was about to have the same effect on her life, and it scared her.

"I know you're dealing with a terrible shock," Fiona said. "Would you like to call a friend or relative?"

Friends. Yes, they had friends. People they met down in Surfers Paradise and at the championship events in Port Macquarie and all along the coast. Johnny was well known in the league, and even Nikki had some recognition, though she'd never made it to the very topmost tier. But since neither of them had racked up enough points to qualify in the past few years, those relationships had fallen off. Now she questioned whether they were friendships at all. Maybe they were just very pleasant business associations.

Nikki was thinly acquainted with a couple of neighbors at the apartment complex, but she wasn't sure they even had an apartment anymore. That had been one of the several nightmares Johnny had revealed to her right before the crash—they were being evicted.

Relatives? Johnny's parents were divorced. His mum lived with a boyfriend in New Zealand, and his father was across the country in Perth with a second family. Nikki had never met them. She wasn't even sure how to get in touch with them.

"There's no one to call," she admitted to Ms. Costello. "He's never been in touch with his folks. I don't think they'll be part of this, so . . . I mean," she said, regrouping, "I'll be handling this on my own. I'm . . . I can do it. I have to do it."

Fiona gave her a card. "This is a crisis counseling service," she said. "They're very good."

Nikki pocketed the card without looking at it. "I can . . . I have to figure this out," she said. "I just . . . I need to know what to do right now."

"You and . . ." She glanced down at the folder from the hospital. "You and John are so young. Did you ever talk about end-of-life preferences?"

Only that they would love each other until the day they died.

"No. Of course not. We barely talked about end-of-*month* issues." Somehow, she'd managed to avoid thinking about the bills piling up. The dun notices and warnings. In the past fifteen years, they'd managed to muddle through the times when money was tight. Some seasons, they were able to cobble together a living with sponsorships and side gigs. Other times, they would find temporary jobs, coaching or lifeguarding. Johnny always told her not to worry. He always said he would take care of things. She had trusted him to take care of things.

Nikki had been blissfully unaware that the eviction process—a first, even for them—was well underway. Johnny had managed to hide it from her. He was a master of magical thinking, and apparently he'd wished away the dilemma, hoping for a windfall just around the corner.

When the removal company had shown up at her door, brandishing a sheaf of official-looking paperwork, she had been certain there was some mistake. No, they'd assured her, this was not a mistake. It was all there in the papers. There had been a default judgment and an Order for Possession. They had seventy-two hours to vacate the premises.

Nikki could still feel the sensation of all the blood draining from her face. Stumbling through an explanation, she assured the removal people that she and her husband would work something out. Then she'd grabbed her phone and stabbed in Johnny's number, but predictably, he didn't pick up.

He was at the Gunyama breaks, practicing for an upcoming invitational. In a fury, Nikki jumped aboard the beach transit, her foot tapping in such agitation that other passengers eyed her as if she were on drugs.

The area behind the beachfront hotels and campgrounds was rough, the street corners and alleyways haunted by hustlers and panhandlers who hung around the dollar stores and news agencies. She ignored them as she made her way to the beach. A red flag warned casual swimmers of a dangerous undertow. Johnny was out at the break with a few others. Even at a hundred meters, she could pick him out by his easy posture on the board, and the unhurried grace with which he rode his chosen wave. No matter where he was in the standings, Johnny always bore himself like a champion.

When he spotted Nikki, his face broke into a smile—the smile that never failed to melt her heart.

On that day, it failed.

"Hello, gorgeous," he said, coming toward her. "I love it when you surprise me at work. The guys and I were going to head to the pub after—"

"When were you planning to tell me we're being evicted?" she demanded without preamble. She brandished the packet of papers.

He stopped short, wiping the saltwater from his face. "Ah, that nonsense. Sweetheart, it's got to be a mistake. I've been working out a plan with the building manager."

Her heart felt like a stone in her chest. "Apparently the plan is that within seventy-two hours they're taking all our things and locking us out."

"Ah, no. I'll talk to the manager. We'll be fine, sweetheart."

She had always believed him—until now. This was all too real.

He loaded his board into the ute—a battered old Land Cruiser—and pulled out onto the highway.

"How long have you known?" she asked.

"I told you, it's a mis—"

"Jesus, Johnny, would you stop with that?"

He glanced over at her, seeming to be taken aback by her anger. He practically mumbled, "I got a Notice to Quit two months ago. Listen, I'm going to fix this."

As he sped homeward, the quarrel escalated.

They almost never quarreled. They weren't used to it. Agitated, he drove erratically—too fast, no seat belt.

The funeral director sat quietly as Nikki struggled to breathe through the flashes of memory. Then Fiona said, "Well, he was your husband. You know him better than anyone, right?"

That was true. Nikki didn't just know him. She *understood* him. She knew the way his mind worked—and the way it didn't. She knew his heart, and his spirit, and his sense of pride.

"In my experience," Fiona said gently, "your loved one would want whatever gives you the most comfort."

Nikki nodded. She stared down at her hands in her lap. "He wouldn't want a lot of . . . you know, flowers and wreaths and prayers and stuff. We don't . . . We didn't go to church."

"So maybe a small gathering. Are you thinking there would be a casket and viewing, or . . ." Ms. Costello glanced down at the hospital folder. "Or cremation?"

The woman had probably spotted a disturbing detail in the record. Nikki's last glimpse of Johnny's ruined face as the paramedics extracted him from the ute had nearly made her soul leave her body.

On his driver's license, Johnny had ticked the box signaling his intent to be an organ donor. They had both checked that box. Everyone did without giving it much thought; to do otherwise seemed stingy. Yet in the end, giving away all that was left was all that mattered. At the trauma center, every usable shred of him had been harvested. His heart was already beating in a stranger's chest. Someone else would soon be seeing the world through his corneas. His liver and lungs were powering a stranger's body. His kneecaps belonged in different bodies now, as the medical team said they could be used in transplantation. Maybe his skin was helping to heal a burn victim.

She clenched her hands in her lap. Trying to piece him back together for one final glimpse would not make this any less painful.

"He should be . . . you know," she said.

"Cremated? It's a popular and very loving choice." Fiona showed her a brochure with the various "packages." Some of the price tags took Nikki's breath away. Dying could be very expensive.

"Uh, well, this one, I guess." It was the lowest option on the list— "Simplicity." $894. Plus VAT.

Nikki knew they didn't have that much in the bank. Based on what Johnny had reluctantly disclosed to her during the argument, there was actually nothing in the bank. She would have to charge the expense and worry about paying the bill later. That had always been Johnny's way. The American way, he jokingly called it. As an Australian, he had readily embraced the concept.

Miss Costello didn't look surprised by Nikki's choice. Her expression was neutral. "I can take a deposit now," she said, "and the balance upon completion."

Nikki's hands shook as she unzipped the security pocket of her jacket and took out her billfold. Her sleeve was flecked by blood. She handed over the credit card, then filled out and signed an authorization form without reading it. She didn't actually want to know exactly what she was authorizing.

A moment later, Fiona said quietly, "Sorry, the purchase has been declined. Do you want to try a different card?"

"I don't have a different card." Nikki bit her lip. *Oh, Johnny.*

"Maybe check your auto insurance policy," Fiona suggested. "Some of them cover funeral expenses."

Nikki squirmed in her seat. "It was . . . we were uninsured." The policy had been canceled due to nonpayment. The card in the glove box was months out of date. She had found this out only last night. She'd been sitting on the tailgate of an emergency vehicle, wrapped in a thermal blanket while the jaws of life extracted her husband from the driver's seat. Someone at the scene had found the registration card along with the expired insurance card.

Ms. Costello hesitated for a moment. Then she handed over a printout that was separate from the brochure. The "unattended funeral" option ran $275. "There's an aid organization that can cover this. I have a form you can fill out."

"Thank you," Nikki said. For some reason, her cheeks burned with embarrassment. What was she embarrassed about? So they were broke. It happened. So he had died in a terrible wreck. It didn't mean he was a terrible person. "He wasn't drunk or anything."

Miss Costello looked up from her paperwork. "How's that?"

"Johnny. My husband. He wasn't driving drunk or high. It was . . . He was distracted." *By me*, Nikki thought. *He was distracted by me.*

"Ms. Mercury," said the guy from the highway patrol. "These are your husband's effects. And, um . . . other items recovered from the vehicle."

Standing in the doorway of the small apartment, Nikki regarded the man through a fog of grief and agony. He looked very young and carefully put together, his uniform crisp, the sleeves of his pale blue shirt ironed knife sharp, his cap tucked respectfully under one arm. He was sweating as he shifted from one foot to the other. He must have drawn the short straw, having to make this grim delivery.

She took the bag from him and tried to say something. Should she thank him? Did you thank a person for bringing your dead husband's things from the car he'd died in?

He hesitated for just a beat. "Very sorry for your loss," he said, and stepped from the open door. "And also, er, good luck. Ma'am."

She winced at the irony. Luck was not her friend.

He returned to his car. He paused there, lifted his cap, and put it on.

Ma'am, she reflected. That was how people addressed older women. She was only thirty-three but Nikki felt a hundred, a thousand, a million years old. She moved through each hour in a thick fog. The well-meaning advice from the grief pamphlet made no sense.

Her life was terrible and there was nothing to do but ride out each moment like a rogue wave, even knowing it could be the one that would destroy her. But she was already destroyed. She didn't move through the phases of sorrow they said she was supposed to experience— shock, anger, denial. The feelings surged and receded in unpredictable waves, not the sequential progression outlined in the literature.

She didn't want to be told what to feel. She wanted to know how to find a reason to take the next breath of air.

Moving slowly and gingerly, she turned back to the apartment where she and Johnny had lived for the past year. The property manager had given her a few extra days before the eviction company would be back. She missed Johnny, but she wouldn't miss this place. They tended to move frequently, always looking for accommodations where the rent was low and the beach was nearby. Their fortunes fluctuated depending on where they landed in the rankings and how generous the sponsors were. The past few years had been rough, disrupted by the pandemic and then by Johnny's hamstring injury, and they'd ended up making a lot less than they spent just to stay with the league.

Now she set down the plastic tote, stamped with the Queensland highway department logo and 90% RECYCLED MATERIALS. She didn't want to look at the contents of the bag. It was going to be unbearably painful to go through the things Johnny had left behind.

She'd lost her husband on Valentine's Day. And *lost*, of course, was a cruel misnomer. She knew exactly where Johnny was—in a molded plastic urn that was currently propping open the screen door to let in a breeze while she packed up the last of her belongings.

Drawing a deep breath, Nikki forced herself to open the parcel. There was a box of soft passion fruit licorice (because chocolate tended to melt in the sun) and a card in a sealed envelope with her name on it in his handwriting.

She put the card in her pocket, unable to bring herself to open it, and carried the candy to the trash.

At the last second, she took back the box of licorice and shoved it into her backpack. She might need it later.

Valentine's Day had always been their special time. Each February fourteenth for the past fifteen years, they would celebrate with a bottle of champagne and a meal at a luxurious restaurant, followed by a night of vigorous lovemaking.

They marked the occasion every year without fail, because even after all this time, they loved each other deeply. He was her first thought upon waking and her last as she fell asleep each night. Strumming on a ukulele bearing a long-ago sponsor's logo, he used to sing love ballads from the nineties, and sometimes he surprised her at work for no reason. When they were apart, she yearned for him with an intensity that burned deep.

There was just a hint of self-congratulatory indulgence, a bit of smugness as they celebrated each milestone. It was an almost universal fact that people who fell in love as teenagers never stayed in love. Johnny and Nikki were defying the odds.

Although Nikki suspected that no one would believe her, she had known the moment she met Johnny that he would be the biggest, most important part of her life. The summer they'd met, she had been haunted by Mark's death, and the people of Alara Cove were polarized over her accusations. Then Johnny came along, as attractive as a teenage daydream, offering an escape.

That first summer had been a whirlwind. After receiving a provisional qualification for the surf league, she finally knew what her future looked like.

The first time she spent the night with him, he asked her to stay forever and she did. It wasn't really even a decision. Simply the next logical step in an unplanned journey. Being in love made her feel like a different person, like someone she had never met before. She liked who she was when she was with Johnny. She liked who she was when she was away from Alara Cove, a girl without a past, a girl with only the future in front of her.

She was selected as an alternate for the exhibition tour, and she participated in events up and down the West Coast. In between events, they both picked up side gigs. She found work as a lifeguard at the Redondo Beach surf club, where the planes from LAX thundered overhead and cruise ships steamed past the horizon.

At the end of summer, Johnny's work visa expired, and he told her he had to go back to Australia. He asked her to come with him, and she hesitated only long enough to get a passport. When the document arrived in the mail, it looked so very official, so important. That was the moment Nikki knew. She did not want to be a person who ended up regretting a chance she didn't take. She was going to Australia.

When she announced her intention to move overseas, the plan was met with a chorus of cautionary advice. No one believed her relationship with Johnny would last. Her father told her so in no uncertain terms. But Nikki was determined to be with the man she loved, to live a different life, and to make the journey far from Alara Cove.

Most people probably expected her to dabble a bit in life as an expat, and then come back, to . . . what? Settle down? Or just settle?

There was a tearful farewell with Shasta and Miss Carmella. Afterward, she rode her bike up to the Bradshaw place, where she and Cal had exchanged an awkward hug. Johnny picked her up and the two of them drove away in a borrowed convertible with the top down.

In that moment, as she took in her final glimpse of the pretty, flower-hung main street, the bookstore with its enticing display window, the cafés and shops with their striped awnings, the marina and the bars where the Navy guys hung out, Nikki had felt an unexpected sense of nostalgia, knowing she was leaving Alara Cove for good.

She was young, so impossibly young, and she resisted examining her decision. She resisted making a plan. Johnny was wonderful, and she fell hard for him, and she couldn't imagine staying in Alara Cove, so it seemed the planets had aligned for her.

Screw this dumb little town, she thought, seething with the rashness and impatience of youth. She wanted to get on with her life, build a whole new life, far from home.

Every once in a great while, when she had a bad day in the water and nothing seemed to be working, she caught herself wondering about USC. Had she not told the truth about Mark's death, had she not blown up her own future, she would have been a happy college undergrad who wore the polish of a first-class education at a fancy private school. Instead, the only one who'd paid a price for speaking the truth was Nikki herself.

If college had still been an option, would she have gone off with him? Or was she just running away because it wasn't?

One glance at Johnny banished all regrets. He drove with a grin on his face, wrist hung casually over the steering wheel, the wind rippling through his hair.

Her mood had soured when they passed the Sanger law firm, its expensive offices occupying a gracious, tree-shaded historic building. Even after the truth came out about the night Mark had died, the only consequence was that the Buccaneers Club was permanently banned from Thornton. Judd Olsten had graduated but then went to some strict evangelical college back East. And Nikki's notoriety blew up her plans to attend college and sent her into exile. Other than that, things went back to business as usual.

She and Johnny fell into their life together the way they had fallen in love—it was unplanned but inevitable. In Australia, they stayed busy all the time, helping each other cobble together a way to stay in the league. They both did well in local qualifying events, but the way of life was every bit as hard as people said.

To make ends meet, they both worked a variety of side gigs. Johnny made a bit of money delivering things. Apparently there were plenty of folks who needed items brought to their door, and it turned out he had a knack for finding people and returning objects to their rightful owners. He was also good at serving documents to people who didn't want them. His most lucrative gig was working as a subagent for a registered field agent, delivering official court documents.

Nikki worked at the surf rescue station and gave private lessons, and sometimes it felt like an upside-down version of her life in Alara Cove. Yet as always, surfing was her refuge. When she was in the waves, she tended to forget where she was, and every once in a while, she looked at the shore, half expecting to see the broken neon sign for Beachside Caravans. Johnny suggested that maybe she wasn't done with Alara Cove yet, that she had unfinished business there. She was always quick to dismiss the notion.

Her favorite beach was called Cooloola. The sand flats were rimmed by brakes of coastal cypress—another reminder of home. The native word was suggested by the sound made by the wind in the trees. There was an older man who came sometimes with his pochade box and easel. He'd sit in the shade, a brimmed hat covering his bald head, lost in the scene he was painting. Watching him, Nikki often felt a twinge of longing. She even thought about getting a few supplies and making some art but there never seemed to be time.

She sent messages on WhatsApp back and forth with her dad and with Shasta and Carmella and Cal, but over the years, the contact diminished, and memories faded like the colors of an old photograph left out too long in the sun.

Now she pulled her mind away from those thoughts and sat down in front of her laptop, cribbing a Wi-Fi signal from somewhere out in the ether. The hospital social worker's checklist advised her to gather all financial records. With mounting tension, she logged into their Westpac account and stared at the screen. Harsh reality glared back at her.

Oh, Johnny. How had she missed this? Their budget had always been tight. It was squeezed even tighter by the pandemic. She'd brought it up several times with Johnny, wondering aloud if they should get steadier jobs, maybe skip some of the faraway events.

She should have read something in his silence. It hardly mattered now.

The email queue was clogged with messages of shock and sorrow. People urged her to be strong, to carry on surfing, to live the dream she'd shared with Johnny.

Nikki deleted those notes. Without Johnny, she knew she wouldn't have the heart to chase a ranking in the league. Her dream did not exist without him.

The digital search led her deeper and deeper into the grim state of their finances. Culling through Johnny's email, she found dun notices, overdue notices, eviction notices and warnings dating back months. He'd kept it all from her, masked by his heart-melting smile and can-do attitude. They never seemed to get ahead, but Johnny's optimism never flagged. He kept assuring her that a big sponsorship was just around the corner. She assumed he took care of everything. As it turned out, she had assumed a lot. Trusted a lot.

She was shocked but not surprised. He had so much pride bound up in his role as a provider. At the same time, he was a free spirit. She had adored that about him.

He had given her so much love. He always seemed to know how to delve into the rich part of life. But his expansiveness was also reckless and impulsive. He was happy enough to abandon work in order to head down the coast with her for a day of adventure. He loved finding a new surf spot, turning practice into play. Afterward, they would grab a bite to eat and lie in the shade on a blanket, gazing at clouds. At night they would curl up together on the sofa and watch movies on an old DVD player that somehow still worked, and later they would make love, sometimes more than once.

He could stop time with a kiss. He could banish worry with a smile. On a good day, he could shred with the best of the best, cutting up a wave with his board.

Johnny had many gifts. He just didn't know how to deal with finances.

Nikki stared at the screen until her eyes glazed over with tears. Then the grief ripped through her with fresh claws and she sobbed so hard she almost couldn't breathe, and the salt of her tears burned her skin. After a while, she was too exhausted to feel anything at all. She got up and forced herself through a series of yoga stretches.

Her injuries were minor, the worst being a severely sprained wrist, but she knew her heart would never heal. She ached all over as she filled large black trash bags with Johnny's clothes and shoes, his belongings. There was actually very little for the eviction company to seize. In their peripatetic life, she and Johnny had accumulated only a few belongings. Their home was sparsely furnished with thrift-shop finds and objects no one else seemed to want.

With Johnny gone, it was hard for Nikki to want anything, to care about anything. She had a collection of novels she meant to read and others she couldn't bear to part with, mainly aspirational books featuring places she and Johnny planned to go . . . one day. It was always "one day" in the unspecified future. One day they would get a house, adopt a pet, have a kid. One day . . .

Nikki decided to save only a few items: A faded denim shirt he wore on the weekends. A baseball cap with a logo, the one he wore on deliveries because it tended to put people at ease when he approached them to hand over a summons they didn't want. A cap was inherently friendly, he used to say. Folks trusted faded jeans and sneakers, baseball caps and T-shirts, so long as they didn't display controversial slogans.

Sarah and Jess, the neighbors on either side of the flat, showed up to help. Nikki knew them only by nodding acquaintance, but they came over to offer a kind word and to see if there was anything they could do.

"Thanks," Nikki said. "I . . . no. There's really . . . I'm still trying to get my head around what happened. I didn't realize things were so bad. With our finances, I mean. I was sure the eviction notice was some kind of awful mistake."

"Oh, Nikki. I saw you rushing out of here when that van showed up. What an awful day for you," said Jess.

"I can't imagine," Sarah said. "Truly, I can't. I'm so sorry."

"He was a lovely man. You were a beautiful couple, and he loved you so much," said Jess. "Where do you plan to go next? Back to the States, maybe?"

"That's . . . Wow. I don't really belong there anymore." *I don't belong anywhere.* "I can't imagine going back. I never thought I would."

"Sounds like it's your home, though," Sarah said gently. "I bet there's still a place for you there. People who love you. Who'll take care of you."

Jess nodded. "Sarah could be right. Figure out the real reason you left. I bet it's not what you think."

The reason she had left was Johnny. And now Johnny was gone.

"So, is there . . . Do you have a plan?" Sarah asked. "I mean, you could have my couch for the night, but—"

"No." Nikki was so exhausted by grief she could barely think straight, but she was touched by their concern. "Both of you have been really kind, but I won't impose." Jess had two kids, and Sarah's place was a tiny studio where she gave English lessons to immigrants. "I never pictured what my life would look like without Johnny. I guess I'm about to find out."

They tried to get her to eat something, but she had no appetite. Her final chore before the movers arrived was to clear out the mailbox. She went down to the car park and unlocked the box labeled "Mercury" in smudged marker. It yielded mostly junk mail, and what she now recognized as overdue bills. There was an official-looking letter from the Department of Home Affairs. She assumed it was something to do with one of Johnny's side gigs, but on second glance, she saw that it was addressed to her.

She opened the letter, read it twice, and nearly threw up.

"Does this mean what I think it means?" Weary to the bone, Nikki pushed the notice across the desk of the Home Affairs agent. She had spent the night on a lumpy sofa at her friend Kalinda's place in Chermside, a suburb near the city. Outside, the busy streets of Brisbane seethed in a powerful heat wave. She had come up from the coast by motor coach, because the court authorized the eviction company to take possession of her car.

The clerk—Mr. Clive Hibble, according to his badge—nodded gravely. "It says you have no status in Australia, your visa is long expired, and you're obliged to go back to the United States."

"I don't understand. I'm married to an Australian. *Was* married."

Mr. Hibble peered at her through thick-lensed glasses. He had kind eyes and an earnest expression, the sort people seemed to cultivate when they shared bad news. "I've been looking into your case. I've gone over all the information you submitted. Unfortunately, it appears the marriage was never registered and recorded."

"What? No. There was . . . we had a wedding fourteen years ago." She remembered every moment. A sunset ceremony on the beach, surrounded by friends from the surf club. The officiant had been Cadbury Swain, who had once reigned as GSL champion for several years running.

After the ceremony, they played loud music through the speakers of the surf rescue station, and the feasting, champagne, and dancing had lasted for hours. Later that night, Johnny had taken her to the top-floor suite in a grand hotel overlooking Surfers Paradise, and he'd peeled off her lacy dress and made love to her, and she'd felt like the luckiest bride in the world.

Mr. Hibble cleared his throat. "A wedding ceremony is just that. A ceremony. But if it's not been recorded, it can't be recognized."

"So we were never married." Her voice was raspy with disbelief.

"Not in the legal sense, no. Another related issue is that your late . . . husband's name change was never formalized. Legally, he was John Merceski."

"He was never one to sweat the details," she said faintly.

Her options, the agent told her, were complicated. It might not even be possible to register a marriage when one of the parties was deceased, particularly when the deceased used an assumed name. She would be compelled to arrange a consultation with a lawyer. She'd have to find witnesses to the original event, and then try to appeal the deportation order. There were immigration law firms that might be able to help, but they were backlogged and expensive.

"I don't have money for a lawyer," she quietly told Mr. Hibble. "I don't have money for anything."

He gave her a sheet with contact information on assistance agencies. She would have to register as an indigent and file a request for aid. "If you're being deported to the States," he told her, "then you should apply to the US embassy down in Canberra."

She could scarcely afford bus fare back to Chermside, let alone a trip to Canberra, six hundred miles away.

"And if . . . if I don't have money to get to the States . . . ?"

"It's likely the aid organization will help you apply to the embassy or consulate. If you don't have the funds, they'll urge you to get your family or friends to pay. If you can verify that they are unable to do so, then and only then will the government provide your ticket. You'd be required to repay the loan. If you do choose this option, your passport will be confiscated and replaced with a single-trip passport that will allow you to reenter the United States but is invalid for any other travel."

He looked up the cost of a ticket from Brisbane to Los Angeles. One way.

Panic battered Nikki's insides like the wings of a caged bird. Reality hit hard. She had to leave Australia. The prospect of going back to the States was daunting, but without Johnny here, Australia was not her home. It only made sense with Johnny. Even so, she was horrified by the idea of returning to Alara Cove, a place that had discarded her years ago. She held on to the edge of the desk until her knuckles turned white. And then, as the reality of her dilemma settled into her bones, she did something she never thought she would do. She looked up at Mr. Hibble and said, "Is there . . . a phone I can use? Mine was ruined in an accident."

He paused, his gaze shifting from side to side. There was a hum from the other cubicles in the office space, but everyone seemed busy. He nodded at the phone on his desk.

Nikki frowned. She didn't know anyone's number other than Johnny's. "Um, I'd need a smartphone with WhatsApp. Sorry," she said. She was saying *sorry* a lot. Being suddenly widowed and flat broke altered her spirit. She had an inexplicable impulse to make herself and her troubles seem smaller—so as not to upset other people.

He hesitated again, then took a phone from his drawer, unlocked it, and slid it across to her. "You can log into WhatsApp," he said. "I need to step out for a moment, yeah?"

She nodded, grateful for the moment of privacy. She didn't know many of her log-ins by heart, but she managed to guess her way into WhatsApp. Most of the contacts there were related to surf league business—the GSL regional office in Coolangatta, people she'd met through competitions and exhibitions. She found her father in the contacts list.

Nikki stared at the screen. She didn't know what time it would be in the States. She didn't even know if the call would go through.

Her dad was an ocean away, and sometimes he seemed as distant as the moon. Mostly she and Guy stayed in touch through messages and snapshots on WhatsApp. She tried his number and listened through a minute or so of beeps, followed by a disappointed blip that ended the call.

Then she entered a message—*something happened, it's urgent*—but she already knew a reply was unlikely. She and her dad rarely talked, using the time difference as an acceptably valid excuse. He didn't always check his messages or bother to reply, either.

For a while after she'd left Alara Cove, Nikki had been diligent about staying in touch with her father and Carmella and Shasta, but as time went on, her efforts had dwindled, and so did theirs. The truth was, it was simply too easy to forget to nurture her connections with people at home. Leaving Alara Cove kept her away from memories of Mark and made the pain feel less sharp. Now she realized she'd never lost those memories, and the pain was still there, camouflaged by the passage of time. Losing Johnny dredged up reminders of the trauma that had driven her from home.

Scrolling through the text bubbles, she saw that the last exchange with her father was three months old; she'd sent him a report on a competition in Bali and he'd responded a few days later with a thumbs-up emoji.

These days, her dad had problems of his own. A couple of years ago, he'd knocked up a woman half his age and she had left him with a baby. When he first told Nikki the news, she thought he was nuts, but—oh, well. Her dad had never been much for planning ahead.

He named the baby Gloria. In pictures, the little girl looked adorable. Guy looked tired, and also baffled by this unexpected plot twist.

After leaving the message, Nikki gave her father another try, tapping the phone icon.

This time, her dad picked up right away. "Has hell frozen over?"

"Can I come home?" she asked. There were a million things to explain, but she didn't know where to begin.

"What the hell kind of question is that?"

PART THREE

There's nothing more beautiful than the way
the ocean refuses to stop kissing the shoreline,
no matter how many times it's sent away.

—*Sarah Kay, American poet*

10

Dazed by exhaustion, Nikki deplaned in LAX, leaving her back-of-the-aircraft middle seat behind. After the long flight, people unfolded like moths from cocoons, yawning and stretching as they surged toward Customs and Immigration. After shuffling through the cordoned-off line for half an hour, she approached the CBP booth and handed over her temporary passport, which featured a picture of a stranger who looked a hundred years old. The agent swiped it through a scanner. He glanced from the document to her face several times, then tapped his computer keyboard and studied the screen.

"Lost your passport?" asked the agent—M. Hernandez, according to his badge.

Nikki merely shrugged. She didn't want to be questioned yet again about the sequence of events that had brought her here. Didn't want to explain yet again that this was how an indigent, no-status person ended up. The guy hesitated a bit longer, tapped the keyboard again, then waved her through the airport terminal to the baggage claim area. Most people had their phones out, but Nikki was phoneless. Her father had insisted on picking her up, so she'd given him the flight information. She hoped he could find her in the international terminal, though that was probably a leap of faith. To her recollection, he'd never picked up anyone from the airport.

She waited, half asleep on her feet, by the luggage carousel, wondering if he would figure out how to collect her at the baggage claim that corresponded to her flight. She spotted her lumpy wheeled duffel coming toward her on the conveyor belt. The bag was covered with a patchwork of badges from various surf competitions and venues—Teahupo'o in Tahiti, the Hawaiian pro, the Asia Open, and the Margaret River pro, where their winnings had totaled $30,000 one year and they'd felt like millionaires. So many events. So much excitement. So many memories.

The bag felt leaden as she wrested it from the carousel. The customs line moved quickly, bored agents taking their declarations cards and waving people through. She prayed they wouldn't single her out for a search. She did not want to explain the urn of ashes buried in the middle of her bag.

An agent glanced at her card and waved her through. By the time she reached the other side, arrows of pain were firing in her injured wrist. The physical therapist at the hospital had advised her to exercise the wrist, but she rarely remembered to do so. She felt oddly guilty about her minor injuries, when the crash had killed Johnny. She didn't actually want to feel less broken. But the pain was real, the bag was too much for her, and she dropped it with a thud.

She swayed on her feet, too tired to do anything but stare at it for a moment.

"Nikki!" Her father, tall and broad-shouldered, approached her with assured strides. He reached her side as she was taking deep breaths, trying to fight off another wave of panic.

An unexpected flood of relief weakened her knees. She had not anticipated being so moved by the sight of her father after all these years. He looked both the same and different. Even in the glaring airport light, he was the quintessential beach boy in his vintage T-shirt and jeans, his hair in a ponytail, baseball cap worn backward, single hoop earring. He still had the coloring of a man who spent his life in the sun, the same disarming smile. Yet his hair was now more salt than pepper, and his handsome face bore the creases of age.

"Hey," he said.

"Hey." Tears crowded Nikki's throat.

"I'm glad you came home," he said.

"I had no choice," she said.

He opened his arms. Their hug was brief and a bit awkward. There was no real comfort in it; she was beyond comfort, but the human touch felt like a kind of shelter.

"You've been through the wringer," he said. "I wish I could have come to you and helped more."

"I know, but . . ." Everything was too complicated. She knew he didn't have the money for a plane ticket, let alone a passport. He had a little kid now, too. "You're here now. Thanks for being here."

He still drove the ancient white utility van, which was nearly as old as Nikki herself. The van still held the same familiar smells of motor oil, surf wax, and old neoprene, and she found it oddly comforting.

There was a car seat strapped to the back bench. "That's different," Nikki said.

"Oh, yeah. Gloria's my copilot, same as you used to be. Patsy's watching her for me today. She'll probably keep her overnight."

Nikki shook her head. "You got yourself into a situation." That was how he'd characterized it when he broke the news to her. A situation.

"That I did," he admitted.

"What in the world were you thinking?"

"There was no thinking. There was a condom fail. But wait until you meet Gloria. Best fail ever."

"Yeah? And her mother?"

He sighed. "Worst fail ever. I hardly knew Marnie when we hooked up. I got her to stay clean—mostly—during her pregnancy. Right after the baby was born, she took off with her dealer." He navigated through the airport and out onto the freeway. "Her parents tried to take Gloria but I wouldn't let them. They're the ones who raised Marnie. Think I'd give them another kid to ruin? Gloria is my second chance."

"Because you blew your first one?" Nikki was too sad and exhausted to be polite. Why couldn't he have been this way with her?

"I did what I did. You're an incredible person and I take no credit for that. But I don't take the blame, either."

He indicated a blanket and pillow behind the passenger seat. "Thought you might be ready for a snooze," he said.

"Totally." The pillow smelled like the commercial laundry at the park. With a deep sigh, she reclined the seat and melted into an exhausted sleep before they even exited the airport.

When she woke, it was nearly dark, and they were just approaching the caravan park. She blinked at the sharply familiar sight of the neon roadside sign. It was still missing two key letters, as it had for years. From the southern approach, the sign read B _ _ CHSIDE CARAVANS. Like some sort of word game puzzle.

No doubt the locals still called it Bitchside, a moniker Nikki herself had embraced when her friends came around, pretending it didn't bother her.

She sat up as they rolled through the property, passing the lamp-lit Airstreams, and parked at the end unit by the storage shed and utility buildings. Her dad came around and grabbed her bag and carried it to the door of Unit 7. During the low season, most of the units were vacant.

"This one's all ready for you," he said. "Patsy got it ready."

Nikki nodded, swaying on her feet. "Okay."

"Come on inside," he said, leading the way to his place. "You should eat."

"I'm not really hungry," she said. The knot in her stomach tightened as she tried to make sense of her life. *Not now*, she tried to tell herself. Not now.

"We can have Frito pie," he said. "I got a pot of chili on the stove. Take me just a minute to warm it up."

"I'll have a bit." She went into the cramped bathroom, noticing that nothing had changed about the place. He'd made an effort to spruce up. There were clean towels and a fresh bar of soap in the surfboard-shaped soap dish she'd made him one year for Father's Day.

She noticed a small collection of baby things, which looked oddly out of place.

In the galley kitchen, she built her Frito pie the way she always had, with a layer of chips, chili, cheese, sour cream, and onions. The taste of the hot, spicy concoction turned time backward, and she managed a brief smile. "This is good, thanks. This was always my favorite after surfing," she said.

"I got a bottle of wine I can open. Or a beer? Geez, last time we were together, you weren't old enough to drink."

She was too tired for wine now. "Water is fine."

He fixed a bowl for himself and sat down across from her. The dining booth was the same, too. Hula girl salt and pepper shakers, and a diner-style napkin dispenser next to the old-timey tabletop jukebox. "I remember," he said. "Man, we had some epic days."

"We did." Surfing was the one thing that held them together. Or was it? She questioned everything now.

"Listen, I'm sorry for what you're going through. I want to understand. I want to help. I mean, if you're okay with talking about it. Maybe you could tell me more about what happened. What you're facing. I mean, all you said is he died in a wreck."

"It's . . . a long story. Well, maybe not long, but complicated. We . . . he . . . it turns out, we were having money troubles. Like, major troubles, only I wasn't aware of how major until a crew from an eviction company came to the door with an official notice."

"Oh, shit," he said.

"I was sure it had to be a mistake. Johnny was practicing for a qualifying round that's coming up, so I went to the beach to find him. As we were driving home, we quarreled. Like, a lot. I said some things . . . we both said some things." She shut her eyes but couldn't block out the shock and grim defensiveness in his face. She could still picture his expression, bright and hard with anger. His movements were swift with impatience as he gripped the steering wheel and accelerated around a sharp turn. "He drove too fast on the way back and . . . it's a blur for me after that, just snatches of images. The car flipped, and his neck was broken. And his face . . ." She gasped with pain. "The medical team said he lost consciousness instantly and wouldn't have known what was happening to him." *Please let that be true,* she thought.

"Oh, honey," her dad said, drawing her into a hug. "Oh, my girl."

"He had . . . they said he had a traumatic brain injury. He . . . there was no brain activity. He never regained consciousness. Life support sustained him only long enough to . . . for a surgical team to harvest his organs." Johnny's heart was beating in someone else's chest. How could that even be?

She shuddered and slumped back.

Her dad wiped his eyes. "Shit," he said.

The silence felt weighty as she finished eating and stifled a yawn.

"You're dead tired," her dad said. "You need to sleep some more."

"Yes. I can't even tell you what day it is."

"It's the first day of the rest of your life," he said, "to coin a phrase."

She sighed. She'd never envisioned the rest of her life without Johnny. "It wasn't his fault," she said, once again feeling the need to explain. "He worked hard. We both did. He meant to catch up on the bills. He tried to protect me from knowing exactly how broke we were."

"You married a clone of me," Guy pointed out.

She shrugged her shoulders. "People marry their issues."

For the first few seconds when Nikki woke up, Johnny was alive. He was in the bed next to her, his body warm and pliant and comforting, his breathing soft and relaxed. Smooth skin, tattoo on his left shoulder, and his smell, unique and heady. His lips would make a sleepy trail to hers, and—

Inevitably, reality intruded like a rock thrown into a pool of still water. Nikki opened her eyes to find herself staring at the curved top of the Airstream. The glimpse of sky through the window made it seem, momentarily, as if no time at all had passed. And yet an entire lifetime had gone by. Johnny's lifetime. It was over in the blink of an eye.

The reading Nikki had done about grief told her to expect a barrage of emotions. She was advised to seek support, to feel her feelings, and keep moving forward with her life to a place of acceptance.

Despite the compassionate and well-meaning literature she'd been given by the hospital social worker, some new words would need to be invented for the feelings that engulfed her. In her darkest, bleakest moments, she wondered if she could even go on. And if she could, why would she want to?

She had always considered herself a positive person, but *this*. The grief went round and round in her head, and the only refuge was sleep. She couldn't stop what-iffing that day. What if he'd leveled with her about the eviction? What if she hadn't been so angry? What if they'd realized their marriage had not been properly recorded?

The only thing that felt real to Nikki now was her grief. And as painful as it felt, she clung to the awful, clawlike sensation. She was afraid that if she moved forward with her life, she would lose even her memories of Johnny. And that would be a level of agony she would never survive.

She found herself thinking about Mark McGill, the friend she'd lost so long ago. Sometimes, she could picture him exactly as he'd been, vibrant and bright-eyed, his infectious laugh a loud peal of joy. Other times, she could scarcely conjure up the memories. They had faded, becoming part of the undifferentiated landscape of her past. If that happened to her memories of Johnny, she would never forgive herself for failing to keep him alive within her.

The distant boom of the ocean called to her. That, and her bladder. It was astonishing to Nikki that any part of her could function after the crash. Despite a sadness so overwhelming that it felt as though everything inside her had died, life went on. Body functions went on.

In the tiny efficiency kitchen, she heated water in the kettle and made herself a pour-over coffee, watching it drip into a thick china mug with the Beachside logo. Coffee seemed as pointless as everything else, but the aroma from the mug penetrated her lethargy. She took a sip and felt almost guilty over the pleasure it gave her.

She flipped on the kitchen radio. It was tuned to its usual station, Alara AM, which featured hourly surf reports. The host announced that it was unseasonably warm for February. This morning promised a primary short period swell from the west, mixing with a secondary swell from the south southwest. A three- or four-foot surf beckoned.

She finished her coffee and got up from the table. Through the window, she saw her father puttering around in the shed. He must have heard the report, too, because he was dressed for the waves. Nikki hurriedly pulled on her suit and went out to join him.

"You going without me?" she asked. She grabbed a wetsuit from its hanger—women's small—and pulled it on.

"I didn't want to wake you," her dad said. "You know me. I like to go surfing first thing in the morning—"

"—in case it's the last day on earth," she said, speaking the old adage in unison with him.

Had Johnny known it was his last day? Of course he hadn't. He hadn't known anything. But at least he had gone surfing.

"I don't usually get to go most mornings lately because of Gloria," he said. "What about your wrist?" he asked.

"I have a brace. Besides, exercise is supposed to help." Her dad had no idea how many times she'd surfed and competed while injured. It was part of the job. "What about Gloria?"

"She's still at Patsy's, and she usually sleeps late. Patsy'll watch her."

"Patsy's a saint."

"Let's go," Guy said. "I'm sure your mind could use a break."

He was right. When she was out in the waves, her thoughts turned off entirely. There was something about the undeniable force of a green-faced wave that demanded total focus, leaving no room for anything else. She willingly subjected herself to the visceral power of the ocean, her senses filling with the taste of salt, the color of the water and sky, the boom of the surf, and the energy of the board skimming along beneath her bare feet.

For a few moments, she was in another place. After several rides, she felt more like herself. In balance. Surrounded by a walled enclosure made of saltwater.

Her father was a good surfer. Not great, the way Johnny had been, but strong and sure. The most striking thing about Guy's style was his clear exuberance, whether he caught a wave or just missed it, whether he rode true or wiped out. This had always been their common passion. From the very start, he taught her things about the water, urging her to let the ocean itself show her the way. Even as a little kid, she understood the feeling in her core.

She and Guy both loved it. Both came alive in the waves, like creatures of another species. On her board this morning, she was surprised to find herself remembering in great detail every minute in a way she had not in a very long time—the sound of her father's laughter and his calls of encouragement. The feeling of accomplishment when she did well. The sheer pleasure of the sport, unencumbered by all the stress of competition.

After an hour, the waves settled and dispersed while the crowds increased. People came out to the beach for their morning walks or yoga sessions, or to set up for a day of family fun. Even in the off-season, folks loved the beach. The food kiosks rolled out their awnings and put up their tent signs.

Nikki and her father waited beyond the break for the final ride that would take them home. Without exchanging a word, they chose a wave that split at its peak, and rode separately to shore. He did his old trick of matching her pace so it appeared that the tame wave would drop them off at the same moment like a local bus.

"That was good," Guy said. "Thanks for joining me."

She nodded, shrugging into her oversized sweatshirt. Her dad carried both boards across the beach and up the path toward the park.

Under the curve of the bluff, a young family was setting up for the day—blanket, umbrella, picnic hamper, baby gear. The mom hovered over the baby, offering toys and making bright, chirpy mom sounds.

"Does Gloria like the beach?" Nikki asked her dad.

"I suppose. Not the way you did, though. I could tell when you were only a few weeks old that you were part dolphin."

"You say." She eyed him skeptically. "How would you know?"

"You loved the water. You came alive when I took you in."

"Wait, you took a tiny baby into the waves?"

"When you were born," he told her, "my folks said you had to be baptized."

She slowed her pace and looked at him. "You never mentioned that."

"It was kind of a thing with them."

"Because they're Italian, right?"

He nodded. "They like the traditions. The ceremonies and mysteries of the church, I guess. Don't ask me why. I didn't have much to do with them after I left Cape May, but when you were born, I kind of wanted to reach out, you know? Honor a tradition."

"And was I?" she asked. "Baptized, I mean."

"Not the way they wanted. They expected you to be christened in the church. You know, in a long white gown with a bonnet and prayers, the whole bit. Your mother and I told them no." He nodded toward the outdoor shower. "You go first. I'll wash down the boards."

In the driftwood enclosure, she peeled off the wetsuit and let the warm stream from the shower pour over her, noticing that the faucets were old and rusty. Baptized? What the hell? She barely remembered her father's parents—Nona and Papa. Although they lived back East, they came to visit a time or two when Nikki was little. She recalled lots of food, loud voices, yelling sometimes. They had been nice enough to her, in that doting, generic way old people seemed to have with little kids. As she got older, they stopped coming, claiming the trip was too long and expensive. But really, they just didn't get along with her dad. After a while, it was just the yearly Christmas card, and lately, even that had tapered off.

She got dressed and went to the kitchen of her dad's place, rummaging for food. Once again, that feeling of disloyalty flickered inside her. How could she be hungry when Johnny was dead?

Because she was hungry, she perused the cereal selection—her dad had eclectic taste—and poured herself a big bowl of Honey Bunches. She hadn't tasted American cereal in years, and it was amazing. The taste of her childhood. The taste of simpler times. She ate slowly, studying an old photo album with a faded spine. The book had sat on a shelf above the table for as long as she could remember.

There were so few photographs from those times before phone cameras and the internet. The gummy pages held a few faded prints of her parents, smiling broadly and looking impossibly young, posed in front of her dad's quiver of surfboards. At their wedding on the beach, Lyra had worn a daisy-printed sundress and heeled sandals, and she looked up at Guy as though he was her whole world. A few pages later, there was a picture of Nikki, a tiny baby held between her parents, and another of her lying on a beach blanket, wide-eyed and limbs splayed, while Lyra and Guy gazed at her.

Her parents had been as young as Nikki and Johnny were when they'd first met. There was no hint in those smiling faces that they were a tragedy waiting to happen.

She browsed through the album, trying to figure out if she remembered the moments in the pictures. There were some shots of little Nikki, stick-legged, gap-toothed, but always grinning. In one of them, from her fifth birthday, Nona and Papa sat in the background under a striped awning hung with balloons. All of Nikki's birthday parties had been celebrated at the beach. She used to think the beach was the only place a kid could have a party.

Her dad came in, freshly showered, his hair damp and curling at the ends. He had a stack of mail in one hand, and a toddler perched on his other arm.

Nikki gaped at the baby. Holy crap, that was a cute baby. "Hello there," she said. "I'm Nikki."

The little girl tucked her head against Guy's shoulder, then peeked bashfully at Nikki.

"Your sister," Guy said. "It's cool to have both my girls in the same place."

Gloria had big brown eyes and a thatch of dark hair, the same color as Nikki's. In fact, she sort of looked like the little kid in the photo album.

"You noticed it, too," her dad remarked, watching her glance from the pictures to the toddler. "You two look just alike."

"I have a baby sister," Nikki said. "How crazy is that?" When she was far away, the situation had seemed surreal. A careless impulse her father was dealing with. Now here was this flesh-and-blood person—*Gloria*. The little girl stared openly at Nikki, and Nikki stared back. The baby was so incredibly cute that Nikki smiled for the first time in days.

Guy threaded the child's legs into a high chair and sprinkled some cereal on the tray in front of her. She picked up one morsel at a time, studying each piece before slowly putting it into her mouth.

Guy fixed himself a bowl of cereal and set the mail on the table. "She's not much of a talker yet," he said. "Are you, pipsqueak?

She says the occasional word but mostly, she's still at the babbling stage."

"Why did you tell them no?" Nikki asked him, indicating the photo album. "Your parents, I mean. About the baptism."

"I . . . Your mother and I weren't believers. Not in the Catholic way," he said, shuffling through the mail.

"In what way, then?"

"I guess, you know, we didn't need all the pomp and ceremony. The ritual stuff. When I was a youngster, I spent too many hours in catechism class. Those nuns—man, they could talk kids out of believing in anything." He abandoned the mail sorting and held up one hand, palm out. "See that there?" He indicated a faint, whitish line. "They used to smack us with a ruler, like that was gonna win our hearts and minds."

Nikki recoiled. "You were just a little kid."

"Right? And your mother—she wasn't raised Catholic, but she wasn't any better off. Her mom was . . . I guess she never said. Her people were Midwesterners."

"That's not a religion."

"No. Belief system, though. She said they believed in stuff like spare the rod and spoil the child." He gave Gloria a sippy cup filled with water and put a few blueberries on her tray.

"Nice," Nikki said. "So, no baptism, then?"

"We did it our way."

"You baptized me?"

"That's right. Carried you out into the surf and let a wave wash over you. Your mom thought you'd scream bloody murder, but you didn't. You blinked your eyes and sputtered a little bit and kind of smacked your lips. I lifted you up high, Lion King style, and said your name. Your full name—Nicoletta Fabiola Graziola. Then we wrapped you up like a burrito and had a beer in your honor." He pulled the photo album toward him and flipped to a picture. He was grinning as he held the baby bundled against his broad, bare chest. Lyra stood next to him on the beach, looking off into the distance, not smiling. Just . . . gazing. "Your baptism day," he said.

Nikki was incredulous. "You never told me that story."

"It was a long time ago." He pressed a button on the tabletop jukebox—J-47—and "Happy Together" by the Turtles began to play softly through the tinny speaker. "It was a nice day." He gazed at the picture again.

Nikki was surprised to hear a wobble in his voice. Then he cleared his throat, looked away.

"What?" she asked.

"It was our last nice day," he said.

She slipped the picture from the album, turned it over, and saw the date on the back. Her heart dropped. "She died that night."

"Yes."

"You've never talked about it."

He shrugged. "Not much to say."

"Dad."

"Your mom had a rough time when she was pregnant. And after."

"What do you mean?" Nikki was curious. He hadn't ever talked about her mother's pregnancy. Because he was a man, probably. In her experience, women talked about their pregnancies even decades after the kids were born, but men never did.

"She was sick a lot," he said now. "Morning sickness, but it went on all day."

"And after?" asked Nikki.

"After you were born, she had a hard time."

"Every new mom has a hard time." Back in Surfers Paradise, she'd heard hours of crying from her neighbor Jess's place. Johnny used to cover his head with a pillow and mumble about rethinking their plan to have a kid one day.

"I'm not talking about a normal hard time," her dad said. He handed Gloria a string of plastic toys.

"What are you talking about, then?" Nikki asked.

"Something was going on with Lyra, and neither of us recognized it. In retrospect, I'm sure it was a full-blown postpartum depression. I learned that too late. We were young. I was stupid. I had no idea what was going on. I didn't know enough to ask why she was tired all the time, no energy at all. I couldn't figure out why she was sad, why she cried so much when we had this awesome little baby. I thought maybe she was missing her mother, but she said no. She and her mother never got along."

Guy and Lyra would have been nineteen and twenty, Nikki calculated. Nobody knew anything at that age.

"That day—the day we baptized you—I thought doing something fun might cheer her up, you know. Maybe it did for a while." He studied the picture. "I had to drive up to Pismo to pick up some propane. I told her I'd bring back dinner. Her favorite from a place called Burger Spot."

Nikki put the photo back in the album and smoothed her hand over the plastic. She wondered what was going on in Lyra's head that day. She was gazing off into the distance, and Guy was grinning from ear to ear.

Nikkie glanced over at him. "Did something happen while you were away?"

His shoulders slumped. He shoved his splayed fingers through his hair. "I was only gone a few hours. Maybe four or five, taking care of business. When I got back, I heard you crying before I even got inside. Man, it was the worst sound I'd ever heard. It was a kind of crying I hadn't heard before. Like . . . a panic. I ran, nearly yanked the door off the hinges. You were in the crib, your face all red. Bright red and sweaty, your eyes like slits. And your mother. She was just . . . I called 911 but it was too late."

Nikki stared at him. Her stomach churned. "You always said it was an accidental drug interaction."

He didn't speak. Didn't move a muscle.

"Dad."

"She took something. On purpose."

Nikki felt chilled to the bone. "What? Are you sure? How do you know it wasn't a drug interaction?"

He paused. Stared at the tabletop. "She left a note."

"*What?* What kind of note? You mean a suicide note?"

"The note said she was in a black ditch. She said you wouldn't stop crying and she was afraid you'd never stop. She didn't know how to make it stop. She was scared that she might not be able to keep herself from harming you, and she couldn't take it anymore."

Nikki winced, too easily able to picture the scene. "How am I just hearing about this?"

"It was so damn painful," he said. "I felt so damn guilty. Like, why the hell didn't I see? Why'd I leave her alone all day? And why the hell didn't she walk away, go ask somebody for help with a crying baby?" He lifted Gloria from the high chair and set her on the floor next to a small bin of toys. "That's the reason I didn't object when this one's mother took off. I was afraid she might be too much like Lyra."

"I can't believe what I'm hearing," said Nikki.

"I'm sorry to be telling you now. Was I wrong to tell you?"

"For telling me the truth?" she asked. The picture she'd created in her mind of Lyra, her distant, missing mother, was altered now. Lyra was no longer maternal, laughing, ethereal. Now Nikki imagined a woman who was fragile, shaken by despair. "Do you have the note?"

He went to the sink and started washing the dishes. "The ocean has the note."

Nikki sat at the table, flipping through the ancient jukebox selections. It explained a lot about the way he'd been with her when she was growing up. He'd always kept a distance between them. He'd seemed apprehensive around her, almost afraid. Because she was her mother's daughter?

"We both lost our person," she said quietly. "What are the chances?" The gaping hole of grief yawned wide again.

"There's a part of me that will never be okay," her dad said. "I figure there's a part of you that will never be okay. But after a while you get better at coping. You go on."

She sat quietly for a long time. Outside, there were signs of the park waking up, people coming out of the units, stretching, loading up for the beach. Then she got down on the floor with Gloria. The baby studied her briefly, then offered a drooling smile and handed her a board book.

"Johnny and I kept putting off having a baby," Nikki said. "It always seemed pretty impossible when we were touring. And when we weren't touring, we were too broke."

"I bet you'd be a good mom," said Guy.

"No chance of that now."

He nodded toward Gloria. "Never say never. But don't ever think it's easy. It wasn't for me, anyway. That one—she's easier than you were. Or maybe I'm just better at it."

"I wasn't an easy baby?"

"There were nights that seemed like they'd never end. For some damn reason, your hunger peaked at three a.m. every night. It went on for weeks."

Nikki pictured him staggering to the kitchen to warm a bottle.

He massaged the back of his neck. "You liked certain songs. I'd put on some music and sometimes you would settle down. All those numbers in the jukebox—those were your favorites. And you liked looking at art—I was sure of it. You'd stare up at the ceiling, so I put pictures of faces on it."

"You never told me that. You never told me any of this," she said, slowly turning the pages of the board book. "Why are you telling me now?"

"I figure one of us needs to start talking."

"I just got here."

"Then I figure you'll talk when you're ready." He gave the baby a ripped envelope to play with, and she crowed with delight.

Nikki would never be ready. But she was learning that the world didn't wait for a person to be ready. She nodded at Gloria. "Is *she* baptized?"

"She knows her name."

"And she's easier than I was."

"She's different. *I'm* different." He bent down and fluffed the kid's hair. "She goes to daycare in town. Patsy helps out. Patsy does a lot." He sat down and went back to his mail.

Nikki was tempted to ask if he was planning to give her to Carmella one day, but she resisted. "Well, I never thought I'd see you going all single dad at your age."

"Sorry, what?" He was staring at the printed letter he'd just opened. He looked suddenly ill, his face ashen and his brow scored by creases.

"Something the matter?"

"I got problems with the city."

"Yeah? What kind of problems?"

"I got behind on some payments."

"Wouldn't be the first time, would it?"

"This is different. They're challenging my status as a recreational area, and without it, my taxes will double." He rubbed his temples. "I never owned a thing in this world except this collection of run-down trailers." He gestured at the letter. "Now they're threatening to tow them all away."

"What? Tow them? Have you decided what you're going to do about it?"

"Well, obviously, I'm going to have to figure it out. That is, unless I'm okay with the city hauling the Airstreams to the boneyard."

"They can't do that. The caravans have been here forever. You have a lease on the land."

"They want to move them out, make way for progress. Probably let some developer put up a high-rise here. I don't know."

"Are you just . . . going to let them?"

"Not much I can do."

"That doesn't sound like you."

He folded up the letter and tucked it away. "That's enough about me. This is all bullshit compared to what you're dealing with."

She studied his face, noting the tension around his eyes and mouth. "It's okay to think about stuff other than me, even under these circumstances."

"Yeah, all right, I'm . . . I want you to know how glad I am that you're back. But all I feel right now is worry."

"I'll figure this out," she repeated. Yet even as she spoke, she felt zero conviction. Everything had collapsed so quickly that she had barely managed to catch her breath. She truly didn't know what she was going to do for a living now that she was back in the States. She didn't even have a high school diploma, let alone a college one or career training. She knew how to swim and surf. That wasn't a career. These days, it was barely a living. "Look," she told her father, "I'm not asking you for anything."

"I just wish I had more to offer you. I mean, you're welcome to stay as long as you need to, but my days here might be numbered. Jesus." He shuddered, reached over, and switched to another selection on the jukebox. *Lola.*

"I can't believe that thing's still working," Nikki said.

"I've had to fix it a couple times."

She stared at the vintage machine. "When I was little, I used to wonder where all the songs came from."

"And I used to tell you it was magic."

"I still don't know," she admitted.

"Then I guess it's still magic."

She could feel his eyes on her, and she realized the worry had a deeper meaning. "Dad. I never even knew my mother. There's no way I could be like her. I won't kill myself," she said at length. "I can't promise I won't feel depressed. A lot. But I won't do myself in."

"I'll hold you to that."

Her dad finished the dishes and put things away. She watched him, feeling a wave of appreciation for what he'd just shared. Even though it was terrible, she appreciated knowing.

She felt a new kinship with him. A new closeness. They had both lost beloved spouses in a horrible way. They had both endured the unendurable. The unthinkable. The unfathomable.

And they were both still standing.

11

Nikki busied herself with the mundane chores of putting her life in some sort of order. The small tasks—figuring out where to get a cheap mobile phone, applying for a debit card with a small loan from her father—filled the moments between sadness and panic. She found it hard to care about her future. Without Johnny, it was a bleak, formless cloud. Still, that didn't mean she could drift. She had to make a life for herself.

Today's project—a visit to a free clinic in Santa Maria to get something for her anxiety and sleeplessness. She went to Patsy Hayward's unit and knocked.

Patsy opened the door and stepped down. Her smile was soft, her arms wide with welcome. "My lord, look at you, Nicoletta Fabiola. You're finally back."

"It's good to see you," Nikki said. Patsy had hardly changed a bit. Her shoulder-length wavy hair had a few gray streaks, and there were fine lines fanning out from her pale gray eyes, yet she exuded the same quiet gentleness Nikki remembered. "I guess my dad told you."

"Just enough to worry me. I want to help. I mean, I know nothing's going to help, but—" She gestured at the small café table, set with two glasses of lemonade. "We can talk if you feel like talking."

Nikki did feel like talking, which came as a surprise to her. She didn't have words to describe her grief, but she told Patsy about the midnight panics, the emotional roller coaster ride that wouldn't stop, the fiery ache in her solar plexus that made it hard to breathe.

"You poor thing," Patsy said. "I'm glad you're seeing somebody about it."

"I gave up trying to beat it back."

"You don't have to beat it back. Just . . . try to manage it from one moment to the next, maybe."

Nikki almost wept with relief when she heard that. "Oh, Patsy. You're right. It might mean dragging myself through the day, though. You know what lifts my spirits? Gloria. Who would have thought at age thirty-three, I'd have a baby sister?"

"She's a bright spot, that's for sure." Patsy's smile melted with fondness. "A glimmer of hope."

"I'll take a glimmer. My dad sure is grateful to you for helping with her."

"I like to help."

"You always have, Patsy. He's so lucky that you've stuck around for him all this time."

Patsy's smile faded a bit as she gestured toward her unit. "When my kids were little and my ex was after me, your dad made all the difference. This turned out to be a good spot to raise my kids and feel secure. And then . . . staying and working here became a habit, I suppose. Turns out, I love this place as much as Guy does."

Nikki wondered if her father realized what had been in front of him all along. "So, did he tell you about his problem with the city? The city's threat to take some kind of action against him?"

Patsy shook her head. "Again, just enough to worry me. He tends to keep his trouble under wraps."

Like Johnny did.

Nikki rubbed her wrist. It was still swollen and tender to the touch. She probably shouldn't have gone out surfing so soon.

"Get that looked at when you're at the clinic," Patsy said. "See if they'll prescribe something for the pain. Just because he's gone doesn't mean you need to keep hurting."

"I will. I'm waiting for my dad to get back with the van. He's dropping Gloria off and running errands."

"You can borrow my car. I'm not using it."

"Don't you need your car?"

Patsy took a quick sip of her lemonade. "I'd drive you myself, but my license was suspended. I got one too many speeding tickets. I'm not a bad driver, but I have bad timing, I guess." She looked around the courtyard. "Is it true they're going to try to get rid of this place?"

"I'm not sure. It sounds serious. I don't know what he'll do if he loses the caravan park. He hates to lose things," Nikki said.

Patsy knotted her hands in her lap. "I don't know what I'd do, either." She gestured at the Airstreams. "This is the life you get when you don't make a plan." She took a deep breath. "I'm not complaining, though. I've never been good at planning ahead."

"Join the club," Nikki said. "I wonder if there's a support group for it."

Patsy shook her head. "Sit tight. I'll get you the car key."

Nikki knew she had to focus on choosing to live her life. Living from day to day had come so naturally with Johnny. Now she couldn't even remember how it was done.

Patsy came out and handed her a key on a surfboard fob. "Try not to speed," she said. "It's a gutless old car, but it's been known to exceed the speed limit."

"I'll be careful." Nikki hadn't been in a car since Australia. Her palms were already sweating. "And thanks, Patsy. You've been really good to my dad for a long time. I hope he appreciates it enough."

The county clinic was adjacent to the hospital and ER. Nikki had been taken there a time or two when she was a kid. Once, she'd needed stitches in her chin after banging it on her surfboard during a wipeout, and another time when she'd dislocated her shoulder while playing around on a stand-up paddleboard under the Radium Island bridge. The Navy security officer who had transported her to the ER had lectured her about the dangers of the swift current at flood tide, telling her she was lucky to be alive.

At the clinic, the nurse practitioner showed equal concern for Nikki's situation and her wrist injury.

"Probably not the best idea to go surfing with this," the woman said. Vivian Burke. No-nonsense, reading glasses perched on her nose, strong hands that flew over the keyboard as she asked questions. Now she was fitting a brace on Nikki's wrist.

"I got used to surfing with injuries when I was in the league," Nikki said, holding her arm still while Ms. Burke adjusted the brace.

There was a detailed questionnaire about Nikki's mental health. Did she worry all of the time? Never? Somewhere in between? Did she ever consider self-harm? Did she have trouble sleeping, concentrating, or making decisions?

"This is a good time to give yourself a break." She handed over the prescription slips. "Practice self-care the way you'd practice care of the person you love most."

"I lost that person," Nikki said softly.

"You checked 'widowed' on the information sheet," said Ms. Burke. "I'm very sorry. Now more than ever, you need to look after yourself.

"I know it doesn't seem possible right now, but there will be others. You'll find others." The nurse's tone was firm.

As she followed the sinuous coast road back to Alara Cove, Nikki clung to that thought. Being sad all the time felt like a slow, agonizing death. She had to remember how to feel something else.

The scenery passed in a blur, with only the deepening colors of approaching sunset tracking her journey. Photographers called this time of day the golden hour, when the colors of the sky and water and sand were at their glorious peak. When she and Johnny used to pose for their sponsors' promotional shoots, these were the prized moments, the moments that made them look as if they lived in a dream world. There were times when she believed it was true.

Now she was returning to Alara Cove the same way she had left—her future out of focus, with no clear plan for moving forward. She had lost everything—the life she thought she lived, the dreams she used to dream. Everything had gone so wrong, so quickly, like an explosion. She kept trying to make sense of what had happened, or at least to find some kind of meaning in it, but the answers eluded her. She knew only that she needed to find a safe haven where she could heal. And then she was going to have to rebuild her world from the ground up. The last time, she had voluntarily scuttled her own future. This time, the destruction had been forced on her, which made it feel even more shocking and unjust.

You didn't lose everything, she reminded herself. Thinking about her father and the child he was raising, Nikki made a silent promise. *I won't lose what I have to what I just lost.*

As she approached the town center, she noticed a few changes, starting with the billboard sign at the city limits: *Welcome to Alara Cove—Jason T. Sanger, Mayor.*

Wait. What?

The steering wheel wobbled, and she quickly corrected it. *Jason Sanger.* She shouldn't be surprised. Of course Jason Sanger was the mayor. The Sangers had been in charge of everything for generations. By all reports, they still controlled the county—and apparently now the city as well. Suddenly Nikki realized that her father's trouble with "the city" was actually trouble with the Sangers.

She used to think she would never come back to this town. After Mark died, it had been so inhospitable to her. Still, as she drove slowly along the main street, she felt this place in her bones. Alara Cove was where she'd learned to surf and where she'd fallen in love with painting and art. A familiar, almost comforting nostalgia warmed her as she passed the places she knew so well—the White Rabbit Bookshop with its hand-lettered *Feed Your Head* slogan over the door; ZuZu's

Petals Boutique, where she had worked one summer just to get the employee discount; Carmella's gallery; the many cute cafés and gift shops; and even the public library, which had once been her refuge. It was a relief to see places she remembered with fondness rather than fear.

When she passed the sign indicating the turn-off for Thornton Academy, her thoughts shifted. Looming in the uplands east of the highway, its gleaming grand entrance was surrounded by sun-gilt walls and manicured gardens. The whole institution was a monument to learning, but also to privilege and, she knew now, artifice.

Dogged by a past she wanted to leave behind, Nikki scowled away the memories and accelerated up the winding road toward the caravan park.

A quick, insistent *yip* drew her glance to the rearview mirror. The reflection framed swirling blue lights and the dark green of a local police department vehicle.

Wonderful, she thought, letting out a frustrated sigh as she signaled and pulled over. In fifteen years in Australia, she'd never been pulled over. Now she was making her first drive through town, and trouble had already found her.

If she ever needed a sign that coming back here was a bad idea, it was currently walking toward Nikki on the shoulder of the road—six-feet-something with slim hips, wide shoulders, tall boots, mirror glasses, and a brimmed patrolman's hat, backlit by the lowering sun.

She cranked down the window, then placed her hands on the steering wheel where he could see them. That was what one did here in the US, she recalled, bracing herself.

The smell of the ocean swept over her senses, and the deep sound of the surf mingled with the crunch of boots on gravel.

"License and registration please, ma'am," said a deep, studiedly polite voice.

Nikki frowned, hearing a note of familiarity in that voice. She tilted her head to look at the guy. He used one finger to push the mirrored shades up the bridge of his nose.

For the first time in days, she felt something other than grief and despair. "Cal," she blurted out. "My gosh—Calvin Bradshaw."

He took off his shades and tucked them in an upper shirt pocket next to his shoulder radio. "And *my* gosh, Nikki Graziola. Wow, it's been a while."

"It's been forever."

"Seems that way." He stepped back and regarded her with a wondering expression. She felt a nudge of familiarity, catching a glimpse of her old friend in his smile.

Gesturing at the handbag on the seat beside her, she asked, "Do you still need—"

"No." He waved a hand. "Of course not. Now, what's your hurry? You were speeding."

"I was? Sorry about that," she said.

"And you've got a brake light out."

"Oh, shoot. I didn't know. I just borrowed this car—literally—this afternoon."

"And the tags are expired." He checked the windshield sticker. "Emissions test, too."

She didn't know about that, either. No wonder Patsy said she almost never drove it.

"Thanks for pointing that out," she said. "I . . . I'll look after it." What a strange, unexpected encounter. Calvin Bradshaw, after all these years. "Mind if I get out and say a proper hello?"

"Hey, I'd be insulted if you didn't."

She opened the door and stood up, moving gingerly because she felt oddly fragile. It wasn't just the injury, but the sense that she carried an awful tragedy deeply hidden inside, and if she made any sudden moves, it would escape. She stepped back and looked up at Cal. Like, really up. He was quite tall now, and well-built, like an amped up version of his teenage self, much changed from the undersized boy she remembered. The uniform shirt was borderline too small on him, hugging an impressively muscled chest and biceps that strained against the fabric. "Hey," she said.

"Hey, yourself." They exchanged a brief, awkward hug and she stepped back, leaning against the dusty side of the car. "You're a cop."

"That I am."

Nikki found it disconcerting to see her oldest friend wearing a gun in a holster. She had a million questions. If she started probing now, she'd never finish. Cal Bradshaw, local cop. How had that happened?

"Sorry, what?" She realized he was asking her something.

"Just wondering what brings you back after all this time."

"Desperation," she blurted out, forgetting they weren't friends anymore. "Tragedy."

"Whoa, Nikki. Seriously? What happened? What's going on?"

Since she was already blurting, she decided to spill, all at once to get it over with. Like ripping off a Band-Aid. She couldn't stand talking about Johnny in the past tense, but she forced the words out. "I lost my husband in an accident last month, right after I picked a horrible fight with him. And then it turns out, our marriage was never official and my visa had expired, and I got deported. I had to pack everything up and come back here, because otherwise I'd be living under a bridge somewhere in Queensland." For some reason, she could say these things to him without collapsing. She'd always been able to talk to Cal. In this moment, it felt as though no time had passed since they were teenagers.

He didn't move a muscle for a few seconds. Then he said, "Damn, Nikki. Damn." And with that, he drew her into a hug.

It wasn't awkward this time. It wasn't comfortless like the hug with her dad. It was a moment of ridiculously welcome human contact. She didn't realize how vital it was to feel a connection with someone who knew her. Cal's gentle strength, even his silence, caused something inside her to melt completely. The icy armature that had been propping her up all day suddenly collapsed, and for a few moments, the only thing supporting her was Cal Bradshaw's embrace. She sobbed from a place so deep and fundamental that she felt hollowed out, emptied of everything except the pain of loss.

Cal didn't say anything. He simply held her while her tears soaked his uniform shirt. After endless moments, a car swished past. Then another approached more slowly, and the driver rolled down her window. She was an attractive woman with shiny auburn hair and designer sunglasses. She briefly bit her lower lip and peeked over the top of her glasses. The late-model SUV had a realtor logo on the door.

"Everything all right here?" the woman asked. Then she seemed to recognize Cal. "Oh, hey. You good?"

"I'm good. Thanks for checking, Della."

The woman drove away and Nikki stepped back, suddenly self-conscious. "Della Avery?" Nikki remembered her from middle school, a hundred years ago. Noting the flush that darkened Cal's ears, she wondered if there was some kind of vibe between them.

She used her sleeve to wipe her face, and when she looked up at him again, the blush was gone and all his attention was focused on her. He was probably mortified by her unexpected burst of emotion. "Oh, my God. I . . . Cal, I didn't . . . I guess you didn't see that coming."

"Seems like it probably came from everything you just told me. Seems like you've been through a lot."

"I'm not 'through' anything," she said softly. "I don't know if I'll ever get there."

"Well, it's good you came back. I'm sure you still have plenty of friends here."

She didn't know what to say to that. She didn't know what she had. "I'm glad I ran into you, anyway, Cal. I should get going. I'm going to be staying at my dad's place until I—" Until what? She had no idea. "For the time being."

He took out a card and a pen, and wrote something on the back. "My mobile number. Call anytime. I mean that. Any time of the night or day. No WhatsApp messages or Facebook stuff. *Call.*"

"Thanks. Really, Cal. Thank you." She tucked the card into her back pocket.

"Take care, now." He touched a button on a square device on his shoulder.

"Body cam?" she asked.

"All on tape," he said. "Don't worry. It won't be reviewed. It's a small department. We only review stuff if there's an action."

She nodded and got back into the car. As she drove slowly and cautiously the rest of the way home, her mind lingered on Cal Bradshaw. They hadn't lost touch completely, but through the years, their contact had dwindled to the occasional "like" or emoji on social media. Seeing him again in the flesh reminded her that he was a *person*, not an icon on a phone screen. He had changed so much. But his kindness reflected the guy she'd always known.

And he was a cop. How had that happened? The move seemed at odds with his oft-stated goal to get away and explore the world. He used to talk about traveling to faraway places, but maybe that was just a kid talking. Doing the job of a kid, which was dreaming about everything.

Nikki had learned all too well how to dream, and now she realized that maybe the job of a grown-up was to unlearn that dream. Or at least to bury it.

12

Cal Bradshaw draped his wrist over the top of the steering wheel of his squad car. As he made his way home at the end of his shift, he let his thoughts wander. He'd been surprised as hell to find Nikki Graziola behind the wheel of the old hatchback. After all these years, the girl who had once occupied way too much of his head-space was back in town.

He remembered the day she'd left Alara Cove in a blaze of glory. That was what it had looked like to him. He had always pictured her conquering the surf world with her rock-star husband. Judging by the Global Surf League postings he'd seen online, she had done exactly that—for a while. Although Cal didn't go looking for the in-formation, Shasta—the town's head librarian and data hound—kept up with Nikki's rankings.

But the numbers didn't really tell the story. The rankings didn't explain how Nikki had ended up married—but not really married—to a guy who used a stage name. The numbers didn't explain the terror and tragedy of a fatal wreck.

Now she was back. Cal knew very well that everybody faced tough breaks. He had weathered plenty of his own. But rarely had misfortune piled on a person all at once, so thick.

He pulled into the drive of the house where he'd grown up and where he still lived. He parked in his usual spot. The place was as small and plain as a box of saltine crackers. The walkway and front stairs and porch were spare and painstakingly neat, not because he was particularly picky about the place, but because of his dad.

Rule number one of living with a blind guy was to remove all obstacles, and to never change things. Never rearrange furniture or place objects where he could bump into them.

His dad's big power tools—the tools of his trade—were long gone from the adjacent shed. Al still did some hand carving, but only with soft, pliable wood or resin. Sharp objects were no longer his friends.

Cal picked up a package that he been left on the porch and went inside. China, on her pad, thumped her feathery tail to acknowledge him. His dad, relaxing in his favorite chair, took out his earbuds and set them carefully in the holder by his phone. He favored Cal with a familiar smile and the same greeting he offered every day. "How's life in the big city? Did you bring in any bad guys?"

"All in a day's work," Cal said. "How about yourself?"

"Went to a board meeting—more talk about affordable housing, but of course, no progress. Had a cribbage match with the gamers. Did my ten thousand steps with China." He tilted his head toward the phone. "Started another novel from the bookmobile. A police procedural. I had no idea law enforcement was so sexy. You don't ever talk about that."

"Right. Never a dull moment."

"Oh, and Destiny wants to reschedule my lesson for tomorrow night."

"Fine by me." Cal's dad had signed up for guitar lessons, hoping Cal would hook up with Destiny. She had a fantastic voice and a fine talent on the guitar. She just happened to be single and looking. Maybe he would invite her for a drink. Probably not, though. Hooking up wasn't really his thing.

As he did after work every day, Cal hung his hat and left his boots by the door. Then he went upstairs to shower and change. He could hear his dad practicing on the guitar, laughing aloud at himself as he muddled through "Hey There Delilah."

Al's positive attitude was a daily wonder to Cal. Despite his challenges, Alfred Bradshaw was living his best life, staying connected to people in the community, making the most of each day. It's what the cancer taught me, Al would say. Our time on earth is a gift.

Cal knew he needed to be more like his dad. Some days, it was hard to do that. Some days seemed to drag on forever.

He had grown up thinking he would leave Alara Cove. He always planned on seeing new places, meeting new people, finding a new life.

As it turned out, life had other plans in store for him. His travels ended at California Polytechnic, over in San Luis Obispo. He'd been accepted to Brown, on the East Coast, but there was no money for an Ivy League school. At Cal Poly, he studied social and criminal justice administration and Spanish. Shortly before graduation, the call came in. The good news was that his dad's cancer was in remission. The bad news was that Al had experienced a stroke, which was a known risk from the chemo. The damage to the optic nerve had caused permanent blindness.

Alfred Bradshaw swore he was just glad to be alive. And he was determined to go it alone. "I'm going to figure out a way to live with this," he told Cal and Sandy. "But you don't have to."

While Cal finished his degree, Al went to blind camp—as he called it—working with local and state agencies to learn to live independently. He and his first dog, Calyx, moved to a sheltered residence in Los Angeles. Working with occupational therapists and orientation and mobility specialists, he learned to shop for meals, pay bills, make his way around the neighborhood, clean his toilet, brush his teeth with toothpaste.

Al Bradshaw gave his all to making the transition. He joined support groups, accessed resources, stayed active and engaged, took Spanish lessons, dedicated himself to being the best blind guy he could be.

But when Cal went to visit him, bursting with the news that he'd qualified for a Fulbright scholarship, he knew something was wrong.

He told his brother, Sandy, that their dad was failing. Sandy, who played bass for an up-and-coming band, didn't buy it. He pointed out that there was nothing wrong with their father's health now. After years of struggle, he had beaten the cancer and he was sound of body and mind.

Cal still believed something was wrong. Al had no appetite. No motivation. His face was pale, almost grayish in tone.

It didn't take long for Cal to figure out the reason. His dad was depressed. Al had been forced to move away from the house he'd renovated with his own hands, surrounded by his flourishing gardens and woodworking shop. In the city high-rise, he could no longer feel the sea breeze or smell the eucalyptus wafting down from the hills behind the house.

"We're moving home," Cal had announced one day shortly after graduation. It wasn't even a decision. It was simply the next logical step.

There was an unguarded flash of joy on his father's face, but it quickly collapsed into a worried frown. "No, son," he said. "My care team says the Alara Cove house is too remote for me to safely live there alone. The old place is too much for me."

"Not for me."

Another flash—hope and yearning, swiftly disguised by a skeptical shake of the head. But not quickly enough. Cal saw.

"We'll live there together," he said. "Just like always."

"Hold your horses, son. You've got other plans. You got a goddamn Fulbright scholarship. You're not going to move back home to be a nursemaid to your old man."

"First, you're not old. And second, I'm no damn maid. You're not going to talk me out of it. Listen, Dad. You fixed up that house to give me and Sandy a place to grow up. You sacrificed for us, worked your ass off for us. Took out a second mortgage so I could go to school. Now I have a chance to step up, and I'm proud to do it."

"Son, no. I—"

"It's settled," Cal had said. "We're going home."

Al had hemmed and hawed plenty more, but Cal knew he'd won when his dad's face lit up and his posture changed—chin up, shoulders square. In his studies and criminal justice training, Cal had learned to read a person's most subtle signals. He recognized the hope and relief on his father's face. Even the dog seemed more animated, picking up on Al's mood.

Cal got on with the police department. It seemed like a good fit. He already had the education. All he needed was twenty weeks of procedural, tactical, and weapons training. All of that, of course, had not been his plan. But he discovered that plans were incompatible with obligations.

It took no effort at all for him to knit himself back into the fabric of Alara Cove. Unexpectedly—almost against his will—he grew to love law enforcement. At its most basic level, the job was an opportunity to help people with their most profound needs. There were days when the toughest moment might involve helping an old woman find her mailbox key or fixing a hole in someone's garden fence.

He learned to appreciate those days, because there were other times that presented more complicated challenges. All too frequently, he was called to handle allegations of abuse, assault, or burglary. Since the department was too small to have divisions, a case usually belonged to him from start to finish. He dealt with fender benders, child custody disputes, barroom scuffles, and bail jumpers. Some of his work was out on the water, in the department's safe boat. There wasn't a full-time marine officer, although the DNR had a conservation officer in the district. In this area, everyone was spread so thin that the different departments often had to cover for each other.

Cal never knew what his next twelve-hour shift might bring. All around town, he moved among the people he served: victims, suspects, and witnesses. School pranks, minors with booze, missing pets—all in a day's work.

He encountered plenty of folks who couldn't handle their kids.

Youngsters were definitely a challenge, especially in the teen years. Underage drinking, joyriding, sneaking out—a lot of kids were on a mission to do it all. Here in Alara Cove, there were added temptations, like the naval facility on Radium Island and the local marina with its boats and water toys of every shape and size.

The job wasn't sexy like the one in the novel his dad was reading. And it created its share of awkward moments, like the time he was volunteering at a Helpline House fund-raiser in the concession stand and found himself partnered with a woman he'd arrested more than once for meth manufacturing. Or when he answered a domestic call and the rich lady of the house hit on him. Or when a guy he brought in for drunk driving turned out to be his dad's best cribbage partner.

Or when a woman he pulled over for a broken brake light was his childhood crush who ended up sobbing in his arms.

Yeah, that was awkward.

After his shower, he cracked open two beers and set them on the kitchen table. "I brought meatball subs from Oliva's," he said. "Hungry?"

"Always." His dad came into the kitchen, China at his heels. "I need to feed my girlfriend here first." The dog supply cabinet was perfectly organized with China's food and supplements in braille-labeled containers. The canine diet of raw, grass-fed organ meat and organic produce was made by a local farmer. It wasn't cheap, but China wasn't just any dog. It's obvious that she's my eyes, Al liked to tell people, but she's also my heart.

Cal took a swig of beer and bit into his sandwich, still warm from the wood-fire oven at Oliva's. Heaven.

His dad joined him, his face reflecting the same sort of bliss. "I don't know what they put in their sauce, but it's addictive."

"Witchcraft," Cal agreed.

"Speaking of witches—guess who was driving the bookmobile today."

"Undoubtedly the world's sexiest librarian," Cal guessed.

"That's right, son. I swear, why the two of you don't get together is beyond me."

"Dad."

"I mean it. Did you know library card applications have quadrupled since Shasta Kramer took over as head librarian?"

Cal grinned. "You say." He was probably right, though. Shasta had found something she liked as much as books—shopping for clothes. She liked wearing form-fitting dresses and high-heeled sandals, hoop earrings and colorful highlights in her hair. She'd confessed to Cal that more than once, one of the rich talent agents in town had asked her if she had any interest in acting or modeling.

"It's true," his dad said. "I heard it at the senior center just the other day. Guys go to the library just to watch her purse her lips and shush people."

"Right." Cal chuckled, then tucked into his sandwich again. His dad wasn't wrong about how attractive Shasta was. And how cool she was. For the past several years, he and Shasta had been training together for Ironman competitions and triathlons. They competed regularly, as individuals and in team events.

Some of Cal's other friends had the same idea as his father, suggesting he and Shasta should be a couple. They both found it funny—and impossible. They had been friends for years, but there was never a spark of romance. Not even a glimmer. Chemistry was a mysterious thing, they both agreed.

"Anyway," his dad continued, "it's a documented fact—the increase in library patronage is real. You can check for yourself. It's on her campaign website. I mean, she would never claim it was due to her looks, of course. But her predecessor was a guy who looked like Shrek, so . . ." Al shrugged.

Cal had not checked out Shasta's campaign website, though he was aware that she had filed her candidacy to run for mayor of Alara Cove. It was a thankless, poorly compensated position, but she loved the community and wanted to help make it a better, more inclusive, safer place. Cal admired her community spirit, but it was doubtful that she'd win the position, because her opponent was the current mayor—Jason Sanger.

"What's on your mind?" asked his father. "I can hear you thinking."

His dad had a spidey sense. Cal's daily routine scarcely varied, but today felt different to him. Something out of the ordinary had occurred. And somehow, Al had caught wind of his mood.

"Nikki Graziola is back in town," he said.

"Nikki Graziola. There's a name I haven't heard in a while. Guy Graziola's girl. How's she doing?"

"Actually, not so hot. Lost her husband in a wreck in Australia. So I guess . . . Not good at all. Sounds like she'll be staying at Guy's place for a while."

"Oh, man. Devastating. Think she'll be all right?"

"Probably not anytime soon."

"Wonder if she knows about Guy's troubles."

Cal gave a humorless laugh. "Which one? Raising a toddler on his own or fighting with the city."

"Both, I guess. Maybe Nikki will help him out."

"Dunno."

"You used to carry a torch for that girl," Al remarked.

"'Carry a torch.' Who says that anymore?" Cal took a swift gulp of his beer. "What does it even mean?"

"Ah, you know what I mean. She was a looker, that one, like somebody from *Baywatch*. Bet she still is."

Right. Cal didn't need to be reminded. His entire adolescence had been filled with dreams of Nikki Graziola at the beach. Even in a full wetsuit, she looked incredible, like a posable action figure in human form. He never did anything about it, of course. He was too awkward. Undersized. Unathletic. Not her type at all.

"And now?" his dad asked.

Cal shook himself back to the present. "What's that?"

"Just wondering. Is she still a looker now?"

Yes. Hell yes. "She is dealing with a massive tragedy, man. She's got a lot going on." He didn't say a word about the other things she'd sobbed out while he held her in his arms. That was no one's business but hers.

His father shrugged unapologetically. "You've got the weekend off, and I bet she could use a friend."

And that, of course, was what Cal had always been to her—a friend.

Whether she needed him or not.

13

Nikki stood by the new arrivals display at the library, watching Shasta in action. It was near closing time and Shasta was just finishing for the day. The library was the town's beating heart, located at its geographical center. With its signage promising to uphold the first amendment, to offer a safe space for all, and to protect individual privacy, it was the buzzing hub people flocked to, a place where everyone was treated with dignity and respect. To Nikki, the role of town librarian seemed like the perfect fit for Shasta.

Looking around the bright, welcoming space, Nikki felt something unexpected—eagerness. The feeling slipped through her grief, reminding her that reconnecting with people might just be a lifeline. Especially when the person was Shasta, who had once been Nikki's sister in every way that mattered, except biologically.

Life had happened to them both, and they'd drifted apart, imperceptibly at first, but as time went by, the distance between them was as wide as the Pacific Ocean. Why did people do that? Why did people who were important to each other let their friendship slip away?

Shasta in her element was a wonderful thing to behold. She had changed so much from the insecure, reticent, bookish girl she'd once been. Now she was a bold, dramatic presence behind the main circulation desk, which was a circular pod in the center of the building's atrium. The counter featured an oddly pleasing arrangement of computer terminals, metal and wooden sculptures, stacks of books, and file folders. Shasta was like a sunflower blooming in the middle of everything, dressed in a form-fitting shift that made the most of her lush figure. Her black hair was shot through with an electric blue streak at one temple, and she wore hoop earrings so large they nearly touched her shoulders. Her makeup was flawless, highlighting her full lips and thickly lashed eyes. There was a tattoo of a daisy on one forearm.

Back when they were girls, Shasta used to carry her extra weight like a suit of armor, perhaps to help her bear the burden heaped upon her by a mother whose troubles were too heavy for one person to handle. Shasta had hidden her watchful, suspicious eyes under a thatch of frizzy bangs, and she'd sought escape between the pages of a book. She read books the way most people breathed the air, like a necessity to sustain life.

Shasta used to joke that 23andMe did not have enough combinations to figure out her ethnicity. When she had to check race on forms, she often wished there was a category for confused, or at least ambiguous.

Miss Carmella used to soothe Shasta when she came home crying because she'd been teased at school or no one had asked her to the eighth-grade banquet, or some stupid boy said she was ugly.

"You're not ugly," Carmella used to assure her. "You're just getting started. One of these days you'll grow into your true self, and it'll be 'watch out, world.'"

Miss Carmella had been absolutely correct. Time and experience and maturity had transformed Shasta from an ordinary girl into someone who looked as if she'd stepped off a full-color superhero movie poster—a fierce, magnetic vision in stiletto heels, with a metallic manicure and statement jewelry.

Library patrons seemed drawn to her, waiting patiently in line to check out or ask a question. She offered a warm greeting and a smile to everyone, from the little kid peeking over the top of the counter to the dude who looked as if he wanted to hit on her but didn't quite dare, to the elderly woman with a walker and a bad attitude.

Nikki waited until the last patron had checked out. Then she set her stack of books and worn plastic library card on the counter. "No idea if my card is still valid after all this time," she said, eyeing the digital card reader. "I kept it just in case."

Shasta looked up from her screen and froze. "Holy shit." Her face bloomed into a brilliant smile. "Holy shit. Come here, you." She bustled around from behind the counter and folded Nikki into a long hug, so close that Nikki could feel their hearts beating together.

Finally they separated, and Shasta stepped back, keeping hold of Nikki's shoulders. Both women were crying.

"I was so excited when I got your text," said Shasta, holding out a box of tissues. "My God. I can't believe you're here."

"It feels surreal to me, too." Everything felt surreal, as though she viewed the world through a lens distorted by time.

"What the hell took you so long to get in touch with me?" Shasta demanded.

"Honestly, it's taken me a while just to remember to breathe," Nikki said. "Trust me, I'm not fit company for anyone. I'm like a walking open wound."

"You think I can't deal with a wounded bird?" Shasta demanded. "You underestimate me. I've been in therapy since Carmella took me in. I know stuff."

Nikki nodded. "You do. I would have sent you a text sooner, but I had to set up a new phone." It wasn't exactly new. She had managed to find a secondhand phone that had been refurbished. Now that she had finally grasped the abysmal state of her finances, she had to make every penny count.

At least the library was free. Shasta swiftly updated Nikki's card and checked out her books. The stack Nikki had selected seemed like a snapshot of her life at the moment. *Dealing with Grief. How to Repair*

Your Finances. The Airstream Survival Guide. She'd also selected the latest Bridgerton book and a thriller with a neurodivergent detective. Like all good librarians, Shasta didn't comment on any of the selections, but Nikki knew there was a big conversation looming ahead of them.

They left the library together, with Nikki's books in a swag bag over her shoulder. Walking along Front Street stirred so many memories in Nikki. The street was as unselfconsciously charming as ever, lamplit and hung with flower baskets, the shops displaying their best offerings and the nicest tables of the restaurants spilling out onto the sidewalk.

Nikki noticed a couple of new places. The Internet Café was now a trendy-looking tapas bar, probably because smartphones had made internet cafés redundant. Tucked in amid the old, familiar boating, fishing, and camping shops were a kombucha stand, a henna salon, a pet spa, and a new tasting room named after a flamboyant tech billionaire.

Mostly, though, the town was virtually unchanged, as if time had stood still while she was gone.

She considered this place to be her past, not her future. She'd been so very far away, living her busy, up-and-down life with Johnny. For the longest time, her world had seemed complete, each day filled with their love, their adventures, surfing and camping, driving along the Gold Coast and the Sunshine Coast of Queensland, making trips to places of legend, like the Great Barrier Reef and Fraser Island. They attended surf events in Capetown and Indonesia and Hainan. Caught up in her life half a world away, Nikki had let Alara Cove fade from memory.

Yet here she was once again, feeling echoes of familiarity, distorted by time and memory. At the dinner hour, people were strolling about, getting off work or coming in from the beach or boating, looking for a place to relax for a drink and a bite to eat. A few Navy guys with their signature haircuts and ramrod-straight posture gathered at the brew pub's outdoor tables, sizing up the locals the way they always had.

A couple of them seemed to drool visibly when their gazes stalked Shasta.

Nikki glared at them until they looked away. "Some things never change," she said.

"True." Shasta sighed and quickened her pace. "Even now, when guys are supposed to know better."

"What's your favorite spot?" Nikki asked her as they passed a noisy bar. "Is there a place where we can talk?"

"We can go down by the marina dock and grab an outdoor table."

Along the way, they paused to check out the window display at the Carmella Beach Gallery. The paintings and pieces on display sparked a memory in Nikki. She used to get so excited about art. Carmella's place had always been an unabashed showcase of talent. The dramatically lit samples in the window were celebrations of light and texture and energy. Just the sight of the art pieces coaxed Nikki away from her grief for a moment.

"She still has the most exquisite taste," Nikki said. "How is she doing?"

"Fabulous, I'm glad to say. She can't wait to see you, either."

"I'll go around to her place soon," Nikki said. "I'm trying to pace myself. Reentry is hard."

"Everything is hard."

Nikki felt a flicker of guilt. Yes, she was dealing with a crushing loss. But more than anyone she knew, Shasta understood the hard things of life. She had experienced most of them by the time she turned twelve. "Sorry," she said. "I know you've had your share of trouble."

"That's not what I meant. We all have our shit to deal with. It's not a race to see who was dealt the worst hand of cards."

They went to the Boat Shed, a restaurant at the marina with an extensive weather-worn deck that projected out over the water. While they waited at the hostess station, Nikki studied the community bulletin board, which displayed a collection of flyers and business cards for local services and help wanted.

Help wanted. She was going to need a job. She browsed over the listings—landscaping, retail, clerical, skilled labor. Nothing that matched her skill set. Most employers weren't looking for someone who knew how to swim and surf.

In the middle of the display was a campaign poster for Jason Sanger. She studied the picture of her old nemesis. He had barely aged since high school. He still had that cocky, orthodontically perfect grin. She wondered if she was the only one who could read the diamond hard glint of insincerity in his eyes. Even his campaign slogan sounded slick and disingenuous—*Real progress, not empty promises.*

"So my dad tells me you're running for mayor," Nikki said.

"I am. Crazy, right?"

"Probably. Where's your poster?" She indicated the display.

"You won't find one here. The owner is one of Jason's golf buddies," Shasta said. "Jason makes a lot of promises to local business owners."

"He was awful in high school. Is he still awful?" Nikki asked.

"Duh." Shasta brightened. "Hey, you know who else is running for office? Marian McGill, for county district attorney."

Nikki had a visceral reaction to the name. Since the accident, she had thought of Mark more frequently than ever. Did Marian carry her brother with her? she wondered. What was it like to lose someone who had shared a womb with you? And then the first eighteen years of life?

"Really?" she said. "So Marian went into politics like her mom."

"Yep. Became a lawyer. She started out working for a big private law firm in LA. She must have done really well, because she bought a place up on Crescent Beach."

Crescent Beach was one of the most expensive neighborhoods in the area. "Then she has to know the Sangers have been in control of the DA's office forever."

"She and I both think it's time for a change."

"You're allies, then."

"In some things, I suppose."

They followed the hostess to a table at the far edge of the deck. Below the weathered gray planks, they could see harbor seals and pelicans, kids dipping their nets and capturing things in buckets, people in dinghies and kayaks and standup boards paddling around the calm, protected area.

"What made you want to run for mayor?" Nikki asked as they took a seat.

"Because . . . well, you know I love this town. I always have. But that doesn't mean it's perfect. I have tons of ideas for making things better."

"It sounds like an uphill climb, though. I mean, Jason Sanger? Seems like he'd be a nasty opponent."

"I expect he has plenty of tricks up his sleeve. But I'm going to give it my best shot. The Sangers have been in charge of things for too long. I'm tired of it. From what I hear around town, a lot of people are tired of it."

"Well, if anyone can get things done, it's you," said Nikki.

A server came to offer them drinks. His face lit up when he recognized Shasta. "Hey, Ms. Kramer," he said, simultaneously grinning and blushing.

"Leo." She smiled up at him. "Nice to see you." She turned to Nikki. "Leo has been one of our most consistent patrons at the library."

"Wouldn't have made it through high school without the library," said the young man. He seemed to notice Nikki checking out his campaign button—*Jason Sanger for Mayor*. He blushed even deeper. "Uh, the boss wants us all to wear these," he said.

She was tempted to tell him to find a boss who let him think for himself, but she held her tongue. Many people didn't have much choice about their jobs. And at the moment, she was one of the many.

"I'll have a Kir royale," Shasta said to Leo. "What about you, Nikki?"

A Kir royale sounded heavenly, a magical mixture of champagne and crème de cassis. But no. "Make mine a tonic water, please."

The server nodded and hurried over to the bar, and returned shortly with the chilled flutes.

"To you being back even though everything is awful," Shasta said, and they clinked their glasses together.

"Cheers," Nikki said.

"You don't drink?" Shasta raised her eyebrows. "Are you in recovery? Oh my God, are you pregnant?"

Nikki actually laughed at her expression. It felt good to laugh a little. "No, and no. I'm on pain pills." She held up her wrist with the brace on it. "Besides, I told my dad I'd watch Gloria. You know about Gloria, right?"

"He had a kid and the mom took off. That's what I heard."

"That's about it. I was pretty shocked when he told me, but it didn't really register until I got here. I have a sister three decades younger than me. And that's not even the strangest thing about my life." She rested her chin in her hand and gazed at a group of kids on one of the marina docks. Thornton kids. Even though they were out of uniform, she recognized the polish of privilege they wore—the casual but expensive clothing, the ease with which they moved amid million-dollar yachts, the ineffable air of confidence they exuded.

Shasta noticed her staring. "Memories of your school days?"

"A bit, I suppose. I never fit in at Thornton, even after four years. I did everything right, but the fit was wrong."

"Speaking of much-younger siblings," Shasta said, "the guy in the turquoise polo shirt is Jason Sanger's younger brother. Can't remember his name, but he can be a handful when he comes in to the library."

"Milo," Nikki said with a flash of remembrance. "He was a little bitty kid when I left. I guess he'd be a senior now." As she watched, the kid cocked his arm around a girl's neck and hauled her against him in a proprietary way.

"When you left, I never dreamed you'd stay away so long," Shasta said.

"When I left, I never planned to come back."

"Oh, Nikki. Tell me everything. Let's talk the way we used to talk at Carmella's."

Nikki swallowed the lump in her throat. She'd made some friends on the tour, but she'd never had a friend like Shasta. "It's hard to know where to start."

"It started with Johnny Mercury," Shasta prompted. "I remember the first night he came to find you. My lord, he looked like a dream. I think I knew that very night that you'd end up together."

"Same here. It shouldn't have worked, should it? We were so, so young. But the summer tour was good that year, wasn't it? He dominated at Oceanside and Huntington Beach, and I won my first longboard championship, and everything looked golden. And sometimes it was." She toyed with her wrist brace and looked out at the water. "And sometimes it wasn't."

"Everything," Shasta said. "I want to hear everything."

Nikki kept her gaze on the horizon, letting the ocean and the sky meld together, blurred by sadness. She did her best to explain the inexplicable. Her life had turned into a house of cards, collapsing on every front.

As Shasta listened, emotions chased across her face like wind-driven storm clouds—slack-jawed shock, delight, devastation, and worry, all in rapid succession. Every few minutes, she took a healthy gulp of her champagne cocktail.

Yet Nikki felt a tiny ripple of relief as she summed up her ordeal for Shasta. A good listener was a kindness, and her foster sister had always been a good listener.

"You're in the middle of a shitstorm," Shasta said.

"I don't see a way out."

"Remember Miss Carmella used to tell us, 'If everyone put their problems in a pile on the floor, you'd end up picking yours back up because it was probably the smallest pile in the first place.'"

"I remember that. All those talks during our angsty teenage years."

"Well, I'm pretty sure that doesn't apply to your current situation. You get the prize for the biggest pile."

"Yeah, that's a prize I can do without."

"Aw, Nikki. What can I do to help? What's the first thing in front of you?"

"Sometimes it's just taking the next breath of air. I need to figure out a future for myself, but I have no idea what that looks like."

"Maybe start smaller. What does this week look like?"

"Getting over this wrist," she said, indicating the brace. "Looking after Gloria. For some reason, helping out with her seems to help me. A bit, I suppose."

"That's cool. Do what feels right to you. Have you had a chance to look in to finding care for your wrist yet?"

"I had an appointment at the county health clinic down in Santa Maria. I'm supposed to have physical therapy." A fresh wave of discomfort hit her. "In order to access care at the county clinic, I had to fill out forms proving I'm indigent. It was so humiliating."

"No one should have to do that," Shasta murmured. "Oh, Nikki, I'm really sorry." Shasta's extravagantly lashed eyes blinked fast, letting loose a couple of tears. "I hate what happened to you. It's beyond awful. I'm glad you came home, though. I want you to let us take care of you." She scanned the menu, then looked across the table at Nikki. "How are things going with your dad?"

"Um . . . okay, I suppose. Still getting used to the idea that he has a little kid. We've gone surfing a couple of times."

"It's okay to surf even though you're injured?"

"Not really. The nurse at the clinic said I shouldn't overdo it, but she didn't forbid a ride or two. It's . . . at the moment, it's the one time I feel normal, even for a little while."

"Then you should definitely keep it up. Oh my gosh, I used to watch you surf and I'd think you were a true goddess. I know you practiced your ass off, but you also have a gift."

"It's the one thing I can thank my dad for."

"Have you ever thanked him?" Shasta asked.

Nikki knew that Shasta's father was nothing but a name on a document. She'd always been fascinated by Nikki's dad. She paused, then said, "We're talking like adults."

"That's new." Shasta smiled.

"We both lost someone, which is not a great thing to have in common, but it gets us talking, you know?" She swallowed hard, feeling her way through new territory. "He told me that my mother committed suicide."

Shasta fanned herself with her menu. "What? That's . . . for real?"

Nikki nodded. "I had no idea. According to my dad, she had an undiagnosed postpartum depression. When I was just a couple of months old, she was alone with me one day, and my dad was out of town on an errand. When he came home, I was . . . I guess in a crib, crying my head off. And my mom—Lyra—was dead. She left a suicide note. She said she couldn't get me to stop crying. My dad destroyed the note and never said a thing about it to me until just recently."

"My lord. What a thing to hear."

"It explains a lot. I guess. And Dad and I kind of . . . bonded a little bit, I suppose you could say. He's someone who gets what this kind of loss feels like."

"I'm glad you're talking, Nik."

"He really opened up to me. Said he went to therapy and has a single parents' group—can you believe it?"

"Sounds like he's trying."

"He says that what happened to my mom kept him from trusting himself to be my dad, so much so that he sent me away. He never remarried. Never loved again. He says Gloria is his new chance. Like, he failed with me after my mother . . . Did she do it because of me?"

"Don't even," Shasta said. "Now, listen. And I mean this. You're here now. There's no hurry to figure out how to live your life. Meanwhile, you're going to get all the support we can muster. What happened to your mother is a terrible tragedy, but I'm glad your father told you."

"So am I, but you're right. It's . . . it was terrible. For my dad when it happened, and for me, now that I know."

"And we're here to help. Maybe this is a chance for you to make a new start with your dad."

"After thirty-three years?" She shrugged her shoulders. "We'll see. I came at a bad time. He's having trouble with the caravan park."

"Oh, no. What kind of trouble?"

"I mean, he's always struggled to stay ahead of the bills, but this is more than the usual trouble. The city is trying to change his tax status as a recreational property, which will make his taxes unaffordable. And if he doesn't pay his taxes, the city can invalidate his lease on the property. He says the Sangers would love to see that happen so they can make a deal with a luxury resort developer."

"Ugh. Not a word of this surprises me," Shasta said. "See, that's one of the reasons I decided to run for mayor—to keep developers from destroying the local character of Alara Cove. I'm even a volunteer with the town historical society. The Sangers are way too friendly with outsiders who want to turn the whole place into a theme park surrounded by strip malls."

"Why would anyone want that?"

"It's all about expanding the revenue base, but that's completely shortsighted. The best thing this town has going for it is that it's unique. It has that kind of beachy charm you can't find anywhere else. Without its special character, this place could turn into just another sprawl city. Right?"

"Sure. You know, when we were in the surf league, we traveled to beach towns all over the place. Too many of them look the same— fast food, dollar stores, parking lots, housing with no character at all." Until she'd seen other parts of the world, Nikki hadn't appreciated the uniqueness of Alara Cove. "People here would be crazy to lose the flavor of the town."

"I hope I can convince them of that by election day. I ran for mayor four years ago and only lost by a few percentage points. I think I can make it this time."

"Really? That's so cool, Shasta. I hope you win. If I can help—"

"Yes, *please*. I'm going to need all the help I can get. But first, you need to look after yourself, Nikki. And help your dad, if that helps you."

Nikki squinted at the sunlight glinting off the hulls and masts and the outriggers of the fishing fleet in the marina. The teenagers had gathered on the top deck of a big yacht at the end of a dock. "To be honest, I don't know what my dad would do without the caravan park. He's made it his whole life."

Shasta drummed her shiny, intentionally mismatched nails on the table, then snapped her fingers. "Suppose the park could be designated as a local heritage site."

Nikki gave a dry laugh. "A trailer park?"

"Airstreams are classic Americana. There's a statewide program dedicated to preserving traditional landmarks. And the city has a community fund for purchasing places that preserve the local character." Shasta looked up something on her phone. "Right here, it says a qualifying property is 'distinctive in character, interest, or value, and exemplifies the cultural, economic, social, ethnic, or historical heritage of the city.' Oh, and it's supposed to embody elements of design, detail, material, or craftsmanship. I think your dad's place qualifies."

"Remember, he doesn't own the property. Just the trailers."

"I don't think it matters."

"Really? Dang, Shasta, that would be amazing. We should definitely pursue it," Nikki said.

"Absolutely, but we need to figure out what all the requirements are." She checked her phone again. "We can apply online to the historical foundation. And there's a link to apply for a community development loan, and . . . ooh."

"What? Was that a good *ooh* or a bad *ooh?*"

"There are community foundation grants available for approved projects. *Grants.*"

"What, they just give money away?"

"If you know how to ask."

"I have no idea how to ask," Nikki said. "I've been a surfer for the past fifteen years."

"I'm a librarian," Shasta reminded her. "You know what I'm good at? Getting grants. That's what I'm good at."

"Cool. I should probably do some research before I tell my dad about this. I don't want him to get his hopes up."

"Good idea. I imagine there'll be a lot of hoops to jump through," Shasta said.

"I . . . my dad's a surfer, too. Not much for jumping. Doesn't sound like something he could manage on his own."

"Well, he has you now. And you have a secret weapon."

Nikki caught herself smiling at that. "Would that secret weapon have a blue streak in her hair and a metallic manicure?"

They ordered burgers. Shasta asked for a plate of French fries with fry sauce. "I get one night per week to indulge," she explained. "You are this week's indulgence." She smiled at Nikki's quizzical expression. "The rest of the time, I have to watch what I eat. And drink. You think this rockin' bod just happened?" She shook her head. "We weren't all born with a figure like yours."

"I saw the way people at the library watch you. Seriously, Shasta. You seem like you're exactly in your right place. Your sweet spot."

"That's how I feel most of the time," Shasta said.

Nikki heard something in her tone. "But not all of the time."

"My sweet spot is elusive sometimes. Don't get me wrong; I have plenty of friends—library patrons and board members, workmates and campaign volunteers. Just . . . really late at night sometimes, this feeling, it hits me. And I feel horrible saying that to you, after your loss. I get lonely—and I suck, talking about loneliness when you just lost Johnny."

"You don't suck," Nikki objected. "Just because I'm in a black hole doesn't mean you can't say you're lonely. And listen—I'm sorry you feel that way."

"It just seems petty compared to—"

"Don't compare. It's not a race, remember? Talk to me. Why are you lonely?"

"I don't know. I shouldn't be. But I feel this yearning, you know? To have something . . . it's hard to explain. You had this huge love, and I'm so happy for you that you had it. I wish I could know what that's like."

"It's like having something so important that you're scared to lose it. And then when you do lose it, the world ends."

Shasta studied her for a moment. "Except the world didn't end."

"The world didn't end. I keep waking up to a new day every day, wondering how I'll make it through. So maybe you should steer clear of that kind of love. It's dangerous."

"I know you're hurting now, but look what you had. Johnny's death is incredibly sad, and it always will be, but *you* don't have to always be sad."

"I'm working on it," Nikki said. The grief came in like waves after a storm, some intense, others dull and formless. But the one thing worse than the grief was the idea of never having found the love she'd shared with Johnny. "I guess if everybody felt that kind of love, we would have . . . I don't know. Maybe world peace."

"Exactly. Can you blame a person for wanting that kind of love? I suppose you don't get to see it coming, and you sure as hell don't get to know how it ends. But you should always allow for the possibility that it could happen, right? Even though it's dangerous."

"Sure, okay," Nikki agreed. "For all you know, the love of your life could walk right up to you and change everything."

At that moment, Leo arrived with a large tray. "Two veggie cheeseburgers, extra pickles, extra fried onions," he said, setting their plates on the table. "And fries with fry sauce."

"You're right," Shasta said to Nikki after he left. "The love of my life is right here." She dipped a French fry into the sauce, a magical combination of catsup, mayo, sour cream, and pickle juice, and rolled her eyes in ecstasy. "I'm just going to marry fry sauce and live happily ever after."

Nikki laughed briefly, then stopped. "It feels wrong to laugh," she said. "It feels wrong to be happy or to enjoy anything at all."

"Come on. You're starving, and the burger is delicious."

She savored her first bite. "I know, but liking something— anything—feels like a betrayal of Johnny. And yeah, I realize that sounds ridiculous. He wouldn't want me to be miserable forever. But guess what? He's not here. I'll never know what he wants or doesn't want." She was crying and eating at the same time. How could she be eating a delicious meal on a beautiful evening when Johnny wasn't in the world anymore?

"Help me with these fries." Shasta pushed the plate toward her. "But I warn you. I'm ordering dessert. Training starts next week, but until then, it's game on."

"Training? For what? For who can be the hottest librarian?"

"Ha. No. Ironman triathlon up in Morro Bay. We start a new train-ing program next week. It'll be our tenth event."

"Our? You and . . . ?"

"Me and Cal Bradshaw."

Nikki's face must have betrayed her, because Shasta laughed at her expression.

"Yes, *that* Cal Bradshaw. We teamed up a few years back. Decided to challenge ourselves, and we've been doing events together ever since."

Nikki chewed slowly, rethinking her friends from the past. They were athletes now. Triathletes. That explained why Shasta looked like a real-life action figure. And why Cal had gone from skinny-bones to superhero, straining the seams of his cop uniform.

"I saw him," she told Shasta. "Cal, I mean. He pulled me over for speeding and a broken taillight. At first I didn't even recognize him. He's almost as hot as you. I can't believe how much he's changed."

"Maybe people get better when they're living their best lives," Shasta said.

"And that's what Cal's doing?"

She nodded. "I believe he is. Always seems to have a smile on his face. He's been an awesome friend."

"I'm glad you're still friends. He's always been an awesome friend, ever since we were in grade school."

"I like hanging out with a cop. Keeps guys from bugging me when I don't want to be bugged, you know?"

Nikki knew how to keep guys from bugging her, and she didn't need a cop. Shasta might require extra security, though.

"So he's your training partner," she said. "But not a romantic partner?"

"Please."

"What? Oh, he's not single?" Of course he wasn't. A guy like that.

"He's single—at the moment. He's dated some. But he's not . . . we're not . . . We work better as friends, is all." She paused and stared across the table at Nikki. "And you and I—*we* work better as friends than we do as connections on social media. I hate what happened to you. I mean, I hate it with the fire of a thousand suns. But selfishly, I'm glad you're back. Thank you for coming back."

"It seemed like my only option," Nikki said. "I didn't know what else to do." She gazed back at Shasta and felt a welcome rush of gratitude. "You make me glad I came home, too. It's been a long time. I met a lot of people over there, did a lot of things. But I never had a friend like you."

"Same. I'm here for you, Nik. Whatever you need. Got it?"

"Got it."

14

The clean, hot smell of clothes dryer exhaust was a throwback to Nikki's childhood. Her dad used to call the seemingly endless cycle of bedding, linens, and towels the circle of life. When the park was fully occupied, keeping up with the laundry was a nonstop process.

She found Guy and Patsy and a couple of the day workers in the commercial laundry, dealing with the daily chore of sorting linens. There was a particular camaraderie among them as they chatted together through the mundane chores. This was her father's comfort zone. His life. He'd be lost without this place.

Nikki caught his eye and gestured him and Patsy outside, and they sat together at a picnic table. "So this might be a bit of good news," she said. "Shasta and I are looking into a way for you to keep the city from forcing you out."

"Yeah?" Guy leaned forward. "I'm all ears."

"If we can get it designated as a landmark, then we can appeal to the city council to preserve the park, and you can keep your lease and tax status."

A flash of hope lit her father's face. "For real?"

"For real. It's not a slam dunk, though. We'll need to comply with the town historical commission guidelines." She handed them each a printout from the website. "There's work to be done. If it's going to be a historical landmark, it will need to *look* like a historical landmark."

Patsy eyed Guy cautiously. "So we'll need to fix things up around here."

"We'll probably have to do more than fixing," Nikki said. "The units should be restored to look the way they did when they were new. This park is a true piece of Americana. But we have to establish the historical significance of the place."

"It sounds like a lot," said Guy.

"That's because it is a lot." Nikki noticed the nervous pucker in his brow. "We can apply for a development grant and take out a low-interest loan. Shasta thinks we'll have no trouble qualifying."

"Damn. A local heritage site." Guy rubbed his jaw. "Who knew?"

"So how do we go about this?" Patsy asked.

"One hurdle at a time. We'll have to create a proposal to submit to the historical foundation's board of directors. When they approve the plans, we'll do the renovations. The last step is to put it in front of the city council. After that, this park will be registered as a local heritage landmark."

"It might take a long time to get everything done. I guess we could close for the winter. That's the low season, anyway."

It was gratifying to see the flicker of hope in her father's eyes. Ever since Shasta had suggested the idea, Nikki had been working on a plan. That was the key, she knew now. Not making a plan for the previous fifteen years had led to chaos on top of the heartbreak of losing Johnny. It had been far too easy to drift—or rush—with him from day to day, chasing waves, hanging out with the squad, racking up ranking points, collecting swag and doing promos for sponsors, refusing to worry about where the next day might lead.

Life had seemed effortless back then, and it was all too easy to put off making a plan of any sort.

Adulthood had come crashing down on her in a single moment—eviction, a fight, a death, financial collapse.

She was determined to avoid the mistakes of the past. Making a plan was her new plan.

She started at the library—Shasta would have it no other way—
and delved into a crash course in project management. Each night,
she surrounded herself with a stack of books and a laptop Shasta had
loaned to her from the library.

"Here's the first phase of the plan," she said to her father, placing
the pages in front of him. "If you decide to give it a shot, that is.
There are certain standards we have to meet and document. We
have to list all the repairs and renovations needed, and come up
with a budget for the grant. We'll have to keep tabs on the cost of
everything, right down to the last . . . I don't know, rivet or whatever."

Patsy and Guy looked at each other, and she put her hand on his
shoulder. "See?" she said. "I've been telling you there's a way through
this."

"Nikki," he said, "I don't know how to thank you."

"By rolling up your sleeves, that's how. You have to get permits
for any major renovation. Restoring the Airstreams is not going to be
easy. You have to research the color and design of each unit to bring
is as close to the original state as possible. But if you do it right, the
landmark designation will keep this place intact."

"Are you kidding? Of course I'm going to give it a shot," he said.
"But when I think of everything that needs to be done, I want to cry.
I mean, nineteen units? Really?"

"I know it seems like a lot, but you have a secret weapon."

"I do?"

"You don't have to do this alone."

Carmella Beach looked like a monarch butterfly in a fluttery orange
and black smock and black-framed cat's-eye glasses. She had always
loved to dress dramatically, even on an ordinary day. Nikki felt a rush
of emotion. Carmella had hardly aged, and the light in her eyes was
as bright as ever.

With a warm smile, she drew Nikki into a hug. Then she stepped back, keeping hold of both her hands, and brought her into the house. "It's about time you came around to see me," she said.

"It's been a whirlwind. Or, as Shasta puts it, a shitstorm."

"Then I won't make you tell me everything all at once. I have a feeling you've done enough of that."

Nikki looked around, taking in the familiar foyer and parlor. This was where she had first met Johnny, the moment her world had shifted on its axis. "Everything is the same. And everything is completely different."

"As are we," Carmella said. "Come and meet my kids. Portia's just getting them ready to hit the beach." She led the way to the big, sunny kitchen. The housekeeper was loading a bag with towels and sunscreen. At the sink, a boy and girl were filling their drink bottles. Dark-skinned, with dark, curly hair, they were unmistakably brother and sister. The boy seemed wary and had the first faint shadow of a mustache and long, gangly limbs; the girl, a bit younger, was round-cheeked and moved with a child's eager, coiled energy.

"Ana and Tony, this is Nikki," said Carmella.

They offered bashful smiles. "We're going to the beach," Ana said.

"Town Beach?" asked Nikki.

Tony nodded.

"I spent a lot of time there when I was your age," Nikki said. "What's your favorite thing to do?"

"Boogie board. Skim board." They both spoke at once.

"Good choices," Nikki said. As the kids grabbed their bags and headed out, she felt a wave of nostalgia. "Have they been with you long?" she asked Carmella.

"About six months now." She led the way out to the garden, as beautifully tended as ever, and furnished with art pieces and a fountain. "Their parents were deported to Guatemala."

"Oh, no. I hope they can be reunited."

"That's up to the immigration judge." Carmella sighed. "Meanwhile, I'll do what I can."

"You do so much," Nikki said. "Why do you do it? It's funny, when I was with you, I never wondered about that. About why you're so good to kids who need something good."

"You were a child," Carmella said, "living your life. It wasn't your job to wonder about me."

"Well, it's amazing that you share your life with kids who need you."

"There's something in me that needs them, too. Being able to help is a gift. It helped me through terrible times."

That brought Nikki up short. Carmella had always seemed so serene and centered. "What kind of terrible times?"

Carmella took a seat on a concrete bench and invited Nikki to sit. "Back in the late seventies, when I was in college at Occidental, my parents were killed while doing civil rights work in the South."

Nikki felt a lurch of horror in her gut. Carmella kept a picture of her parents hanging in the front room. Smiling, good-looking, nicely dressed—as good-looking as the mom and dad in a TV series. "Oh, Carmella. I didn't know you'd lost them like that. I never . . . I just assumed . . . you only ever said they passed away."

"It was a racial incident. You can look it up—the Gavin Beach incident in Kilgore, Texas. My parents had been working with a civil rights organization to register voters, and the local police pulled them over on some pretext, and according to police reports, the incident escalated. The cops called for backup help, and my parents were both killed. The police claimed self-defense, and there wasn't even an indictment."

"Oh, Carmella. That's horrible. I'm so sorry."

"After it happened, I came here to live with my grandparents, and for a long time, I was practically a recluse, certain I'd never heal. The injustice was . . . it was searing. I was filled with a kind of rage that consumed my soul. It's hard to describe what that feels like. I've never taken poison, but perhaps that's how it felt. My grandparents were never the same. My father was their only child. The loss just diminished them, to the point where my grandmother seemed to be wasting away. That was my wake-up call. They needed me more than I needed to grieve and rage. I devoted myself to taking care of them."

"I'm glad they had you, Carmella. And that you had them."

She nodded. "Painting became my refuge. I spent hours and hours in the studio, producing picture after picture. Then one day, the family next door asked me to teach their daughter to paint. She had—she was neurodivergent. I suppose that would be the current term. Her mind worked differently and she was struggling in school. But she loved to paint, and I loved painting with her. Working with that child brought me back to life." Carmella covered Nikki's hand with hers. "I learned that I could find happiness even though the grief never ended."

"Point taken," Nikki said. "You're so gifted, and everybody loves you. But you never married or had kids of your own. I mean, not that you should, but . . ." She let the thought trail off.

"There are so many ways to make a family," Carmella said.

"You're right," Nikki said. "What a dumb thing to say. I'm grateful that I was a part of your family."

"You'll always be a part of it." Carmella patted her arm, then stood up. "Let's go to the studio."

Nikki had been looking forward to seeing the place where they'd spent so many hours painting together, listening to music or working in silence. The moment the smell of paint and the slant of light through the windows and skylights hit her, she was startled by a rush of memories. The space contained so many reminders of her growing-up years. Suddenly, she felt close once again to the dreams she used to dream, and to the pleasure of making art.

She looked around at the paintings and photographs on display, the works-in-progress propped on easels. In flashes and flickers of memory, she saw her younger self eagerly perusing the canvases of all sizes, stacked a half dozen deep against the walls. She used to spend as much time painting as she did surfing.

"Of all my kids, you were the most passionate about art," Carmella told her. "Definitely the most talented."

"I always thought painting would be my life, like it is yours," Nikki said. "I've missed this. So much."

"What have you done with your art since you left? Have you been painting?"

"Not at all," Nikki admitted. "Not one single stroke. It's like I left it behind along with everything else when I left here."

"Why?"

She hesitated. "It wasn't really even a choice. We just . . . It was a different life. I was different with Johnny. A different person. We were always chasing down his standing in the league, making plans to climb the ladder, finding sponsors, and working in between practices and competitions. It filled every minute of every day. We never stayed in one place for long. I guess I avoided making art because it reminded me of a life I couldn't have." She scanned the colorful space. Carmella's beautiful world was filled with light and art and creativity. Yet she had created it in the aftermath of a terrible grief. "I guess that's what's so hard about this, Carmella. Now that he's gone, I don't know who I am. I know I'm supposed to move on, open a new chapter. But when I think about doing that, I feel Johnny slipping further away."

"Oh, honey. You lost yourself in a magnificent love, and that was a blessing some of us never get to experience. And now, you owe it to yourself to find a new way to be happy. Starting now. Think about the life you *can* have. You can't live in heartbreak forever."

That brought her up short. *Yes,* she thought. And ouch. For decades, her father had dragged his grief around like excess baggage. His constant sadness and worry had formed a wall between them, Nikki realized now. She'd never known a father who wasn't grieving. Carmella had been grieving, too, but she'd still found ways to connect to people and to make art.

"You're right," Nikki said. "You're absolutely right. But I don't know how to start over. I don't know how to rebuild my life, because I don't know what it should look like when I'm done. I feel as if I'm doing it all wrong."

"There's no wrong way to do it. Live each day, Nikki. But don't let life come to you. Go out and seize it." Carmella brought her over to a storage rack in the corner. "I have something to show you. Remember this girl?" She pulled out a large, flat portfolio made of sun-faded heavy card stock and set it on the drafting table.

Nikki slid the pages out and regarded them as moments from the past came to life, like lights winking on in the dark. Her whole history lay before her, from her earliest childish efforts to the portfolio she'd submitted with her college applications. "You saved these for me."

"I certainly did." Carmella checked her watch. "You said you'd come back for them. And here you are. Now, I'm going to make some lunch for the hungry troops. They'll be starving when they get back from the beach."

"Let me help."

"You stay right here and take a trip down memory lane," she said.

Nikki took a seat on one of the drafting stools. "Carmella, thank you."

Carmella paused in the doorway and turned back. "Listen. I understand that this is hard. But I've known you, Nikki, for your whole life. I know you can do hard things. Just remember that you don't have to do them alone."

Nikki studied the artwork she had done so long ago. She remembered each one with startling clarity—the time of day, the way the air felt on her skin, the set of her mind as she went about capturing a scene. There were seascapes rendered in bold strokes with vibrant colors. She'd experimented with pencil drawings of found objects, like a pile of rope and netting on a weathered dock. There were pictures of the cypresses at Three Tree Point, the dun-colored sea cliffs, and flame-brushed clouds piled on the horizon at sunset.

Some of the art surprised her, because she couldn't remember being that skilled or that observant. Other pieces were flawed but sincere. Yet even in the poorly executed ones, there was something she recognized blazing across every picture, and that was conviction. Some of the colors were savage, almost angry, spilling off the edges of the page. There were paintings of softness, too, and lightness, a whole range of adolescent emotion in the artwork Carmella had saved for her.

Nikki felt as if she were visiting someone she used to know but had forgotten about. What had happened to that girl? At one time, everything she had ever dreamed of was contained in these works of art.

And then, the moment she met Johnny, those dreams had been set aside. She didn't recall making a decision. It was as if everything had suddenly been decided for her.

Their lives had revolved around his passion. She'd had no problem with that, because her passion was Johnny, and he took up all the space her other dreams used to occupy. Now he was gone, and Nikki had no idea what to do with herself. She was waking up from a long sleep and facing a formless void. Her dream was gone and couldn't be recaptured. She looked around the studio, and it seemed for a moment as though the past fifteen years had simply not happened.

Except for a daily reminder. Johnny was gone. Their marriage had never been official. When filling out forms for the clinic and bank, she hadn't known what to check. Single? Married? Widowed?

She closed her eyes and tried to remember Johnny while forgetting the pain. Impossible. When Johnny made love to her, she forgot everything. It was easy to recall the last time they'd had sex—the morning of the day he'd died. Slow, sweetly sleepy morning sex that left them replete and reluctant to leave the bed. Afterward they'd done a silly rock-paper-scissors challenge to determine who had to get up and put the kettle on for coffee. She'd lost—her scissors bested by his rock. After coffee, Johnny had kissed her goodbye and left for his practice session. She'd made the bed and tidied the flat before preparing to head off to work for the day. Her period had started, something she greeted with a tense mixture of relief and regret. They did talk about having a baby—someday. It was always *someday* in the indeterminate future.

Johnny was usually the one who resisted the idea. She hadn't understood his reluctance. She knew money was tight, but she always thought that if they had a child, they would find a way to deal with their finances.

And maybe they would have. She would never know if her conviction was the result of youthful optimism or willful naïveté. Finances had been the last thing on her mind the day the eviction notice had arrived at her door. She couldn't recall what was on her mind that day—the notice itself or the fact that Johnny hadn't told her how much trouble they were in.

With a shudder, she turned her attention back to the art portfolio. The pieces reflected so many lost moments from long ago. Staring down at all the shapes and colors and movement she'd captured with her brushes or pencils brought back those moments. Nikki felt something stir inside her. A ripple. An urge. A sharp ache of yearning.

The feeling pushed through her grief and rose to the surface. So much had been taken from her when Johnny had died. But maybe she could still make art. Maybe she could try to find the beauty in something terrible. Seeing the old pieces connected Nikki with a part of herself she'd ignored for far too long.

"You're very quiet." Carmella came back into the studio. She held out a box of tissues.

Nikki didn't realize she was crying. Again. "I have to put myself back together, and I don't know how."

"You'll figure it out, child."

"I will. I have to." She hugged her arms around her middle. "It's . . . a lot. It's overwhelming."

"Come and have some lunch. There's egg salad sandwiches and a fresh watermelon from the farmers' market," Carmella said.

"In a minute." Nikki dabbed at her eyes.

Carmella regarded her thoughtfully for a moment. "What's your next logical step?"

"I need to help my dad." She told Carmella about the idea to transform the caravan park into a heritage site. "I've never designed a thing in my life, but I think I can do this."

"Of course you can. But ask yourself—is this what you want? Not just for your father, or for Gloria. For yourself."

"I suppose I'll find out. It will give me something to do. For fifteen years, my purpose was loving Johnny. Now that he's gone, I need something else to keep me from falling to pieces."

"And the caravan park is something else."

"It's something, at least."

"You can do this, Nikki. Believe it." Carmella put the portfolio back together. Then she handed over a pad of art paper and a set of paints. "Let's go have some lunch. And take these with you."

A few moments later, a teenaged girl arrived, bustling with energy. "Hey, Miss Carmella. Sorry I'm late. I was helping a friend with her math homework." She took a chilled mason jar from her backpack. "They had a batch of your favorite at the kombucha stand."

"That's so thoughtful. Thank you, dear."

The girl wore artfully torn denim overalls, turquoise and kohl eye makeup, and a look of eagerness that reminded Nikki of herself, back in high school. Being in the art studio chased away all teenage surliness. To someone who loved to make art, walking into the studio was like a visit to the candy store.

Carmella introduced her to Nikki. "This is Zoe Camden. Zoe, this is my friend Nikki."

Nikki noticed seams of paint color under the girl's fingernails. She recognized that, too, along with the daubs of paint on her overalls.

"Zoe is a Thornton student," Carmella said. "She's doing an internship with me for the spring semester."

"Oh, good choice," Nikki said. She liked this kid immediately. Good eye contact and an easy smile. Zoe seemed effortlessly cool, unafraid of being herself. "Miss Carmella's studio used to be my happy place."

Zoe beamed. She had a constellation of freckles across her nose and cheeks. "Me too. I feel really lucky to be here."

"Is Mr. Wendell still the art teacher?"

Zoe nodded, then shrugged into one of the smocks that hung on a hook by the door. She turned off her phone and set it aside. "Yep. So you went to Thornton?"

"A long time ago. I was one of the local kids." Even now, Nikki felt compelled to make that distinction.

"Hey, me too. It's different, right? I mean, not living on campus." She wove her improbably colored hair into two stubby braids. "I wish I could live in the dorm, but my folks can't afford it."

"I bet dorms are overrated," Nikki said, though she had no evidence to back it up.

Zoe opened a portfolio to display several versions of a painting. Sign of a good artist, Nikki thought. Willing to work to get something right. "Wait a minute," Zoe said. "You're Nikki Graziola. The whistle-blower."

She wasn't Nikki Mercury anymore. As it turned out, she never had been. "A long time ago," she said again, trading a glance with Carmella. "I can't believe people still talk about that."

"My ex talked about it—Milo Sanger. I went out with him last fall." Zoe cast her eyes down. "I was totally in love with him. When we broke up, I thought the world was going to end."

Nikki shook her head. "A wise woman once told me that when you're young, every bump you hit feels like the end of the road. Turns out, it's not. It's actually just a speed bump taking you to the next new place."

Zoe looked up at her. "Milo turned out to be a jerk." Alarm flashed in her eyes. "No, that's mean. His dad is . . . kinda harsh. And his dad never liked me."

"Then I suppose it's good that he's your ex," Carmella pointed out.

Zoe settled onto a stool and studied the top painting in her portfolio, a well-executed watercolor of a sailboat in the harbor. She used bold, confident strokes with a graphic edge that had a kind of retro-sixties vibe. "So Milo doesn't even like me anymore, but he's being a complete dick to my new boyfriend, Teddy Matson. Teddy's aunt has this awesome boat—the *Sunset*. I made this painting of it after she took us out sailing."

"I hope young Teddy Matson is as awesome as the boat," Carmella said.

Zoe grinned. "He might be. And if he's not, at least his aunt has an awesome boat, right?" She looked at Carmella and then over at Nikki. "I think about boys all the time. Even when I'm painting. My mom says it's normal. Do you think it's normal?"

Nikki sighed. She'd changed her entire life for a boy she couldn't stop thinking about. "I'm sure it's fine. But I'm the last person you should ask about what normal is."

Nikki loaded a number four brush with cerulean and a tiny speck of steely gray, then made a steady stroke to define the edge of a cloud. Getting back to painting was one of the few decisions that came easily to her. It felt like reconnecting with an old friend. She had spent an hour on the bluff, painting Three Tree Point just as the late afternoon sun deepened the colors and lengthened the shadows. Like the act of surfing, painting took her away from herself, a welcome respite for her mind.

Although she was out of practice, the picture pleased her, capturing a particular mood with a slant of the light and a layering of water and sky. She brought her work inside to put the final touches on the piece. A proper plein air painting was created eighty percent outside, so she had only a few final refinements to make to the original.

She carefully removed the frog tape from the edge of the paper, then stepped back to view her creation. *I am painting again*, she said to

Johnny. *You never knew me as a painter. I can't think why I never showed you that side of myself.*

He would probably laugh and sweep her into his arms and say something goofy like, *Let me paint a masterpiece on your bare skin.*

Lately, she'd taken to talking to Johnny as if he were present and imagining his replies. It was a silly practice, but as the weeks passed, she had been feeling him slip away, and that worried her. She didn't know how to keep him close. Even watching his *In Memoriam* reel on the Global Surf League website made him feel further away, somehow.

Nikki let out a sigh and set aside the painting. With meticulous care, she cleaned the brushes and capped the paint tubes. The key to fitting into an Airstream was, of course, keeping things neat and in their place.

Like Johnny. Was he in his place?

It seemed impossible that someone who had been her whole world had been reduced to a budget "eco-friendly" container of ashes, which she still hadn't done anything with. Currently it was in a cubby over the fridge, next to a tin of PG Tips and a half-empty bottle of Jameson.

She opened the cupboard and took out the urn. She'd brought it to the States in her carry-on bag from Brisbane to LA. Her albatross. At the airport in Brisbane, the X-ray image of her bag had triggered a security search. A melancholy Nikki had sat in the terminal, shuddering with sobs, while the apologetic agents inspected the strange parcel.

"Aw, Johnny," she said, staring at the urn, "what should I do with you now?" She had no idea where to put him, the same way she had no idea where to put the love that had once filled her life to the brim.

On impulse, she took the urn from the cupboard and put on a swimsuit. Then, carrying the urn awkwardly under one arm, she went to the shed and geared up in a wetsuit. She found a dry bag rucksack for the urn, chose the biggest longboard she could find, waxed it, and hauled it to the beach. There was a chill in the air and the day was nearly done, although some oversized sets of big waves kept rolling in. There was an undulating, unbroken expanse of water in the backline.

A red flag flew, warning that the surf was dangerous today. A few people strolled ankle deep in the swash, and several dogs raced along the beach, churning up the shoreline and chasing birds. Nikki wasn't fazed by the conditions. The tide was up, and the incoming sets of big waves didn't seem dangerous. What seemed dangerous was being without Johnny.

With the dry bag on her back and the board leashed to her ankle, she waded slowly into the surf, letting the wetsuit warm the water to her body temperature. She duck dived under the incoming waves at the break, feeling resistance from the parcel she carried, and from the bigger than usual board. The waves pounded her, reminding her of the hazard flag, but she forged ahead. She knew how to tackle big surf.

Once clear of the break, she sat atop the board to wait. She was in no hurry. She took the rucksack from her back and unrolled it and held the sealed container between her legs.

She broke the seal and removed the lid. Inside was a paper-wrapped parcel like a flour sack. It was filled with a grainy, undifferentiated dust. This was not Johnny. He was well and truly gone. This could have been anything—leftover ashes from the fire pit. Roadside dust. Sand from the beach.

"I don't know how to say goodbye, so I won't," she said through chattering teeth. "Our time together was too short, but *forever* would have been too short. Oh my God, I wish I could have just one more moment with you, just to make sure you knew how much you meant to me. You brought joy to my world, Johnny. I don't know if I'll ever figure out how to do that on my own. But I guess . . . well, I can surf. And you can go where the ocean takes you." She tipped the container over the edge of the board. The ocean received him with indifference, and she watched the ashes disperse in pale clouds, formless and colorless, that swirled briefly and then began to sink. "Oh, Johnny. Maybe I'll see you around sometime."

Nikki followed the particles until every last one had disappeared. Then she put the container back into the bag and slipped her arms through the straps. The final remnants stained the deck of the surfboard until a wave washed it clean.

She laid herself prone on the board, centered for attack but not moving. Her cheek pressed against the cold surface of the fiberglass. Gulls wheeled in the sky and cried out, and a few rollers passed beneath her. Then a big one arrived, a fast, powerful, destructive wave, and she recognized the opportunity—a glassy, muscular curve of water beckoning to her.

She paddled fast to join the wave at the shoulder as it rose, feeling a surge of adrenaline as she found her moment. It was a big swell with an unexpectedly steep slope. As she grabbed the rails and popped up, pain shot through her bad wrist. She focused on the wave peels scooping her up, but then the barrel closed, and she lost her line.

Caught inside the wave, the nose of the board dipped. She hadn't found the perfect spot on the unfamiliar board, or maybe she was unbalanced by the rucksack. Whatever the cause, she pearled and wiped out and was caught inside the wave. It was too heavy to escape. The water held her pinned down, and as wave after wave pounded her, she just could not catch her breath.

Nikki knew better than to fight for her life, because in a fight against the ocean, the ocean always won. She simply surrendered, thinking of Johnny, wondering if she would see him, somehow. She felt no fear. She'd never been one to let fear keep her from doing the things she dreamed of. Maybe she had picked a dangerous wave on a dangerous day on purpose.

The swish and thunder of the ocean filled her head, and she simply let go. It was easy to be in the moment if you didn't know you'd make it to the next moment. Had that thought gone through Lyra's head as she'd faded into sleep for the last time?

Nikki's limbs relaxed, and she lost herself and let the wave take her. A lifetime passed, and then the wave brought her to the other side.

She tumbled into the shallow swash as if the foam had expelled her, vaguely aware of people rushing toward her. Lifting a hand to signal that she was okay, she tipped her head back and took a deep breath, grateful to find the air again.

This was the profound lesson of surfing—to let go. To find the air again. All she had to do was breathe.

PART FOUR

Live in the sunshine, swim the sea, drink the wild air.

—*Ralph Waldo Emerson*

15

When Cal's personal mobile phone started playing "Für Elise," he almost let it go to voice mail. At one time, he would have snatched it up without hesitation. At one time, he had learned to play the familiar piece on his guitar just to impress her. But he hesitated now. For one thing, he was at work. For another, he and Elise Matson were exes.

They'd dated last year. They'd had some good laughs and good sex. And one night, after a fine few hours of lovemaking aboard her sixty-foot Beneteau yacht, she had told him with dewy-eyed earnestness that she was in love with him.

Cal wished he could have welcomed the declaration. He wished he could reciprocate it. He had tried his best to get there with her emotionally, because there were so many reasons that she was right for him. She was interesting, attractive, and as the heir to a shipping fortune, she was loaded. And she wanted to have kids.

Cal wanted kids, too. He wanted to be in love. He tried to convince himself that he was—but it felt forced, artificial. He didn't know why. Didn't know how to push himself into that state of bliss.

Not only had Elise told him she was in love with him; she'd also said he could quit his job and come away with her, anywhere they fancied. She said they could hire a live-in aide for his dad and the two of them would travel the world together. It would be an all-expense-paid vacation to forever.

A part of him had felt a flash of temptation. But when he thought about actually doing it—actually joining his life with this very nice, very attractive woman, he realized it made no sense. He would find himself in the lap of luxury with a person he admired but didn't love, with whom there was no emotional intimacy at all. That was no way to live. Not for him.

It was a difficult conversation, but he and Elise were both grown-ups and they got through it. Cal knew he'd made the right decision when the knot in his gut unfurled with relief and gratitude. Things didn't always end so amicably with other women he'd dated. He'd had a couple of past relationships that had gone on too long because he couldn't figure out how to end them. With Elise, there were tears, assurances that they'd stay friends, a final hug, and clarity. Grown-ups.

It kind of sucked that he was getting pretty good at ending things. He needed to get better at starting things.

Now the phone screen flashed a picture of Elise Matson's smiling, very pretty face. He surveyed the pile of work on his desk. Then he swiped up. "Elise," he said.

"Cal, I need you right away at the marina," she said. "Someone broke into the *Sunset* and it's a mess. Things were stolen, destroyed, defaced—you name it." Her voice was taut with exasperation. "Graffiti, filth . . . a real shit show."

"Oh, no. Sorry to hear that. Are you all right?"

"Yes. Everything was in perfect order when I took her out over the weekend, but I got here this morning and found this nightmare. Cal, I just feel so . . . so creeped out. Violated. Who would do a thing like this?"

"Is the conservation officer there?"

"The . . . sorry, who?"

"The conservation officer. The marina's under the jurisdiction of the DNR law enforcement division." Most people didn't realize that, nor were they obliged to. Alara Cove was covered by a patchwork of agencies—the local police, the sheriff's department, the DNR, and, thanks to the Radium Island facility, the US Navy. The district conservation officers dealt with enforcement actions in posted areas, checked on anglers, taught safety classes, and looked into property theft and damage to watercraft.

"It's—I don't see anyone like that. The only person around is the guy from the harbormaster's office, I think," said Elise. "Cal, it's really creepy. Can you come? As . . . as a favor for a friend."

Cal took one more glance at the work piled on the desk and queued up on the computer. "Sure." He stood up and grabbed his gear. "I'll be there soon. Sit tight, and don't touch anything."

En route, Cal had the dispatcher send a message to the conservation office, requesting assistance. It wasn't that he didn't want to help, but his department was small and understaffed.

Elise was waiting on the dock by her boat, a sleek yacht gently bobbing as the water lapped at it. The hollow sound of rigging and masts thrummed rhythmically in the breeze. She looked lovely in white pants and sandals and a silky yellow top, her blond hair in a ponytail. But when she pushed her expensive-looking shades up on her head, he could see the furrowed brow, the eyes darting nervously.

He knew the look all too well. People who were victims of crime, however petty, were always rattled by the experience. Even if no one was injured, there was a feeling of violation that drilled deep into a person's psyche, upsetting or realigning the way they viewed the world. Cal didn't love everything about his job, but he did like helping people. He did like the fact that when he showed up, ready to help, he was usually greeted with relief.

"Hey," he said, "how are you doing?"

She stepped forward as though she needed to lean on him. To his relief, she stopped short, respecting a professional distance. "Not so hot. I was planning to take my nephew and a group of his friends out for his birthday today. My brother's boy Teddy is a student at Thornton." She gestured at the boat. "Obviously I had to cancel that plan."

Cal's phone signaled a message—the CO was tied up with a case forty miles up the coast.

Cal messaged back that he'd take the report himself and submit it back at the station. Elise would need the documentation for her insurance claim. Judging by the crude graffiti sprayed on the hull and stern, the incident appeared to be an act of pointless mischief. As he worked methodically through the scene, he asked himself who would benefit from this crime. Was Elise's boat targeted?

He noted that a trolling motor had been wrenched from a moored dinghy, and the locked hatch door had been forcibly opened. Inside, furniture and gear were upended, cabinets ransacked, electronics and navigation gear stolen or destroyed, storage lockers raided. The bed in the main stateroom smelled of piss. He took pictures and made a list of things Elise thought were missing. She said there had been no firearms on board, but some emergency flares were gone, along with food from the galley and bottles of liquor from the bar.

While Elise paced the dock on a call with an insurance agent, Cal collected a few stray items and bagged them—a wrench that had probably been used to break in, a mat with a shoe impression, a small metallic button, a couple of spray paint caps and bottle caps, a hair tie, a piece of vape pen that smelled of weed.

He checked in at the harbormaster's office. He was assured that the marina practiced good security, but someone had managed to get around the coded gate, or perhaps had the code. The security cameras weren't working, which no one had realized because no one had checked the feed. Bird poop on the solar panels—an ongoing problem. The harbormaster said he would check with the other vessels in the marina, since some of the bigger boats had their own video security systems. Maybe one of them had picked up some activity.

Cal took some more photos and looked around again. "I'm really sorry this happened," he told Elise. "I'll work with the DNR to get the word out. We'll do our best to get some answers."

"Thanks, Cal." Elise shuddered and then hugged herself, rubbing her arms up and down. "It's so unsettling, you know? I can't stop thinking about strangers ransacking the *Sunset*. This was one of my happy places, remember?"

He did remember. They'd made love in the stateroom that now smelled like piss.

"Am I ever going to feel secure here again?" she asked.

"You need time to process," he said. "It's a shock right now. Might be a good idea to hire a cleaning service and do some refurbishing. Maybe look in to installing a security system."

"I thought the marina was secure," she said. "Jesus, who does this shit?"

"Punks," he said. "Tweakers, or kids up to no good. Unfortunately, there's never a shortage of drifters from outside, and locals." Property crimes were always hard to solve. In a town the size of Alara Cove, it wasn't too hard to find likely suspects. This mess was almost certainly the work of juveniles. Tweakers usually left telltale signs, but he hadn't observed any here—disposable lighters, disassembled pens, rubber bands, dirty lanyards, syringes. He had a few ideas about which kids were apt to sneak out after hours and where they liked to hang out, but the marina wasn't usually their first choice. Several things about the case were unexpected. There hadn't been a pattern of anything like this.

"And why the *Sunset*? There are dozens of boats here."

"There's graffiti defacing several boats. Yours appears to be the only one that was boarded."

"It's just . . . gross." She gave another shudder.

"I know. Again, I'm sorry." He gathered up his gear. "I'll get the preliminary report ready so you can submit it to your insurance carrier. And I'll get the word out to the other departments."

"Yes. Okay." She took out her phone. A breeze ruffled her pretty blond hair. Her brow was creased with trouble.

"Take care, Elise, okay?"

"I will."

As he walked away, she said, "Hey, Cal."

He turned back. "Yeah?"

"I, um . . . just, thanks for coming. It's good to see you again, even in this crappy situation."

He nodded. "Likewise, Elise. Take care," he said again. "I mean that."

After exiting the marina, Cal surveyed the parking area. There was only one camera, crusted with bird shit like the others. He observed an array of tire tracks in the sand and gravel, including some from the bike rack. An old key chain with no key on it in the dust. A crumpled candy wrapper. He took more pictures. As he drove back to the station, he tallied up everything on his plate. It never seemed to end.

The station was adjacent to city hall and the municipal offices and city courthouse, the buildings arranged around a green space with walkways close to the center of town. The municipal offices were buzzing at midday, people coming and going in a constant bustle. Cal ran into Jason Sanger in the hallway by the city clerk's counter. Cal had never thought much of Jason, and he suspected the feeling was mutual. But the two of them had a working relationship, of necessity.

"How's your day going?" Jason asked. His bored tone indicated that he didn't really care about the answer.

"It's going. Vandalism incident at the marina. Probably juveniles."

"Man, that's too bad. Guess you'll be rounding up the usual suspects?"

Jason always assumed the petty juvenile incidents were the work of local high school kids. He was often right, but Cal didn't like how quickly the mayor's finger pointed in that direction, never at the gleaming halls of privilege at Thornton.

"We'll see," he said to Sanger.

He laid the bagged items on the counter. "Recognize anything?"

Jason briefly scanned the evidence in the clear plastic bags. He straightened his tie. "Nope. Sorry."

"So the boat's a sixty-footer called *Sunset*. The owner's nephew is a student at Thornton."

"Your point?" Jason lifted an eyebrow.

"Your younger brother's a Thornton student. Wonder if he'd know of a connection."

Jason's face turned hard. "Watch what you're asking, man."

"Just doing my job. Man."

"Right."

"Okay, well, I'll be turning all of this over to the CO of the DNR. It's their jurisdiction. Maybe tell your guy there he's understaffed." Cal rarely had much luck with cooperation from the upper level of the DNR assigned to the county. The chief of the law enforcement division just happened to be Vernon Sanger—Jason's uncle. There were Sangers in office everywhere.

Jason glanced past Cal and his expression changed. His eyes narrowed and turned sharp, though he broke into a smile. "Well," he said, "if it isn't our trailer park queen."

Nikki had just come from the city planner's office. She regarded Jason with an icy glare. "Restoration specialist to you," she said, adding a sniff of superiority that only made her look more adorable. Her expression warmed when she turned to Cal. "Hey there," she said. "Guess who just got final approval on the plans for Beachside?"

"Yeah?" Cal smiled at her. He knew she'd been working with the city planning department for many weeks, seeking a special designation for Guy Graziola's caravan park. Cal had to admire her aplomb. She had dragged herself though a sadness he couldn't imagine, trying to put her life back together after it fell to pieces. She'd been working nonstop to help her dad keep the Airstream park. "That's great, Nikki."

Jason glared at the paperwork in her hands. "It still needs to clear the community development committee and the environmental impact committee."

"You're the mayor, not the planning department. Don't you have better things to do other than interfering in other people's business?"

She turned to Cal. "Jason's been micromanaging the project from day one."

"That wasn't interfering. It was doing my job."

"That was you, trying to screw this up. And your last stunt didn't work." She looked up at Cal again. "He tried to challenge the land lease, but he failed."

"We'll see about that," Sanger said to her.

She scowled at him. "Don't you have someplace you need to be? Doing your job?"

He scowled back. "Apparently I need to be in a policy review meeting about the planning department." He shook his head, exuding condescension. "Do you really think that shithole is worth saving?" he asked, nodding at the documents she hugged against her chest.

As he stalked away, she watched him for a few seconds, then turned to Cal. "Is it possible that he's even worse than he was fifteen years ago?"

Entirely, Cal thought. "No comment," he said.

"So, yes, then." She looked at the clear evidence bags, then did a double take. "Where did you find a Buccaneers pin?"

"How's that?"

She pointed at the small round button he'd picked up. "That's a Buccaneers pin. Used to be a badge of honor for kids at Thornton. They'd give them out as rewards when a member completed a dare. But the Buccaneers were banned from the school after Mark died."

Interesting, Cal thought. Jason Sanger would have recognized that instantly.

"What?" she asked.

"What do you mean, what?"

"The way you're looking at me."

"Tell me more about this project of yours. I'm intrigued." He was glad to see her embracing the Beachside renovation. She seemed more animated, more like the bright-eyed girl he'd known.

"Which project? Getting my dad's park renovated is the big one.

Getting Shasta elected mayor is another. I'm a volunteer on her campaign. Come to think of it, I'm a volunteer at my dad's place. God forbid that I should get an actual job."

"Do you want an actual job?"

"Are you offering?"

He grinned. "Not my department. You're multitalented, Nikki. You'll find something."

"With a high school education and a failed career as a professional surfer?"

"Hey, don't sell yourself short. Seriously, how are you doing?"

She brushed her hand over her hair and sighed. "I have a roof over my head and a new little sister. A dad who needs me. I guess I'm adjusting to this new world order."

Cal wasn't sure why he felt so awkward around her. A throwback to their high school days, maybe. She'd always seemed so sure of herself, a lithe goddess on her board, emerging like Venus from the surf.

"That's good. I know it can't be easy."

Her mood seemed to shift, and she sighed. "I miss surfing. I didn't get out much this summer thanks to my wrist. Now that winter is coming, I'll get out even less." A faraway look softened her eyes. "In Australia it was always possible to find summer."

Australia was one of the many places on his bucket list. In the past fifteen years, she'd probably set foot in half the places on his list. She'd lived a different life for a long time, with a guy who had been her whole world. Cal pictured them like eternal tourists, surrounded by surf and sand, illuminated by brilliant sunsets.

It was kind of beautiful and deeply sad at the same time, watching Nikki find her way through such a terrible grief. Cal had a lot of love in his life—his dad, his brother, his friends—but nothing like the sort of love that wrapped itself around a good marriage.

There was nothing he could do to help her deal with that kind of loss. But he could help. "How about a boat ride?" he asked. "Can you go boating?"

"Sure. If I had a boat."

"How about I take you out?"

"Do you have a boat?"

He grinned, picturing the department's new high-tech patrol boat. "Oh, yeah," he said. "I got a boat."

"Cool," she said.

They checked the weather and the calendar for his next day off and agreed to meet at the city dock. The patrol boat, with its twin 300 engines, wasn't a toy, but the occasional ride-along was permitted if the vessel wasn't in service.

"Cool," he echoed. "See you then."

Nikki gathered up her things and headed for the exit.

Cal stared after her. Even after so much time had passed, she looked exactly as he remembered her, slender and suntanned even after summer was gone, her dark hair shining, her walk as smooth as waves on a calm day. There was never a time in his life when Nikki wasn't there. In preschool, they'd lined up their rest-time mats side by side, and he could still remember the sparkle in her eyes as she tried not to giggle. In junior high, she'd insisted on being his date for dances, even though they weren't boyfriend and girlfriend, thus saving him from ridicule. Their high school summers had been magical, idyllic, and sheer torture, because he knew that if he told her how he felt, it would mean the end of their friendship.

A text notification came up on Cal's phone. Elise Matson. She missed him. She wanted to see him again. For drinks. Maybe for something more.

Elise Matson was gorgeous. Funny. Available. A catch by anyone's standards. Cal didn't know why he wasn't attracted to her anymore.

Then he saw Nikki turn at the end of the hallway and wave goodbye. And yes. He did know why.

16

Growing up in a thirty-three-foot Airstream, Nikki had never regarded the trailer as an icon of Americana. She'd never appreciated her drop-down bunk as a clever innovation, or the boomerang pattern on the Formica countertops, the wooden cabinets and floors as hallmarks of the midcentury. But her research into the origins of the caravans drew her into a whole new world. According to the standards for historic preservation, the design had to reflect the true historical character of the original feature.

Now, with approval from the planning department and a development loan for the renovation, Nikki was immersed in the project. The process was challenging, and often frustrating, but each time she cleared another hurdle with the city, she felt a gratifying sense of accomplishment. She never dreamed she would be in charge of something like this, but there were a lot of things she'd never dreamed of. Without Johnny, it was a different world entirely, but for the first time in her life, it was *her* world.

Glancing at the clock, she shut down the laptop. It was time to meet up with Shasta and Carmella. Shasta had not exaggerated when she'd said she was good at finding grants and writing proposals. In addition to the preservation society's grant, she had found an opportunity for arts funding, provided the renovation project included work from emerging artists. It was a strange but welcome thrill to know she now had a budget for art. Nikki had taken to visiting local artists in their studios and ateliers, seeking unique pieces to display.

Today, Carmella wanted to introduce her to a kinetic sculptor named Kenji Harui, whose installations were dramatic and complex evocations of the atomic age of the 1950s and '60s.

The three of them drove together to Kenji's studio, a shabby building on the far side of the highway. It had a roof of corrugated tin, walls made of reclaimed lumber, and a glass garage door to let in the light. Despite its humble look, the studio had a certain rustic charm. As she looked around, Nikki realized things were placed just so—an iron arbor, a walkway made of driftwood under a grand archway of coastal cypress, and mobiles made of moving parts that swung in the breeze.

"I like him already," Nikki said, checking out a powder-coated ladder of connected dots that led to a loft above the studio.

"Good to hear," said a voice, and she realized Kenji was on a platform at the top of the ladder. Like a gymnast, he climbed down and jumped to the ground, executing a courtly bow. "You must be Nikki. And I like *you* already."

He had reddish hair and freckles, refined Japanese features, and the body of a gymnast. Nikki tried not to stare. She tried not to blush. As he led the way into his studio, she turned to Shasta. *You could have warned me*, she mouthed.

Shasta offered an exaggerated shrug.

The studio was crammed but well organized, with a welding station and materials in bins and on floor-to-ceiling shelves. Lots of metal and found objects. Nikki had already read up on Kenji's career. He'd attended prestigious art schools and had won many juried prizes, but like so many working artists, he struggled to make a living. His pieces were bold and oversized, with a decidedly retro vibe. She could already picture one by the flagpole at the park entrance, or maybe at the fire pit, where people gathered after a day of surfing.

And Kenji himself was charming. More than charming, in fact. He seemed genuinely interested in her. "I have a confession to make," he said. "I looked you up online. You're a world-class surfer."

"Not lately. But thank you," she said. "I'm wearing a different hat these days."

He nodded. "Carmella said you're working on a historic renovation. Man, I love that beach. It wouldn't be the same without the Airstream park."

"That's the idea. To bring it back to life so it never has to leave." She eyed a soaring metal sculpture up and down, thrilled by his use of space and shapes. The objects and structures on the twisted ellipse drew her eye and made it look as if it might soar aloft at any moment. The piece conveyed emotion in some ineffable way—or maybe it made her emotional. "This is wonderful," she said.

"That one was commissioned by a bank down in Orange County," he said, "but it didn't work out for them. Too controversial."

"You're kidding."

"I took it as a compliment. I just follow the shapes as they emerge."

"Can I take a few pictures?"

"Be my guest."

He visited with Carmella and Shasta while she looked around a bit more. She kept sneaking glances at him. Here was a man living in the art world, something she'd once dreamed of doing. Did she still dream of such a thing? It had been a long time since she'd asked herself that question. She almost didn't trust the answer.

On the way out, Kenji fell in step with her. "Thanks for visiting," he said. "So . . . I know you're busy with all of this, but if you ever want to hang out, maybe get a drink . . . ?"

Nikki felt a curl of curiosity in her gut. Was he asking her out? Or was it just an artist-to-artist thing? It was confusing. And not . . . not unwelcome. "How about coming to Beachside one of these days? We are elbows-deep in the renovations, but I'd love to show you what we're planning."

"That sounds great." He stuck out his hand. A manly hand, callused and firm. "Good luck, Nikki. With everything."

When they got in the car, Shasta turned to her. "Well?"

"Well, what?" Nikki was surprised to feel the heat of a blush in her cheeks.

"This town doesn't suck so bad after all, eh?"

"He's a fine artist, isn't he?" Carmella said. "I've booked him for a show at the gallery."

"He's fine, full stop." Shasta started the engine and drove down the gravel road to the highway.

"Don't even," Nikki said.

"I know," Shasta told her. "But it was hard not to notice the way he was looking at you. Who knows? Maybe you'll be friends. Or something like that."

Nikki glared at her. "So I'm supposed to, what, slot in a new guy in the void Johnny left behind?"

"Nik—"

"Don't take it the wrong way, honey," Carmella said from the backseat. "We know how strong your love was for Johnny. It's that very strength that tells me that if you can love someone so much, then you can love again."

"I'd rather be painting," Nikki said to Gloria, looking up from her computer screen. "How about you?"

"Okey dokey." The little girl was on the floor of Nikki's unit, making great swirls of color on a big sheet of paper. Nikki had brought her home from daycare and was watching her while Guy and Patsy worked on one of the Airstreams.

"You like purple, don't you?" asked Nikki, admiring Gloria's work.

"Purple." Gloria held up a fat crayon and mangled the word.

"I love making art," Nikki said. "Painting helps me get in touch with myself again. Does coloring help you, too?"

"Uh-huh."

Nikki grinned, knowing the kid had no idea what she was talking about. It was nice to have Gloria's company today. Working long hours with a CAD program was a new experience for Nikki. Mastering the digital design and planning program was unexpectedly satisfying as she used the software to produce documents for the contractor and planning department.

Gloria kept her company as she finalized the layouts for the smaller units. "You know, in Australia, I was part of a team, but when we were out in the surf, it was every man for himself," she told her sister. "This is a different kind of team. Are you a member of our team?"

"Yep," said Gloria.

"That's great, because we need all the help we can get. We've got Shasta researching the heck out of everything, and Carmella is helping me with the designs. I've got to figure out what art pieces we're going to need, and where to put them, too." It had been sheer pleasure, visiting the various studios and ateliers, finding unique pieces to feature. She had given a presentation at the library and invited serious students to submit art. "I can't stop thinking about the Kenji piece." She paused. "I think about Kenji a lot. I worry that he reminds me too much of Johnny—so bloody handsome and charming. And do I like him because of that? Or because I like him?" She paused. "I'm meeting him at Carmella's gallery later. He has a showing there on Friday. And I need to, you know, talk about his art for the park. He might want to talk about other things . . . Do you think I should go for it? Meet him at the gallery?"

Gloria lifted both hands in the air, palms out. "Yep," she said.

The Carmella Beach Gallery was quiet in the low season, but it was still a fine place to find good art. Carmella's gallerist was on maternity leave, so Nikki had been helping out when she could spare the time. She made sure the lighting and placements were exactly right.

Kenji arrived, wearing ripped jeans and a cashmere sweater, and bearing a box of chocolates from the Sweet Spot, a shop across the street. "I don't know what you like, but I figured chocolate is a safe bet."

"You figured right." She came down off the stepladder, where she'd been aiming a can light at a piece.

"You're good at that," he said, checking out a sinuous piece he'd created. The lighting threw its magnified shadow against a blank wall.

"You think?" Nikki said. "It's not hard to display a piece I know is really good."

"Well, thank you. Carmella said you're a talented painter. She doesn't say that lightly."

"I'm hoping to find time for painting again. I loved it as much as I loved surfing. But the surfing kind of took over, when I was married and we were in the league."

"Are you still in the league?"

She shook her head. "That was another life."

"I'm sorry for what happened. It's good you came back to your hometown."

He didn't know why she'd left. "Coming home was never my plan, but, well . . ." She gestured around the gallery. "Here I am."

"You're pretty great, Nikki," he said.

"So are you," she said. She wished she could feel something more than appreciation for him. He *was* great. "I'm sorry, but—"

"Don't be. Sounds like you've been dealing with a lot. One thing at a time, right? You're going to be okay."

"I'll never be okay."

"You already are. You just don't know it yet."

She was actually relieved to hear him say it. "That's a really kind thing to say."

"My grandmother—she lives in Okinawa—likes to say kindness costs nothing."

"Well, thank you. And I absolutely want to make a deal with you."

After he left, she ate too many pieces of the chocolate while finishing up at the gallery. She felt hollowed out and lonely. It wasn't a date, she reminded herself. But it still felt like a failed date. Did that mean all dates were doomed to failure?

She desperately wanted Carmella to be right. Before she could stop herself, she took out her phone and sent a message—*Let's go boating.*

"I might have done a dumb thing," she said to Gloria the next day. She had spent the past hour at the city planning office, and then she'd picked up her sister from daycare to bring her home for the day. "Look at you," she said, glancing in the rearview mirror. "Two years old, with a lifetime of dumb things ahead of you."

She turned into the park, slowing down to admire the progress. The old neon sign had been restored, and all the letters of BEACHSIDE CARAVANS emitted a cheery glow. The workers were pouring a concrete slab near the fire pit to display Kenji Harui's sculpture. "He's a very nice guy, but I didn't even try with him. And that's not even the dumb thing. I impulsively sent a text to somebody else, and I don't think there's any way to unsend a text, right?"

"Yep," said Gloria.

"And there was no reply, so I don't know what the hell that means. How long does it take to answer a damn text?"

"Damn text."

"I just don't want to be some weird underage widow living in the past, you know? I need to feel like there's something else for me. Some alternative to being sad all the time."

"Daddy," Gloria said as Nikki parked the car. "Dad. Daddy-O."

Hearing a text tone, Nikki checked her messages. At last—a reply. *How about today after work?*

"Hello," Nikki said, feeling a flush on her cheeks.

"Daddy-O," Gloria said again, more loudly.

"Right. Let's go see what Dad and Patsy are up to." She picked up the roll of plans on architectural paper and unbuckled Gloria from her car seat. Outside, the park was a hive of activity. Although it was closed for the winter, there were electrical and plumbing contractors, landscapers, and carpenters working on the place. Other workers were upgrading the hardscape, painting the outbuildings, and polishing the aluminum alloy siding of the units until they shone.

The hardest workers of all were Nikki and her father. Even after the crews left for the day, she and Guy stayed up late, working side by side. They talked a lot during those hours, probably more than they ever had when she was younger.

She brought Gloria and the plans over to Unit 2, where her dad and Patsy had tackled a kitchen. Through the open door, she could see Patsy with a bandana around her head and rubber gloves up to her elbows. The only sign of Nikki's dad was a pair of olive green gumboots protruding from underneath the Airstream.

"How's it going?" Nikki bent down to look.

"Dada!" Gloria clapped her hands.

He had a flashlight in his mouth and a wrench in hand. Even with his mouth full, he managed to emit a stream of cuss words.

"That good, huh?"

Patsy parked a load of cleaning rags out on the stoop. "Hey, short stuff." She beamed at Gloria. "Watcha got there?"

Gloria babbled, held out a bag of Goldfish crackers, then snatched it back.

They heard more swearing from under the trailer.

"Plumbing issues," Patsy said to Nikki. "He'll gripe, but he'll get it fixed. He always does."

The comment reminded Nikki that Patsy had been at the park longer than anyone except Guy. Gloria toddled close to a pile of broken lumber and particleboard, and Nikki pulled her back. "What's all that?" she asked.

"What's left of the cabinets. They were rotted, and since you found out they're not original, I demolished them. I'll put the wood in the fire pit." She caught Nikki's look. "Turns out I'm good at demolition and I like doing it. Puts my bottled-up rage to good use."

"Do you have a lot of rage?" Nikki asked.

"Nah, not really. Not lately, anyway."

"I brought some more layouts and sketches," she said. "Want to see?"

"Hell, yeah." Patsy peeled off her gloves.

"Helya," Gloria echoed.

They went inside, and Nikki's dad took his boots off and joined them. His overalls and baseball cap were crusted with damp sand and smears of dirt and oil. "Plumbing's fixed," he said, washing his hands at the kitchen sink.

"That's great," Nikki said. "And our design has provisional approval from the planning department." She unrolled the master plan, which showed floorplans and elevations of the campers. There were other pages, printed out from the CAD program, that outlined every detail from the layout of each unit to the color scheme and styles she'd found in her research.

Patsy handed Guy a clean rag to dry his hands. "These all look so cool," she said. "You're really good at this, Nikki. How'd you get so good at this?"

Nikki shrugged. To her surprise, she did seem to have a knack for the craft of arranging spaces and making precise scale drawings. It wasn't plein air painting, but it did feel a bit like making art. "Not sure. Desperation, maybe."

"The great motivator," Patsy said. "I think your plan is going to work."

Nikki took a deep breath. "*Our* plan. Teamwork, remember?"

"I sure as hell hope you're right," Guy said, glancing at Gloria. "I'd hate to lose this place."

"That's not going to happen. Check it out. Carmella helped me find the right colors and patterns from the fifties and sixties, and we're going to use original art from local artists."

"I hope you're including yourself in that group," Patsy said. "Make us some paintings."

"Okay," said Gloria.

"Maybe," Nikki said. "I might. Oh, and Shasta helped me unearth a bunch of reference notes about the significance of the caravans. We have magazine clippings of legendary surfers who stayed here, so we'll use those, too." She aimed a look at her dad. "We're going to look through all the old guest books and registries. I found a box full of them in the back of the shed. They date all the way back to the time when Boone Garrity ran the park. Turns out we've had some interesting guests through the years. Surfers and artists and lots of Hollywood types."

"We should go through everything in the storage shed," Patsy suggested. "Maybe we'll find some artifacts to feature in the designs."

Guy drew Gloria onto his muddy knee and studied the sketches and sample drawings Nikki had made. "I love it," he said. "Nice work, Nikki. But it's probably going to take us all winter and into the spring to pull this off."

He used to spend most winters in Costa Rica. He started going down there after sending her to live with Carmella. Nikki used to beg to go with him, but he always said the surf camp there was too rough for a kid, and school was more important. Now that he had Gloria, his winters were spent in Alara Cove.

"It takes as long as it takes," Nikki said. "Isn't that what you used to tell me when you were teaching me to surf?"

"Then we'd better pick up the pace," he said.

"We will." Nikki checked her watch. "Tomorrow."

"What's wrong with today?" her dad asked. He helped himself to Gloria's Goldfish.

"I'm going to knock off early," Nikki said. "To go boating."

"Boating? Who are you going with?"

"Cal Bradshaw. He and I are going for a cruise in the police boat."

"You're . . . Why the hell would you do that?" her dad asked.

She shrugged. "I mentioned that I miss being out on the water, so he offered."

"Hey, that's great," Patsy said, following her outside. "It's good to see you getting out. Never too soon to start dating, right?"

"Oh! Hell, no, it's not a date." Nikki was surprised to feel a flush on her cheeks. "Cal and I . . . We're friends. We go way back."

"That's the best kind," Patsy murmured. She tossed another scrap on the woodpile.

"It's not a date," Nikki reiterated.

"Fine. But it would also be fine if you were to go on a date. It's terrible that you lost someone, and we all wish it hadn't happened, but you're still human. You're incredibly young. And I'm not gonna lie—Officer Bradshaw is quite a catch. Don't let trouble stop you from doing something you want."

Nikki thought about that. "I don't know what I want."

"That's no excuse."

"I need to go get ready," said Nikki, and headed back to her place. *Don't let trouble stop you from doing something you want.*

Nikki wondered if Patsy had taken her own advice. She'd been at the caravan park, looking after the place, for years. Nikki recalled that Patsy had shown up with two little kids and some nasty bruises, and she'd never left. Was this the life she wanted? Or was it what she ended up with because she didn't know?

After her shower, Nikki caught herself deliberating over what to wear, even though her options were limited. It was a gorgeous evening, crowned by clear skies and calm seas. She culled through the small closet and put on leggings and a black sweatshirt and a windbreaker. Then she took off the sweatshirt and swapped it for a thigh-length sweater. She spent too much time on her hair. She put on a touch of makeup.

And for a few moments, things felt normal. For a few moments, she actually did feel as though she was getting ready for a date.

She shook her head to chase away the thought. Not a date. Still, she couldn't resist a final check in the mirror before heading to the city dock. Cal was waiting by the patrol boat. He wore jeans and a city PD jacket, and when he saw Nikki, his face lit with pure delight.

"Glad you could make it," he said, scanning the burning colors of the sunset along the horizon. "Nice evening for a cruise."

Nikki strolled along the dock, checking out the boat as its bumpers nudged the weathered wood. The vessel had huge twin engines and was bristling with gear for navigation, rescue, communication, and security. "That," she said, "looks like a sweet ride."

"Oh, yeah. It's a SAFE boat. Stands for 'secure all-around flotation equipped.'"

"In other words, we're not going to sink."

"Not a chance." He held out a hand while she stepped into the hull. She welcomed the gentle motion of the water beneath her feet. He started up the motors, and she helped him cast off. Although the day was chilly, there was a small pilothouse with a console and an array of equipment. Cal called in to the station to let them know he was doing a ride-along.

They trolled out into the channel, passing the fishing pier and the breakwater. On the other side they reached open water.

"Hang on," said Cal, indicating a handhold on the console. Then he accelerated smoothly. Within a few minutes, the boat was going so fast, it felt like flying.

In the distance, Alara Cove looked like a toy town, its waterfront buildings forming a colorful line under the shadow of the wooded hills in the uplands. Thrilled with the sensation of speed, Nikki looked over at Cal and laughed aloud. "This is awesome," she said, eliciting a grin from him.

As they zoomed past the caravan park, she sounded the horn. The park's neon sign, her beacon when she was out surfing, glowed against the sky. Her feelings about that place were complicated, but she couldn't deny that at this moment, it looked like home to her.

Cal did a couple of donuts and jumped his own wake, showing off the boat's agility.

"So cool," she said, and laughed again, the sensation pleasant but foreign. She still missed Johnny every day. But she was finding out that it was entirely possible to miss him and have fun at the same time.

As they rode around, various messages crackled over the radio. Most of it was incomprehensible to her, but she recognized a remark about the Marina Mart failing to verify ID for alcohol sales.

"Some things never change," Nikki said. "I bet the kids buying booze are from Thornton. They're the only ones who can afford it, right?"

"It's not that simple. The ones who can't afford it just shoplift," Cal said.

She flinched, recalling that long-ago incident at the Marina Mart. Had her failed theft been broadcast on the police channel? *Motherless twelve-year-old female steals tampons.*

They circumnavigated Radium Island. There were signs prohibiting boats and surfers from coming within two hundred feet, but apparently the rule didn't apply to an official vessel. Beyond the rock-rimmed shore, she could see a collection of low, squared-off buildings.

"Last time I was out here, I was chasing bad guys," Cal said.

She was struck by his casual tone. "What? Bad guys? For real?"

"Real as they come. Drugs, assault weapons—they checked all the boxes."

"And you chased them."

"They were smugglers, and the dumbasses got lost. They thought they were in Long Beach."

"Oh. Well, did you catch them?"

"Sure. They were idiots, like I said. A lot of bad guys aren't known for their smarts. They tried to outrun me. Made a sharp turn at a high rate of speed, and two of their guys were thrown out." He shook his head. "They were way too close to these rocks."

"For some reason, I hadn't considered the idea that you actually have an immensely hazardous job, Cal."

"Occasionally."

"That doesn't worry you?"

"I have good training. Huge advantage over dumbass bad guys."

She studied him for a moment, bracing herself against the up-and-down motion of the boat. Mild-mannered Cal Bradshaw had always seemed so cautious, back when they were kids. Timid, even. Always wore his helmet, always followed the rules. A lifeguard with a whistle. Yet maybe what looked like timidity was just a quiet vigilance. As a lifeguard, he'd never hesitated when someone needed saving. He didn't mind taking risks when somebody needed him.

They motored the rest of the way around the island, passing an area surrounded by chain-link fencing and barbed wire. Then the boat entered the channel that flowed between the ocean and the inlet.

"This is a favorite spot for boaters to get in trouble," he said, indicating the pylons under the bridge that arched between the island and the mainland. "The current can get wicked here, and a lot of amateurs don't understand it."

"The locals do," she said. "Remember? We used to get on our boards and shoot the bridge when the tide went out."

"*You* used to shoot the bridge," he corrected her. "I always watched from the shore, praying I wouldn't have to go in after you."

"You were smart," she admitted, eyeing the turbulent water. "It was so damned dangerous. Sometimes I think I did it just to get my dad's attention."

"Did it work?"

She gave a short laugh. "He gave me a high five. That wasn't quite the reaction I was looking for." She glanced over at him. "How's your dad doing?"

"He's good. Retired, but he seems busier than ever. You should come by for a visit one of these days."

She studied the current as it swirled violently around the bridge pilings. "Sure," she said. "I'll have to check my social schedule."

He frowned, then shrugged his shoulders. "Okay. Let me know."

"I'm kidding. I have no social life."

"Maybe you need one."

She looked up at him, feeling the beginnings of a smile. This was not the Cal Bradshaw she used to know. He was there, yes, but she sensed something new about him. Something new about his energy. His body language. His voice. It awakened different feelings in her. Feelings she wasn't sure she was ready for. "Maybe I do."

"Hey, my dad heard about your renovation project. Did you know he has some old signage from the original caravan park? Back when he was a teenager, Dad made some signs for the previous owner, but the guy never picked them up, so they're just sitting in a shed. Bring your dad over and I'll show you."

"On one condition—we provide dinner. We're not so good at cooking, but we can bring takeout."

He navigated back to the marina and they tied up at the dock.

"Thanks for today," Nikki said. "That's some boat."

He nodded. "The job has a few perks."

17

Nikki and her father drove up and down the coast, searching for supplies and materials to use in the renovation project. When it came to historical accuracy, detail was everything. The Airstreams dated from the fifties, sixties, and seventies, so artifacts were plentiful enough. They scoured flea markets and swap meets and yard sales, snatching up odd pieces to play up the period vibe of the campers. Some of the places they visited were ultrahip, featuring live music and gourmet food that catered to well-heeled browsers, but the best ones were eclectic affairs. They were not always well organized, but sometimes the search yielded time-worn souvenirs and ephemera from days gone by.

Guy and Nikki collected architectural salvage, light fixtures and memorabilia. It was an exhausting, exhilarating treasure hunt, poking through the collectibles and cast-off bits and pieces of the past. She felt an inexplicable sense of satisfaction when they came upon just the right thing—like a cat clock with a tail for a pendulum, or an authentic set of Airstream hubcaps in mint condition.

It was also a peek into strangers' lives. In an old set of cupboards, they found a Navy man's vaccine card from 1968; a cribbage board inside a PanAm flight bag; a stack of 45s, the kind that went in the old jukebox; a pair of Seattle Space Needle earrings, still clipped to the card; Pink Floyd's *Wish You Were Here* vinyl in its original wrapping; a weather-beaten wallet filled with French franc notes; a program from a surf competition. Something poignant: a plastic box filled with used pregnancy tests—all negative. Something creepy: a collection of David Hamilton photos from the seventies—seminude prepubescent girls in diaphanous gowns and crowns made of flowers.

What made a person not want something? What made a person hold on to a Led Zeppelin concert ticket from 1975, and then at some point decide it was no longer needed?

Nikki had never been one to keep things. She and Johnny had never had much and they never wanted much. Their souvenirs were limited to sponsor swag and luggage stickers and patches commemorating surfing events.

Now she wondered if she should have been more mindful of the meager possessions she and Johnny had shared, if she should have treasured them more. Would it have helped her to bear the grief? Would she be less frightened that the memories might fade? Thinking back over her years in Australia, Nikki felt a complicated jumble of emotions. Driven by youthful impulse, she had found herself in an upside-down, wrong-side-of-the-road world, totally different from the only home she'd ever known.

Starting a new life there meant adjusting to a new culture, and most of the time it was like finding her way along a dark path, able to see only as far as her headlights would shine. Looking back through the years, she realized she had adjusted and adapted to everything life had thrown at her—a surf camp childhood, a home with Carmella and a Thornton education, and then a headlong plunge into the world of the surf league. Johnny had made it all worthwhile, though, with his huge heart and his appetite for life, his arms around her at night and his total, unfeigned belief that they were an unstoppable team. She worked her ass off at her sport and adjusted to an unplanned life and had adventures in that far-off place, and it had changed her for the better.

Grief had changed her, too, not for the better but it had realigned her perspective on the world. Now that she was back, she saw Alara Cove through new eyes. Maybe she was starting to understand why her father, as a young man, had been so drawn to this world.

And it occurred to Nikki that, for the first time in her life, the future was up to her. There was nothing to adapt to but her own decisions. The prospect was exhilarating and a bit daunting.

Their rambles took them up along the winding highways of the central coast, and clear down to LA and Malibu. She stared out the window of the old van and thought about the reason the memories were so important. They were the story of where she had been. If she lost that, she wouldn't know who she was. Now she admitted to herself that before Johnny, before she'd entwined her life with his, she'd also had a story of her own.

After having been away for so long, Nikki viewed the coastline through new eyes, and it was more beautiful than she remembered. As a bored, impatient teenager, she hadn't appreciated the gorgeous vistas of the seaside byways of the coast—the shadows of the uplands and mountains descending to the craggy inlets and placid bays, the glimpses of wildlife and flowers that bloomed even in winter. As she gazed at the scenery, she remembered to breathe. The sheer, profound beauty healed her, maybe a little. Or maybe it was the strange reconnection with her father, and the tiny new person in her life.

Strapped into her car seat, Gloria babbled and played with a cloth book about kittens, held upside down. "Look out the window," Nikki said to her, gesturing at the ocean. "We might even see gray whales. It's that time of year. Do you even know what a whale is?"

"A snack," Gloria replied.

Nikki turned and handed her some yoghurt puffs in a plastic cup. "You're missing the view," she said. "Don't you want to enjoy the view? We're making memories here, right, Dad?"

"Nah, she won't remember any of this," Guy said.

She heard something in his tone. Regret. Bitterness? "What?"

"Little kids don't remember stuff, even the cool things we did."

Nikki hesitated, trying to think about her earliest memories. The beach. The curve of the ceiling over her bed. The stars winking outside the window. "Tell me something I don't remember."

He drummed his fingers on the steering wheel. "Lots of things. Pretty much everything until . . . what? Kindergarten? We had good times, you and me. I took you on road trips when we could get away from the park. One year, we went down to the Santa Monica Pier and you rode a pony. Remember?"

"No. I rode a pony?"

"You didn't like it much. We had lots of adventures on the road. We stopped at fruit stands and rock shops and roadside attractions. I taught you to pee standing up."

She frowned, then let out a brief laugh. "How's that?"

"When you were first learning. I couldn't figure out about public restrooms, you know? Then if we were out in the woods somewhere, I wasn't sure about the squatting. So you did it standing up. I bet you don't remember that, either."

She laughed again. "I'm not sure I want to."

"How about that time you swam with a whale shark? Remember that?"

"What? I swam with a whale shark?" She pictured the huge, gentle, spotted creatures, but had no recall of swimming anywhere near them.

"We went down to Baja California and swam in the Sea of Cortez. Cabo Pulmo. You were probably four or five, and I taught you to use a mask and snorkel and fins, and you took right to it. There was a nice, protected bay with whale sharks. I held on to a dorsal fin and we went for a little ride. Damn, that was a day. You loved it."

"I don't suppose you have pictures."

"Nah. Too busy keeping track of you, because you could never sit still." He drummed his fingers on the steering wheel again. "Nobody took pictures back then. It's not like now with cell phones."

She and her father had made memories she couldn't remember. In that case, who did the memories belong to? *Gloria's my second chance.* Nikki lifted her phone and turned to the backseat. "Lots of pictures. No excuses."

"Nope." Gloria grinned and drooled a bit.

Nikki caught a sideways glance from her father. "What?"

"I never understood why you left," he said.

She barked out a laugh of disbelief. "I torched my own future," she said. "You saw me do it."

"I wish I could have done more for you then," he said. "It weighs on me."

That makes two of us, she thought. "I did what I did, and I moved on." She sighed. "I have no idea if I made the right choice, but it was *my* choice to live with. Being back here, I see how everyone else has gotten an education and a career. I never did that. I jumped into Johnny's surf life, and sometimes I wonder if it's something I did after everything else fell through."

"Or did you do it because you loved that boy?" her father asked.

She sent him a grateful look. *Yes,* she thought. *Yes, I loved that boy like my life depended on it.*

"Here's our exit." He steered the van off the highway, and they glided down to Seabrook, which boasted a weekly vintage flea market and swap meet.

By now they had a routine. While Guy strapped on the backpack, Nikki grabbed the diaper bag and took Gloria to the bathroom. "Don't let him teach you to pee standing up. It's not a skill you'll be using later in life." She hoisted the toddler onto the drop-down table and made quick work of the diaper. By now, this was a habit she knew by rote, even though at first she had felt completely out of her element. Through Gloria, she was coming to know the challenges her dad had faced when he was raising her alone. "However, if he offers you a pony ride, you should probably take it."

"Love ponies."

"Everybody does." Nikki hoisted her onto her knee so they could both wash up at the sink. She glanced at their faces. "Everybody says we look like sisters. What do you think?"

"Sisters." Gloria garbled the word, but Nikki felt certain she recognized it.

When they stepped outside, their dad was waiting. Gloria squealed with joy at the sight of him and held out her hands with fingers splayed like starfish.

"I foraged for supplies," he said, handing Gloria a soft pretzel. There was a cup of coffee for Nikki. She loaded the baby into the backpack and they went exploring. It was a low-key operation with friendly vendors and an eclectic mix of old things and handcrafted goods. Her dad, who was six-foot-two, looked like Bigfoot with Gloria on his back, twirling his ponytail with her finger. He was still good-looking enough to garner attention, and he still remembered how to turn on the charm to get a better price for a set of antique drawer pulls and some salvaged windows for the new laundry shed. They took their time poking around, because they'd learned that some treasures were easily overlooked if they were in too much of a hurry.

Nikki scanned a display of dashboard hula figurines when something caught her eye—not one of the figurines, but the table itself, which was a battered surfboard set atop two sawhorses. The board had a wood-burned insignia near the tail. "Hey," she said, nudging her father. "Check it out. Is that what I think it is? Renny Sweet's logo?"

"Damn," he said, taking out his reading glasses. "I think it might be."

Reynolds Sweet was famous for having designed one of the first boards with balsa-wood rails and a fin, nearly a hundred years ago. They had been looking for a vintage board for the entrance to the quiver—the shed where all the Beachside boards were kept. A rare antique model would be perfect.

The vendor, a middle-aged woman who had seen too much sun, was happy enough to part with the old piece. "I'll never get around to restoring it," she admitted. She smiled at Guy as he counted some bills into her hand. Nikki helped set the figurines aside. "Take one for your baby," the vendor said. "On the house."

"Oh, thanks. That's really nice of you." Nikki had stopped correcting people who assumed Gloria was her kid. It was even more awkward when they assumed it was hers and Guy's. "How about this one?" She showed Gloria a little grass-skirted figurine.

"Yay!" said Gloria.

"Can you say thank you?"

"Nope."

Nikki sent the woman an apologetic shrug. "Thanks from all of us," she said. "We'll take good care of this board."

It was big and broad, like an airplane wing, so different from a modern board. But the wood and the shape gave it character, and she could already picture it fitting right into the new look of the park.

"Good haul today," Guy said, glancing over at her as they drove home. Gloria was already sound asleep, the figurine clutched in her hand.

"We're a good team," Nikki said.

Back at the park, they stored their treasures in the newly cleared-out shed. Nikki and her father stood back and regarded the items they had gathered. Guy stuffed his hands into his back pockets and tilted his head. "The place is nearly stuffed to the rafters," he said.

"That's a good thing," Nikki replied. "We need to get this right, Dad. Down to the last detail. Carmella always said God is in the details."

"She's full of advice. She was good for you," he said.

"Yes." Nikki paused. Of course he needed to say that. "But you should probably know, it was hard to get my head around the fact that I was living in a foster home."

"I'm sorry it was hard for you. This is not an excuse, but when you were little, I woke up every day feeling like a beginner. You were so smart and motivated and energetic and just so damn cute. I didn't know how to make a life for you. I was barely out of my teens and

I had to make it up as I went along. My folks back in Jersey didn't exactly set a good example. They were all about yelling and hitting."

"I guess I'm glad you didn't follow their example, then."

"I have more confidence with Gloria. I get a lot of advice from Patsy. She did a damn good job with her kids. The older one's a fire-fighter, and the younger one is in college, studying to be a teacher."

"Unlike your loser kid," said Nikki.

"Knock it off. You know better than that. I'm proud of everything you've done." His face flushed and he looked off into the distance. "I took a parenting class, did I tell you?"

She stared at him. "Yes, you did."

"It's weird, right?"

"Absolutely not." Nikki still had a hard time picturing her dad in the class. "I'm proud of you for doing that. It's good you're making Gloria a priority."

"I'll try to get it right with her. I suppose I'll probably screw up, but I won't screw *her* up." His gaze was soft as he looked at Nikki. "I wish I'd been a better dad to you."

She nudged her shoulder against his and let out a sigh. "You didn't screw me up, Dad. I did that all on my own."

"Listen, there's nothing remotely screwy about you. It sucks, what happened in Australia, but I'm glad you came back. Next summer, we should—"

"Whoa there. Next summer? I don't even know if I'll be here then."

"Where are you planning to go?"

"I don't know. I don't feel like I belong here, though." Back in Australia, Jess had advised her to figure out why she'd left in the first place. There were many, many reasons. What she needed was a reason to stay.

She thought about this new life she was leading. There were things about it that appealed to her. She liked the process. She worked as hard on the renovation as she'd ever worked on painting or surfing.

And every once in a while, she sensed a change deep inside. The transition was subtle and gradual, but she realized that it was possible to find something in her heart besides grief.

"Talk to me, sister," her father said. "Is it so bad, being back here?"

"No, not at all. It's just that . . . when I'm doing all this planning and designing and working, I stop being sad for whole minutes at a time."

"And that's a bad thing?"

"It's a thing. I don't know if it's good or bad. It's good when the hurt subsides. It's bad when the memories fade away. I worry that forgetting about the grief is the same as forgetting about Johnny. I'm afraid if I lose the grief, I will lose him."

Her father turned to her. "Hey. It doesn't work that way. I still feel sad about Lyra. But then, every time I look at your face, I see your mother. In thirty-three years, I've never lost her."

Then why did you push me away? she wanted to ask but didn't. "I'm just so scared of losing him forever."

"You're not going to lose him. You get to keep him forever. That doesn't mean you have to turn your heart into a shrine to him. You know the best way to honor his memory?"

"Oh, so you're an expert now."

"Not even close. But I'm old, and I know stuff. I know you belong here with people who love you. Nikki, you could make a life here. A good life."

"I was just a kid when I carved these things. Maybe thirteen or fourteen," Cal's father remarked, sitting at the big kitchen table. His hands were moving over the old signs he'd once made for the caravan park. When Cal had told him about the renovation project, his father had sent him deep into the archives of his old shop, looking for signs he remembered creating for someone named Boone Garrity.

Cal and his brother, Sandy, had found the artifacts in an old crate, wrapped in faded newspaper with headlines about Vietnam and the Watergate hearings. The guy who'd commissioned the signs had never picked them up, because he'd never paid for them.

"These look great, Dad," Sandy said. "Perfectly preserved. The colors aren't faded at all."

"I bet they're just what Guy and Nikki need right now," Cal said. "They're making the park look like a midcentury time capsule."

"So she finally took you up on your offer to come over." His dad grinned.

"Yep," said Cal. "Just Nikki, though. She said her dad couldn't get a sitter."

"A sitter."

"He's got a little kid, remember? I think she's about two."

"Oh, that's right. I heard something about that. Heard the mama ran off and he's doing the whole single-dad thing all over again." Al shook his head. "Damn. I remember those days, raising kids by myself. You two were a handful."

"Just doing our job," said Sandy. As the older brother, he had more specific memories of their mother. She'd gone to Hollywood to find fame and fortune. Instead, she'd found some other guy, and eventually gave up trying to stay connected to her sons.

"I always liked that girl, Nikki," Al said. "Surfer girl, just like the song. She still as pretty as a picture postcard?"

"She . . ." *Yes.* "She's not a girl. And she's great, Dad. Getting herself through a rough time and helping out her dad. I'll take you down to check out the renovation project one of these days. It seems to be going pretty well."

"I hope these signs will give it the finishing touch."

"Hey man, speaking of finishing, I brought a fresh growler to celebrate getting to the end of your class," Sandy said. He brought a chilled jug and some glasses to the table.

"Class? What class?" asked Cal, turning to his father. "You didn't tell me you were taking a class."

"I don't have to tell you everything," Al said, swiveling to face Sandy and then Cal. He smiled and reached down to smooth his hand over China's head. "I'm now a certified speech and language pathologist."

"Wait. What?" Cal stared at his father.

"Cool." Sandy opened the growler and poured three fresh glasses of beer. "That deserves a toast. To you, Pops."

"Well, thanks. Couldn't have done it without you, Sandy." As if he could hear Cal's racing thoughts, Al leaned toward him. "Your brother got me enrolled in a distance learning program. I just finished up finals and did my practicals at the primary school in town."

"When did you visit the primary school?" Cal asked.

"Every Monday and Wednesday when you were on shift. You know I've always liked kids. Never had time to finish my education until now."

Cal was amazed. He'd often been frustrated with Sandy, who'd lit out when their dad was sick, who was super-unreliable, flitting in and out of their lives, his fortunes rising and falling depending on which band he was performing with at the moment. The current one had just dropped an album and apparently it was doing well.

"A speech pathologist? For kids?" he asked, then took a big gulp of beer.

"Sandy's idea. I swear, Sandy, sometimes I think you know me better than I know myself."

"Yeah, bro, you always thought I was a loser," Sandy said.

"I never—"

"You did, and I was, but not always."

"Sounds like the perfect fit," Cal said. His dad really was good with kids. He had endless patience and time. He didn't need to be able to see in order to help. He'd be great at helping with speech problems.

"If I get the job I'm hoping for, you might be looking for a room-mate," Al said.

Cal frowned. "What job is that?"

"My degree was funded by a program in Santa Barbara, and I made a two-year commitment to work in that school district. I'd have to move near the school. Ha, can you see me working in Santa Bar-bara? Maybe I'll snag me a rich widow while I'm at it."

"Seriously, this all sounds great," Cal said. Yet all he could think about was the many things that could go wrong. "But I just don't see—"

"That's exactly the point," his dad snapped. "You *don't* see." He took a breath, put his hand on the dog again. China was finely tuned to his mood. "Listen, I appreciate everything you've done to help me. You changed your whole damn life for me. It's long past time for me to do something else. Find a new path. I'm not a young man. I want the rest of my years to mean something."

Cal felt objections swirling through his head like air traffic over LAX. Santa Barbara was a big, busy city. All kinds of problems could arise. He filled his chest with a deep, cleansing breath, the kind he took when he reached the hardest part of a long race. Now he understood why Sandy had come up from Laurel Canyon for the weekend—not to help excavate the old signs from the shed.

Cal caught Sandy's eye. He lifted his beer glass and mouthed the words *thank you*.

"We're heading down on Monday morning to meet with the school team," Al said. "It'll be my first in-person interview."

"They're going to love you," Cal said.

"Let's hope. I might even—"

China's ears pricked forward, forming triangles of alertness. "Someone's here," Al said. He and the dog seemed to be able to read each other's minds.

Sandy got up to check. "It's your girlfriend."

"She's not my girlfriend." Nevertheless, Cal's heart skipped a beat.

"Good news for me, then," Sandy said, gaping slack-jawed out the window. "Damn, she is smoking hot."

"Hey."

Sandy offered a dismissive wave. "I'm not going to hit on her, man. Give me a little credit." He swept the door open and greeted her with an exaggerated bow. "Milady," he said.

"Sandy! Wow, it's been a long time." Nikki stepped inside. "You look the same."

"In a good way, I hope."

"Of course. I was always a little intimidated by you—the rock star. Are you still a rock star?"

"Depends on who you ask. Still playing in a band and living down in Laurel Canyon. And you do not look the same," he remarked. "You look incredible, all grown up. Definitely in a good way. I had to promise my brother I wouldn't hit on you."

Thanks, bro. Cal shot him a poison glare.

Her cheeks flushed bright red. "Probably good advice. It wouldn't go well for you. But thanks."

She was wearing tight jeans and boots, and a bulky sweater, but somehow, she managed to look, as Sandy had put it, smoking hot. In a town where a lot of the rich women appeared airbrushed even in person, she was a breath of fresh air.

"Let me help you with that stuff." Cal took the large paper bag from her. "Smells amazing."

"Tacos," said Al. "How'd you know they're my favorite, young lady?"

"They're everyone's favorite. I brought sopapillas and cinnamon ice cream for dessert." She placed the carton in the freezer, then turned to Al. "I've heard nothing but good things about China," she said. "I brought her some dried yams. Cal said it's her favorite."

"Thank you," Al said. "Now, take a seat and have a beer and let me tell you about these old signs."

Nikki went to the table and surveyed the signs. They were made of wood with metal accents in abstract shapes, futuristic and spacey with curves and deep, vibrant colors. The signs had been made to point out features and directions, like guest laundry, outdoor showers, the picnic area, the beach. The pop art vibe appeared to be inspired by the shape of a surfboard.

"Oh my gosh," Nikki said. "I'm so glad you kept them all these years. They're fantastic."

"You think?"

"My dad and I have been scouring junk stores for months, looking for things like this." Her face shone as she admired the handmade signs. "Cal said you made them for the former owner, Boone Garrity. Why didn't he ever use them?"

"I was a youngster when he ordered them. I worked on them for weeks, but he never came to pick them up. I felt too bashful to ask him to come and pay for his signs. He was a quirky old guy, anyway. Guess I held on to them because I liked 'em."

"They're absolutely great. Perfect. I would love to buy them for—"

"Whoa, now. This is a donation."

"But I have preservation funds for things like this—"

"I won't have it any other way, young lady." He held up his hand. "Now, let's get these two scalawags to pack the signs up for you so we can eat."

"Scalawags, Pops? Really?" asked Cal.

"Tell me I'm wrong."

"I want to hear the scalawag stories," Nikki said. She stood at the counter next to Cal, helping him set out the tacos and side dishes.

Cal's dad did his best to embarrass him and Sandy, telling Nikki about the stupid pranks they'd played as kids, like locking each other out of the house when one of them was in the outdoor shower or setting trip wires at their bedroom doors. At Sandy's sixteenth birthday party, Cal had replaced every framed picture of his brother with a headshot of Tom Skerritt. Sandy had retaliated on Cal's birthday, writing "find the toenail" in icing on the fancy cake right before the party.

Cal loved seeing Nikki guffawing with laughter. He loved seeing her happy.

"Just doing my job as a big brother," Sandy said. "Did I hear you've got a sister now?"

"Gloria. She's two, so I'm more like an old widowed aunt."

"I heard that, too," Sandy said. "I'm sorry. Glad you have family here."

She looked startled by the statement. "Yeah," she said. "Me too."

"And you might be widowed, but you're sure as hell not old."

Cal served up the tacos, putting a plate together for his dad the way he did almost every night. He didn't let himself wonder who would do this for him if he moved to Santa Barbara. Nikki kept chatting with Sandy, telling him about Shasta's mayoral campaign and asking him about his new album. Within minutes, she had convinced him to perform at a fund-raiser for Shasta in the spring.

Sandy always made it look easy to talk to women. She was already putting her number into his phone. For Cal, talking with Nikki was never easy because the stakes were too high. She mattered too much. He didn't want to blow it.

". . . any leads in that vandalism case?" Nikki asked him.

"Sorry, what's that?" asked Cal.

"That vandalism case, remember? At the marina. Did you figure out what happened?"

"Made no headway as far as I know," Cal said. "In the first place, it's not in my jurisdiction. I just took the initial report."

"Dad said the boat belongs to Elise Matson—your ex," Sandy said.

Cal shot him a look. *Thanks, bro.* "She's not *my* ex. Just somebody I went out with." He felt Nikki staring at him and waved a hand in dismissal. "Anyway, the case is assigned to the DNR and it doesn't seem to be a priority for them."

"Why the DNR?" Nikki asked. "I didn't know they investigated crimes."

"The Department of Natural Resources has a law enforcement division. It just happens to be headed by Vernon Sanger, and under him, the DNR is not known for cooperation with other agencies," Cal said.

"A Sanger." She made a face. "They've contaminated both the DNR and the DA's office. They're like a virus."

Cal's dad chuckled. "Good one, and you're right. I came up through school with Vernon and Neil Sanger. They're thick as thieves."

After dinner, Cal walked Nikki out. She had the borrowed car he'd pulled her over in when she'd first come back to town. "The sticker is current and the taillight's fixed," she said, giving him a nudge.

"I'm off duty," he said.

Cold air swept up from the beaches and she shivered. "My first actual winter in about fifteen years," she said. "I nearly forgot what cold weather feels like."

"Yeah? You staying warm enough?" Cal tried not to cringe at his own words.

She didn't seem to hear the question. She was facing the horizon, her expression hard to read. The breeze lifted her hair, and she looked so vulnerable, he wished he could hug her. "My dad said I could make a good life here," she said suddenly.

"Here. You mean Alara Cove."

She turned to face Cal. Her cheeks were bright from the chill air. "Is that what you did? Or did you stay because of your dad?"

"Well, at first, it was for Dad, sure. He hated the place they wanted him to live. To tell you the truth, it wasn't my cup of tea, either. But the house here"—he encompassed the property with a sweep of his hand—"isn't safe for him to live alone. I moved back home to help, ended up getting a job, and it's just like your dad said. I have a good life here."

"No urge to move somewhere exotic? You used to talk about it all the time when we were kids."

"I travel when I have time off and can get Sandy to stay with Dad."

"And how often does that happen?"

"Not often enough," he admitted. "Once, actually."

"So where'd you go?" she asked.

"Sea of Cortez," he said. "Went there for New Year's last year, and the snorkeling blew my mind. There was a marine park—Cabo Pulmo."

"Cabo Pulmo?" she asked, eyes wide with surprise.

"That's it. You've been there?"

"I have." She paused. "And I have no memory of it. My dad mentioned it just the other day. He said I swam with whale sharks when I was little. Now I want to go back, because it sounds awesome and I wish I could remember it."

"You should. It *is* awesome."

"Maybe I will someday." She hesitated again. "I . . . I might have trouble renewing my passport, though. You know, the whole deportation, indigent issue . . ."

"I bet you could sort it out."

"I'll give it a try one of these days. So did you drive down there?" He glanced away. "It was . . . I went by boat."

"You went by boat. Like, on a cruise?" She grinned, looking up at him. "You don't look like a typical cruiser."

"It was, um, a private boat. There's a marina at Cabo Riviera." His ears caught fire as he realized he'd painted himself into a corner. "What about you? What's the best—"

"A private boat, like Elise Matson's boat?" She laughed at his expression. "Shasta already told me about her. I knew, anyway. Kind of hard to miss the giant freighters with that name plastered on the side."

"Okay, well, she's not the reason I liked the Sea of Cortez so much." This was true. He could have stayed in that underwater world forever, drifting with the rays and whales and sea lions.

"I bought a painting of her boat to put in one of the Airstreams," she said. "The *Sunset*, right?"

"You bought a picture of the *Sunset*?"

"Yep. From a student who's working with Carmella. She's dating a kid named Matson, and she's been on that boat. But that's not why I bought it. I bought the picture because it's wonderful—a poster, actually. It looks like a California travel poster from the sixties."

"Oh. Sounds cool."

She looked up at him, her gaze probing his face. "Why didn't it work out? You and Elise?"

He thought for a moment. When Elise walked into a room, his heart didn't skip a beat. His palms didn't sweat. His stomach didn't tremble, not the way it was doing right now. "Uh, there was nothing wrong with her," he said, knowing he couldn't explain the impossible. "Or with me. We just weren't right together."

"I don't know, if someone took me on a private yacht to the Sea of Cortez . . ."

He grinned. "That's what my dad thought. He thought I should have turned the trip into an elopement." Cal shook his head. "He keeps trying to run me off. Marry me off."

"And?"

"I'm open to suggestions."

She made a brief sound, an exhalation. It gave him no clue as to how his comment landed with her. She must have caught his look, because she asked, "What?"

"Trying to figure out if you're laughing or scoffing," he said, certain his ears were turning red.

"I'm laughing. Could be, I'm also thinking serious thoughts," she said, with a slight smile. "But we're thirty-three years old and I don't have any suggestions for you, Cal. Not now, anyway."

18

By the time winter was nearing an end, every unit was nearly completed. Repairs had been done. Fresh paint and finishes gave all the surfaces a rich sheen. The polished campers gleamed like new. Papers had been filed with the state historical preservation office and with the local preservation commission. The loans and grants had been applied for and secured so that the project could be funded. It was time to get ready for the next phase—the approval process. The preservation committee would need to verify the authenticity and significance of the park.

In researching the provenance of the caravans, Nikki and Shasta had combed through news archives and guest book entries. There were stories hidden in the walls and crannies of the Airstreams, and Nikki made every decision with that in mind. They highlighted anything that would underscore the historic nature of the park.

They discovered that Woody Prentice, a talented beat poet, had once inhabited Unit 4, so Nikki found an antique typewriter and designed it as a little writing den. Unit 7 had a darker history— Quentin Barry, a once-promising actor, had experienced a drug overdose there in 1972. Nikki gave the trailer a theme of self-care, filling it with comforting books and cushy furnishings and soothing artwork on the walls. Another unit had housed a prominent politician who lost his seat when he came out as gay, and then became a hugely successful surfer and activist. She decorated it with a rainbow LGBTQ theme. The decor in most of the Airstreams celebrated the best things about the beach—sunshine, surfing, summertime.

Carmella had created several collages from the guest book entries. Many of the pages were filled with scribbled narratives and sketches that detailed the memories people had made at the caravan park through the decades. It was a place where ordinary people stayed to enjoy the beach, to be together, to fall apart, to run away from the world, to celebrate milestones. As each unit came together, Nikki could see how the old, funky place was part of the fabric of Alara Cove. She was confident that the project would win the approval of the community. She thought she'd done enough to pass the benchmarks set by the local preservation society. The only hurdle on the horizon would be the presentation to the city council. That was the final exam, and it was still several months away.

There were fights with the city at every turn, of course. She attributed the difficulties to Jason Sanger, who kept trying to impede the progress of the renovation. As mayor, he had ultimate veto power, because he held sway over the city council. So far, he'd held off, probably restrained by the fact that Shasta's mayoral campaign was proving to be no joke. She truly did have a lot of community support. Maybe even enough to win the election. Definitely enough to make him cautious about making enemies.

At the end of a long day, Nikki and Patsy kept working after the crew had gone home. It was a cold day, and darkness was falling, but there was still so much to do. They tackled a pile of trash and combustibles that needed to be separated. Although they tried not to add to the landfill, there were meaningless things that had no place in the world now, like ancient mixtapes marked *Rush* and "disco," and cassette tape players that no longer worked. Nikki found something called an Instamatic camera from way before her time and a collection of *Surf World* magazines no one would ever look at again. Johnny had been featured a time or two in the magazines. A few years back, there had even been a sidebar article about Nikki. "Queensland's Power Couple" or something like that. For about five minutes. They'd celebrated by sharing a bottle of cheap champagne and making love.

Nikki let out a sigh as they bagged up the landfill and stacked paper goods and scraps of wood and driftwood in the fire pit.

She shrugged away a wave of melancholy. Focusing on the project lifted her mood—or maybe it just distracted her. It was gratifying to see her vision coming to life. There were so many hurdles to clear, but they were making progress.

Guy showed up with Gloria, having picked her up from daycare. Shasta arrived with supplies for s'mores and a hot dog roast. "Who wants junk food?" she called.

"Yay," said Gloria.

"I thought you were in training for a race," Nikki said, eyeing the basket of goodies.

"I'm stress eating today."

"Aw. What's up? Campaign things?"

Shasta made a face. "Jason Sanger is trying to change the rules of the debate."

"In his favor, no doubt."

"In his favor, of course."

"That's because he knows you'll wipe the floor with his sorry ass," said Nikki.

"Sorryass," Gloria echoed.

"Exactly," Shasta said to her. "How you doing, little one?"

Gloria offered a bashful smile.

"I like this kid," Shasta said. "I want one."

"Yeah? Maybe you should have one."

"I need to work on getting a date first."

"How can I help?" Nikki asked.

"Forget dating. I need to focus on my campaign."

"Agreed. Once we get through this next hurdle—a presentation to the history and cultural committee—I'm going to focus on your campaign. Jason has made this whole process ridiculously complicated. He needs to be replaced. Should we do a practice debate and I'll try to goad you and rattle you?" Nikki suggested.

"Probably," Shasta said. "Not that goading and rattling are going to help my nerves."

"We'll practice," Nikki promised. "Like when we were kids and I quizzed you so you would dominate every spelling bee, remember?"

"Sure, like that, only more nasty."

"We'll figure this out together, Shasta. We'll find his weak spot. You have to catch him with his pants down. He has no power over you and he can't control you. And it's driving him crazy."

"He's awful, but I keep telling myself that there's something good inside everyone," Shasta said.

"Inside Jason?"

"Sometimes it's deeply buried."

"He was a dumb teenager," Nikki said, "warped by privilege and entitlement. Is there any way he can grow out of that? Some people are just bad."

"I would hate for that to be the case."

"Sure, maybe one day he'll prove me wrong."

"Or not." Shasta made a face.

"Speaking of burying stuff . . ." Nikki gestured at the pile of debris.

"Hey, we made some good headway today," Guy said, approaching them with a six-pack of cold beer and a juice box for Gloria. "So now what?"

"Let's make a fire in the fire pit," Patsy said.

"Good idea," Nikki said.

"Beats cooking." Patsy gulped down her beer.

Guy lit the fire, coaxing flames from the old paper and scraps of wood, and they watched the sparks climb into the night sky. Nikki welcomed the blast of warmth on her face.

"You doing okay?" Patsy asked her.

"I'm good. I feel fine." Nikki poked a stick into the glowing heart of the fire. "Shasta keeps me supplied with all the latest books about things I never thought I'd need to know." She put a hot dog on a long-handled fork and gave it to her dad for Gloria. "Like raising a toddler. I've got a lot to learn about you," she said to her little sister.

"Child-rearing books all seem to boil down to a few things," Shasta said. "Safety, respect, and validation."

Patsy nodded. "And snacks. Do not forget snacks. I really liked raising my kids. It was the first thing I knew I was good at. For me, the toughest part was those endless nights. My useless husband was never around, so I had to go it alone."

Guy held the fork over the glowing coals. "I didn't do so hot, all by myself."

"Hey, you did, too." Patsy gave him a nudge. "You raised a good daughter."

"Well, that part is true enough," he said. "I can't take credit for it, though. Nikki was born good."

Patsy gazed at him thoughtfully, her kind, world-weary face soft in the fire glow. Nikki had never paused to wonder why Patsy hung around. Now, observing the look they shared, she finally sensed the answer. She regarded them both, studying their expressions and the way they seemed to lean together, propping each other up.

"What took you so long?" she asked in a soft murmur.

Patsy smiled and cast her eyes at Guy. "Sometimes folks take a while to get on the same page."

A set of headlights flashed as a car turned into the park. Nikki frowned when she saw the silhouette of a police cruiser. "What's this about?" she asked her dad.

"Beats me. No outstanding warrants as far as I know."

The car stopped and the headlights went dark. When the cop got out, she recognized the tall silhouette. And it happened again, an unbidden reaction buried deep in her gut.

"Cal," she said, standing up. Gloria clung to Guy's thigh and hid her face.

"Evening." Cal nodded to Shasta, Guy, and Patsy. "Evening. You got a permit for this fire?"

"It's still winter," Guy said.

"You're supposed to get a permit." Cal took out his pad and pen.

"You're going to write me up? Jeez, man."

Cal scribbled something and handed him a slip of paper. "Here's your permit. In case anyone asks."

"Can you join us?" Nikki asked. "I mean, I know you're working, but—"

"Love to. My shift's already over."

Shasta set out a decadently satisfying feast of hot dogs, mustard and relish, chopped onions and peppers, and a big bowl of chips. They talked about the project, and Shasta's campaign, and the upcoming presentation for the city council. Cal told them about doing a welfare check that ended with him cleaning an old lady's gutters. Nikki sat back and looked at their faces, and she felt something so unfamiliar that she scarcely recognized it at first. It was a sense of belonging, of shared purpose, of connection. They were a *family*.

"Hey." Next to her, Cal spoke softly. "You okay?"

"I . . . yes."

"You got all serious for a second."

She looked over at him and it happened again—a thrum of warmth. She gestured toward the beach—dark-bellied clouds and a seam of light along the horizon. "Let's walk. That is, if you have time."

He stood and held out his hand, palm up. "I'll always have time for you."

She tried not to read too much into his statement. She read everything in his statement. They went to the top of the bluff overlooking the beach and stood there for a moment, watching the waves, iron gray and disorganized, seething with foam in the gullies. Then they took off their shoes and descended, the soft, cold sand giving way under their bare feet. They walked to the tide line, where the sand was packed hard, and let the waves at the beach break swirl around their ankles. Static crackled from his radio, but he touched a button to silence it.

"I used to hate winter," Nikki said. "The cold, the onshore winds . . . I was always resentful of the way it disrupted my surfing schedule."

"And now?" Cal asked.

"There's something kind of magical about the beach in winter," she admitted. "Makes me want to do more painting."

"I hope you're doing it, then."

"I guess this winter has given me time for something other than surfing," she said.

"Fixing up your place," he said.

"That. And—" She cut herself off.

"Nikki. It's me, Cal. Remember? I know you were gone a long time, but you used to tell me everything."

"That's true," she said.

"You still can."

"Maybe not this." They faced the ocean, standing close.

"What do you mean, *this*? I'm a guy, remember? I don't speak in nuances."

"You don't have to remind me that you're a guy."

"But I have to remind you that I'm a friend."

"You don't have to remind me of that, either. It's just . . . I think of you," she said, the admission coming on a shaky rush of air. She kept getting the feeling he wanted to touch her. To be close to her. She kept getting the feeling that she might want that, too. It made no sense, and yet it made perfect sense. "As a friend, but maybe . . ."

"Maybe more?" A gust of wind blasted them.

She turned toward him. Her hand found his. "Maybe more."

He cupped her cheek in one hand. His thumb stroked her temple. "I don't know if this is the right place or the right time to say this, because once I do, things are going to change between us and there's no going back. But I want you to know that I'm in love with you, Nikki. Nicoletta Fabiola Graziola, I love you. I always have."

She caught her breath. "That's . . . Cal, no. It's too much. Too soon—"

"It's about thirty years too late if you ask me."

"I don't know what to say."

"You don't have to say anything. Just be with me, Nikki. Be with me, and let's see what—"

She stopped him with a kiss. She lifted up on tiptoe and kissed him straight on, her lips seeking and tasting with a hunger that had been escalating in some secret place for a long time. He tasted of cold salt air, and he held her as if he never wanted to let her go. Her pulse raced, and she felt engulfed, overwhelmed. It was a kind of surrender, though it didn't feel like weakness. She gave herself up to it the way she surrendered when she was caught under a wave, letting go until it brought her up for air.

When she pulled back and looked up at him, the intensity of the moment pierced her heart. The light had faded. There was no sunset in the overcast sky. Just an absence of light. A gray monotone.

"You're shaking," he said.

"I am." Even her voice shook.

"So am I." He took her hand and turned toward the bluff. "Let's go to your place." But he didn't move. He seemed to be waiting for her.

Things are going to change between us and there's no going back.

And all of a sudden, Nikki realized that was exactly what she wanted.

The crackle of a police radio awakened Nikki. She felt the warm expanse of a muscular male chest beneath her cheek. Beads of condensation clung to the window over the bed in the small trailer, and the first glimmer of weak morning light outlined the mound of blankets covering her and Cal.

He flung out a hand and silenced the radio. Then he pressed his lips to her temple and inhaled deeply.

She stretched and lifted her head and looked at him. "I hope I'm not as bleary-eyed and unattractive as I feel."

"You're bleary-eyed," he said. "But you're beautiful."

His sleepy smile touched her heart. "You said things were going to change between us and there's no going back."

He ran his thumb across her lower lip. "I did say that."

"I think you might be right."

"Hope that's okay with you."

"I . . . ah, Cal. I'm a mess. I don't know . . ."

"You don't have to know. Just be with me. That's all you have to do."

"What if I—what if this doesn't work out?"

"That would suck," he said. "That would hurt. And we'd both sur- vive. So how about this. How about we imagine what would happen if this *does* work out?" He propped himself up on one elbow and trailed his hand down her arm. Her skin tingled where he touched her, re- minding her of the way he'd made love to her last night, with slow deliberation, and a level of skill that took her breath away.

Nikki was suddenly hyperaware of everything around her—the rustle of bedding and the softness of his breath on her shoul- der, her neck. The muted quality of the light through the window. The distant sound of the waves. The unfamiliar but deeply evocative scent of Cal's hair, and the warmth of his skin next to hers.

"You're blushing," he said. "It's cute."

"You're good in bed," she said.

"I'm good with you."

"I mean, you know things." Oh, he did. With his hands and mouth and tongue, with the rhythm of their bodies together, "It's like . . . you know things."

"I haven't been a monk, Nikki. But it's not the things I know in general. It's that I'm into making you happy."

She pressed her hand over his heart. "Last night made me happy." She startled herself with the honesty of that statement. She had only ever been with Johnny. He had been good in bed, and when she lost him, she'd been certain she would never find that kind of love again.

Last night had proven her wrong. Last night made her think that maybe—just maybe—good love and good sex might come along more than once in a lifetime.

"Last night made me happy, too, baby," Cal whispered against her temple. He stretched and slid from the bed, ducking slightly in the small space.

Now that, she thought, eyeing his naked body, *is beautiful*. He was as cut as any champion surfer—long limbs and muscles defined by hard work.

"You know what would make me happy? A cup of coffee, that's what." He put on his glasses and pushed them up the bridge of his nose.

She made coffee and they sat at the tiny dinette in silence. Light filtered into the window over the sink, highlighting the steam from their mugs.

"You're thinking about him," said Cal.

"I always think about him. Probably always will." She blinked fast and looked at him. "I don't know any other way to do this."

"It's fine," he said. "It'd be weird if you didn't think about him. He's part of your story."

She nodded. "We zoomed through life. Seemed like we never stopped. I loved him with all my heart, but he . . . it wasn't perfect. He didn't exactly focus on details, you know? Sometimes I think I married my dad."

"Your dad's a good guy."

"He is."

"You're doing a good thing for him, trying to save his business."

"I just hope it works. He has no Plan B." She studied him over the rim of her coffee mug. "Come to think of it, neither do I. And I probably need one."

He smiled at her. He had a ridiculously sexy smile. Why had she not noticed that before? "I love you, Nikki. I know this is new, but I mean that from the bottom of my heart." He placed his hand over hers on the table. "But I won't be your Plan B."

Something in his tone caught at her heart. "What's that supposed to mean? That you need to be my Plan A? That this has to be serious or nothing?"

"Oh, hell, no," he said. "I'm saying that I can't unring this bell. So if—"

She pressed her fingers to his lips. His soft lips. "Listen. It *is* new. And I don't know . . . I don't have a plan of any sort. But . . . I don't want this to stop."

19

After fifteen years, Kylie Scarborough was even more beautiful than Nikki remembered from their high school days. Nikki had followed her former classmate on social media, and Kylie's feed was filled with aspirational pictures of obscure destinations and adventure travel suggestions, with an emphasis on small, family-run outfits. It appeared that Kylie had pulled away from her famous mother's shadow to become her own person—an influencer and the host of an online travel show with followers that numbered in the millions. She was effortlessly stylish and projected a kind of snarky humor and cool energy that won her lots of attention.

Assuming it was a long shot, Nikki had reached out to Kylie via a contact link, never dreaming she'd get a reply. She was amazed when Kylie sent her a text message saying she wanted to do a feature on the revival of Beachside Caravans.

Kylie arrived in an electric SUV, bringing along a production assistant and a cameraman with something called a steady cam, which made him look like a cyborg when all the gear was strapped on. "Trust me, this won't hurt a bit," Kylie said, laughing at Nikki's expression. "I'm glad you got in touch. I read about what happened to your husband. I should have contacted you when I heard. I'm sorry I didn't."

"You're here now," Nikki said, gesturing around the area. "My new life for the time being. I've, uh, I've kind of avoided Thornton people since I moved back here."

"Most people hate who they were in high school. I always thought you were incredible all through Thornton, and you never got enough credit for it," Kylie said with a toss of her glossy blond mane. "You changed the school for the better as far as I'm concerned."

"Did I?"

"That stupid club—the Buccaneers?—was disbanded. No more hazing parties. That's something. Who knows how many kids avoided alcohol poisoning?"

Nikki shrugged. "One can hope. I just hate it that Mark died. It was the worst thing that ever happened to me until I lost Johnny."

Kylie touched her shoulder. "Well, at least you know you can survive the worst thing ever, right?"

Yes, she'd survived. Now she was in the next phase of survival. She wasn't quite sure what that looked like. Sometimes—and she shocked herself with the feeling—it looked like being held in Cal Bradshaw's arms. She struggled with the feeling, because it was so different from the way she'd felt about Johnny. Her marriage to him had been a roller-coaster ride, filled with unexpected twists and sudden, dangerous hills and valleys, comets and whirlwinds.

When she was with Cal, time seemed to move slowly. There was no head rush of uncertainty. There was a sense of calm security. There was the certainty that she was in the company of someone she could trust.

She thought about him constantly. She craved his touch and the sound of his voice, and the long, searching conversations they had after making love. Cal was an exceptional person. She'd always known that. He was also exceptionally good in bed, something she had definitely not known until recently. He knew who he was. He knew what he wanted. When it came to sex, he knew what *she* wanted.

She knew only that, for the time being, they made each other happy. She was starting to think it might be more than temporary. Yet loving and losing Johnny had made her heart timid.

". . . never thought I'd like it, but it's awesome," Kylie was saying.

Nikki realized she'd drifted off. Thoughts of Cal were very distracting lately. "Sorry, what?"

"Marriage and children. My parents made such a mess of things I never thought I'd go that route, but it's awesome. Vu and I met on a trip to Vietnam, and it's been wonderful. Three kids later, and it's still wonderful."

"Aw, Kylie. I'm happy for you."

"Thanks. All credit to Vu." Kylie showed her a picture on her phone. A gorgeous Vietnamese guy and three stair-step boys. "He makes it easy, you know?"

"Not really, but it sounds great." And honestly, it did—for Kylie. But for Nikki it sounded impossible. Her marriage to Johnny had never been easy. Fun? Yes. Passionate? Undoubtedly. But definitely not easy.

Her thoughts shifted to Cal again. He was the opposite of reckless. He spent a lot of time with local kids of all ages, volunteering at schools, running a youth safety program, and teaching surf rescue.

". . . even better than I expected," Kylie said, looking around the park.

"Really? You think?" Nikki beamed. "Thanks again for doing this. We've bet everything on the project. If the city council doesn't approve the historic designation, the trailers will be hauled away."

"That would be a shame, but I can't help wondering why your dad doesn't just sell the real estate and walk away with a giant wad of cash. At today's prices, he'd have a lot of options, right?"

"Not exactly," Nikki said. "If he actually owned the real estate, things would probably be simple. But the city owns the land. The only thing my dad owns is the group of caravans. Sure, they're collectibles, but at the end of the day, they're just trailers. They won't sustain him and Gloria forever."

"Ah. I didn't realize. I hope the people in charge of the city can see the value in what they have here."

"I like to think that's the case. But . . . there might be a complication. Remember Jason Sanger from school?"

"Of course. His douchebaggery was hard to forget."

"Now he's mayor of Alara Cove, and he's just as much of a dick as ever."

"At least he's consistent. Let's do a preview walkabout and you can fill me in."

The cameraman was already walking ahead slowly, shooting footage. Kylie's productions always featured excellent musical selections, and she was already dictating notes about music into her phone.

Nikki felt a surge of pride as she showed Kylie around. She described the research she'd done, and the forays with her father and sister to bring the past to life. Each unit was a carefully crafted time capsule. There was a Bambi, one of the oldest and rarest Airstreams. Nikki didn't even realize what they had until she started looking into the provenance of each trailer. The Overlander and Tradewind from the sixties were accurately restored right down to the tea towels and the drop-down baby crib.

Along with the campers, the park had a horseshoe pit, a communal library, expertly curated by Shasta with local-interest books and volumes on surfing and nature, and the picnic area and fire pit, now landscaped with driftwood and art pieces.

"This is adorable." Kylie gestured at the smallest unit. "It looks just like a little toaster. Nikki, I'm so impressed. You did a fantastic job."

"It really was a communal effort." Nikki spotted her father pacing in the distance, his gaze darting around as if he was scanning the area for a place to hide.

"Well, I love the vibe here," said Kylie. "There's something for everyone, isn't there?"

"That's the idea. I have to admit, some of the diehard surfers are probably not going to feel the love. It's always been their go-to spot."

"It still will be." Kylie offered a sympathetic smile. "Something I've learned from experience is that change is hard, especially for something that people recall with such pleasure. They want a special place to stay exactly as they remember it."

"You're right. Some folks would always want to book the same unit, and when they arrived, they'd go around checking out everything to make sure it's the same."

"Well, another thing I've learned is that people adjust."

"Now that's something a surfer understands. Adjust or get dragged. I've tried it both ways, and adjusting is better."

Kylie studied her for a moment. "You're going to be all right, Nikki. Better than all right. You have such a resilient spirit. You always have."

Nikki's skepticism must have shown on her face, because Kylie added, "I trained as a clinical therapist, and I know things."

Nikki's expression must have morphed into surprise, because Kylie grinned. "For real—master's degree and state licensure. Did my clinical component at UCLA Medical Center. I figured it was a pretty good way to make sense of all my years of childhood therapy."

"That's . . . pretty remarkable." Nikki felt a mixture of admiration and frustration. Kyle had come such a long way. Nikki was still stuck without even a high school diploma. None of which was Kylie's fault, however. "It's pretty great, actually."

"Thanks. I . . . You saw what a mess I was in high school."

"Weren't we all?"

"The bulimia was so hard," Kylie said. "I figured I either had to figure out how to heal from it or turn into the worst version of myself. So . . . thank you, UCLA. I worked with teen girls who reminded me of myself. Ended up changing careers when the kids came along."

"You've been busy."

Kylie nodded. "So have you." She glanced over at Nikki. "So, have you kept up with anyone from Thornton?"

"Barely. I couldn't wait to get out of here after I blew up graduation. Now that I'm back, I tend to run into Jason Sanger more than I'd like, since he's the town mayor." Nikki sighed. "I think about Mark McGill every day, though."

"His sister, Marian, followed their mom into politics," Kylie said. "I hear she volunteers as a youth advocate, too." She shaded her eyes and watched her cameraman making a circle around the Kenji sculpture at the entrance to the park. "This is going to turn out great. It's exactly what I love showcasing on my channel. A passion project, brilliantly executed."

"Thanks for the vote of confidence," Nikki said. She waved to her dad, who was pacing around with Gloria on his hip. "Come and meet my family. They're superexcited that you're doing this."

My family. She felt an unexpected beat of emotion when she said it. For most of her life, she had not thought of herself as someone who had a family.

She introduced Kylie to her father and Patsy and Gloria. The assistant fitted Guy and Nikki with a tiny microphone on a wire that snaked through their shirts.

"This is nerve-racking," Guy said, eyeing the cyborg-looking steady cam guy. "I'm not so good on camera."

It wasn't Nikki's favorite thing, but the process wasn't new to her. When she was active in the surf league, she got used to having cameras pointed at her. She had learned to mouth platitudes—*the awesome power of the sea and the life-giving force of nature*—and also to thank her sponsors—*I couldn't have done it without the backing of Nehru Hydration and Terra Firma Gym* . . .

"It'll be fine." She took her father's arm and turned him to face the park, glowing now with sunset colors. "Let's take a moment to look at what we did. Look what we made, Dad. We restored these old trailers into California's iconic silver campers. We brought this place to life again, and nothing's going to stop us."

She watched the smile bloom on his face. "You're absolutely right, Nikki. Really. I swear, I don't know what I'd do without you."

Somewhere behind her, she heard Kylie and the cameraman. "Did you get that?"

"Yeah, I got it."

20

Nikki held Gloria on her hip and stood in the doorway of Guy's trailer. "Say bye-bye to Patsy and Dad."

"No," Gloria said, pushing out her lower lip.

"Okay, fine. He's busy being Prince Charming, anyway." She watched in bemusement as her father opened the passenger door of the van and held it while Patsy climbed in with her overnight bag. "They're going on a date—can you believe it?"

"No."

"Right? I mean, they refuse to say it's a date, but it is, totally. Down to Santa Monica, to a Bonnie Raitt concert. And then they're staying overnight at Seadrift—a fancy resort. That's a date, if you ask me. And look at them. All dressed up."

Patsy wore a flowing maxidress and cowboy boots, her curly hair piled like a coronet on her head. Guy was in dark jeans and a new white dress shirt, still creased from the package, his beard and ponytail freshly trimmed. Nikki gave them one last wave and shut the door.

"I think this might be a thing, don't you?" she asked, setting Gloria down next to her bin of toys. The little girl had a thing for small plastic figures, her favorite being the swaying hula girl they'd found on one of their flea market forays. "What an interesting development," Nikki mused. "Dad and Patsy, after all this time. I wonder what finally drew them together, don't you?"

"Beep beep." Gloria pushed a plastic car along the floor.

"Well, I sure do. Did they just wake up one moment and notice each other in a new way? Did she look at him one day and feel this sudden attraction?"

"Where's Dada?" asked Gloria, rummaging through her toys. "Where's Patsy?"

"They went to a concert. They'll be home tomorrow." She went to the fridge and sliced some grapes for a snack. "Imagine, knowing someone for as long as they've known each other, and then suddenly seeing something new in them. Dad and Patsy never seemed romantic when I was little, but I think something developed between them. Maybe it didn't happen overnight, though. Could be it grew out of little things that finally added up to something big. How's that for a theory?"

"Yep."

"Patsy's been here since I was eight or nine years old. Our dad was what they used to call a tomcat."

"I like cats," Gloria said.

"Yeah, not this kind. He was prowling around, going out with different women but never sticking with anyone. Patsy was there for all that. Was she waiting for him to realize he was never going to find what he was looking for? I guess he quit all the tomcatting once you came along, right? I wonder if Patsy worries she might be one of those women who comes and goes."

"Okay." Gloria carefully lined up her toys on the floor.

"I wonder if Cal and I . . ." Nikki took a breath, having a little shiver when she thought of him. On the night of the bonfire, a door had opened, and she had stepped over the threshold into a different world. That was how it seemed, anyway.

After that first time, after Cal had spent the night at her place, everything changed. The next morning, he'd slid his fingers into her hair and kissed her long and slowly, and told her again what was in his heart. Then he had stepped out of the trailer and encountered her dad.

Watching from the window, Nikki had caught her breath, not ready to show the world what was happening between her and Cal. She herself wasn't even sure what was happening. She'd watched her dad and Cal from a distance, her stomach in knots. She was a grown woman, but seeing her father assessing the situation had still made her cringe. There was no question about what had happened in her trailer that night. None at all. Cal's uniform pants were wrinkled, his shirt unbuttoned, his cheeks shadowed by a morning beard. The squad car was still parked by the fire pit.

As the two men met on the lawn, the body language was clear. There was a brief exchange. Mutual nods. Then Cal had gone on his way.

Later that morning, her dad had caught her eye as they were loading things into the van to take to the transfer station. "You good?" Guy asked her.

A blush had shaded her cheeks. "I'm good."

Last night, Nikki had stayed at Cal's place for the first time. Since his father had left to start a job in Santa Barbara, Cal lived alone in the rustic house in the uplands. He had endearingly made her a candlelight dinner with soft music and a good bottle of wine. They had opened the wine and didn't even get halfway through the movie they were streaming when they started making love. The two of them were like teenagers, urgent and insatiable, twining themselves into knots of pleasure late into the night.

Cal Bradshaw. She was hooking up with Cal Bradshaw. It was the last thing Nikki had expected, and now it was all she wanted.

"I wonder if Cal and I are a bit like Dad and Patsy. Like, I went for years without thinking of him, and now I think of him constantly, even when I'm supposed to be concentrating on something else. I never imagined this, Gloria. Never imagined I would like him. I mean, *like* like him. Is that okay?"

"Okay," Gloria said again.

Nikki handed her a cup of sliced grapes. "He wanted to do something special for Valentine's Day," she said. "I told him no. And I told him why—because Johnny died on Valentine's Day. God, I can't believe it's been more than a year."

The nightmares and crying jags had stopped, but Nikki carried the lingering sadness like the constant ache in her injured wrist, which had never healed completely. "I keep questioning my own feelings," she told her sister. "It's totally different from what I had with Johnny, but it feels as though . . . I can't believe I'm saying this, but it feels as though maybe I might really be falling for Cal. Can you believe it—me falling for a guy I met in primary school?"

Her whole life was filled with memories of Cal—the nicest boy in primary school, the overlooked teenager, the friend who was always there for her. It had taken time and distance and adulthood for her to recognize what Cal claimed he'd known all along—that they were meant for each other.

Nikki still couldn't be sure. She didn't trust herself. She'd given her whole heart to Johnny, and she couldn't be sure there was anything left to give. "Let's go to the beach, Glory-bee," she said. "The ocean is where I sort myself out, you know?"

Gloria loved the beach, the way all little kids did. Everything seemed so large and expansive to her. It was too cold to swim, but they took off their shoes and ran across the chilly, hard-packed sand down to the water's edge to chase the waves. Gloria squealed as the foamy inrush of water swirled around her. Nikki took her hand and they ran to the end of the beach, where tide pools formed in the rocky outcrops. They watched little fish darting, poked their fingers at anemones, and found an open abalone shell, picked clean by birds.

"See how pretty?" Nikki said, showing her the iridescent interior of the shell. "Let's take this one home."

Gloria beamed at her as if she'd just discovered El Dorado. Nikki laughed. "You're pretty great, you know that? Think you'll be a surfer one day?"

Gloria found more shells and colorful stones. She chased a flock of birds along the sand and waved to the pelicans. They put their treasures in a plastic pail and sat together, watching the sun go down. Nikki wondered what Cal was doing. He had a night shift for the next two days.

"Some people say there's a green flash the moment the sun disappears." Nikki put her arm around the little girl. "I've watched so many sunsets from here, but I can't swear I've ever seen it."

"I'm hungry," Gloria said.

"Me too. Want to help me fix dinner?"

"No."

"Thanks." She got up and took Gloria's hand. They turned back toward the park just as the lights blinked on. The restored neon sign and the new lighting scheme gave everything a special glow. "Looks beautiful, doesn't it?" Nikki said. "I told Dad nothing's going to stop us. I hope I was right. All we need is for the city council to approve the local heritage site designation, and we're home free, right?" A dark doubt pushed into her mind. "Suppose Jason Sanger tries to interfere? He likes making people jump through hoops. What the hell made him such a fan of the circus, anyway? I hope Shasta wins her election, don't you?"

"Shasta." Gloria bounced up and down. She felt the same way about Shasta that everyone else did.

"She's nervous about the election, and she shouldn't be. She's going to be the next mayor, just you watch. You're little now, but this election is for you. She has to win. She's going to make this town a better place for you. For everybody."

They stopped at the outdoor shower and rinsed the sand from their feet. Nikki's mind flashed on a memory from long ago. She was in this very spot with her dad. He used to pick her up and swing her bare feet in and out of the spray while she laughed uproariously.

She carried her little sister into the trailer. "What am I going to do with myself, Glory-bee? I mean, once this is done and Dad reopens the park. Do I stay here? And do . . . what? Everything scares me now, and I used to be so fearless."

Gloria climbed up to the table and poked her finger at the jukebox. Some random song from the seventies started up. Nikki fixed some pasta with peas and walnut oil and Parm, which was delicious. Gloria picked out all the peas and ate the pasta. She gave Nikki a *nice try* look.

"More grapes."

"We're out of grapes," Nikki said. "You ate them all."

"Please."

"Sorry, kiddo. We're fresh out." She opened the fridge to double-check. "No more grapes. We have berries." She found a pint of early-season strawberries. "Do you like berries?"

"Yep."

Nikki sliced the berries and handed them over. Gloria devoured them, smearing her hands and mouth bright red. She looked at her sticky hands and started to cry. Nikki got a wipe and tried to clean her up, but Gloria fought her off. It was fascinating, the way her mood could swing from unfettered joy to utter tragedy in a matter of seconds.

"Dang," Nikki said. "Here, you can clean yourself off, okay?"

Gloria cried harder. She was probably tired from the beach. "Come on, you," Nikki said. "What are you crying for? There's no reason to be miserable. It's not a good look."

More crying, the sobs ragged at the edges. Nikki thought about her mother, alone with a crying baby, desperate to get her to be quiet. It was painful to imagine what that had been like to a woman who was just nineteen, in the throes of depression, all alone in the world.

Nikki gathered Gloria into her lap and held her, rocking back and forth. "I wish she'd reached out for help," she said, pressing the words into the child's downy head. "Why didn't she just step outside, knock on the door of someone's unit, or go to the pay phone and call someone? It's kind of awful," she told Gloria, "missing someone I never knew. I wonder what's going to happen if your mom shows up. I hope she does. I hope you get to know her."

Gloria wailed and squirmed in her lap.

"Aw. Come on," Nikki said. "Don't give me such a hard time. I'm doing my best here." She found *Bluey* on the TV, and they watched a bit of the camping episode. The familiar Aussie accents of the characters stirred a wave of nostalgia in Nikki. "Sometimes special people come into our lives, stay for a bit. Then they have to go," Bluey's mum was telling him.

Gloria gave a long, sad sigh. She rubbed her eyes until they were red and swollen. "Want Dada."

"You'll see him in the morning."

"Want Dada."

"I hear you. But all you have is me." Nikki glanced at the clock. "I let you stay up too late. Time for bed."

"No."

"Tell you what. Let's both have a sleepover in the big bed."

"No."

"Please."

"More berries." Gloria's cheeks were bright red from crying.

"How about we have berries in bed?"

"Yay!"

Nikki sighed. She gazed out the window and saw a thick mist swirling in from the ocean. On the TV, Bluey said, "I slipped on ma beans!"

Nikki looked at Gloria, curled into a ball of misery. "It's going to be a long night."

"Dude. These items are weeks overdue."

Cal grinned, unfazed by Shasta's signature scolding-librarian look. "My dad's fault." He pushed the stack of audiobooks across the circulation desk. "I'm still digging out now that he moved to Santa Barbara. Started his new job down there with the school district."

"He's amazing," Shasta said, "starting a whole new career. The bookmobile staff will miss him, though. He was one of our best patrons."

Cal nodded. "I hope it works out for him."

"Of course it'll work out. But I get it. You're worried."

"I'm a worrier."

She glanced at the clock, and then at his fresh uniform. "It's almost closing time. Late shift today?"

He nodded. "Twelve hours of small-town mayhem."

"Lucky you. Are we still on for training tomorrow?"

"Sure." They'd signed up for a half-marathon in San Luis Obispo, a fund-raiser for cancer research. "Let's meet at noon."

She came around the desk and walked out with him, under an arbor covered with bougainvillea just starting to bloom. "How are you doing? I mean, now that your dad's gone, you could go anywhere?"

"Believe me, I've thought about it." He paused. The question kept him awake at night—since his dad had moved, what was keeping him here? "But now I've got a reason to stay."

She slowed her steps. "Oh, Cal. That's wonderful. How are you and Nikki doing?"

"Why do you ask?" He felt a jolt of warmth just at the mention of her name. "Did she say something about me? What'd she say?"

"Dude. I think we had this conversation when we were in high school."

"Am I pathetic for still being hung up on my high school crush?"

She shoved his arm. "Stop it. That was then. This is now. It makes me happy to see my two favorite people together. It's all about me, see?"

"Right."

"You make Nikki happy. And *that* is what makes me happy. I hope this is something good for both of you. I hope it lasts." She must have noticed the mood written on his face, because she drew him into a firm, affectionate hug. "Hang in there, partner."

"Thank you." He let out a heavy sigh. "I'm in love, and I'm a patient man. But I have my limits—"

"Oh, hell, Calvin. Just be a fool for love. If you fall apart, the world will not end. It will undoubtedly be a dimmer, sadder place for a while. But the earth will still turn on its axis. It's a scientific fact."

He knew she spoke from experience. Shasta fell in love easily, and she fell hard. When her last serious relationship hadn't ended well, she'd sworn off love for a while. "I'd like to avoid the dim sadness, if possible."

"It's possible. And here's a thought. Maybe the two of you will figure this out, and you'll live happily ever after."

He grinned. "I gotta get to work. See you tomorrow."

His shift was routine that night—until it wasn't. Around midnight, central dispatch sent out a call about a boating collision in the area of Ocean Drive and Radium Creek under the bridge connecting Radium Island to the mainland. Multiple injuries. The call was sent out to emergency medical services, marine rescue, DNR, Navy security, and the Coast Guard.

All hands on deck, he thought, grabbing his gear and heading out. He activated his blue lights and drove onto the deserted highway. A thick marine fog lay in the hollows of the road. This was going to be bad; he felt it in his gut. Juveniles, he assumed. He could think of a handful of local kids who might be involved. At flood tide, the current was swift and unpredictable, and inexperienced boaters tended to get in trouble there. Especially in the dark, on a night of heavy fog.

Cal was the first to arrive. It was so dark that for a moment, he thought the call had steered him wrong. He noticed an incoming call from Nikki. He brushed the screen away. No time for a late-night chat.

Someone must have seen his lights, because the yelling started. *Help us help us help us over here.* Then, through the haze, he saw a flicker of green light—running lights of a boat. He turned on his body cam and paused to light a flare at the side of the road to signal the other emergency workers. Then he ran down toward the water, calling in the info as he made his way over the sandy bank. The dull glow of a cell phone light bobbed along the shore. He heard more yelling, and a female voice, ragged with pain and fear.

Under the bridge pilings, he saw a console powerboat on its side. The smell of fuel hung in the air. A couple of people were moving around. It looked as though the boat had slammed into a piling and ended up onshore.

"Alara Cove Police," Cal said. "We've got more help on the way. Who's injured?"

"Help! Over here!" A girl was on the ground next to a boy holding his jaw and moaning.

Cal stepped over a cooler surrounded by spilled ice and beer cans. He checked the girl for visible injuries, didn't see any. The guy on the ground was moaning and gasping. "What's your name?" he asked the girl.

"Anya." She wore a Thornton hoodie. Her hair was matted with mud, and her teeth were chattering uncontrollably. "We crashed—"

He shone his light on the girl and then the boy. "Who's this, Anya?"

"Milo Sanger. He's hurt, he was going fast, and we crashed."

Milo Sanger. Thornton kids. "Hey Milo, can you breathe?" Cal asked.

"Yeah . . . hurts." He held his face.

"Okay, be still. EMTs are coming. How many were in the boat, Anya?"

"Six of us." The girl spoke through chattering teeth. "Me and Milo. Emmie and Rosco. Teddy and Zoe. My mom. I want my mom." Her voice thinned with hysteria.

One of the girls—Emmie—was in the boat, holding her arm and crying. He found Rosco wandering with his cell phone. The boy named Teddy was wading hip deep in the water, yelling and crying.

Cal waded in after him. "Teddy Matson?" Shit, Teddy Matson? Elise's nephew. "Hey Teddy, you hurt?"

"I can't find her," the boy said. "Where'd she go? I can't find her."

"Who? Zoe?" asked Cal. "Is her name Zoe?"

"Camden. Zoe Camden. My girlfriend. She was scared, he was going too fast. She was in my lap—"

Everyone reeked of beer. Cal raised his light and scanned the water. The current was ripping out to sea. The other agencies began showing up, and within minutes, the area was crawling with EMTs, fire and Coast Guard. A Navy vehicle and a couple of private cars arrived—possibly passersby. Cal swiftly filled them in. "One passenger was ejected and she's missing," he said. "Her name's Zoe Camden." People fanned out, searchlights swinging across the water. "Is the chopper coming?"

"Can't," someone said. A woman in a DNR uniform. "Visibility's too low."

The EMTs and searchers went to work. Cal's mind raced as he moved among the students, piecing together information for the preliminary incident report. The kids were grossly intoxicated, bleary-eyed and sick with panic.

"Where are you hurt?" Cal asked Teddy.

"I'm . . . I don't know. Where's Zoe?"

"They're looking. Can you tell me what happened here? Whose boat is it? We need all the information you can give us."

"We left from the day dock. It's, um, I guess the school's boat. Zoe got scared when we went fast. She kept telling him to slow down."

"Who was driving?"

"I need to find Zoe," he said, his gaze unfocused, darting around. "She was really scared. I fuckin' hate Milo. Did they find Zoe?"

Cal didn't reply. The fog lay heavy on the water, and there wasn't a breath of wind. The first responders were fanning out, shouting, launching rescue watercraft, organizing a search. Cal managed to coax the names and ages of the crash victims out of Teddy Matson. They were all seniors at Thornton Academy. Someone had a key to the yacht club, and they'd helped themselves to beer and ice. A fairly typical, stupid-kid prank with a predictably bad outcome.

Octavia, the other cop on duty, radioed that she had arrived. "Bring the PBT and plenty of straws," Cal said.

"You got it," she replied. "Give me one minute."

"Hold on there." A tall older man in sweats and flip-flops came over, phone in hand. "You're not going to be Breathalyzing anybody here."

"Who are you?" Cal asked.

"Neil Sanger, and the DNR's in charge of this investigation. My brother Vernon is head of the law enforcement division."

As if Cal didn't know. A water incident was not the domain of the local PD. "And I'm assisting the agency," he said, bristling. "I was first on the scene and I'm doing a preliminary incident report, and you're obstructing that. Sir."

Octavia came down the bank, her eyes wide as she scanned the chaotic scene. Cal wondered how Sanger, a lawyer, had shown up so quickly. "Are you Milo's father?"

"I am."

"Your son's over there. The EMTs are taking care of him." Cal gestured at the kid on the ground, still moaning. Then he took the Breathalyzer and straws from Octavia.

Neil Sanger didn't move. "Have you determined who was driving?"

Not a hundred percent. All the kids were obviously confused and in shock. "Sir, I'm investigating."

"So that's a no. You can't Breathalyze if you don't know who the driver was. It's not against the law for a passenger to be drunk, even if they're underage."

Cal did know the law and the procedure like the back of his hand. He knew damn well that testing more than one person could lead to the case being dismissed if charges were filed. But he also knew he could get the teenagers to submit to a voluntary test.

"Go look after your boy," Cal said to Neil. "And let the rest of us do our job."

"Mark my words," Sanger shot back. "No PBTs."

Cal looked over at Octavia. It was going to be a long night.

21

Nikki woke up to the sound of Gloria crying. It wasn't the regular kind of crying or whining. This struck a different note in Nikki. Gloria sounded fearful, and her sobs were more like gasps for breath.

"Hey, baby girl, what's up?" Nikki said, pulling her close on the bed. They'd fallen asleep together while watching *Bluey*. She checked the time—after midnight. "You don't feel so good, do you?"

Gloria sobbed and wheezed. Nikki felt her dewy cheek with the back of her hand. Though it felt warm to the touch, she couldn't tell if the baby had a fever. "I'm going to get you some water, okay? You wait right here. Hang on to Bun-bun." She handed Gloria her favorite stuffie.

She filled a sippy cup with water and dialed the number of the pediatric clinic, which was posted by the old-fashioned wall phone. A recording clicked on: *"If this is an emergency, please hang up and dial 911."*

Nikki rushed back to the bedroom. "Is this an emergency?" she asked Gloria.

The baby gasped and clutched her toy.

Nikki called Cal. It felt like pure reflex, tapping his icon on her home screen to connect instantly. He didn't pick up immediately, which meant he was probably busy at work. She didn't call her dad, either. He was a good two hours from home. This was his one night away. She could handle this. She had to.

"What's going on, little one?" she asked Gloria. She studied her sister for a moment, leaning in close. She angled the reading lamp at the little girl. "Oh, man. You're covered in a rash. Open your mouth, honey. I need to look inside. Can you do that for me?"

"Nooo," Gloria said.

Her mouth opened. Nikki couldn't see any obstruction there. "It's gonna be okay," she said, grabbing her cell phone. She felt a sudden, searing spike of panic, driven by an emotion so pure it was a physical pain.

"911. What's your emergency?"

"My baby sister—two years old—is sick. I think she's having an allergic reaction to something. Woke up with a rash and she's wheezing. There's nothing blocking her airway, but—"

"Ma'am, what's your location?"

Nikki told her. The dispatcher told her to hold, and it seemed to take forever. "You poor little baby," Nikki said to Gloria. "I guess you feel awful, don't you? We're going to get some help. You're going to be all right, I swear." This was different from the way she'd felt when Johnny went out too far or took on a wave that was clearly too big. Yes, she recognized the love and fear, but this was deeper, because Gloria was so little and helpless, completely dependent on Nikki. There was a series of clicks and some static on the line. Gloria wasn't crying, but wheezing and gasping, which was way worse than crying.

"Hello?" Nikki said. "I really think this is an emergency. She looks kind of blue around the lips."

"Is she conscious?"

"Yes. But she's having trouble breathing. How fast can they get here?"

"Ma'am. Both units are out on a run. I'm going to have to try Castillo—"

"That's thirty minutes from here! I'm taking her myself. I can get there faster." Nikki was already grabbing the diaper bag and her backpack. C-A-B—circulation, airway, breathing—the rescue basics she'd known for years—told her that time was of the essence. Gloria was breathing, but not normally. Nikki yanked the car key from a hook by the door. "Can you call the medical center and tell them I'm coming? Two-year-old girl. About twenty-five pounds. Rash and wheezing."

Nikki put the phone on speaker and tossed it into the car while she buckled Gloria into her seat. "Tell them we'll be there in fifteen minutes, tops."

The dispatcher asked her more questions, which Nikki tried to answer while she got underway with Gloria whimpering in the backseat. The roads were deserted, and Nikki sped as fast as she dared. Maybe five over the limit. Fog hung in the valleys and roadside ditches, so she leaned forward, hands clutching the steering wheel, peering through the shroud. As she passed the turnoff to Radium Island, she noticed lights and emergency vehicles on the bridge. An accident, or maybe the Navy was moving one of their equipment barges, which they could only do at high tide.

"I used to shoot the bridge on my board," she told Gloria. "The current made it so much fun. And so dangerous. Don't ever do that, okay? Cal knew better. He was always on the bank, waiting for me. I never had any trouble, but he was there, just in case."

Gloria coughed and gasped. Then she puked. "Yucky," she wailed.

"Holy cow, sweetie, I'll get you cleaned up when we get there. You just hang tight." Nikki glanced in the rearview mirror, praying the kid wasn't choking on her puke. "We're nearly there." She swung into the lot of the county medical center and parked haphazardly in the nearest spot. Then she jumped out and unbuckled Gloria, trying to ignore the barf, and lifted her out of the car seat. She grabbed Bun-bun and the diaper bag and ran for the entrance.

The ER didn't seem busy at the moment, yet Nikki noticed gowned and masked workers gathered near the ambulance bay. She rushed through the automatic doors and went straight to the main desk. She rattled off everything she knew about Gloria, and the intake nurse hustled her to a curtained area with a paper-covered exam table.

Gloria wheezed and whimpered.

"She threw up on the way here," Nikki said, stroking her sister's head as the nurse examined her. "The pink stuff—I guess it's strawberries. She ate a lot of strawberries."

"You did?" The nurse offered a brief smile. "Do you like strawberries, Gloria?" Then she looked up at Nikki. "Looks like anaphylaxis—an allergic reaction. Could she be allergic?"

"She—oh God. I don't know. I just—*strawberries?*"

"It's not uncommon."

"Our dad's away for the night. I don't think I'll be able to reach him."

A doctor arrived, brisk and attentive—MIGUEL ARRODONDO, his tag read—and the nurse reported Gloria's respiration, pulse, blood pressure, and oxygen saturation. "We'll treat the anaphylaxis right away and figure out the cause once she's stable." He ordered epinephrine, and within moments, Gloria's breathing evened out. The color returned to her lips. The nurse verified that her pulse and respiration had improved.

Nikki staggered a little, her knees buckling as relief flooded her. "Oh, Glory-bee," she said. "You look so much better. Do you feel better?"

Gloria gave a weak little nod. "Better."

"We need to do a full exam and keep her here awhile for observation," the doctor said. "We'll give her an antihistamine for the rash. There's a risk of rebound anaphylaxis, and she might need some other drugs—bronchodilators and steroids—if she still has trouble breathing."

"Keep her—you mean like admit her to the hospital? Really?"

"Not likely. She can stay right here for a while. We'll dim the lights and she can get some rest, and after about four hours we'll probably discharge her if she seems okay." The doctor went to the computer cart and tapped some notes. "I'll send you home with an EpiPen and instructions for using it. You need to be sure to follow up with her pediatrician."

"Of course," Nikki said. She nearly wept with exhausted relief. "So we'll just . . . hang out here?"

"That's the idea." He handed her a card with the Wi-Fi information and a website. "You'll find links to information on anaphylaxis and allergy management. I recommend reading up on it."

"I will. Thank you."

The pager on the doctor's waistband went off. A moment later, so did the nurse's. They exchanged a quick glance.

"We'll check back periodically," the doctor said. "Try to get some rest."

Nikki nodded. She didn't even know doctors still used pagers. The nurse handed her some sanitizing wipes. "Ring the call button if you need anything at all."

They left with the rolling computer station, drawing the beige curtain around the area. Nikki kissed Gloria on the brow. The rash was already fading from her cheeks and neck. "I'm so sorry I didn't know about the strawberries. I brought them from the farmers' market as a special treat for our girls' night in tonight." She rummaged in the diaper bag and found a clean shirt and diaper. "You're going to be all better soon. Let's get cleaned up and have a little rest, okay?"

Gloria offered a weak nod. She whined a bit as Nikki changed her and put on the clean shirt. She gave her a sip of water and kissed her again, rubbing her lips back and forth on Gloria's downy head. "See if you can get some rest, okay?" Nikki suggested, tucking Bun-bun in next to her. She sat down on the mesh folding chair. The only other seat was the doctor's rolling stool. She sighed, shifted uncomfortably, and took out her phone to read about allergy-induced anaphylaxis. She decided not to send a message to her father. The crisis was over, and there was no point in alerting him now. He turned his phone off at night, anyway. Time enough to explain in the morning.

She heard a hubbub outside—rushing feet slapping the linoleum floor, swishing doors, beeping monitors, something about multiple victims. It sounded chilling, and Nikki wondered if it was related to the action she'd seen on the bridge earlier. She was curious, but she wasn't about to leave Gloria just to be nosy. Nikki didn't have a great track record when it came to other people's business.

"Snuggle me," Gloria said. She looked so small and helpless in the big mechanical bed. Nikki's heart lurched. She glanced around, poked her head out of the curtained area. People in scrubs and white jackets were rushing around, pushing carts with monitors and equipment trays.

"Sure, I can do that," Nikki said, hoisting herself over the guardrail. "Scoot over, sweetie."

She lay on her side next to the little girl, forming a protective curve with her body. The hospital bed was surprisingly comfortable. Gloria let out a sigh and tucked herself against Nikki. "Dubyou," she said in a tiny voice.

"Oh, honey. Love you, too." Nikki was visited by the strangest emotion as she lay there next to a kid who still smelled faintly of vomit and pee. She felt . . . maybe happy wasn't the word, but it was some kind of contentment sweetened by love, and for those moments, she felt as if she was in the one place in the world where she mattered.

This was her first real taste of what raising a kid was actually like—a roller coaster of terror, relief, elation, guilt, caution, tenderness, and joy. Going through it as a single parent was undoubtedly twice as hard. For the first time, she imagined her father dealing with this on his own. As a child, Nikki had gone to the ER a few times that she could remember, and probably a few more she could not.

Gloria drifted into exhausted sleep. Nikki, too, must have dozed off, because an urgent, low voice startled her awake.

"—going to be all right. We can fix this. Everything's going to be all right." A man's voice, sounding strained.

Nikki held very still. Gloria was deeply asleep. There were people outside the curtained area. Not workers—the man wore flip-flops and the woman, sneakers covered in damp sand.

"I'm scared, Neil," a woman said. "He just turned eighteen. He's not a juvenile anymore. What if charges come at the end of the investigation?"

A brief laugh, like a huff of air. "There won't be charges. Nothing to charge. Nobody took a sobriety test. After two hours, it doesn't matter anyway."

"You know better than that. Investigators have ways to prove sobriety even if no tests were given at the scene. Suppose someone looks into blood records from the hospital? Suppose people at the scene testify with their observations? Suppose—"

"Jesus, calm down. All we need to do is get the kids on the same page. We have to make sure they all know Zoe Camden was driving the boat." A pause. "They can't charge a dead girl."

"Oh my God," the woman whispered. "What a horrible thing to say. I'm sure she'll be found. I pray she'll be all right."

Nikki felt her heartbeat slamming in her throat. Zoe Camden? What the hell . . . ? Zoe was the student artist working with Carmella. Something had happened to her. Something bad.

22

When tragedy struck a small town, everyone grieved together, even people who hadn't actually known the lost girl. The terrible incident somehow touched everyone who heard about it, because it was just so sad, and too easy to imagine—a talented, high-spirited, promising young woman, poised for life's adventure, whose light had been snuffed out in one awful moment. No one was immune to feeling the pain of such a loss.

While the search took place, there was a candlelight vigil for Zoe Camden, attended by hundreds. As the hours passed, hope sank into desperation. The vigil turned into a circle of support for the family.

It took the army of searchers two days to find Zoe. The current had carried her body through the tidal channel and out to sea, among the shipwreck rocks that rimmed Radium Island. According to the news reports, she had died of blunt force trauma and drowning.

Further spontaneous eruptions of support sprang up along the Radium Island bridge—bouquets of flowers, handwritten poems and tributes, tokens of remembrance in the form of toys and jewelry, and odd little keepsakes meant to express the inexpressible. Though years had passed since Mark's death, the heaviness that oppressed the town felt eerily familiar to Nikki. She couldn't escape her memories of her own soul-scarring losses—of Johnny and Mark.

To celebrate Zoe's life and mourn her passing, an evening processional streamed slowly from the gates of Thornton Academy down to the seaside church that the Camdens belonged to. The chilly, blustery weather underscored the sadness of the day.

Nikki attended the service with Carmella, Shasta, and Cal. There wasn't room in the small church for everyone, so they gathered outside with a few hundred others. She caught a glimpse of Zoe's parents as they made their way to the front of the sanctuary. The Camdens had moved to Alara Cove from Oakland, seeking the security and comfort of small-town life. Zoe was their only child. They moved slowly, like accident victims, their faces stony with agony. Nikki recognized their harsh, inconsolable expressions, the same expression she knew she'd worn after losing Johnny—as if everything had been scooped out of them.

Zoe's life was celebrated with song and prayer, and readings by her closest friends and relatives. She was a vivacious, popular girl who loved art and volunteered at the local animal shelter. Her dream was to study art, said Mr. Wendell, the art teacher at Thornton. Nikki felt a jolt of familiarity when she saw him and heard him speak about a young girl filled with talent and ambition.

After the ceremony, she was surprised to see Marian McGill in the crowd milling around the church. Mark's twin sister looked polished in a fitted navy knit suit and low-heeled pumps, dabbing at her eyes with a tissue.

"Marian," Nikki said, holding out her hand. "It's Nikki Graziola."

"Nikki!" Marian's mouth curved into a tremulous smile. "Wow, it's been such a long time. I'm sorry we're meeting again on such a sad occasion."

"Did you know Zoe? Or her family?"

"A bit. Zoe volunteered in my last campaign, so I wanted to come and pay my respects. And . . . this brought up a lot of memories," she added.

"Of Mark." Nikki nodded. "Me too." Just seeing the Thornton kids in their school uniforms, hearing the school's a cappella group singing "Bright Eyes," and listening to the tributes had brought on a sweet, sharp pang of memory. She studied Marian's face, trying to picture what Mark would look like if he were here. The cheekbones and pale blue eyes, the shallow dimple in her chin—Mark had shared those features. "You must miss him so much," she said.

"Every day. I'm . . . and Nikki, I never saw you after that day, but I'll always be grateful that you came forward about the hazing. And I'll always be ashamed that I hesitated. From that day onward, I wanted to be a better person for Mark's sake." She shuddered, inhaling a deep breath as she dabbed at her eyes. "I like to think it's not his death that changed me. It's the way he lived his life. I dedicated myself to being not just the best person I can be, but the person he always believed I could be. God, I miss him. Every time I look in the mirror, I feel his absence."

"You're in public service," Nikki said, moved by Marian's emotion. "Like your mom. He'd approve of that."

"I hope so," Marian said, visibly struggling for composure. "I still remember you being the lone voice for him. Sometimes I think my whole career has been about looking for redemption."

"We were kids, Marian. Sometimes I think the whole job of a kid is to screw up and then do better."

Marian shut her eyes and took a breath. Then she looked at Nikki. "How are you doing? Better, I hope."

Nikki didn't want to go into her whole sad saga, so she changed the subject. "I saw Kylie Scarborough. She said you've been a strong youth advocate."

"That's the job," Marian said.

"Thornton's going to take another hit," Nikki said, eyeing the somber students in their school colors.

"If they can't keep their students safe, then they deserve it," Marian said quietly.

"Can I ask you something?"

Marian nodded. "Sure."

"Are you—Can you say what's happening with the investigation?" she asked. "I suppose knowing the facts won't bring Zoe's family any comfort, but they deserve answers."

"And I hope they get them. The DNR is in charge of the investigation."

"Ah. The DNR. Which is headed by a guy named Vernon Sanger." Marian's lips thinned in annoyance. "I'm aware. At this point, they're investigating it as an accident."

"But isn't it a crime to cause an accident like that?"

Marian nodded. "Word is, Zoe and the others voluntarily exposed themselves to the risk of injury—not a crime. But at the end of the day, a young girl is dead. If the investigation indicates it, charges will be filed."

Nikki bit her lip, thinking about the hospital. "Do you have a card, Marian? I'd like to give you a call about something."

Marian gave her a card with the district logo. "Anytime, Nikki. You take care, now."

Nikki found herself alone for a few minutes, and as she watched people making their way to their cars in the church parking lot, the sadness and sense of loss nearly overwhelmed her once more. She'd barely known Zoe, but she knew loss all too well. She felt Cal come up behind her.

"You doing okay?" he asked quietly.

"It's so hard," she whispered to him. He looked particularly somber in his dress uniform, crisply pressed, the collar brass, nameplate, and insignia gleaming, his boots polished, and his hat tucked under one arm. "Her family's going through a kind of pain that makes you want to lay down and die."

He gently placed his hand at the small of her back. "I'm sorry that you know what this is like," he said.

"I, um . . ." She ducked her head and dabbed at her eyes. "Yes, sorry."

"Listen," he said, drawing her close. "I can handle your sadness, Nikki. I'm here for you." Cal had been in the business of helping people for ten years. Nikki knew he'd seen a lot, including things he didn't talk about. She noticed a tic in his jaw. He had been the first to arrive at the scene of the boat crash, and he'd been there a good thirty minutes before the DNR officers showed up. He hadn't said much about what was found there, but based on the news reports and video from the bridge camera, it was bloody chaos. He'd turned over his body cam and dash cam data and had conveyed the information to the investigation team. She sensed he was frustrated by the process.

"It must be hard," she said, "dealing with people at the worst moments of their lives."

"It is sometimes. But that's also when folks most need the help."

"Oh, Cal. Sometimes I think I'm too broken for—"

"Never," he said quickly. "Don't say that. Don't even think that." He rubbed the small of her back. "Listen, I have to go back to work," he told her. "Why don't you head over to Carmella's?"

Nikki nodded. "Yes. Okay, I'll do that."

She found Carmella and they drove home together. Nikki couldn't shake the feeling of melancholy. "I'm glad Zoe got to work with you," she said.

"She was talented, and so thrilled when you bought that graphic picture from her for Beachside. She was a bright light," Carmella said. "I hurt for her family. I hope they felt a lot of love and support today."

"Do you think it makes a difference?" Nikki asked. "An outpouring like that?" There had been no outpouring for Johnny. Nikki knew there could have been, since he was so well known in the surf community. But with the world collapsing all around her, she didn't engage in any of the spontaneous tributes.

"I don't know." Carmella went to the kitchen and put the kettle on. "I don't suppose it could make this worse."

Nikki added honey to her tea and took a sip. "You always made us tea and toast when we were having a bad day."

"And it didn't make the day worse, did it? Zoe was making something for you," Carmella said. "Come look." They brought their mugs of tea to the studio, and she took out a graphic poster. Zoe was still finding her own style, and this one emulated the bright travel ads of the 1960s. Something about the cheery, innocent vibe caught at Nikki's heart. Zoe's art was crisply rendered and full of confidence. She had nothing to fear from the future.

The handmade poster featured a woman in sunglasses and a bikini, her face tilted to the sun as she held a surfboard over her head. There was a woody station wagon and the beach in the background, lit by a golden glow. Bold letters spelled out "Welcome to Beach Town."

23

It was a hot summer night, and the city council of Alara Cove was meeting in a special session. Nikki was almost sick with nerves, because the purpose of the meeting was to make her final presentation to the council. The public review period was over. Tonight, there would be time for public comment, and a vote would follow immediately afterward.

Guy parked the van and extracted Gloria from her car seat. Patsy went on ahead to set up the laptop and projector for the photo display. Kylie's team had shared a collection of photos from her visit to the caravan park that made it look like a wonderland. The "Welcome to Beach Town" poster made by Zoe Camden was already on display in the lobby of the auditorium.

"C'mon with me, surfer girl," Guy said to Gloria. "You're gonna love this—a meeting full of grown-ups."

"Nooo." Gloria shot him a suspicious look.

"It'll be fine. We can go for ice cream afterward."

"Yay!"

"What's that look?" Guy said, noticing Nikki's smile.

"You know, when I was in the ER with Gloria, it gave me such painful insight into what it takes to raise a kid. And I realized that everything I've learned—the good stuff, and the hard stuff, and everything in between—started with you. And the ocean. You're a wonderful dad, and we are lucky girls."

He hefted Gloria on one hip and pulled Nikki into a hug with his other arm. "I'm the lucky one," he said with a suspicious roughness in his voice. "Don't you ever forget it."

Patsy came back from setting up the projector. Shasta was waiting in the parking lot of the city hall complex when they drove up in the van. She had dressed up like a sixties model in a summer dress with a cinched waist, oversized glasses and a hair band, bare legs and coral-colored flats. She and Nikki and Patsy had all decided to come in period dress. They'd scoured the vintage shops to find just the right outfits. Patsy wore cuffed jeans with socks and sneakers and a Beachside Caravans T-shirt. Nikki had found a yellow-checked fitted sheath and jeweled sandals. Her dad and Gloria didn't need anything special. They always looked ready for the beach.

"I hear music." Nikki tilted her head to listen.

"Yes, you do." Shasta took her by the shoulders and turned her toward the village green in front of city hall. "Come see!"

Guy and Patsy led the way, swinging Gloria between them. "What's going on?" Nikki asked Shasta. Then she heard the strains of a Beach Boys song and stopped in her tracks. "What did you do?"

"It wasn't me. It's a little something Cal arranged."

Sandy's band was in the covered pavilion in the middle of the green. They wore Beachside shirts and shaggy hair as they played the old classics. Drawn by the bright sounds and irresistible rhythms, a huge crowd had gathered, dancing and tapping their feet.

"Unbelievable," Nikki said, feeling a rush of joy. Then she tempered her mood. "This might be premature. They still haven't voted yet."

"A mere formality, I swear," Shasta assured her. "I mean, it would be simpler if I'd actually won my election . . ."

"God, I wish you had," Nikki said.

"I'll try again in two years. Third time's the charm, right?"

"Look at all these people," Nikki said. "Do they even know about the council meeting?"

"Plenty of them came to stand up for the caravan park," Shasta said. "The council has to meet in the main auditorium. There isn't enough space in the council chamber to hold everyone. You can thank your friend Kylie Scarborough for that. Her video about Beachside has millions of views."

"We only need five votes, right?" Nikki asked. There were eight seats on the council, and the mayor was the deciding vote.

Shasta nodded. "Four votes are rock solid in favor. Only two are rock solid against. Greenlee and Garcia are toss-ups, but I'm sure we'll win them over tonight. I mean, look at this."

Nikki smiled. It was like something out of a dream—the beautiful evening, the beach music, her dad twirling Gloria in circles, people swaying and dancing to the beat.

"It's perfect," Shasta said. "What could possibly go wrong?"

Nikki was carrying an old-fashioned pocketbook as part of her outfit. She opened it to get her phone for a picture. "My phone," she said. "That's what. I left it in the van. I'll see you inside, okay?"

She rushed back to the parking lot and found her phone in the drink holder. The crowd was even bigger when she returned. She recognized Elise Matson, the woman Cal used to date, and Teddy Matson, who had given an emotional tribute at the memorial for his girlfriend, Zoe Camden. There were surfers—Manny and Chassie and others from the original squad had come out for the caravan park. She saw a number of local merchants—her elementary school friend Irma, who now ran La Tienda. People who worked in the fishing fleet. Vendors whose kiosks fed the ever-hungry surfers. Navy people and tourists. Nikki took some pictures, then stood at the back of the crowd, listening and marveling, taking it all in. This was her town. Her community. The place where she lived. Where her heart made its home. Maybe her dad was right. Maybe she did belong here after all.

"Good to see you, Neil. And good to finally get that business behind you, eh?" said someone behind Nikki. The voice was raised to be heard over the music.

She glanced over her shoulder to see a well-dressed older couple and another man in a business suit, carrying a stack of envelopes.

"Indeed," said the first man. "And thanks for your help with . . ." Nikki missed the rest as the music crescendoed.

". . . hope you're doing something to celebrate."

"We're meeting the boys for dinner at Chez Michaud later. Jason has to get through the council meeting first."

Cal showed up then, and she waved to get his attention. When he saw her, a smile lit his face. "You, my dear, are a knockout."

Nikki was distracted, even from that smile. "Who are those people?" She indicated the couple walking toward the parking lot.

"That's . . ." He pushed his sunglasses up the bridge of his nose. "I think that's Neil Sanger and his wife."

"Jason's parents?" she asked. "Milo's parents?"

"Why do you ask?"

"What's going on with the Zoe Camden investigation?"

"That? It's over. I got the memo in my email today. The DNR will release it to the press tomorrow."

"What do you mean, it's over?"

He checked something on his phone. "The investigation concluded that Zoe Camden was driving the console powerboat that crashed into the bridge pylon."

"Zoe wasn't driving," she said with gut-level conviction. "That's just something people said so none of the other kids would get in trouble."

"The case is closed," he said. "That's the conclusion of the DNR, and it's their case. I turned in my cam footage and preliminary report, made a statement. But at the end of the day, it wasn't my case to investigate. There'll be civil suits, probably several of them, but there won't be an indictment. There's no one to indict." She heard an edge of frustration in his voice.

"They can't charge a dead girl," Nikki murmured.

"What?" Cal stared at her.

"I heard them say that. At the hospital the night of the accident."

"Heard who? At the hospital?"

"The Sangers. I mean . . ." She hadn't actually seen anything. But she knew, because she knew the Sangers. "I didn't actually see them. I didn't see anything, but—Cal, it's the Sangers. I heard them when I was in the ER with Gloria. They had to be talking about the accident. I didn't realize . . . I guess I assumed everything would come out in the investigation."

"My stars and little catfish," Carmella said, bustling toward them. "You look absolutely divine. Both of you. Let's get together for a picture before everyone scatters." She rounded up Guy, Patsy, Shasta, and Gloria and took a few photos on the steps of the municipal building.

"We need to talk later," Nikki said to Cal. "About what I heard in the ER."

He touched her hand. "We can. But it'll be nearly impossible to get something into the record now that the case is closed."

The auditorium looked huge to Nikki, and people kept streaming in, filling the rows of seats along multiple tiers, all facing the presentation area. The council members were already gathered on the stage at a long conference table with pitchers of water, glasses, notepads, and pens. On one side was a lectern with a microphone, haloed by a spotlight, and a large screen filled the back part of the stage.

Nikki was as nervous as she used to get before a competition. Her nerves buzzed and she could hear her pulse beating loudly and steadily. This was the final exam. Her last chance to convince people that the caravan park was a local heritage site worthy of protected status.

She took a seat in the front row, awaiting her turn at the microphone. The first to speak was Carmella Beach. She was poised and polished as she spoke simply and persuasively about the importance of preserving the character of the town. She spoke briefly and eloquently about her ties to the community, highlighting what it meant for her to find a safe haven here. "We have a chance to keep what's special about Alara Cove," she said. "Or we have a chance to turn it into any other characterless coastal town, indistinguishable from any other."

One of Jason Sanger's cohorts—a man named Parker Ames, who owned a few local restaurants—offered a different argument. "These people"—and he indicated Guy Graziola with a withering glare—"are trying to swindle the city out of funds and future revenues in order to receive preservation monies, not to mention tax benefits and incentives."

Nikki watched her father visibly struggling to restrain himself. The veins stood out on his neck and his face turned red. *Don't lose your cool,* she silently begged him.

"Remember, the trailers occupy city-owned real estate," Mr. Ames pointed out, "and we all know the value of real estate in this area. It's a *trailer park,* ladies and gentlemen. They're asking for taxpayer money to fund a *trailer park.*"

Patsy quickly put her hand on Guy's arm and whispered something. He took a deep breath and slipped his arm around Gloria.

Nikki breathed a sigh of relief. If her dad lost his temper, he'd only be proving Parker Ames right.

When the sergeant-at-arms turned the timer in Nikki's direction, and it began counting down from three minutes, she stood and made her way to the lectern. "I grew up in that *trailer park,* Mr. Ames. To me, it was home. To this town, it's an icon."

"Ooh, yeah," said the surfers she'd grown up with, applauding.

Nikki stifled a grin and looked out at the audience. "Ask yourself why you came to live here. Why you like living here. Why you're willing to pay the local real estate transfer tax to fund preservation efforts. Because Alara Cove is unique, right? If you don't preserve the character of this community, the reasons you moved here will vanish."

"It's a health hazard," someone claimed from the floor. "The water treatment is inadequate."

Nikki's father surged to his feet. "Bullshit," he said.

"B'shit," Grace echoed, clapping her hands.

Patsy gathered the little girl into her lap.

Guy didn't need a microphone. "Every inch of the system is up to code, Earl," he said. "Which you'd know if you had bothered to read the—"

"A hotspot for crime," yelled the local bank manager.

"You want to talk about crime?" Nikki said into the microphone. "What about banks that process debits before credits when they come in on the same day?" In the past year, she'd become painfully familiar with shady banking practices. "What about minimum deposit penalties—charging people to keep their money in your bank?"

A buzz rippled through the auditorium. The timer went off, and Nikki didn't have a chance to speak further. The sergeant-at-arms banged a gavel, ceding the discussion to the council members. Frustrated, Nikki returned to her seat, feeling more nervous than ever as the debate carried on. Some of the members characterized her father as an opportunist and tax cheat. Others praised him as a steward protecting an iconic feature of the community.

We only need five votes, she reminded herself. But as the discussion went on, her hopes wavered and started to sink. The four council members in favor held firm, but Greenlee and Garcia, the swing votes, made it clear they wouldn't vote in favor of the landmark designation after all. The sergeant-at-arms announced that there would be a recess before the vote. Out on the lawn, the music started up again.

Nikki stayed in her seat, feeling ill. Her father moved over to the seat beside her. He let out a long, heavy sigh. "It's not going to work, is it?"

"We need five votes, and we only have four. Jason will be the tiebreaker, and he'll vote against us," she said.

"It appears that way," Guy said.

"I'm sorry. I did my best."

"We all did, honey. We worked like rented mules on the park. Turned it into a regular showplace."

Nikki held her father's gaze with hers. "I'm sorry," she said again.

"Hey, it's not the end of the world. I'll figure something out. Maybe now that the campers are fixed up, they might be worth something."

She couldn't ignore hard tension in his jaw. He was devastated. The park was his life. Starting over was going to be an ordeal for a man his age, with a kid to raise. He had no Plan B. He'd been so sure that this would work out—because she'd promised it would. Now she felt guilty as hell. She'd been overconfident, too. She'd misled him.

"Dad, I'll make it up to you, I swear. I'll figure something out."

He patted her hand. "We'll get through this. We've been through worse before."

She tried to smile. "I'm going to step outside. Get some air and hope for a miracle."

She took the exit door by the stage. Her stomach dropped when she saw Jason Sanger there, talking on his phone.

". . . Milo with you," he was saying. "Got it. Nine o'clock at Chez Michaud." He spotted Nikki and ended the call. "Well, hey," he said. "I guess you're not having the best evening, eh?"

She ignored the taunt. "You're going to Chez Michaud." She'd never been. It was known to be the most expensive restaurant in town.

He offered a phony smile. "Want to join me?"

"Your family has something to celebrate, apparently," she said, her voice very flat and quiet. She spoke slowly, although her mind was racing. "Sounds like there's a celebration because you managed to keep Milo out of trouble."

His whole body stiffened, and his eyes turned hard and mean. "What the fuck are you talking about?"

"You Sangers have a way of weaseling out of trouble," she said. "As long as I live, I will never forget what you did to Mark."

"Fuck off, Graziola. Quit blaming me because your gay friend overdosed a hundred years ago."

She didn't allow herself to react. "That's not what happened to Mark, and you know it. And Zoe Camden wasn't driving the boat the night she died," she said. Her voice shook, because she was bluffing recklessly, but it was possible that *he* didn't realize that. Could she bluff him into making an admission? Could she? "The investigation will be reopened, because some new information is about to come out."

"What the hell—"

"Someone else was driving the boat," she said.

His eyes turned even harder and meaner. But the color of his face drained to white. "What's your game, Graziola?" he demanded, his voice a low rumble, like a growl. She didn't say anything, knowing her silence would unnerve him. "I get it," he said. "I know what you're after. So you'd better think about what's more important—your dad's park? Or getting my kid brother in trouble?"

She hadn't mentioned Milo specifically. Interesting. And she hadn't been *after* anything. And yet . . .

"Why, Mayor Sanger, are you offering to make a deal?" She batted her eyes with fake innocence. "If I keep my mouth shut, you'll vote my way?"

He extended his right hand to her. She stared at it for a moment. Was he really doing this? Trading his vote for her silence? All she had to do was keep quiet, and the council's approval would be assured. The project could go forward. She'd be a fool to pass up a sure thing like this. Except . . .

She looked Jason in the eye, seeing a man shrouded in the mantel of entitlement, of privilege. Of corruption. Then she turned on her heel.

"See you inside," she said, and went back to the auditorium. The council reconvened, and there was a final call for questions and remarks before the vote. Nikki sat unmoving, though her stomach churned.

"All right, then," the secretary said, straightening her notepad. "Let's get to the—"

"I have something to say." Nikki's voice sounded foreign to her own ears. She stood up and went to the microphone.

Keep your mouth shut and save the park. Preserve your dad's security and Gloria's future.

To do otherwise would be selfish. But to bow to Jason Sanger's will, to knowingly cover up a crime, made her as corrupt as he was. He would always know he'd found her weakness—and nothing would stop him from exploiting it again and again. She had to figure out a way to keep her integrity without ruining her father. Right this minute.

She adjusted the mic and took a deep breath. As she let it out, she scanned the people gathered in the auditorium. "Fifteen years ago, I stood up in front of everyone and told the truth about a tragic incident involving the death of a classmate at Thornton Academy. And just now I heard that the investigation into Zoe Camden's death has been closed and there aren't any charges.

"The conclusion was that Zoe was driving the boat the night she died. I believed the investigation would bring out the truth, but apparently it has not." She paused while questioning murmurs drifted from the crowd.

In the front row, Marian McGill came to stiff attention. She picked up her phone and pointed it at Nikki. A few rows behind her, a teenaged boy stood up—Teddy Matson. The woman next to him grabbed his arm and whispered something. Nikki recognized her— Elise Matson. A moment later, Elise and the boy came down the aisle, headed toward the mic.

The sergeant-at-arms rapped her gavel. "This has nothing to do with the matter before the council."

"It has to do with the integrity of our leadership. I have more information about that night," Nikki said, "and Jason Sanger knows it. Only moments ago, your mayor offered to trade his vote for my silence. He expects me to secure the council's approval of my family's home by not bringing up what I know about Zoe's role in the boating accident."

"Oh, for Chrissake," Jason snapped.

Cal stepped into a side aisle. Even from a distance, she could see the tension in his muscles as he stood there, vigilant.

It was risky to expose Jason in the open meeting, but this might be her only chance to be heard. She wasn't a kid anymore. She wasn't going to be run off this time. And judging by the determined look on Teddy Matson's face as he came to the front, she wasn't going to be the only voice this time. Teddy had been among the victims of the crash. Like her, he'd probably assumed the truth would come out. Like her, he probably realized he needed to speak up.

The gavel banged and the room erupted, sounding like the ocean in Nikki's ears. She realized she'd lost control of the meeting, so she stepped back and made for the exit. She had to get away, had to find some headspace to figure out what to do now that she'd blown up the evening. This time it wasn't her own future Nikki had destroyed. It was her father's, and Gloria's. She had derailed the entire evening to uncover the truth about Zoe's death. "They can't charge a dead girl," Neil Sanger had said that night in the hospital. But Jason had shown his hand. His offer meant he was covering up for his brother Milo.

Nikki felt sick. Her father stood to lose everything. She had to figure out a way to make things right. She had to.

She strode past the village green and headed straight for Town Beach, a block away. The minute her feet touched the sand, she took off her sandals and waded straight into the water, letting it swirl around her ankles. She stood there for a long time, feeling the salt air on her skin and the breeze in her hair. A few people and dogs went by, and out past the break, a lone surfer sat on his board, patiently waiting.

This evening could have turned out so differently if she'd simply gone along with Jason. By now, they'd all be toasting the newest landmark in Alara Cove, and looking forward to the grand reopening. Instead—

"I figured I'd find you here," said a voice behind her.

"Cal." She turned to him and felt a wave of gratitude.

"You're like one of those newly hatched turtles. You always head out to sea."

"I . . . how did the vote go? Was it bad?"

"The vote didn't go. They're probably still fighting. Marian McGill is already talking to Teddy Matson."

"Good. I know you said it's nearly impossible to reopen a case, but she has to make it happen. She has to get the other students who were in the boat to say what really happened. If you could have seen Jason's face when I said that I knew Zoe wasn't driving, you'd know he's hiding something." She leaned against Cal, exhausted by frustration. "I never dreamed the investigation would fail to get to the truth," she said.

"It happens. The Sangers are fixers."

"They fixed the Mark story," she said quietly. "Please say there's a way to reopen the Zoe investigation. Otherwise, I trashed my dad's place for no reason."

"You didn't trash anything," he said. "You told the truth. Marian McGill is going to be the next DA. She won't let this slide. Jason'll be out on his ass, too."

She leaned into him, resting her forehead against his shoulder. "Oh, Cal. What's going to happen now?"

"Well, I'm going to take you to that fancy wine bar on Front Street, and afterward, we'll go to my place and I'll ravish you. Maybe more than once."

"No, I mean, what's going to happen with—"

"Shh." He touched her lips with his finger. "Not tonight."

"But—"

"Shh." He kissed her. "Tonight is wine and sex. Tomorrow we can sort things out."

She let out a long sigh. "Wine and sex sounds good to me."

"Right? Now that my dad lives down in Santa Barbara, we have the house all to ourselves. Rumor has it, he's dating someone." Cal took both her hands in his. "Listen, Nikki. You need to get used to being happy again. You have to trust it. I've watched you rebuild your life from the ground up, making your dad happy, and Gloria happy, but now it's your turn."

His words brought tears to her eyes, because he had the uncanny ability to see her the way no one ever had before, not even Johnny Mercury.

"You're my person," she whispered, feeling the truth of it like the warmth of the sun. He was the one she could laugh with or cry with. Stay up late with. She could reach out at night and feel him next to her. He was the one she could make dinner with, confess her dreams to, and trust with the deepest secrets of her heart. Her person.

"You were here all along," she said. "When I was a mess, when I didn't know what to do with myself, you were here."

"I was here," he echoed, and he held her while the ocean swirled around their ankles, burying their feet in the sand. "I always will be."

24

"hey never entered my cam data into the investigation," Cal said to Marian McGill, pacing back and forth in her office. "And that's just the start." He was seething. It shouldn't take a public accusation from a private citizen to make the system work. But apparently that was the way to deal with the Sangers.

"I'll take everything you've got," she said. "I've already spoken to the judge." There was a crease in her brow, accentuating her look of sadness.

Loss left its scars, he thought. "It's probably bringing up old reminders," he said. "I'm sorry."

"I get a reminder every day," she said softly. Then she tapped her keyboard. "Let's go over the data you submitted."

He knew each second of the flashing lights, the noisy panic and chaos of the traumatized kids. Teddy Matson's confusion and terror made his statements seem ambiguous, but the sworn statement he'd made after the council meeting broke up clarified a fact that had never made it into the initial investigation—Zoe Camden could not have been driving the boat, because she had been sitting in his lap. He'd lost her on impact.

It all boiled down to rivalry over a girl. The break-in and vandalism on Elise Matson's yacht had taken place after Zoe broke up with Milo Sanger. Despite the fact that the school had banned the Buccaneers Club, it had merely gone underground and continued in secret.

Ultimately, the other students corroborated the facts. Zoe wasn't driving the boat. Milo Sanger was. In light of the new information, Marian—now duly elected—sought and obtained three indictments from a grand jury. Milo Sanger was charged with one count of boating under the influence resulting in death, and two counts of boating under the influence causing great bodily injury. If convicted, he could face prison.

The scandal rippled through Alara Cove, leading to Jason's resignation and a censure against his uncle from the DNR. The changes were long overdue. The city council appointed a temporary administrator to take over and resume the business of running the town. When the election rolled around, Shasta would run for mayor unopposed. And one of the first items on the agenda was Beachside Caravans.

Nikki and her dad sat across the table from each other in the host unit where she'd grown up. They were going over the final paperwork from the city. Guy's face shone as he paged through the documents designating the park as a cultural heritage site.

"You know, thirty-six years ago, I sat at this same table with Boone Garrity when he transferred the park to me. I never thought I'd have a prouder moment, but I was wrong. This is better."

"It was a near thing," Nikki said, wincing at the memory.

"It's all good," he said. "The city just kept us in suspense awhile longer."

The final vote had taken place quietly, in the council chambers, and the heritage designation was granted. The grand reopening of the park was a week away.

"I sure do wish you'd stick around," Guy said. "Things won't be the same around here without you."

She smiled at him. "You need number seven for guests, Dad. It's booked every night for months." The unit she'd occupied was called

the Atelier, and it featured some of her favorite art pieces. She'd outfitted it with art supplies for the guests to use. "This is your world,
not mine, Dad."

"I get it. But I'll miss having you around."

"All that free labor. Nope, I need a paying job."

"In that case, I'll be okay. I think we're all set." He studied her
face, and she wondered what he saw when he looked at her. The
past? Her mother? Or the person Nikki had become? "You hungry?"
he asked. "Frito pie?"

She grinned. "Sounds good, but I'm meeting Cal at Town Beach
after he gets off work." She felt a shiver of nerves. In the flurry of final
preparations for the park, she'd barely had time to spend with him,
and she missed him with unexpected intensity.

"That's cool," Guy said. "I always liked that boy."

Her grin softened. "So have I, Dad. So have I."

"Don't keep me out too late," Nikki said to Cal. "I have to go to work
in the morning."

"Work." He frowned.

"You know, that thing people do in order to make a living . . ."

"At Beachside, you mean."

She shook her head. "I have a job at the Carmella Beach Gallery.
I'm going to be her gallerist. I get to choose the art and find new
artists to exhibit."

"A gallerist. Very cool, ma'am," he said.

"It is," she agreed. "I made a proposal to Carmella, and she said
she thought I'd never ask. I curated my first window display this
morning. Want to go see it before the beach?"

"Hell, yes."

It was a tribute to Zoe Camden, her paintings elevated by beautiful frames and dramatic lighting. Cal gazed at the display for a few
minutes. He wiped away an unabashed tear, and she took his hand.

"So I take it this means you're sticking around," he said. "Here in Alara Cove, I mean."

She could feel her gaze soften as they walked down Front Street, under the lamplight and flower baskets with the hush of the waves in the distance. "This town. This damn town. I think we can make our peace with each other."

They went to the beach as the sun was going down. People were out paddling in the shallows, tossing balls for their dogs, enjoying a stroll. The sand still held the heat of the day, and the waves formed gentle rollers, just big enough to play in. Then she asked him the question that had been nagging at her. "What about you?"

"What about me?"

"You and this town. You stayed because of your dad. Now that he's moved on . . ." She swallowed, surprised at how hard it was to ask the question. Because the answer mattered so much. "You used to dream of traveling the world."

"I still do," he said. "But the thing about traveling is that you can always come back home."

"True. But it took me fifteen years."

"I couldn't handle fifteen years without you," he said, direct as always.

"Cal, you're finally free to see the world. I won't be the thing holding you back."

"Listen," he said, "you're not a thing. You're the woman I love. And you're not holding me back. You have a job now. A life here. Why would I want to be anywhere else?"

Nikki looked up at him, feeling the love shine from her. Then she took his hand and walked with him into the waves.

EPILOGUE

Gloria Graziola felt the sea breeze tugging at her mortarboard. Surreptitiously, she reached up to make sure it was secured by bobby pins. She didn't want to miss a moment of Thornton Academy's keynote guest speaker—her sister, Nikki. Gloria was super-proud of Nikki, definitely as proud as their dad, who sat in the VIP row with Patsy, Cal, and the kids—gangly teens about to start their own high school journey.

Gloria knew that Nikki had spent days and days crafting her speech. She knew it would be a message of striving and stumbling, meeting life head-on, knowing when to hold on and when to let go, learning to ride out troubles like turbulent waves.

Actually, Gloria didn't need to hear what her sister had to say, because Nikki had always lived her life out loud, hiding nothing. Even though they were years apart in age, they'd stayed close through thick and thin. Nikki had taught Gloria to swim and surf. Gloria had been the flower girl in Nikki's wedding; when the babies came, Gloria had helped look after them.

Nikki had supported Gloria when Marnie came to town, declaring she wanted to be in her daughter's life—for all of four months, before she disappeared again. And Gloria had held on to Nikki when

Carmella Beach passed away, bequeathing the art gallery to Nikki. The sisters had celebrated their dad's retirement, a bittersweet time when he handed off Beachside Caravans to his old surf buddies Manny and Chassie, who were delighted to take on the task of running their favorite spot on earth.

It had been a fine, long ride for the sisters, and this morning while they were getting ready for the ceremony, Nikki had declared it a full-circle moment.

Gloria wasn't so sure that applied to her, though, because she was about to step outside the circle—very far outside. Today was her beginning.

And for Nikki, it was an ending of sorts. Her portrait now hung in the school's hall of distinguished alumni. Yet she'd never gone to college. She'd never won a fancy prize like a Pulitzer or an Oscar. She had never made a world-changing discovery. But she'd distinguished herself by making a life that mattered in a place that meant the world to her.

The headmaster went to the podium to introduce her, and when he started to speak, Gloria realized there were still a few surprises in store. "Nikki Graziola was valedictorian of her class here at Thornton," said Mr. Ellis. "And even though I'm going off-script here, I'd like to address some unfinished business from that day. Although she has earned this honor many times over, there is one formality left undone. Nikki, could you come up, please?"

Nikki approached, her head tilted with caution. The breeze caught at her robe, and she touched her cap to keep it on.

"Now, without further ado . . . Nicoletta Fabiola Graziola Bradshaw." His voice rang out as he handed her a rolled document tied with a ribbon in school colors. "Congratulations." They shook hands; then Nikki faced everyone and flipped her tassel from one side to the other. The applause rolled like a wave through the audience. She looked much the same as Gloria imagined she'd looked all those years ago—pretty, athletic, full of confidence—a woman on the verge of an amazing life.

Nikki smiled and took in the crowd. She leaned toward the microphone and said, "Ladies and gentlemen, students, faculty members, and distinguished alumni, let us commence."

ACKNOWLEDGMENTS

Deepest thanks to my fellow writers, who are always the safest place to "cuss and discuss" the process of writing a novel. I'm looking at you, Anjali Banerjee, Lois Dyer, Sheila Roberts, Kate Breslin, Maureen McQuerry, and Warren Read.

I'm also grateful to Cindy Peters and Ashley Hayes for keeping everything fresh online. The cool posts and TikTok clips are their good work; the embarrassing ones are entirely mine.

Every book I write is enriched and informed by my literary agent, Meg Ruley, and her associate, Annelise Robey, and brought to life by the amazing publishing team at HarperCollins/William Morrow Books—Rachel Kahan, Jennifer Hart, Liate Stehlik, Tavia Kowalchuk, Lindsey Kennedy, Lisa Glover, and their many creative associates who make publishing such a grand adventure.

Special thanks to the HarperCollins Global Publishing Team, especially the UK, Spain, Germany, Israel, Hungary, Poland, the Czech Republic, Italy, Scandinavia, France, Portugal, Brazil, and Holland. I'm so proud to be published in faraway places.

About the Author

Susan Wiggs's life is all about family, friends . . . and fiction. She lives at the water's edge on an island in Puget Sound, and in good weather, she commutes to her writers' group in a twenty-eight-foot motorboat.

She's been featured in the national media, including NPR, PRI, and *USA Today*; has given programs for the US embassies in Argentina and Uruguay; and is a popular speaker locally, nationally, internationally, and on the high seas.

From the very start, her writings have illuminated the everyday dramas of ordinary people facing extraordinary circumstances. Her books celebrate the power of love, the timeless bonds of family, and the fascinating nuances of human nature. Today, she is an internationally bestselling, award-winning author, with millions of copies of her books in print in numerous countries and languages. According to *Publishers Weekly*, Wiggs writes with "refreshingly honest emotion," and the *Salem Statesman Journal* adds that she is "one of our best observers of stories of the heart [who] knows how to capture emotion on virtually every page of every book." *Booklist* characterizes her books as "real and true and unforgettable."

Her novels have appeared in the number one spot on the *New York Times* bestseller list and have captured readers' hearts around the globe with translations into more than twenty languages available in thirty countries. Her novel *The Apple Orchard* has been made into a film for TV.

The author is a former teacher, a Harvard graduate, an avid hiker, an amateur photographer, a good skier, and a terrible golfer, yet her favorite form of exercise is curling up with a good book. She divides her time between sleeping and waking.

Visit Susan Wiggs's Website

susanwiggs.com

Social Media

facebook.com/susanwiggs
pinterest.com/beachwriter1
twitter.com/susanwiggs
goodreads.com/SusanWiggs
instagram.com/susan_wiggs_
bookbub.com/authors/susan-wiggs

Susan's Amazon Page in the US

amazon.com/Susan-Wiggs/e/B000AQ1FJO

Susan's Amazon Page in the UK

amazon.co.uk/Susan-Wiggs/e/B000AQ1FJO